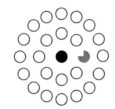
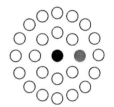

What We Think We Know

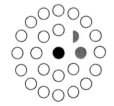
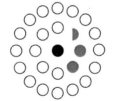
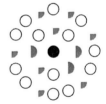

Short Fiction by **Aaron Schneider**

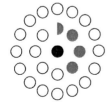
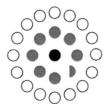

GORDON HILL PRESS

Edited by Shane Neilson
Cover and book design by Jeremy Luke Hill
Proofreading by Carol Dilworth
Set in Linux Libertine and Open Sans
Printed on Mohawk Via Felt
Printed and bound by Arkay Design & Print

LIBRARY AND ARCHIVES CANADA CATALOGUING IN PUBLICATION

Title: What we think we know / short fiction by Aaron Schneider.
Names: Schneider, Aaron J., author.
Identifiers: Canadiana (print) 20210212381 | Canadiana (ebook) 2021021239X |
    ISBN 9781774220290 (softcover) | ISBN 9781774220306 (PDF) |
    ISBN 9781774220313 (HTML)
Classification: LCC PS8637.C515 W43 2021 | DDC C813/.6—dc23

ONTARIO ARTS COUNCIL
CONSEIL DES ARTS DE L'ONTARIO
an Ontario government agency
un organisme du gouvernement de l'Ontario

Gordon Hill Press gratefully acknowledges the support of the Ontario Arts Council.

Gordon Hill Press respectfully acknowledges the ancestral homelands of the Attawandaron, Anishinaabe, Haudenosaunee, and Métis Peoples, and recognizes that we are situated on Treaty 3 territory, the traditional territory of Mississaugas of the Credit First Nation.

Gordon Hill Press also recognizes and supports the diverse persons who make up its community, regardless of race, age, culture, ability, ethnicity, nationality, gender identity and expression, sexual orientation, marital status, religious affiliation, and socioeconomic status.

Gordon Hill Press
130 Dublin Street North
Guelph, Ontario, Canada
N1H 4N4
www.gordonhillpress.com

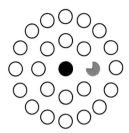

The Cara Triptych

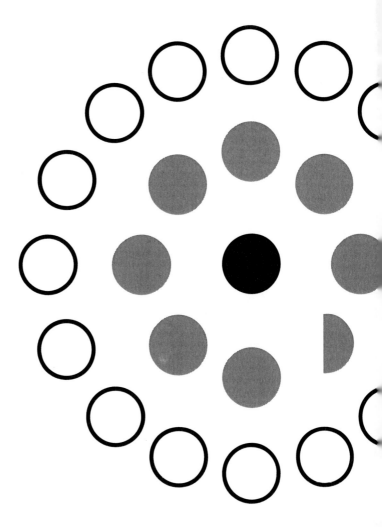

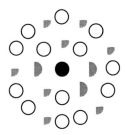

Cara's Men (As Told to You in Confidence)

Cara tells you about the men that she has slept with, across a table in a crowded campus bar over a series of Friday afternoons in the fall when you are both a little drunk and the light is easing you into the evening. You have to lean forward to hear her clearly. The clamour of graduate students and professors talking together, their noise and closeness, how they keep bumping into your elbow, the back of your chair, and apologizing, closes a circle of privacy around you, contains and deepens the intimacy of the conversation:

Her first boyfriend was a Jehovah's Witness. They were both in Grade 8. His parents didn't want him dating her, or dating at all, and he told them that she was a classmate and that they had been assigned to work together on a project that term. She waited in the entryway of his apartment, and felt: the massing silence. The shining parquet. The atmosphere of piety, certainty and disapproval. They climbed the stairs of his building to a locked door that opened onto the roof and made out on the top step pressing against the steel of the door. The echo in the stairwell magnified and restrained their movements. She was wearing a skirt. He pushed inside of her, and she felt nothing. No pain. Nothing. It was only for a few seconds, and then he stopped. The next day he told her he had wanted to see if she would let him do it. He was already distant when he said this, not expressionless, but withdrawing into disdain, and they broke up.

Cara makes an issue of the strange and hurtful behavior of her exes. She asks you, "Why?" Her voice dramatic, irate, almost panicked, uncomprehending. In these moments, her face is open, caught between surprise and bewilderment. Why would he do that? To me? But she never says anything like this about her first boyfriend, the first man to be inside of her. It is as if she accepts him, as if his behavior is explicable, not excessive or aberrant, a common, understandable cruelty.

She tells you about him and the echoing stairwell before she should, before she knows you well enough to share her oldest hurts. You are flattered by her trust. You like what this says about you, and the kind of man that you are: you want to reach out to comfort her, to take her hands that are sitting folded, still, forgotten, you think, on the table in front of her. You want to touch her resignation into tenderness, but you don't: it's not yet time. You wait, for now. And listen.

*

In high school, Cara dated a boy from a home like hers—breaking, but not yet broken. He was erratic, and she now wonders if he is a manic depressive, maybe a sex addict. He liked her to bite down hard on his penis. Hard! He cheated on her and they broke up. She went to university and he became a photographer and a bon vivant, an offbeat dandy. Right now, he has a mullet and a potbelly, wears a novelty belt buckle that he bought in Calgary, and that he tucks ostentatiously under his gut. He is considering moving to Kingston for its history and its market square. He travels on assignment or on a whim. Next month, he is going to watch a rocket launch in Kazakhstan. "Why?" you ask. "Because he can," says Cara, "because he wants to." You are fascinated and a little bit horrified by the people Cara knows: they are self-absorbed, recklessly unapologetic, and utterly unlike you.

This ex calls her sometimes and talks about how much he misses her. Cara tries to explain to you the silence she hears collecting around his need, the emptiness reverberating on the other end of the call. She imagines him hunched, taut with confession, an arch terminating in the phone: he has never stopped caring about her. It was always her. It will always be her. Becoming more hysterical, more sincere: his next girlfriend would deep throat him on the living room couch. Deep throat him. And all he could think about was her. He offers this as a demonstration, a grand gesture, to make a point about the depth and intensity of his obsession. He doesn't mean to be hurtful.

You nod. You are sympathetic. But you can't touch any of this, her understanding, the tenderness of her condescension. Does she still care about him? Does she like these intrusions, these eruptions of the past into the present, or merely tolerate them? When she tells you about him, her voice turns soft, calm, and you can hear her disappearing into herself.

*

Cara did it with two boys in the yearbook office. She isn't normally elliptical, but when she talks about this, and she only does twice and briefly, she uses words that stop short of the possibilities they suggest. Her eyes, which you expect to be locked on yours, to demand your attention, drift away. You wonder if this is a pleasurable reverie, a memory of pain, or the aftereffect of having given over control, a lasting diffuse blankness. Is that what sex is for her? A surrender? You think about this often and at length, but what you imagine is as vague as Cara's words: you arrange the three bodies, but the arms and legs and mouths won't fall easily into place; the tableaux you invent are tentative at first, blurred by generality, and then too precise. The teenagers take on the sharp unreality of porn actors, and you shy away from what comes into focus. You can never make it happen the way it must have. You are disoriented by the excessive, predictable intersections of flesh, and repelled by the same force that attracts you.

*

During her undergrad, Cara dated another Creative Writing student. In an author photo she shows you, he is round. Round glasses in a round face smoothed by fat. Rounded shoulders and his chest rounding into the gentle promise of a gut cut off by the border of the image. He has never been attractive. Cara tells you that when they were dating he looked like a half stuffed sock. You say he looks overstuffed now, and she tells you not to be mean. Cara's exes belong to her like a family, and you can criticize them in solidarity with her, but that is the limit.

Cara, her ex, and a woman she doesn't like to talk about competed for the best marks in their class; in the end, Cara came second, and he came third. Last summer, he published his first book. She went to the launch, and saw him with his new girlfriend, and thought about how it could have been her, how it should have been her, drunk, elated, thanking everyone loudly for coming. You tell her that, yes, it should have. It can still be her. You are emphatic, encouraging, and you almost believe yourself.

*

Cara went back to his room with the captain of the York cross country ski team. (Does York have a cross country ski team?) He looked Norwegian, maybe Swedish, tall, blonde, lean but muscular, blankly, impassively beautiful. The athletic type. They had nothing in common. She didn't even like talking to him. Cara wants to know: "Why do men expect women to go down on them during one-night stands? Why do they take it as a given when sex is still uncertain? And why do they never reciprocate?" Your answers leave you both unsatisfied.

*

Cara was raped in first year. Another student roofied her and walked her back to his room. She woke up half-naked on his bed. He was watching her from the chair next to his desk. While she was still semi-comatose, stunned by what had happened and the residue of the drug, he told her what he had done to her, how he had fucked her, in detail. She couldn't report him. It was her word against his. What you feel when she tells you this: rage at first, but not unironically. You are aware that it is what you should feel. And you feel it uncertainly—does Cara want your anger or your sympathy? After it, replacing it, a cold sickness close to despair. And then a revulsion at what men can do, at what they are capable of. You draw back from Cara, but not visibly. You conceal your discomfort, and maintain the distance between you; instead of pulling away, you sense her isolation and do nothing, consciously do not reach out with either tenderness or desire: some victims can repel us with what they make us feel. You think about this regularly, probing the incident and your response, as if the hurt belongs in a way to you, but never when Cara is present.

*

During her MA, Cara had an on again, off again, mostly off again, never quite a relationship with another graduate student. He was an eighteenth centuryist with delicate bones and a darting quickness who approached everything he did, from scholarship to relationships, with the same adamant drive, as if the key to life was deliberate persistence. He worked as a research assistant writing entries for an online encyclopedia of eighteenth century culture. She tells you this with pride. He is a doctoral candidate now, and he has a small penis. The first time they slept together was in a closet down the hall from the graduate student offices. When he put it in, she couldn't feel it. You wonder if this is an exaggeration. It reminds you of a line from *Sex in the City*. Cara isn't quoting, but she often speaks in formulas. He is still pursuing her, she says, and she still answers his calls, sees him regularly, although not for sex. You notice how she lets men who want her, who have loved or still love her, stay in her life, how she keeps them at a remove, at the end of a long distance phone line, but never entirely leaves them behind. You notice too that you always sit across from each other with an arm's length of table between you, only talk like this on Friday afternoons, and live in opposite directions.

*

Cara's first boyfriend in graduate school, her partner really, was a philosophy PhD from Edmonton who was writing a thesis on Heidegger's materialism. He once presented at a conference attended by Derrida. Cara never tells you how they met, or when they moved in together. All she talks about is what came after. He was an alcoholic who went on day-long benders, bar hopping across the city, and stumbling home, incoherent, always belligerent, at odd hours, in the middle of the afternoon or in the blind darkness of the morning. He once found himself at a New Year's Eve party thrown by Russell Smith, but didn't know who he was. Cara told him where he had been after the fact, when he described the host to her. He won a SSHRC and started doing cocaine. He came home, still high, his euphoria declining into a lucid sedation, and asked her if she knew that you could smoke cocaine. "Oh my God," she said, "you smoked crack," and he didn't seem bothered.

They had a two-bedroom apartment, and the second bedroom was his office. He wouldn't let her into it, not even to clean. Dust coated the desk. Dust softened the lines of the monitor. Spiders strung webs between library books, and he wouldn't let her get rid of them. He said he needed them to think, and slammed the door.

He hated that she could only come with a vibrator. She hid it in her underwear drawer, or at the back of her closet, but he would find it, and break it.

There were the good times, like the period when they went to restaurants. They went to ethnic restaurants, Thai, Cambodian, Ethiopian, an Eritrean restaurant that they made the mistake of calling Ethiopian, or searched out undiscovered gems, trying to find the next big thing before it got big and they couldn't afford it. They went on long streetcar rides to these restaurants. On the way back, they sat together in the almost empty cars, touching comfortably, feeling sated, a little superior. They saved up, and went to North 44 for an anniversary. They agreed that it was better on TV.

And then there were the fights, wild, hysterical screaming matches, and worse. He smashed a plate against the wall, and she called a cab. He followed her out to the street, and they fought on the sidewalk, yelling, crying, coming undone and not caring who saw them. When the driver pulled up, he asked her if she wanted him to call the cops. "The cops," says Cara. The word is an offering. You ask, did he hit her? She is cautious, evasive. What she means, and what you understand, is yes, but not in the way men hit women, in rage, in frustration, to hurt; he was lashing out at the impossibility of the situation, not at her. She may have hit him back. You are shaken by the violence, and by the intensity of the emotion: Cara has been caught up in an attraction that didn't stop at destruction. You think of her on the sidewalk, painfully revealed, but in silhouette, a picture of herself. Coming undone. Not caring. She is set apart in your mind, and in hers. She never tells you how it ended. It isn't how it began, or how she got away that matters, what counts is the tangible fact of the trauma, that it happened.

When she met him, he wore Nine Inch Nails t-shirts. Those were the ones she recognized. The rest were shirts for industrial and metal bands she didn't know. Some of their names were German. All of the shirts were black with hard-edged lettering in reds, greys and metallics. They were faded, frayed at the hems, beginning to disintegrate, and he wore them over jeans that were old enough that his mother could have bought them for him. She took him to The Gap for basics and to Club Monaco for professional attire. She convinced him that his shirt size was medium not large, and persuaded him to buy a pair of khakis. She told him what to wear to conferences, lectures, and department functions. The next time he applied for teaching, he got a section of Intro to Philosophy. "I got him that course," says Cara. She is bitter, proprietary, pre-emptively defensive.

The fall is edging into winter, the afternoons are dulling into evenings, and your conversations are turning clipped and listless: she is getting tired of the pressure of your attention. And you are getting tired of listening.

*

Cara tells you that she met her most recent boyfriend, the one she might still be dating (she doesn't know, or won't say, and you have been careful not to ask), at a party. She didn't like him at first, but then she decided that she liked him. She wasn't sure if he liked her. He is casual, inattentive. It is a relief to not be cared about too much. She took him bathing suit shopping, and he encouraged her to buy a knit two piece. It wasn't until she was walking out of the water at Wasaga Beach last summer that she realized it was see-through. He didn't seem worth getting mad at. He took her to Niagara Falls for the weekend, and got a suite with a heart shaped hot tub. She asked him if he was being ironic. He looked surprised. After sex, he turned on the basketball game. They lay there in the hotel room and the flickering light of the television. Neither of them talked. And Cara didn't mind. She tells you it was peaceful, almost reassuring: she could exist, she could breathe for as long as she wanted to, in the stillness of being his girlfriend.

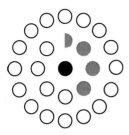

Sex (With Footnotes)[1]

The first time Sebastian has sex with Cara, real, penetrative sex,[2] they start out lying on her bed. They talk for a long time, past midnight, softly but emphatically, without effort: there is always something to add, to say or tell, to reveal, and no room for silence.

The sounds of the house become sharper and more remote. The cars go by less frequently outside the window. They notice their intimacy: Sebastian strokes her forehead to the slightly oily fringe of her hairline, to the delicate prickle of scalp and the smooth and shifting filaments

---

1   Neither Sebastian nor Cara is capable of having sex unselfconsciously, without second, third, fourth, fifth and etc. thoughts: during the act, these consist of detached observations whose clinical objectivity would be bitterly cruel if it were intentional, flashes of memory, and the doubts, second guesses, and unspoken desires of two people who are still discovering each other together; afterwards, they include a probing review of every detail–in Sebastian's case privately and in Cara's over the course of three discussions with her roommate–and retrospective fantasies that prompt a dozen bouts of masturbation between the two of them; here, they take the form of footnotes.

2   They made out on her couch once before, and on her bed, and the last time they lay here, in this same spot and configuration, a little drunk, restless with discovery, anxious also, she had slowly jerked him off while they kissed: they were face to face on their sides. He felt her skin, her warmth against him, and the cold air in the empty places between them, a tender discomfort against his blood flushed cock. Her hand was small and hot and insistent. She wanted to fuck, but he hadn't brought a condom, and she didn't have any.

She stopped and rolled onto her back.

"But there's other stuff we can do," he said, and was immediately ashamed of the word "stuff" and even more of the half-whining adolescent voice in which he said it. He will still be ashamed of it years later. He will hunch and tuck his chin when he thinks about it so that the memory of the word is indistinguishable from the sensation of reducing himself.

She told him he could finish himself off, and he wanted to come, but not like that, alone, with Cara unreachable, superior and disappointed, beside him. He tucked his deflated penis back into his jeans. They slept in their clothes on top of the sheets.

He resented her stopping and taking away her hand, withdrawing her desire with it, but, more than that, he resented the need she had revealed in him, the smallness and vulnerability. Now, that night and how she had rolled dismissively onto her back make him careful, almost fastidious, and slow at first.

of her hair laid flat along her skin,[3] and then the looseness of her hair falling in a ripple away from her head, the curve of her ear, and the almost undetectable fuzz of her neck. The fingers of his second hand follow her hip to the open warmth at the small of her back where her shirt rides up over her jeans. The tips rest there, light—he thinks, barely felt[4]—and ready to withdraw.[5]

Cara kisses him. She is gentle, inviting without urging, and he matches her gentleness.[6] His fingers keep working in the crevice between her waistband and her rucked hem: they advance by delicate steps, as if by accident, as if they are separate from him, from each other, and detached from intention. They lift by steps the bunched folds of her shirt. They inch it. They push it higher. Until. He palms the small of her back and she arches against him. The movement is both decisive and equivocal— she bends away from his hand and into his body—and it leaves room for doubt. He firms his hand to feel the depressions on either side of her spine, below that bone easing to the lushness of flesh and the beginning of her ass. His cock is hard. It binds inside his jeans. He shifts and there is a brief confusion about whose leg goes over whose. Sebastian smiles. Cara frowns. She starts to undo his shirt.

When she tugs the last button free and draws the fabric over his shoulders, he can tell that it has been decided: they are going to have sex. This liberates him from the constraints of ambiguity.[7] The lead up to sex has always been like this for him—questioning, defensive encouragement, followed by certainty, and the restrained pleasure of finding out a woman's limits, deciding what he wants to do, and discovering what she will let him

---

3   He is used to coaxing women towards sex. He has always masked uncertainty with tenderness, compelled, insisted softly, and waited for them to reciprocate.

4   She feels him thinking this as much as she feels the hovering, now half-weighted, tips of his fingers.

5   The lightness of his touch communicates his reticence to Cara. She is used to sleeping with men (even when she thinks it, she gives the word depth and resonance, fills it with the force of her diaphragm) who are confident, even aggressive, men who insist with their bodies, and have to be resisted, controlled. She can tell that Sebastian needs permission; he needs to be encouraged. In his fantasies, women ask him to do things to them. His passivity makes her conscious of her power, and annoys her: it is immature, adolescent, almost childish, and she hates childishness in men, especially during sex. She can tell already that Sebastian will have to be led, that even his demands will be restrained. He will wait, delay, he will make her take the initiative, and she will respect him less because of it.

6   He remembers that she doesn't like stubble, and he is conscious of his face, even though he shaved that afternoon, the friction of their skin, and the fine hairs on her face. He thinks about her small and perfect teeth.

7   And from a kind of tact that he substitutes for respect.

do.[8] Cara feels his hands and stroking fingers become firmer, more definitive, but Sebastian still stops them short.

They undress each other: he pulls her shirt over her head. She completes the process of taking off his shirt[9] and unbuckles his belt.[10] He fumbles with her bra. She frowns again—he can feel the tension harden through her body—will she pull away?—and helps him.[11] Her breasts[12] are small,[13] a further softness after her forehead and her back. He marvels at their olive skin, lighter here, more yielding, and more delicately itself.[14] She inhales when he touches her

---

8   As he has gotten older, he has gotten better at reading his partners, and grasping this moment. When he was younger, a teenager and then a young man, sex was a prolonged uncertainty: periods of foreplay during which he searched for the confirmation he needed to be confident, and then worrying while they were fucking whether what he was doing was right, and welcome, edging, even as he worried, towards what his partner wouldn't accept. He often felt like he should apologize after it, and did once.

9   Although he has lost weight over the past months, he notices his stomach, the looseness and pucker of leftover fat, the frizzle of hair on white flesh. His skin follows gravity when he lies on his side. He rolls onto his back, it settles flat, soft and muscleless, and he can ignore it.

10   She likes men who are thin, lean, their skin taut over spare muscle, their bodies avid, contained in hardness. Sebastian is not thin. She reflexively sees the best of him, the brackets of his collar bones, the bumps of his hip bones showing over the waistband of his boxers when he lies back, and his happiness that she lets herself believe is grateful and uncomplicated.

11   She wants to forget herself during sex, to do without thinking, easily, fluently, and his clumsiness prevents this. Sebastian likes these moments of awkwardness: they are for him moments when intimacy breaks through the formula of performance: lovers laugh at themselves, laugh together, and are safe from judgement in their shared ridiculousness. Cara is reminded of the immaturity she sees in Sebastian. She already suspects that they are not right for each other.

12   He remembers: the first time he saw a breast in person, touched the skinflesh of a breast, and felt nothing unusual. Adolescent anxiety erased surprise, desire, wonder. It was simply skin and flesh; warmth was a temperature. Now: he is smiling widely, unselfconsciously. Cara likes this apparently, and its insistence, how it imposes, but hides nothing.

13   He has never slept with a woman with large breasts. He wonders what they feel like, if they have weight—they must—and what kind, when he watches porn, or when he is walking, or doing anything else. It is one of a dozen things he misses because he has never done them, like anal sex or a woman kneeling naked in front of him asking to suck his cock, but not like they do in porn, sensually, aestheticizing her own exploitation, like women do in Leonard Cohen poems. Sometimes he is ashamed of making sexual checklists, sometimes he cringes internally and thinks about objectification and what he learned in undergrad about structures of power, but usually not.

14   She has thought of getting boudoir photography done, and she returns to this idea as she watches him touch her breasts: a set of tasteful nudes. She told him this earlier. They stood at the dresser in the corner of the room, and she showed him jewelry passed on to her by her grandmother. Silver from the 1920s. Dull and intricate necklaces. Bracelets that colour every movement with sound. He imagined her posed in black and white, on a stool, half turned towards the camera, fabric falling in pleats from her shoulders, draped over her lap and falling from her thighs. Faintly sepia. Revealed. And impervious. She told him that she wanted to remember what she looked like now when she got older. He thought this was superficial, but did not say it. He checked his face and the line of his stomach in the mirror over the dresser.

nipples. She unbuttons his jeans,[15] takes out his cock,[16] and starts to suck it.[17] He watches her suck it.[18] She bobs, pausing to put half of it in her mouth[19] and look up at him.[20] She stops before he comes,[21] and they start kissing again.

He sits up, and they finish undressing, facing each other in the middle of the bed. While she is working out of her jeans, he puts on a condom.[22] He is on his knees, and she bends forward to suck his cock again, but she feels the condom in her mouth and leans back into the pillows. He looks at her,[23] in the

---

15   He is a little bit embarrassed by his boxers. They are a faded navy blue, and there may be a hole in them. In grad school, a woman he had a crush on (blonde, angular hair, a jittery energy, and a tendency to hold forth) told a table of students that she loved men in Calvin Kleins, the band of white elastic above their jeans. He was surprised by this casual revelation (impressed by a confidence he lacked) and by the dramatic exclamation of desire with which she punctuated it. She didn't reciprocate his interest or notice him much. (He understands now that the lack of attention was her way of resisting the pressure of his desire.) He was the only man at a table full of women listening to them talk to each other as women. He remembers feeling privileged and irrelevant. He will feel the same way in those moments when he can tell that Cara is following a formula, when her movements are choreographed, and he is at once necessary and negligible. Cara manages not to notice his underwear.

16   Sebastian is uncircumcised, and this makes sucking his cock harder, less obvious; she has to think about what she does as she does it.

17   He is used to women who tease and delay. The last woman he slept with kissed his chest, his stomach, and the tops of his thighs, pausing between each kiss while he watched her through a mask of arousal, thought, why can't she just suck my cock?, and concentrated on keeping his erection. He likes how direct Cara is. There is no demureness, no reticence, feigned or otherwise; she wants to do this as much as he wants her to do it, and he can enjoy it without guilt or feeling that he is somehow compelling her.

18   He wants to put his hands on her head, direct her, push her up and down at his own rhythm. He remembers an old girlfriend wondering why men do this. She was puzzled, a little offended. He brushes Cara's shoulders and hair, lightly, diffidently, and then lets his hands fall to his sides.

19   Only one other woman has done this to Sebastian. She told him that he had the second longest penis of all of the men that she had slept with. Cara will tell him the same thing several weeks later, and he will recognize that she is flattering his ego without being absurd. He will be disappointed, but still proud.

20   Cara has learned that men have to be looked at during sex, recognized, and Sebastian is no different.

21   Several months later, when they are having phone sex, she will tell him that she loves it when he comes in her mouth, and he will think that he has never come in her mouth, and carry this kernel of resentment forward with him.

22   Neither of them likes condoms. They make it hard for him to come, especially when he is drunk. She says that she can't feel his warmth when he wears one. She also tells him that she likes how his penis thickens at the base. When they don't use a condom, he feels guilty (most of sex is like this for him—a mixture of guilt and desire—dogged by the sense that he should be better than what he is doing), and pulls out. When they do use a condom, he has to fuck her hard to come. Several months from now, they will do it twice in one night. The second time he will pretend to come. Cara will see the empty condom, and panic, thinking that it has broken or leaked. He won't believe his own explanation.

23   Her pubic hair lies flat over her groin. She doesn't shave, but it is sparse and silken. He will learn that it reaches around, between the cheeks of her ass, and, when he sees this, remember an ex-girlfriend telling him about a friend of hers who slept with a woman whose pubic hair went almost to the base of her spine. They will be 69-ing.

dim light of the shaded lamp, against the soft shine of the pillowcases[24] and the metal bars of the headboard, and thinks about going down on her, but doesn't.[25]

He crawls[26] on top of Cara and enters her.[27] He starts slowly, feeling the softness of her breasts on his chest, resting his weight on his elbows, cupping her head with his hands, and kissing her. She pulls up her knees, and angles her hips towards him. He can feel her hands on his back. Cara is attentive, focused, drawing him in. She is making soft, reassuring sounds of pleasure. Sebastian is silent[28] and takes his time.[29] He speeds up, and slows down when he builds himself up to coming, delaying his orgasm, prolonging

---

He will see a tiny freckle of shit by Cara's sphincter. The image will stay with him. He will privately hold this indiscretion against her. Two weeks later, she will read an article about labiaplasties and the shapes of pornstars' vaginas, and complain bitterly that she has to worry about what *that* looks like now, too. He will be sympathetic, complimentary, and a little impatient with her.

24   The olive sheets, and olive and heather pillowcases are the first set of linens she has ever bought new, and for herself. She used her student loan money. She tells him this with the dramatic frustration with which she sometimes responds to minor problems, naked, next to a wet mark on the edge of the bed. He had been fucking her, although not really (she had said, just stay inside me), hardly moving, while she used her vibrator. When she came, she ejaculated. No woman had done that before with him. He wasn't expecting it, and he was a little revolted, and hid it. She explained that her parents were poor (divorced when she was young, an alcoholic carpenter and a waitress), and she had never had nice things. He was uncomfortable, vaguely jealous that she had a past that he couldn't touch. The stain was faint, and washed out.

25   He will later, almost making her come, but he has never done this with a woman before he is comfortable with her, with their bodies together, and, when he does it, it is a gift, no matter how many times it is given.

26   She is disappointed by the occasional awkwardness of his movements, but he transitions to moments of strength, of assertive confidence and tangible force, and the interplay between the two extremes make it seem like he is both emerging and retreating.

27   She is wet, and his cock slides easily into her, without resistance, or fumbling, without pushing ineffectually, shifting and pushing again. The mechanics of sex, its patterns and vectors, are effortless for them. There is an ease to it, a familiarity. This is rare for him. Other women have arched their backs, and tilted their pelvises away from him, or lain straight with their legs stretched out flat, or watched him passively as he struggled to enter them, unresponsive to his awkwardness and frustration. With other women, he has had to learn spontaneity. He knows already, although not consciously, that he will remember the effortlessness of being with Cara, suspect it a little, and miss it, like the tone of her skin or the way she looks at him when she sucks his cock.

28   He is always like this: attentive, deliberately focused, and just as deliberately silent. He has always been too reticent to verbalize his pleasure. Whenever he has said something during sex, it has been in response, repeating a variation of a woman's words back to her, and Cara never says anything to him.

29   In high school, a friend of his who had had the same boyfriend since Grade 8, and who talked openly about her sex life, and especially to Sebastian because she knew he was a virgin, told him, "A gentleman waits for a lady to come." He resented her experience, the knowing, aggressive tone in which told him this, and what it said about him at seventeen. He remembered it. For a long time, without meaning or wanting to, he repeated it to himself during sex. Even after he moved past its echoes, he still tried to hold back until his partner came, and was discreetly proud of how often he did.

a tense and elevated state of anticipation. He does this repeatedly, and she goes with him, getting louder, rolling her hips, and then giving up control, surrendering to the routine of ecstasy, each time. He can't tell if she is coming or not. Her responses are regular. Her eyes are closed or turned away. She is distant, and he feels suddenly lonely and exposed.[30]

He lifts her right leg over his left hip and starts to roll them over onto their sides.[31] She tenses, looks at him with surprise and a touch of confusion, and asks, "How do you want to do it?" He tries to show her, but the yielding complicity of her body has disappeared. They fumble for a while. Her uncertainty feels like resistance; he gets none of the reassurance or closeness he wants, so he rolls back on top of her. She relaxes into the familiar pattern, and he starts to do the work of coming, which is work because he is a little drunk and it is late and he is unsure of her and wearing a condom, thrusting hard, watching her, but concentrating on his own sensations, and thinking to himself[32] that he is fucking her. That he is fucking her hard. Cara moans along with him, louder now, but in tandem with him like before. He takes it as encouragement, and he is too focused on his own pleasure to question its regularity. His reticence and tenderness fall away from him. He puts her legs over his shoulders[33] and enjoys

---

30   This is often the case with him when women come. They withdraw into themselves, close their eyes, and become opaque. They cry out, separately, and not for him. They never say his name. Afterwards, they come back to urge him to orgasm.

31   He used to do this with an old girlfriend. He likes the comfort and sensuality of the position. He doesn't have to support himself on his arms, and he can thrust gently, deliberately, kissing and watching his partner. It fits with his idea of sex as a connection to be prolonged, and reminds him of those moments, fixed in his memory, preserved in fantasy, when he discovered a way through clumsiness into conscious sensuality. Cara resists this and other positions that slow sex to the pace of contemplation, that give Sebastian the time to reach out with the same tenderness with which he stroked her forehead. She becomes passive, awkward. He is a little surprised by the narrowness of her repertoire. Sometimes he thinks about her favourite fantasy: two people talking, but not touching, talking until they come. By chance, maybe by an invisible logic, this leads him to one of her earliest memories: as a small child, she would look out the window and imagine aliens landing in her backyard and taking her away. She would rest her front teeth on the wood sill and bite down. She showed him on his forearm, leaving a brief semicircle of indentations in the skin. Her therapist says this was because her parents fought and then divorced. Sebastian agrees. He refuses to think about the other possibilities.

32   He often thinks about what he is doing to help himself come, forming sentences like "I am fucking her hard," describing himself, flirting with slurs like "whore" and "slut," words he would never say aloud, and forms timidly, cannot even fully commit to when he thinks them. Or he remembers other women, a familiar handful of moments, to which Cara sucking his cock will soon be added.

33   Several days later, when Cara tells him that she talked over sex with him with her roommate (she does this with every aspect of their relationship), and Sebastian asks her what she told her, she says, when he put her legs over his shoulders. He is disturbed by her openness, uncomfortable that she has shared that, a rare moment of sexual assertiveness, almost aggressiveness. Her roommate asked if she liked it, if that worked for her. Cara tells him she said, "Yes." And he forgets to be offended.

bending and pressing on her body.[34] The metal frame of the bed shakes, and the headboard bangs against the wall,[35] briefly distracting him until he looks up from watching himself fuck her and she is looking back at him intently, her face open, her eyes eager and demanding.[36] He smiles when he comes.[37]

There is a pause during which he is still inside her, but not moving or wanting to move, a moment of neutral intimacy. She touches his face. He rolls off of her,[38] and removes the condom sitting on the side of the bed with his back to her. He struggles to tie a knot in the latex, and then walks naked to the bathroom. It is hard to urinate because he is still half erect, and he scans the contents of the medicine cabinet to the left of the toilet while he concentrates on his full bladder, on loosening and forcing, until a weak stream splashes on the porcelain and he has to look away from the makeup and her roommate's anti-depressants.

She is waiting, naked, in the bed, and he smiles again.[39] They smoke and talk. When she turns away to ash her cigarette, she looks back at him over her shoulder, and he can see her face above the curve of her ass.[40] Cara gets up, and walks around the room. She does a handful of yoga poses on the

---

34   This is the first time he shows Cara unrestrained pleasure, enjoyment that has not been adjusted to her, that has not been curated, a selfish pleasure that breaks the mold of his careful and attentive tenderness.

35   The noise will become an issue for them. It carries through the old house, and can be heard distinctly in the other rooms—their rhythm, even the squeaking of the bedsprings as they shift. Cara's roommate isn't home, but, when she is, they will do it on the rug on the floor, sometimes after putting down her duvet, or Sebastian will sit on a chair and Cara will straddle him. The floor will hurt his elbows and knees, even through the duvet. He will dislike being motionless on the chair, and how, when he tries to thrust, she presses her calming hands down on his chest. The ease of sex with Cara will get bound up with these minor difficulties and irritants. It will stumble over practicalities, like the rest of their relationship.

36   Sebastian can tell from her openness, from her face and open eyes, that she is not coming. Her moans are a performance. They are about him, and he doesn't care that they are a performance.

37   Later, she tells him that she likes this. It is different than the faces men usually make when they come; it is bright, intimate in its exposure, not pinched or grim with interiority. He has never thought about this, but he will after she tells him, and, for a while, he will be conscious of how he looks when he comes.

38   He remembers jokes in high school about nailing the dismount and the anxious knowingness with which teenage boys talk and laugh about sex.

39   Moments of happiness are like this for him: they take place, in part, at a remove, and are tinged with unreality. He is offering her his gratefulness, holding out an abbreviated version of his self, a version who can't believe that he has grown up, that he has gotten this woman, and he is walking naked towards her.

40   Early on, she told him that she doesn't like sex from behind, that it reminds her of animals. It was an odd moment of prudishness on her part, and a disappointment on his, one of the occasional unexpected shifts of position that reminded him that he hardly knew her. He agreed. He wants it now, and is ashamed of wanting it, of not asking for it, and of it being so common.

rug, and comes back to bed. After working himself up to it, warily, casually, as if he only half cares, Sebastian asks her if she came. She tells him no, and then explains that she can only come with a vibrator.[41] They talk until the early hours of the morning. She falls asleep against his shoulder. He shifts her head to the pillow and rolls onto his side so that he doesn't snore.

The End[42]

---

41   He can get her close to coming with oral sex, but never quite there. She tells him that if he could go longer she might come. She is objective when she says this, not resentful or demanding. He tries every time he goes down on her, but he can never move his tongue fast enough, and his jaw always cramps. The last time they have sex, closed in a room, in the middle of the night, shutting out the reality of their decayed relationship, holding back the fact that they are already both almost with other people, she climaxes with him, and tells him it is the first time she has come from intercourse. He chooses to believe her.

42   ...is not clean. They break up, and get back together, and break up, and talk about getting back together. Eventually, they move on, but neither of them is satisfied. Sebastian thinks about the relationship regularly. His memories of the sex take on the shape of fantasy. They become a collection of scenes, of set pieces that he fast forwards, pauses and rewinds as he masturbates, they become predictable and convenient, but they never lose the difficult precision of reality or the prickly halo of regret.

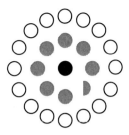

Appendix C: Happiness and Related Scalars

Section 1: Raw Relationship Data

Relationship Data: dates, locations and emotional beats of major romantic relationships from teenage hood to the present as verified by Cara, her significant partners, and independent observers who responded to inquiries. When observers did not respond to specific inquiries, their silence was accounted for in the weighting of the relative significance of data points. Where data was found to be incomplete, it was generated through conjecture, extrapolation from established patterns, and a set of machine-learning-based psycho-affective prediction algorithms (contact researchers) to generate complete entries for all partners.

*Dates both partners and external observers agree on are in normal type. Dates disputed by one partner are in bold. Dates denied by both partners, but confirmed by external observers are in italics.

**Shared Activities are ranked in descending order according to number of hours dedicated to them per week and the relative significance of those hours weighted according to the recollections of both partners.

***Most Lasting Memory is what rises most readily to the surface of consciousness when Cara hears a partner's name. Not what she tells the person who said the name, but what she thinks for a brief moment before she decides what to tell them, what she thinks so quickly that she is left with only the fleeting impression that she has thought something without knowing precisely what.

**** Reason for Ending the Relationship is not the sentence that permanently severed their connection and sent their lives reeling off on separate trajectories, but the words that first pried open a fissure between them.

Partner: Mark Hunter

Dates: October 9, 1993-November 27, 1993

Locations: Toronto, ON

Shared Activities:
- Walking slowly along the fall streets, talking in a listless circular way that flattened time into the perfect, continuous, unbearable present of being together.
- Sitting with a space closing between them in a carrel in the junior high school library.
- Considering privately and separately whether and how much they should touch.
- Working quietly on their homework in Mark's apartment on the dining room table that was covered with a white cloth, a lace cloth and then a clear plastic sheet through which Cara could feel the muted ridges of the lace pressing into her elbows.
- Waiting. Waiting for Mark to tell his mother about his school day so they could go back to walking the streets where the light was already blurring into the uncertainty of evening. Waiting on the shining parquet of his foyer. Waiting for class to finish. Waiting a beat, often two beats, too long for him to fill in the emptiness that opened after her words.

Most Lasting Memory:
The silence that held and magnified their movements as they pressed together against the metal door at the top of the stairwell in Mark's apartment building that was the same silence that hung over his dining room table and sometimes felt like a weight pressing her bare forearms down onto the ridges of lace and that mutated into the silence that filled up the space after she spoke and before Mark responded which turned inevitably into the silence that was her waiting until it wasn't anymore; it had become the silence he disappeared into once he said (see below).

Reason for Ending the Relationship:
Mark: "I wanted to see if you would let me do it."

Partner: Simon (for a decade now, variably Si or Simon depending on his mood) Richards

Dates: *May 27, 1996-May 30, 1996*
June 15, 1996-**March 12, 1997**
March 20, 1997-March 27, 1997
July 2, 1997-**September 8, 1997**
October 12, 1997
October 17, 1997
October 31, 1997
November 21, 1997-November 23, 1997
November 29, 1997-February 6, 1998
March 30, 1998-*August 11, 1998*

Locations: Toronto, ON

Shared Activities:
- Refining their opinions of their friends and acquaintances, of the strangers they watched walking past as they blew the smoke from their cigarettes out the bay window of Simon's mother's apartment.
- Making fun of terrible films they rented from Blockbuster and then of the hairstyles of MuchMusic VJs who they sometimes saw on the street and were always surprised by how human and vulnerable, how much smaller, they looked in person and then re-watching the films to see the parts they missed because they were laughing so hard they stopped paying attention.
- Fucking on the couch in front of the TV that was playing a movie they would rewind and watch again from the beginning when they were done, Simon experimenting with her body, inventing things to do so that he could demand them from her, trying and failing to make her come until he got tired of trying and fucked his frustration out on her.
- Arguing about the state of their relationship, about whether they were together, whether they could be together, and whether, before they were old enough to even begin to understand what the future was and how that unknowable reach of time and possibility wears on everyone's decisiveness, they had a future together.
- Telling each other in the middle of these arguments what was wrong with each other and that they weren't trying hard enough, that they weren't trying, that they didn't care, at all.

Most Lasting Memory:
Not a memory. Simon called her out of the blue for a decade after they broke up for good the summer after Grade 12, not often or regularly, but often enough that what they had lived together for almost two and a half years remained for the time that he was calling immediate and raw. It never rested. It never settled. It never sedimented into memory. And, when he finally stopped calling, she discovered that everything she recalled about them was filtered through the faint sound of him saying "Hi" or "Hey" or just "Cara," through all of the need contained in those compact attenuated syllables, through the sound of his desperation following the signal along the line to arrive in her right ear like the fading echo of adrenaline, and through the conversations that always decayed into the boredom of talking him down for what felt like hours, and sometimes was. When she thinks of him, if she does at all anymore, it is through a portal opened in time by the feeling of her ear turning numb where the hard plastic of the receiver pins it to her head.

Reason for Ending the Relationship:
Cara and Simon at different times, and once together: "I don't love you."

Partner: Stuart Robby

Dates: October 22, 2000-April 11, 2001
              September 18, 2001-April 23, 2003

Locations: Toronto, ON

Shared Activities:
- Debating writing in general and the quality of each other's work in particular. Her telling him that his poems about rural Ontario were good, and then asking if they were him? Was he in them? Really? And meaning that he had grown up in a house on a cul de sac with an above-ground pool in the backyard and trying to make him see everything that that said about him and his art. Him telling her that her interest in boxing was too predictable. Too obvious. And then saying something rude about Joyce Carol Oates' logorrhea. Agreeing that the world needed a new kind of poetry and they were going to write it in different ways together.
- Fucking, although Stuart didn't like the word, not for the slow, barely rhythmic rocking that let him cup her head in his hands and look steadily at her, that let him feel his gentleness, his sensuality, and that for her was sometimes wrenchingly, beautifully, almost painfully intimate, and sometimes, most of the times, tedious.
- Waiting for Stuart to tell her what he thought of a suite of poems she wrote where the white geometries of women's bones were hidden in holes, at the backs of deep closets, in locked chests. Waiting that lasted for only a few minutes but that reached out past the time it took him to read the poems so that, for weeks afterwards, she was poised, expectant.
- Working silently together at a table in a coffee shop. Not touching but feeling each other across the intervening space.
- Calling and leaving a message. Listening to a message and returning the call to get the same leave a message recording. Tonight? Tomorrow night? Yes. No. Not then. An hour later. Finally falling into a pattern of leaving class together and keeping up the phone calls that were never picked up and the meetups that were pre-empted as soon as they were arranged as a pretext that carried them to the next class they could leave together.

Most Lasting Memory:
Was it spring or fall? Late evening or heavily overcast? They walked through the sort of easy cool that lets you wear a jacket to feel your warmth glowing around you or fold it over your arm so that the cold fringes your skin. They walked down a street that seemed to go on for a long way, for as long as they walked, without changing. What street? It feels now like a dream or a memory mixed up with a dream. It has all the precision—the light, the temperature—she wore a long wine-coloured coat and pushed her hands into the feltedsoftalmosttoohot of the lined pockets—and all of the passing ambiguity of something that cannot be real. They were in 3rd year. They talked in that hopeful, jockeying way that lovers who are also classmates sometimes do, like people who are in the middle of that brief period of their lives when they are learning to produce their adult selves, when they are both young and yearning not to be young anymore, and they were able to talk like this while walking down that vague street because their futures had begun to emerge and were filled with possibilities that were still far enough off, still strange and distant enough, still as vague and precise as the street, to feel like certainties. It is not a memory to which she returns often, and, when she does go back to it, it is only incompletely, half-disbelieving, as if waiting for the evening to revisit a dream from which she has not only woken, not only let slip away, but against which she has set the long hours of the day.

Reason for Ending the Relationship:
On the campus of York in the late fall, in the middle of a relationship that always seemed to be faltering in one way or another, with a finality that had nothing to do with

the brutalist architecture that they both agreed was ugly, the stretches of close-cropped lawn greased in goose shit or the clouds that had locked together into a low, corrugated ceiling over the city, into a drab, unreachable surface that didn't say anything about what they felt in that moment, but that would, in time, say everything that needed to be said: "Goodbye."

Partner: Derek Laghari

Dates: **October 28, 2004**
November 12, 2004
November 13, 2004
January 27, 2005
March 18, 2005
March 19, 2005
March 20, 2005
May 7, 2005

Locations: Toronto, ON (exclusively the U of T campus, and mostly the Jackman Humanities Building)

Shared Activities:
- Gossiping about the faculty and the other graduate students, debating their merits, talking with a restrained veneration about the careers of senior scholars, and finding reasons to feel superior to everyone they talked about.
- Listening to him tell her about the eighteenth century, its importance, the richness of its...his words blending into the background of everything happening in her life.
- Sitting at separate terminals in the graduate computer lab at hours that seemed normal to them but were strange to everyone else.
- Confronting the force of his conviction, explaining to him that they were not dating—"they were friends"—which she offered as a consolation rather than a statement of fact.
- Arranging their clothes before and then after the suddenness of sex.

Most Lasting Memory:
A shelf in the storage closet down the hall from the graduate computer lab where she and Derek went to fuck a handful of times that were all, in Cara's mind, discreet events with their own motivations and inciting moments, and, no matter what Derek said or wanted, did not connect to form even the beginning of a relationship. Despite their obvious similarities, there was for Cara a unique and specific texture to the experience of each of the encounters that took place in this closed, generic room, whose clutter was arranged in a pattern that was specific to it, but whose cinderblock walls, beige metal shelves, decades of abandoned journals, rows of identically bound theses from long enough ago that no one remembered their writers, and general aura of disuse could be found tucked away in one configuration or another at the end of an empty hallway on every campus in the country. Did she sense the countless versions of that closet every time they closed the door? Did she feel them when they stood close to each other under the pair of fluorescent tubes that lit the windowless space without lifting the shadows behind the books or the

dimness that half hid the walls? She noticed particularly that shelf with its uniform row of *The Journal of Canadian Studies* whose final volume had fallen over and was leaning at a forty-five-degree angle against a metal divider. It was beginning to bow, and she found herself drawn, even during sex, especially during sex, to the gently increasing concave of its spine and the black lettering that she remembers to this day: Volume 18, Number 4, Winter 1983-1984.

Reason for Ending the Relationship:
Cara to Derek in a hallway in the middle of a weekday afternoon like any other: "I need to go."

Partner: Mark Dorsey

Dates: September 27, 2004-February 12, 2006

Locations: Toronto, ON

Shared Activities:
- Listening to him talk about his PhD thesis in which he was making the case that Heidegger was actually a materialist, and exploring the implications of this insight for reading his inheritors and critics.
- Arguing about his work, about her work, about him disappearing for unpredictable stretches of time, about him coming home dazed into a mumbling semi-consciousness by a mixture of alcohol and drugs, about cleaning, about having sex, about not having sex, about anything until arguing was about the impossibility of the two of them doing anything but arguing together.
- Picking a restaurant to go to that week, talking about the meal on the streetcar on the way home, comparing it to the one from last week, the week before that, aware that they were filling up as much time as they could with this one thing they had found that they could share and agree on, or disagree about without fighting.
- Listening to him talk about Calgary, his family, the people in high school who had hurt him.
- Telling him about her parents, about her childhood, about Mark Hunter, and watching him as he reached out across the table, across the bed, across the rocking streetcar, and covered her hand with his, and wondering as his fingers settled light and warm and calloused still from a summer he had spent as a welder over hers if this deliberate offering contained everything that he would give her.

Most Lasting Memory:
Their apartment without him. The rooms that belonged to both of them, but that, in his absence, in the stillness that opened behind him, were determined by the residue of his presence that was both the echo of his departure, a fading thing, and a guarantee that he would return, sometime, often when she had given up waiting, when she had let go of her frustration and begun to expand to inhabit the space, to live fully in the sounds of herself moving through it alone. The bedroom that they shared. The second bedroom that was his office and that he wouldn't let her clean because the dust that banked in the corners and furred the irregularities on the walls

helped him think. The open kitchen/living room/dining room where they always ended up when they fought, as if they needed the room to fly apart, to yell the way they couldn't in the closeness of the bedrooms, and from which they threatened to tumble screaming onto the street, which they did explode out of incandescent with disaster how many times? Most of all, the pine table with the tacky varnish that the summer heat would weld to the skin of her forearms as she waited and then stopped waiting for him.

Reason for Ending the Relationship:
Cara when the cab she has called pulls up to find them fighting on the sidewalk in front of their apartment and the driver asks her if she wants him to call the cops: "No."

Partner: Mike Spurr

Dates: March 2, 2006-[. . .]

Locations: Toronto, ON
            Windsor, ON (mostly a room in the casino hotel)
            Toronto, ON
            Niagara Falls, ON
            Toronto, ON
            Wasaga Beach, ON
            Toronto, ON
            London, ON (for half a weekend)

Shared Activities:
•   Watching TV with their bodies laid out long on his couch, more often his bed, sometimes a hotel bed. Basketball when it was on. Or whatever. He wasn't picky. She didn't care.
•   Listening to him tell her about his friends that never became her friends, about the ones he played basketball with, the one he went to musicals with, the one who complained that he couldn't buy good basil in Toronto.
•   Shopping. Really, walking slow circuits through stores, picking things up and telling each other what they thought of them.
•   Going on weekend trips to Niagara, Wasaga Beach, and planning but never taking a trip to New York.
•   Fucking in a perfunctory way that was as casual and uncomplicated as watching TV.

Most Lasting Memory:
The callous, almost contemptuous, way she talked about him when he wasn't present: he had ridiculously (she turned each syllable into its own word) thick legs. When he put on jeans, it looked like he was wearing two pairs of pants. Two pairs! His friends didn't make sense. Who plays basketball one day and goes to Chicago with a group of guys. Just guys! The next? He's probably gay. And the distance that always expanded between them. How he seemed impossible when he wasn't right there, solid and breathing beside her in front of the flickering television. How that let her say these things, say whatever she wanted to, so easily and guiltlessly.

Reason for Ending the Relationship:
Over the course of that half a year, Mike, but mostly Cara, thinks about calling, and doesn't: "..."

Partner: Sebastian Schade

Dates: September 30, 2006-December 7, 2006
January 11, 2007-January 28, 2007
March 17, 2007-April 3, 2007
September 21, 2007-September 23, 2007
February 19, 2008

Locations: London, ON (the house on Oxford Street at the crest of the hill west of Western Road that she shared with a single roommate, and once the semi-detached in the subdivisions in the northwest of the city that he shared with three other postdocs who were all away for the weekend when she came and stayed for three days until she couldn't anymore and panicked and wanted to walk home but let him call her a cab at 3 a.m.)

Shared Activities:
- Talking about everything that she had talked about with both Marks and Stuart and Simon and not talked about with Mike, going on in a rush past tiredness and the last of the cigarettes until their voices turned rough with talking, racing towards dawn, driven forward by the euphoria of re-discovering themselves through each other.
- Discussing the fact that he was a post-doc and she was only starting her PhD and they couldn't let anyone in the department find out about them because of what it would say about him, but, mostly, because of how she thought people would look at her. And understanding but not telling him that it was also because of her uneasiness with him, because of the coursing intensity of their conversations, and because of his blanket acceptance of her and how it meant that she couldn't trust him.
- Explaining to him that she couldn't be in a relationship, even a secret one, not right now, not after Mark (Mike didn't count), not while doing her degree, not when there were papers, comprehensive exams, and her own writing, so much she wanted to do, so much she had to do, and she had taken a year off, and she had worked as a bartender and hated it, and she was older than her cohort, but everyone had read more than her, and she was already behind on everything.
- Talking on the phone because he couldn't—she told him and he agreed, he always agreed as a way of ingratiating himself with her, and that was half of the problem— come over to her house because of her roommate and the front door that opened onto a busy street that people walked on and took the bus on and drove along on their way to the university.
- Having sex with a slow and conscious urgency, as if that time—right then—in the early morning—always in the blind dark before dawn—would be their last.

Most Lasting Memory:
The nights when he showed her a new version of herself, and the mixture of shame and elation (in its sharpness worse than the shame) that went along with this and that seemed, at the time, both unbearable and necessary. Now, on those few occasions when

this memory returns, she will let herself feel that surge of emotion for a difficult moment, she will examine it like she would inspect a strange and delicate object whose purpose she can`t understand, she will turn it carefully over in her hands, and then she will set it just as carefully aside.

Reason for Ending the Relationship:
Cara, twice, both times in a terrified voice in the middle of the night: "We can't be together."

Partner: Jon Neeves

Dates: August 14, 2011-November 29, 2014

Locations: Toronto, ON (at first, in the neighborhoods where the two cities that they knew and had lived in separately overlapped, and then in neighborhoods neither of them knew, and then in the neighbourhood around their house and then just their house that they shared with the easiness of two people who like but don't care about each other anymore)

Jon's parents' farmhouse, west of Collingwood (the dining room that was small and square and fit a too-big table and had chairs whose backs banged against the wall if you stood up abruptly, the woodlot behind the house, and the trails that branched cold and deserted through it and that wound their way along fence lines and more woodlots to the shore and then back up the mountain)

Shared Activities:
• Working on the house they picked out together in the east end of Toronto, and that he put the down payment on with the money that he had saved by living with his brother in the same basement apartment for more than ten years and topped up with the hiring bonus that he got when he started as a project leader at Constellation Software.
• Doing things separately that they could show to or share with each other: he started a small online literary journal named after the Scarborough Bluffs, and read her the poems he published. She remembered some of the names of the writers from her undergrad. She started cooking. She bought a crockpot and learned how to make cornbread with bacon grease that they both ate too much of whenever she baked it.
• Taking long weekends at his parents' house outside of Collingwood, particularly in the winter, when his parents were in Greece or Mexico or, one time, Argentina. Sitting around the kitchen table drinking whiskey and smoking and talking with his friends who were now her friends, and the next day going for long hikes, sometimes winding through the trees up the mountain until they could turn back and look out over the open slate gray of Georgian Bay trimmed in ice. At first doing this half ironically and then wholeheartedly because of the way their hangovers made everything colder and sharper and closer.
• Talking about her job at a textbook publishing company, about how little time or energy she had to write, and about how much of her student loans she still had to pay off.
• Letting themselves disappear into the everyday tasks of living together.

Most Lasting Memory:

The feeling they shared when they had finished something. That mixture of pride and satisfaction that was, at its base, a flatness and stillness that followed the moment of completion when they stood back and looked, looked at the planted garden, at a freshly painted room or the hiking trail they had climbed to its summit, stood and looked at what they had done for as long as they wanted to without any urgency, and that wasn't, in the end, enough for either of them. Or maybe it was too much, too alluring. And that explained the calmness with which he helped her pack the moving van after they decided to go their separate ways without fighting or yelling or pleading, and, when everything was loaded, how they hugged with the awkwardness of new strangers on the porch of the house (he was keeping it), and then how she got in the front of the U-Haul, and they both thought about waving but didn't, and she drove off.

Reason for Ending the Relationship:
Jon: "Done?"
Cara: "Done."

Partner: Alexander (Alex to Cara and a handful of old friends) Campbell

Dates: October 3, 2014-Ongoing

Locations: Toronto, ON (the Starbucks on Queen Street West east of Bay Street, a room in the Royal York whose curtains didn't entirely block out the early afternoon light, his loft at Queen and Parliament, travel destinations across Europe, once Mexico because they didn't want culture, they just wanted a week to loll in the sun with their books open face down on the tile beside their sun chairs, their fingers reaching sometimes to touch the spines, to feel the hard concave ridge that reminded them that the books were still there, returning always through Pearson to that loft and then to a condo from which they could see the clouds gathering over the lake to the south of the city but not the water)

Shared Activities:
- Eating the meals that she cooked for him by herself in their galley kitchen because he was working, and talking, as they ate in the evening, in a puddle of light with the lateness of the hour pressing around it, talking in a quiet, aimless way that was comforting without being demanding, and that blended seamlessly into working side by side in front of a show they both felt like they should be watching.
- Traveling, first, to a reunion of his MA class at Cambridge after which they spent a week in Iceland and ate Pylsa (lamb hotdogs) for lunch every day, and then to France, Italy, Trieste, Friuli, the village to which she could trace her mother's side of her family. Walking strange cities. Alex carrying their things in a small backpack with security pouches. Taking pictures of each other mimicking the poses of statues in a way that she knew she would have hated and said was juvenile before she met him and she travelled on her own and slept in pensions, but that was now frivolous and adorable, instead of definitive, because of the hotels that they walked back to, the white sheets that accepted their exhaustion at the end of the day and the concierges Alex spoke to with a casual familiarity she was learning to replicate.

- Navigating the tests and infertility treatments and in vitro fertilization and her miscarriages and the long and painful decision to get a surrogate and the torturous legalities that followed from that and felt like another unnecessary, unavoidable trauma and waiting and hoping and waiting and one day holding their son and naming him Stephen in a late afternoon hospital room and taking him home that evening.
- Marveling at Stephen and the occasional wonder and constant demands of parenting.
- Giving each other the room to be themselves independent of who they were together: Alex working on a big contract, a merger or acquisition, late into every night for two weeks. Cara disappearing into herself at her desk in the living room to write another chapter of her book, not talking to or looking at him or Stephen for several days at a time, eating microwave popcorn, pacing and fretting like she was in grad school again, but without that old wildness or desperation because she was in their condo above the city in Yorkville and she had a book contract and editor's notes and a looming publishing deadline with a press whose launches she went to when she wrote poetry that she hardly remembered anymore.

Most Lasting Memory:
Not a particular moment or a single event, but, in many moments, when events are moving quickly around them, how she turns to his face, and finds it there, and she is reassured, not by his sympathy or concern, but by its reliable presence, by its steadiness, by its length that always surprises her when she notices it, and by the way that his hair falls over his forehead and makes him look a decade younger than her even though he is close to that many years older than she is, that makes him look almost childish. In these moments, she wants to reach out and push his hair back, and sometimes she does.

Reason for Ending the Relationship:
N/A

Section 2: Changes in Emotional Commitment Over Time
(Cara and Selected Long-Term Partners)
and Relevant Secondary Variables

Note: Solid lines indicate emotional states/intensities confirmed by the partner and supported by external observation. Gaps indicate an absence of reliable data. Broken lines indicate a discrepancy between reports from the partners and external observers. In these cases, values have been weighted according to the reliability of the informants, and adjusted to match trends in the reliable values in the data set. Values are presented in a numerical scale that ranges from -10 to 10 and represent relative intensities rather than absolute quantities. This facilitates comparison, but it is important to keep in mind that values are relative within the context of the specific comparisons listed below, and not necessarily across multiple comparative contexts.

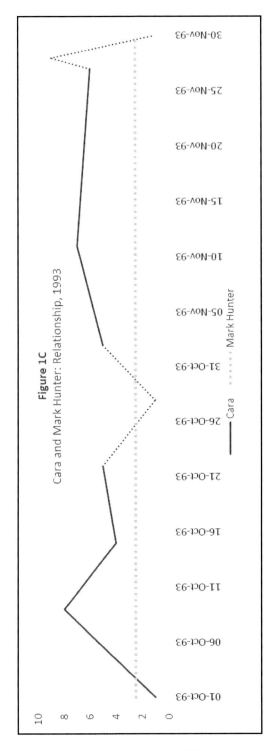

Figure 1C: Cara and Mark Hunter. The lack of variability in Mark's emotional investment in the relationship reflects the absence of any reliable evidence beyond his silences, and even those intervals, their regularity, duration and substance remain speculative. The impact on Cara of their brief relationship cannot be disputed. It registers in both the qualitative and quantitative data for decades after those two months in 1993 as a weakening signal that never disappears, as an asymptotic value approaching something other than the zero of forgetting. We have been left with the indisputable fact that Mark Hunter was, and we have chosen to resolve the problem of representing the absolute and featureless certainty of his existence for Cara with a flat line.

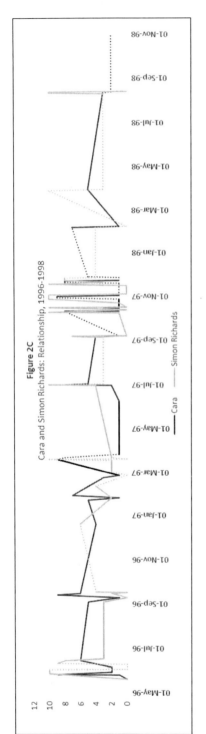

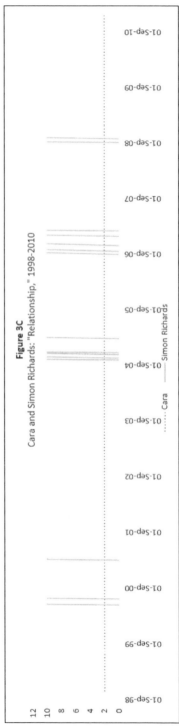

Figures 2C and 3C: Cara and Simon Richards. Figure 2C documents their engagements over the following decade. Figure 3C documents their relationship. Cara's commitment to Simon must have varied between 1998 and 2010 but there is no data for those ten years beyond the fact that (as confirmed explicitly by two roommates, her mother, Stuart Robby and Mark Dorsey, and tacitly by Sebastien Schade) she took his calls.

Appendix C: Happiness and Related Scalars

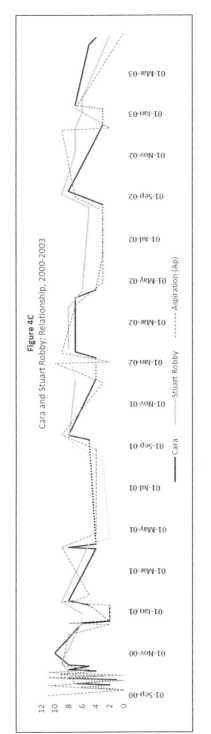

Figure 4C
Cara and Stuart Robby: Relationship, 2000-2003

Cara —— Stuart Robby ------- Aspiration (Ap)

Figure 4C: Cara and Stuart Robby. Cara and Stuart Robby's emotional investment in each other is presented alongside her aspiration to become a published author. Aspiration (Ap) represents a weighted average of her desire to achieve this outcome, her sense that it was a possible/likely outcome of the means by which she was pursuing it (in this case, her degree at York), the time which she dedicated to the work of achieving it, and the attentiveness and enthusiasm with which she did this work. There is a weak to nonexistent correlation between Cara's ambitions to write, or to, as she would have said at the time, "be a writer" (a word that, regardless of where it falls in a sentence, she still capitalises with a barely detectable pause preceding it followed by a similarly subtle lengthening of the first two consonants), and her and Stuart's investments in each other, but Cara, Stuart, three of their mutual friends, and a professor who taught both of them, albeit in separate classes and different years, collectively insist that it was at the time and remains in retrospect impossible to untangle these two strands of her life, that, despite the data, they form a single thread running continuously from September of 2000 until the end of the Winter term in 2003. The researchers would like to note that both immediate perception and memory are fallible, and that recent studies suggest that the gap between what is/was and what is perceived/remembered widens the more broadly a perception/memory is distributed throughout a population, and would add, in addition, that we are often not who we think we are nor who we are thought to be.

31

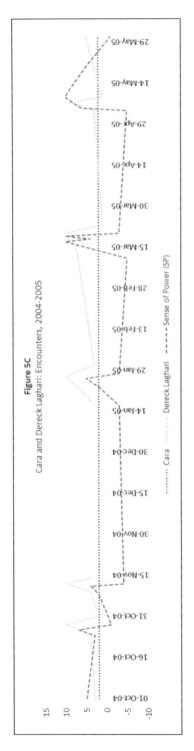

Figure 5C: Cara and Dereck Laghari. All values are disputed by the parties involved. Dereck Laghari's investment reflects an equal weighting of his and Cara's assessment of it. Cara's investment reflects her reports exclusively. Dereck Laghari provided multiple contradicting descriptions of her investment whose values were discounted on the basis of their variability, and whose existence was reflected by indicating that Cara's investment was the subject of a discrepancy between multiple (her single and Dereck Laghari's several) accounts. Sense of Power (SP) represents Cara's relative perception of her own agency, not her absolute ability to control her own life as such (which remained more or less constant through the period), but her subjective perception of her capacity for agency, or, more properly put, her relative capacity to access her own agency. The timespan of this graph overlaps exactly with the first eight months of Cara's tumultuous relationship with Mark Dorsey, and, consequently, SP is significantly determined by data not included in this figure (see Figure 6C). Finally, it is important to note that SP consistently peaks several (1-3) days before encounters with Dereck Laghari (coinciding in this figure with peaks in his investment) and declines sharply during and after the encounters. The exception to this is their final encounter in May 2005. In this case, SP rises to the encounter, peaks several days after it, and declines at a much slower rate. What connection, if any, there is between this anomaly and the end of their encounters remains unclear.

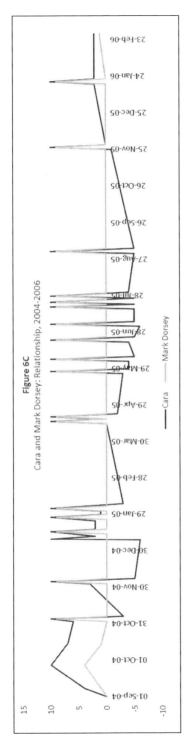

Figure 6C
Cara and Mark Dorsey: Relationship, 2004-2006

Figure 6C: Cara and Mark Dorsey. All of the values are agreed upon by Cara, Mark Dorsey and external observers. The varying intensities of their investments in each other are certain, only the absolute value (ie. the objective impact of the relationship on each of the parties' emotional health) remains in dispute. It is of particular note that the respective peaks of Cara and Mark Dorsey's investment in each other coincide exactly. This pattern begins with the initial peak on November 4, 2004 and continues through to the end of the relationship on February 12, 2006. Furthermore, these simultaneous spikes in affect, these moments when they are both most deeply committed to each other and their relationship, do not precede their fights. They also do not follow them. They do not reflect either mutual apologies or their even more intensely mutual reconciliations. Instead, they coincide exactly and in each case with the worst of their blow-ups, with those very moments when they were threatening to fly apart, and the cold eye of the data reveals, whether we (or they) agree with it our not, whether we (or they) are willing to reach out and grasp what is there for us to so easily take hold of, that when their ragefrustrationfury finally wrenched itself free of their frames that had turned parenthetical with hours of feuding, when it became a third electric thing between their frozenflailing bodies, in these moments of apocalypse that belonged entirely to themselves and nothing else, they were most Cara and Mark Dorsey.

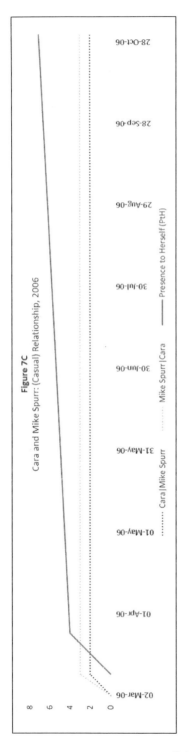

Figure 7C
Cara and Mike Spurr: (Casual) Relationship, 2006

.... Cara|Mike Spurr   ········· Mike Spurr|Cara   ——— Presence to Herself (PtH)

Figure 7C: Cara and Mike Spurr. Both parties' accounts are mirror-true reflections of the relationship, or, in other words, correspond exactly in their outlines and constitutive details, but transposed: Cara reported that Mike Spurr was as invested as he reported she was and vice versa. In this case, both the data and its attribution are in dispute. We have represented both lines and used "|" to indicate that each line may represent the investment of either Cara or Mike Spurr, but not both, so that assigning one line to one partner automatically, assigns the second line to the other partner. The two lines must be read as equally significant, definite in their values, but indeterminate in their referents. Presence to Herself (PtH) represents Cara's presence in the moments of their being together in the small, self-contained universe that every couple creates around themselves no matter how casually and incidentally they are connected. For Cara, these oases of enclosure combined with Mike Spurr's essential indifference to create a stillness through which her sense of herself could slowly return, could come back to her, like a person who arrived on foot from a long way away, a figure that she watched as it became clearer and more definite by the barely measurable units of footsteps, that neither hurried nor delayed, that approached at a rate that was uniquely its own, approached for what seemed like an impossible length of time, until suddenly it was there within hailing distance, and its face was her own.

Figure 8C

Cara and Sebastian Schade: Relationship, 2006–2008

—— Cara   —— Sebastian Schade

Figure 8C: Cara and Sebastian Schade. No reliable data exists. Both Cara and Sebastian Schade confirm, either explicitly, by implication, or by telling omission, the existence of a relationship stretching from late September of 2006 to February of 2008. However, neither provided sufficient or sufficiently consistent data points to produce even an hypothetical representation of this relationship. External observers likewise confirmed beyond a shadow of a doubt the existence of the relationship but could provide no specific data on its nature, intensity, fluctuations, etc. Sebastian Schade climbed the five steps to Cara's house on Oxford Street an unspecified number of times. Cara climbed the two steps to his townhouse in the north-west corner of the city at least once. Those two doors closed behind them and remain sealed to this day. Despite our best efforts, we have been unable to pry them open.

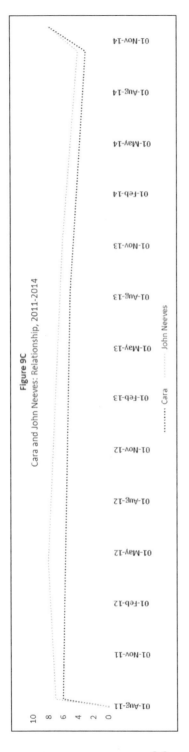

Figure 9C
Cara and John Neeves: Relationship, 2011-2014

.... Cara   .... John Neeves

Figure 9C: Cara and John Neeves. Both partners' investments in each other are represented with broken lines, not because they are in dispute (both Cara and John Neeves described their entire relationship and its limited but still detectable fluctuations in reliable detail, and their descriptions were uniformly reflected in reports from external observers), but because they represent something other than romantic love and its various affective cognates, something closer to friendship, really (as both Cara and John Neeves made clear, but which neither would specifically confirm) the comfort of someone whose life and interests you share without friction, with whom you never argue about what to watch or which restaurant to order dinner from on Friday night or how to love each other, and, if you argue (everyone does, do they not?), you do so only with an easy calmness that makes disputes synonymous with debates. As they both realized on a Tuesday evening in the middle of October when the city was cool without being cold and Cara looked at him from across the room and said, "I'm moving out," agreement is not synonymous with commitment.

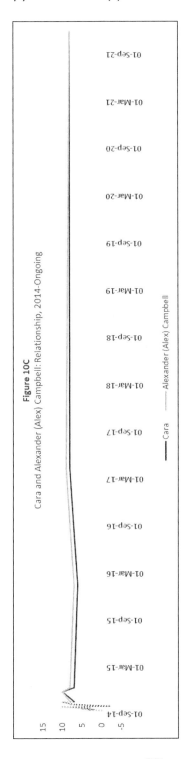

Figure 10C: Cara and Alexander (Alex) Campbell. There is, in these two unbroken lines reaching with little variation from November 2014 through the moment at which you read this into the vanishing point of the future, happiness of a kind whose accumulating depth and breadth exceed the crude representation of this pair of lines and forces us, the researchers, to reckon with the limits of our tools, devices, frames, etc.—in short, with all of the apparatus of investigation, and, consequently, with the investigation itself. In its gnomic simplicity, the right hand side of this figure confronts us simultaneously (as if the two sentiments are on, at first, parallel, and, then, gently but inevitably convergent trajectories; as if they are in some way indistinguishable from the collection of data points to which we have reduced Cara and Alexander Campbell) with our inadequacy and our shame.

Section 3: Changes in Aspiration
and Relevant Financial Variables Over Time

The following three figures present the fluctuation in Cara's Aspiration (Ap) in the context of the financial data that determined the limits of her Ap, of the material conditions of her life as she lived it, and, consequently, the immaterial limits of how she could imagine living it.

The figures cover, in order, the period from mid-high school to the end of the summer before she began her Master's, the entirety of graduate school (both her Master's and her Ph.D.), and her subsequent professional life through to the present. Financial Variables are Cara (Net Income), Cara (Debt), Partner (Net Income), Partner (Assets) and Cara/Partner (Combined Net Worth). Partners are restricted to long-term partners with whom the duration and nature of the relationship provided Cara with a reasonable claim on her Partner's Income/Assets, whether she chose to exercise it or not, and, either supplemental to that claim or persisting in the absence of it, a basic sense that what belonged to one of them belonged, at least in a limited way (see the following discussion of Cara(Debt) and Cara(Assets)) to the other. Partners fulfilling these criteria and included in the data set are Stuart Robby, Mark Dorsey, Jon Neeves and Alexander Campbell. Their names are not listed on the charts. Our primary concern is with the relationship between Ap and the Variables that most accurately represent Cara's material conditions. Affective Variables are a secondary consideration which we have chosen to deemphasize by presenting Partner Variables anonymously.

We have opted for Cara (Debt) instead of the broader category Cara (Assets). Over the period covered below, Cara's debt fluctuated from 0 to a maximum value of $122,581.71. During the 23-year span from 1997 to 2020, she had no appreciable assets, beyond a few pieces of dull silver jewelry given to her by her grandmother, a small filigree mirror frame that she thinks is from the late Victorian period but which she hasn't had dated because she is afraid to find out that she is wrong, a set of olive sheets and matching olive and heather pillow cases that was the first nice thing she bought with her own money for her room in a house she shared with a roommate who was not a partner, a blown glass vase she purchased to put in her dorm room window in first year and whose delicately fluted mouth has survived how many moves?, a collection of Moleskine notebooks that contain sentences she can remember writing, but that turn stranger the longer she waits to return to them, a handful of other objects that are of measurable sentimental value, but no monetary worth, and her claim on her partner's assets. Until she married Alexander Campbell, this claim was at best weak, based on the goodwill that is taken for granted in relationships and the solemn promises that matter more than contracts in the moments they are made, that are offered and received with full conviction (in the closed rooms, always in the closed rooms, that contain the secret two people create between each other), the voice catching on its seriousness, that are tearful and joyful at once, but that are never written down in so many words, that have never and can never have any legal force, that cannot compel anything more than the heart. In short, for the majority of the period in question, Cara (Assets) is reducible to Cara (Debt), and the assets she acquired through marriage to Alexander Campbell are effectively reflected in Partner (Assets) and Cara/Partner (Combined Net Worth).

Ap simultaneously represents Cara's specific belief in her ability to realize the possibility of becoming a writer and her broader intuitive understanding of her capacity to actualize herself. It is juxtaposed with material Variables, but Ap should not be viewed as the result of a rational calculus. It is best, although not completely, understood as the contingent possibility of forward movement, as the horizon of life, as that blueing at the edges of distance, that visible uncertainty that draws out the first step, and then pulls each subsequent one out of it in an accelerating cascade of progress. It is the limit that never comes closer, but that sharpens, becomes clearer and more definite the further you walk, and that is separate from but continuous with dignity. Ap is a relative variable and in each chart is adjusted to a range bounded by the absolute min/max value of the segment of data in question.

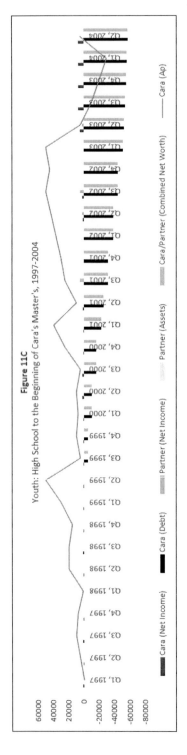

Figure 11C

Youth: High School to the Beginning of Cara's Master's, 1997-2004

Cara (Net Income) — Cara (Debt) — Partner (Net Income) — Partner (Assets) — Cara/Partner (Combined Net Worth) — Cara (Ap)

Figure 11C: Youth: High School to the Beginning of Cara's Master's. Ap climbs relatively steadily through the final two years of high school, stepping up with a series of confirming successes (publications in the student newspaper, praise from a teacher, a poem she watched break a friend open into absolute sincerity), and dipping, but never too much, with minor setbacks, failures that bruised and mattered, but couldn't follow her imagination when it reached out beyond the confines of that building, those halls, and the classrooms filled with restless, urgent bodies. Ap peaks with her graduation in the summer of 1999. When she walks down the stairs of a thrust stage constructed of battered black risers, across a stretch of parquet gym floor carrying two medals and a certificate of distinction rolled into a tube and tied with a synthetic blue ribbon, the ratio of Ap to Financial Variables reaches its absolute maximum. The abundance of white space between Cara (Ap) and Cara (Net Income) in Q2 1999 marks a moment of liberation, one of those brief intervals of time when hopefulness breaks free of the contingencies of life and everything you can dream seems real and possible. Ap declines sharply with the disillusionment of her first year in university, and then climbs steadily, in proportion to her student loans, as if those numbers on the monthly statements which she mostly does not open contain the compressed or rarified substance of her experience, its weight and what that allows her to imagine. Ap declines towards her graduation, and becomes a negative value during the year between her Undergrad and her Master's when she works as a bartender, dates one customer after another, but none of them seriously, doesn't save enough to make even her interest payments on her loans, and, for reasons she cannot understand or will not admit, locks herself out of the life reified in that debt.

40

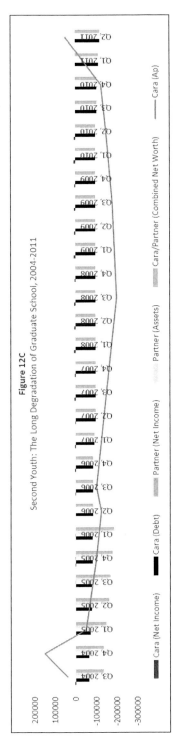

Figure 12C: Second Youth: The Long Degradation of Graduate School. Ap peaks in Q4 2004 at the start of her Master's, her reorientation towards a new set of possibilities and the opening up of new futures which she can appropriate to herself. Ap then dips sharply, and remains negative from the midpoint of her Master's through to the fifth year of her Ph.D. This dip is, in part, the effect of the dead weight of student loans, of the debt that operates as a sort of Nietzschean bad conscience, that lives as a continuous, never entirely absent sense of her own culpability in every minute of the day, and that has its own gravity, its own stultifying allure. This negative value is also an effect of the discovery that the new futures she saw so clearly at the start of her Master's and could imagine again, albeit more gingerly, during the first weeks of her Ph.D. belonged to generations of people who had come before her, that they had already been claimed and defined, and that everything she did would be an exercise in fitting herself into old formulas. Ap begins to climb at the exact moment when she decides that she is done, done with graduate school, done with the anxiety and disappointment of conferences, done with networking that is just another word for flirting, done with Friday afternoons at the Graduate Club declining from dry shoptalk into drunken confessions, and, most of all, done with endlessly thinking about and not doing her thesis. This shift happens on a dull November morning that is no different than any other except that it is the one on which, staring at the counter in the galley kitchen that is too small for her and everything in it, she discovers her determination, gathers herself to make her escape, walks into the living room, sits down at the table at which she once waited through the summer days for Mark Dorsey, and begins to write furiously. Ap climbs as she types, until, five months later, she has written, with both front and back matter, 234 pages on Oscar Wilde and the New Journalism that sit on that table next to her laptop and say with their heft that she is, finally, emphatically, DONE.

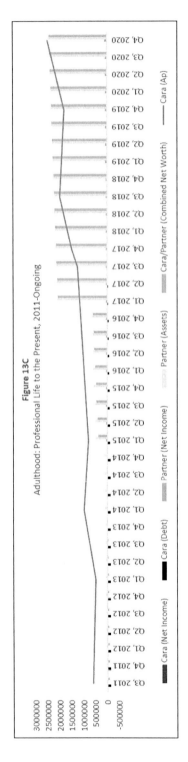

Figure 13C

Adulthood: Professional Life to the Present, 2011-Ongoing

Legend: Cara (Net Income) | Cara (Debt) | Partner (Net Income) | Partner (Assets) | Cara/Partner (Combined Net Worth) | Cara (Ap)

Figure 13C: Adulthood: Professional Life to the Present. Although it declines at several points, Ap remains positive throughout this period, and points at which its rate of growth is negative must be understood in the context of the much more dramatic declines of Figure 12C, Figure 11C and the overall upward trend of the value in this figure. Despite the apparent correlation, Ap should not be understood as responding to the crude and direct influence of the changes in Cara's material conditions. The value should not be viewed as a direct, affective reflection of financial variables, but as responding to the impacts of money as it concatenates through Cara's life, to the sense of security that it carries with it, but also of freedom, of that liberation of the future into possibility that is the inverse of the closing down of debt, to time that expands as the decade progresses, that opens a space in her life that she can fill with writing, to the easy certainties of Jon Neeves' house, to the light that falls through the floor-to-ceiling glass windows of Alexander Campbell's condo, to the way several dozen planes press the full length of her body against the seat as she is hurled forward into the air. Ap peaks when she meets Jon Neeves, declines until they buy the house, and peaks again when she is standing in the living room holding a wet roller, drawing the chemical slurry of the moisture-heavy air into her lungs, and pausing for a moment to look at what she has done and what she still has to do. Ap then drops steadily until she changes jobs and meets Alexander Campbell and it begins to rise consistently, only declining with the inevitable disappointments of her book contract, the editorial back and forth, the box of advanced copies that are beautiful in ways she never imagined, but not in ways that she did, the launch, the festivals and interviews which are at once overwhelming and fewer than she hoped for, until all of that slips away and she is left with a slim volume sitting on the shelf above her desk on whose spine she can read her own name in black letters, and, when she does this, touch the permanent certainty of that accomplishment.

Section 4: Emotional States and Fulfillment Over Time (2008-2020)

Figure 14C: Emotional States and Fulfillment Over Time (2008-2020). Sadness, Despair and Happiness are among the most basic emotions, and are essential affective elements out of which more complex emotions (ennui, grief, hopelessness, melancholy, elation, etc.) develop as emergent properties, at once containing and exceeding these primary feelings. Fulfillment is the multifaceted sense of achievement/satisfaction/accomplishment/completion that marks the alignment of desires (both those that are explicitly stated and those we cannot admit, even to ourselves) with the lived experience of the world—in short, a symmetry that finds its expression in contentment.

Figure 14C

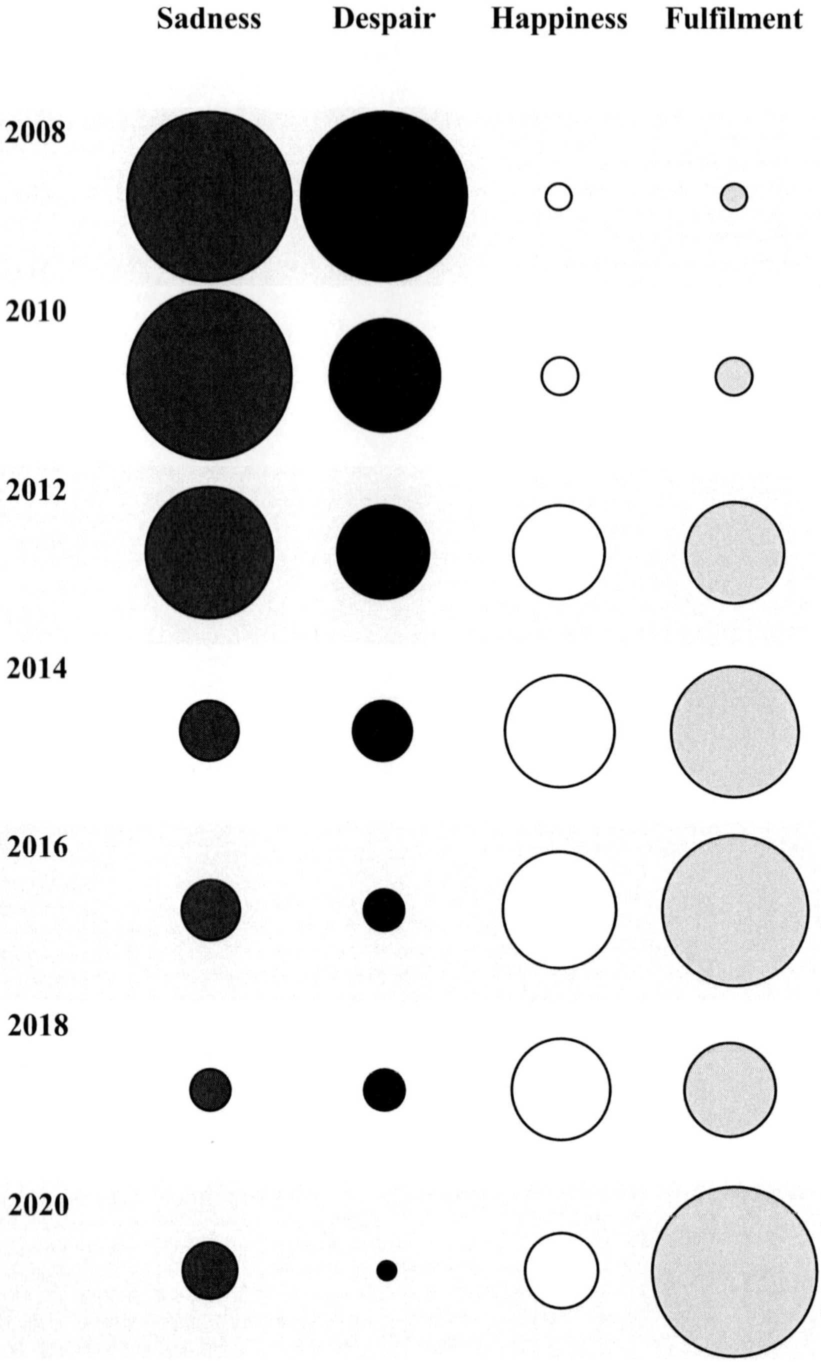
Sadness
Despair
Happiness
Fulfilment
2008
2010
2012
2014
2016
2018
2020

Taxonomies of Loss

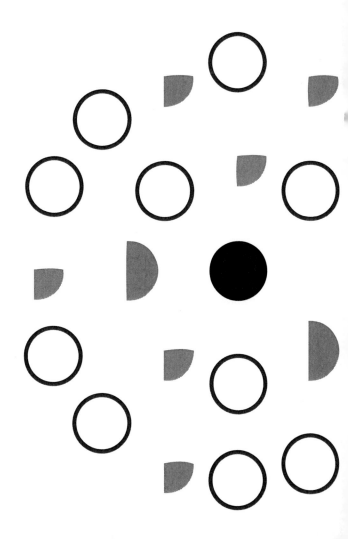

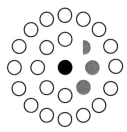

Dugouts

When Margaret told him, Jonathan remembered the dugouts. Their smell. The mud that pinched your skin when it dried. The must of decaying leaves. He didn't know why he remembered them. It didn't make sense, but then nothing made sense.

"They were girls," she said, "young girls."

It was Thursday afternoon, and he had a sudden feeling of vertigo, as if everything had shifted down and sideways and then come to rest. If he took a step, he would miss his footing.

Margaret told him how she had found the pictures on Rob's computer. She hadn't been snooping, she said, although it wouldn't have mattered if she had been. Rob had moved out two months ago. She needed the contracts from the last two quarters for the accountant—Rob ran a small plumbing and electrical company called Rob's Pipe and Socket. Jonathan pictured the logo: Rob in capital letters over an X made by a pipe wrench and a lightning bolt.

"His desktop was a mess," Margaret said. "You know how he is."

"Yes."

"I was just opening folders at random." She described clicking on "Work2" and then "Documents" and then "Clients" and then "New Folder" and then "New Folder" again. "I don't know why. I thought he might have forgotten to name it. It was full of JPEGs. You can see the thumbnails before you open the files. They..."

Her words were spare, exact, hedged against pain, against the hysteria that throbbed in her precision. He could tell that she had rehearsed them, repeated them to herself in an empty room until they had becomes real and true, until she had turned them into testimony. And as she had rehearsed them, she had cut them down to just enough, no more than needed to be said, and part of that just enough were these details: the names of the folders. The girls. Some of them were clothed. A few partially. A handful not at all. She noticed that a lot of them wore their hair in braids. She counted 319 pictures in total. These were facts, these were solid, a substance that had weight, that had heft that he felt as she passed them to him one by one.

"I thought you should know," she said.

"Thank you," he said.

"Someone needs to tell your parents," she said, "before the police..."

"Yes," he said

"Thank you," he said again.

When he hung up, he was surprised that his first response wasn't disbelief, only that sudden unbalancing, that reorientation that left him tilting through the rooms of the house, floating, unmoored, until he touched down in the dirt and leaves of the dugouts.

*

They were Jamie Sterling's idea. Jamie was one of a handful of kids,—Andrew Lucas, Brent Carson, Mickey Holm, and the Berrick brothers— whose houses, like Jonathon and Rob's, backed onto the ravines. In Owen Sound, a ridge runs along the west side of the sound, parallel to the water, and they all lived on top of it, on the edges of a rough semi-circle that ancient streams had carved into the slope. Where the sunny expanse of their backyards stopped, and their green lawns ended in a weedy fringe and a wall of leaves, the land fell away into shade and a closed off stillness, and Jonathan followed it: trees grew there. They had long trunks. Tall and smooth. And branches that started too high up to reach. Jordan, the middle Berrick brother, could shimmy up the skinny ones, but Jonathan's parents said he was half monkey. The tall trees with long trunks blocked the sunlight and the sound of the town, creating a separate space, a columned silence set apart from the streets and cul de sacs around it.

The boys could walk easily along of the tops of the ridges between the ravines, and in their muddy bottoms, but they had to grab onto trees or roots to climb the slopes and dig their hands and heels into the dirt to control their descents. They loved the fearful, whooping exhilaration of sliding down an almost vertical incline greased with damp leaves, skidding their feet ahead of their half-falling bodies, and making a hard, satisfying landing in the dirt. They did it one summer until they wore tracks in the slopes and ground mud permanently into the seats of their pants. It was how Mickey Holm broke his leg. He caught a foot on a root, flipped over headfirst, cartwheeled. and folded it awkwardly under him. He tried to stand up and couldn't. They had to get his father. He slung Mickey over his shoulders, held him on with one hand, and used the other to pull himself up the slope to their backyard. No one told them that they had to be more careful, less reckless, but they knew, and they were, warning each other with serious voices, for a little while.

Unless they brought them to settle a dispute, or dragged them by the hand to show them what they had built, or, frantic, racing ahead, led them right to where Mickey was lying and trying not to cry, no grownups went there, not even to walk their dogs. The ravines belonged to the boys. They played hide and seek, king of the hill and war in them. They competed to see who could jump over the widest parts of the stream that ran through the deepest ravine, gathered in small pools, and slipped away, quick and silent and clear, before winding through a spongy meadow that was half marsh, and disappearing into a storm sewer. One time, Andrew Lucas missed a jump and sank up to his armpits in the shoal of mud under the bank in the meadow. When they pulled him out, he was covered in black muck that stank of rot. His mother made him strip down to his underwear on the lawn and sprayed him off with the hose before she let him in the house. The cold water accordioned his ribs. He squealed and ran in circles like it was a game, and she yelled at him to knock it off, and he did, but they could tell that she was only pretending to be mad. Later that summer, they pushed an old log across the stream and used it as a bridge.

Sometimes, they would crawl up the slopes and spy on their own houses from the shelter of the trees. They watched their mothers, their sisters sunbathing, their fathers mowing their lawns, as single people when they thought they were alone. They looked disarmed, different than the boys were used to, a little like strangers, and the boys felt like they were doing something illicit, dangerous. Jonathan remembers spying on his father. He was reading a magazine on the back deck. He turned the pages and let a hand dangle and swing. He traced loose, distracted patterns on the planks with his fingertips. He seemed smaller somehow. It was hot. Sweat spread in patches from his armpits, and darkened a line where his gut folded into his rib cage. Jonathon watched him for half an hour, luxuriating in the difficult prickling sensation of something like guilt, before sliding back into the cool silence of the ravine.

Sometimes, they created elaborate fantasies, mixing together their favorite TV shows, movies and books, mapping an imagined geography, Castle Grey Skull, Tatooine, and Minas Tirith, over the real one. But most of the time, they built forts. When they were younger, these were simple structures, sticks leaned against trees, low, loose walls made of rocks and mounded dirt, screens of dead branches stabbed into the ground. When they got older, they borrowed their fathers' tools and built platforms where the trunks were close together.

Jamie Sterling always took the lead. He was bad in school, and every year his teachers debated holding him back, but he loved to make things, and he was good at it. He took out books from the public library, old Scouts manuals with plans for lean-tos and tree houses in them, and big, hardcover books about castles and fortifications with two-page, full color illustrations. He always had the best ideas. He showed them what a Quinzee was, and they built one one winter. They used it as a hideout until a pair of warm days caved in the roof. He would go into the ravines alone to work on their latest fort, and he would stay after they got bored and wandered off or went home. He liked to see things finished.

When Jamie was twelve, he got into Vietnam. Before that, he had been into the middle ages, and he had made swords and plywood shields and tried to build a catapult. Before that, it was Voltron, and he still had the full set of robots that fit together to make the super robot Voltron in his room. They all got into Vietnam. They watched *Platoon*, and talked about Charlie and Hueys, and debated whether M16s were better than AK47s. But Jamie took it further than the rest of them. He recorded episodes of Tour of Duty, the TV show based on Platoon, and re-watched them on the combination TV/VCR his grandparents gave him for Christmas. He bought the Platoon video game, and played it so much that he could repeat the route through the jungle level, "down, left, down, right, up...," from memory. He got the idea for the dugouts from the second episode of Tour of Duty, the one in which the squad discovers a tunnel complex under a Vietnamese village. The tunnel rats they send in find bedrooms, offices, storerooms, armories, even a mess hall, a whole, second, invisible village carved out of the earth.

When Andrew Lucas and Jonathan found him, he had already drawn out a tunnel and a round room with his shovel on the floor of the driest ravine, and started to dig. They got their own shovels and helped him. They were getting too old for forts. They were at that stage when they were trying to escape childhood by rejecting the things they used to love, but this felt different than the wood platforms or the Quinzee, it felt bigger, more permanent, more serious, and the work was harder. They dug down at least four feet, until the sides came to their shoulders, and, in Calum Berrick's case, to his eyebrows. They hacked through roots and levered free rocks. Their hands blistered. Their backs hurt in a pleasant, reassuring way, and they periodically straightened up and stretched like they had seen their fathers stretch when doing yard work. In a few days, they had a trench leading to a round hole the size of a family tent. They made a roof by laying down logs and thick branches, and then cedar boughs, marsh grass and plastic they scrounged from Brent Carson's garage. They piled the dirt they had dug out on top of this, and covered it with dead leaves for camouflage.

When they were done, it was a low, symmetrical mound in the ravine floor with an arm reaching out from one end. It didn't look like much, but they climbed into the opening at the end of the tunnel and it was close and dark and real. They had to crouch and grope their way forward. The sides brushed their shoulders. And then it opened into the room.

There was enough space for all of them to sit in a circle. They dug seats out of the walls and covered them with garbage bags. Jamie opened a smoke hole in the roof and built a fire pit out of stones in the middle of the room. Even he knew better than to start a real fire so close to the beams of the roof, so he stuck candles on the stones. The flames lit their faces when they leaned forward, and filled their contours with shadows. Just being in the dugout felt private, conspiratorial, like they were doing something wrong, and getting away with it.

It was the last fort they built together. Jamie kept working on it, regularly at first, and then fitfully, when the mood took him, well into his teens, building more tunnels and smaller rooms, repairing the sections of roof that collapsed over the winters. The rest of them stopped helping him. But they didn't stop coming. It was the one place they could count on being alone.

Calum and Jamie stole porno mags from the bottom of the stacks in their fathers' closets and hid them in a hole in the wall. The boys took them out and passed them around. They inspected the pictures. They talked about sex. They talked about blowjobs. Do they actually blow? Calum said they did. He blew on his hand, changing the intensity of his breath and the shape of his mouth. He looked focused and a bit confused, like he was trying to solve a difficult problem. He was a literalist. He liked building models with tiny pieces that he needed tweezers for and that took days to glue together. His room was filled with replicas of battleships and famous buildings that his mother yelled at them not to touch. Calum stopped passing the magazine. He turned it one way and then the other. He was looking at a picture of a woman getting fucked from behind. The man and the woman were both standing up and the woman was facing the camera. The boys could see the man's head over her shoulder, and his hands grabbing her hips and breasts—"tits" they liked to say. Her legs were spread, showing her shaved genitals, and Calum was looking at them closely. "There must be a hole for it to come out of once it goes in," he said. They argued about this. Jonathan, whose parents had given him an elaborate talk and a copy of *The Joy of Sex*, said it wasn't possible. But the boys wouldn't listen to him. They didn't want clear, sanitized facts. They wanted the magnetic experience of revulsion, not lessons, and Calum was adamant. He swore he could see the penis coming back out. Standing in the kitchen, staring out across the deck into the backyard (how long has he been standing here staring like this?), Jonathan feels once again the atmosphere of confusion and arousal, the discomfort of hiding the hardon that rubbed against his jeans, and the frustration that they wouldn't listen. The tang of mud. The closed walls. He hears Calum saying "look" like he is pointing to a map.

They drank beer they paid older teenagers to buy for them. They smoked pot they bought themselves, plugging the hole in the roof to keep the smoke from getting out. Jonathan's childhood memories of the ravines are precise and clear. His teenage memories are blurred, smudged by substances, a restless anxiety, too-loud voices, shoving that was starting to move past play into the edgy toughness of boys trying to be men.

*

Jonathan stands in the steady light falling through window over the sink. Today's newspaper is open on the island to the headline "Woman Charged After Striking and Killing Dog." And standing there looking out over the deck at the back of the house across from him but seeing the wall of leaves at the end of his childhood yard, he remembers the details of the story: a middle aged woman hit a man walking his dog. It happened at a stop sign at a suburban intersection. She waved them across and then ran them down. The man got out of the way, but the dog didn't. The man. The dog. What Jonathan thinks about now is Rob. Not Rob the way their parents knew him, not Rob who needed glasses to read, who was good at board games, and who was three years younger than Jonathan and needed to be protected from him. He thinks of Rob the way he was with other kids, away from adults, in the intimate spaces of childhood. Rob behind those leaves. Rob as himself in the ravines.

He was a part of a group of younger brothers, Jordan and Mark Berrick, Steven Lucas, and Will Holm, who formed a smaller, looser knit analogue to Jonathan's circle of friends. They tagged along in ones and twos, whining to be included. Sometimes they were. More often, they weren't, and, when they weren't, they hung around out of reach and complained. It wasn't fair, they said. The older kids didn't own it. They weren't the boss. Sometimes they formed a small gang and staged raids on the ravines, creeping down from a backyard, breaking things, knocking over forts, scattering and running like mad when the older boys went after them. Some days, these raids would evolve into games of war with bases, sides and battle lines.

Rob was always at the head of the younger kids. He complained the loudest, the most fiercely, refusing to accept the rules of childhood, their unfairness. He organized the raids. He convinced his friends to stake out a portion of ridge as their own and defend it. He didn't like to run. He wanted to stand up for himself, to fight, and he often did. He couldn't win, and he never won, but that didn't stop him. He was short for his age and pudgy, one of those kids whose bellies are a hard, round curve, and whose arms and legs look too short for their frames. He turned red and wild when he got angry. His freckles stood out like bruises, and he forgot that he was small and fat.

Jonathan remembers: they were having a fight with clods of dirt. The summer had dried the stream to a trickle and baked the exposed mud until it cracked into fist sized squares. They gathered these by the armload and carried them back to their bases. They were like snowballs, but harder, heavier in the hand, bursting into puffs of dust on impact, and more satisfying. At first, they threw them at each others' feet, yelling "Grenade!," imagining the dust was smoke, but then Mickey hit Jordan Berrick in the face. He said it was an accident, but no one believed him, and the fight got serious. They started throwing them hard, to hurt, and right at each other.

When Jonathan hit Rob, Rob was looking over the crest of a ridge. Jonathan could see Rob's head and shoulders. He crouched behind a tree. He waited until Rob turned, and then nailed him right on the top of the head. He shouldn't have done it, and he knew that. Even in the middle of the fight, they were aiming at each others' bodies, avoiding their heads and faces. But he did it anyway. He can't remember why, but he remembers that it was a perfect shot, from sixty feet away at least, long and arching and precise. He remembers the feel of it leaving his hand and watching the high, breathless flight.

Rob never saw who threw it. His head jerked from the impact. The dried mud exploded in a spray of grit. And he went stiff with rage.

He got so angry that he broke a shard of glass out of an old window that someone had tossed into the ravines. It was the length of his forearm, curved and wickedly sharp along the edges, like a knife an exotic bad guy uses in a movie, the kind he pulls with a sadistic flourish on Sylvester Stallone or Arnold Schwarzenegger in the climatic fight scene.

He chased the older boys, swinging the shard in wide, careening arcs. He was going to get them. He was going to fucking kill them.

They scattered, laughing, scrambling out of the way and taunting him. They yelled "Spaz!" They jumped and winced with real terror when he got too close. It was a game, a good one because it was cut with fear as sharp as the glass.

Mickey threw the first clod. Rob was going after Jamie, and Mickey hit him right in the small of the back as hard as he could. Rob seized like he'd been shocked, and whipped around, but Mickey was already darting away. The rest of them joined in, forming a loose circle around Rob, throwing when his back was turned, and then dodging and running. They wouldn't have done it normally. It wasn't fair. The six of them against Rob. Hitting when his back was turned. But the shard suspended the usual rules. And his wild rage. And the thrill of throwing and hitting. And of pushing him further.

Rob was wearing a blue baseball jersey and black track pants. The dried mud left light brown marks where it landed. Jonathan hears the projectiles striking flesh. The hardsoft thud. The bruising sound. The dust stuck to Rob's face and bled down his cheeks.

Rob lunged and tripped. He caught himself with his free hand, holding the glass up, and rushed again. His face was streaked and purple. He started making a hard, high keening noise, an animal sound, the wrenched howl of frustration and fury that would not fit into words, and that collapsed into gasps before starting again.

Jonathan can see him: flailing, hysterical, overcome by and impotent with rage.

Rob stumbled, tried to right himself, but couldn't because he was holding the shard like a glass of water, and went down. It hit a rock and shattered.

They pounced on him.

They pinned his arms and legs and started to talk about what to do with him, how to punish him for being a little shit, how to teach him a lesson. Mickey wanted to beat his ass. Jamie was already trying to give him an Indian burn. Calum took charge. He said one punch in the arm from each of them was fair. Mickey argued for two, but Calum said one. There was a sense that things had already gone too far, and the rest of them agreed.

They held him down and took turns. Rob fought them the whole time. Jonathan remembers: the feel of holding him, the hot, solid flesh of his right arm, and the ease with which they did what they wanted to. Jonathan relaxed, let Rob flex and struggle, gave him room to fight, maybe hope, and then clamped down. There was the frisson of shame and the vicious, detached joy of strength and then it was his turn.

None of them worried about Rob telling, not even Jonathan, not when they were holding and hitting him or when they let him up and he ran home. They did things there that they weren't supposed to, that they wouldn't do elsewhere, beyond the shade of the trees, beyond the high, steep slopes, and the stillness that closed out the world, and no one told. Rob wouldn't tell. And he didn't tell. That was the understanding. That was what made the ravines special. No one ever told.

*

Jonathan and Rob were never close. There was the age gap (three years), but that was the smallest of the differences that divided them. Jonathan liked books and Rob liked sports. Rob played basketball on the driveway in the summer and in rec leagues in the winter. Jonathan did well in school and

Rob struggled. They both liked video games, and they played them together, but always against each other, in long sessions, arguing about whose turn it was, who cheated to get a high score, or who got to play which Street Fighter character (both of them wanted Blanka because of his Beast Roll), and who won mattered.

In high school, Rob started skateboarding and smoking pot. He lost a lot of weight, and wore baggy clothes that showed off how thin he was. The pot gave him a hard, wet cough. He started dealing drugs, mostly pot and hash, to his friends, and then, according to him, more seriously. When Jonathan came back from university, they would climb down into the ravines and smoke Rob's pot. Rob had a good spot, a couple of logs around a fire pit next to the dugouts. Jamie had stopped repairing them years ago and the dugouts had collapsed into holes filled with leaves, rotting branches and plastic. There was a place under one of the beams and a decaying tarp where Rob hid his stash so that their parents wouldn't find it if they searched his room, which they did sometimes. He kept it in an old tackle box, filling the lure compartments with neat, Saran Wrapped bundles of bud.

Rob knew everyone now, and he liked to talk about the people he knew, people in Owen Sound who Jonathan had never heard of and who all had nicknames—Dirty, Sketchy Steve, Tripper. He talked tough and knowledgeable. He called Jonathan "Bud." Jonathan heard his own voice get rougher, his sentences get shorter, fill up with monosyllables.

When he graduated from high school, Rob started a general contracting course at Georgian College in Owen Sound. He did it because their parents said he had to do something. He dropped out in November. That spring, he hitch-hiked out west. He made it as far as Banff and then doubled back to Calgary when he couldn't find anywhere to stay. Then Edmonton. For a couple of years, he lived in a house with half-a-dozen other burnouts and sold drugs to the oil workers down from Fort Mac. Then he smartened up and got his shit together. He started framing houses in the suburbs going up around the city. He got new roommates and the names of his friends changed. He went to the Northern Alberta Institute of Technology and graduated with his electrician's ticket. His apprenticeship. The frustration of working for other people. Then Margaret. Rob's Pipe and Socket. A house in a suburb he had helped to build. The kids. The frustration of other people working for him.

At first, Rob came back a few times a year, staying in his old room until it felt like he'd never left, and then only at Christmas, and, once he had the kids, for a week every second year. Sometimes Jonathan saw him. Sometimes they missed each other. Mostly they talked on the phone. Like the visits, the calls got less frequent, more abbreviated and perfunctory. The truth was that Jonathan didn't know Rob, what he was doing, what he was making of himself and his life anymore. Not really. Not in the ways that mattered. And he knew that he didn't. But he still imagined Rob going on like he had since childhood, changing in a predictable pattern, following an obvious trajectory, fitting more closely the less he heard from him into who Jonathan thought he was.

*

Margaret is right. He has to tell his parents.

Jonathan rests his hands on the counter and returns to the newspaper story and the woman driving the car. He can see the intersection. The white lines of the crosswalk. And her behind the wheel. She raises her hand. The gesture is curt, polite but brisk, as if she is in a hurry. And then the car jumps, accelerates into the suspended moment of disbelief: it is happening and the man doesn't yet know it is happening. He can't let himself. And then he is starting to understand, but too slowly, because these things don't happen. Not here. Not to him.

Jonathan can see her, but he can't see her face, and, like the man, he doesn't understand. He doesn't understand why she did it any more than he understands why he threw the clod. He can't touch that moment before its long and hanging flight. Or maybe he can: sometimes you want to hurt someone. Sometimes you hurt them.

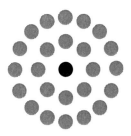

Rembrandt's Etchings

Amsterdam is cold in December:

(But not cold like the Bruce Peninsula, the crooked finger of limestone between Lake Huron and Georgian Bay, where I am from and where they are having a record snowfall. My mother posts pictures on Facebook: drifts mushroomed on the roofs of cars, the buried backyard, and the top of my father's toque, a brown crescent of wool, barely visible above a snowbank. In some of the pictures, she has been carried away by the event—"a once in a generation storm!!!" she writes in a caption—and she has allowed herself a rare artistic liberty. These aren't practical shots of recognizable objects, shots she can point to in the future and say, "See, the snow came up to the handle of the front door, to the eaves of the gazebo. It buried the shed." These are abstract compositions of white and grey under ice-blue slabs of sky, shots of the undulating, half-recognizable geographies of winter, of the lines of snow combed off the lips of drifts. In the images, the wind has a light touch, the lines blur, curl and dissolve into delicate frills and arabesques of dust, but I remember how it cuts. I remember walking backwards into it. I remember my body and how it hunched protectively around its heat.

There, the cold is dry and hurts. Here, it is damp and numbing. Dishwater grey clouds hang over the city, a low, drab ceiling during the day and a pale haze at night. Sometimes, they drop a fine rain, more like a heavy mist than a real shower, a rain that stays in the air, that gives it texture and density. A layer of pinhead droplets collects on my clothes and dissolves into a clammy dampness. Other times, what falls is a heavy sleet. Flakes too soggy to be snow clog the streets with slush. The temperature hovers close to zero, but it never freezes, and, because it never freezes, everything is wet. The bricks of the buildings are darkened with water. The cobblestones are slick and dark, and my shoes are perpetually sodden. My pant legs wick water almost to my knees. My coat is saturated in the evening and still damp in the morning when I hang it to dry. The moisture penetrates, soaks through, and lies close to the skin.

I have inherited bad circulation in my fingers from my mother, and Amsterdam's damp cold turns them a buttery white. It drains them of sensation: I can move them, but I can't feel them or what they are holding. In cafés, a coffee comes with a cookie in an individual wrapper. I order the coffee for the heat of the porcelain cups, and fumble with the plastic foil on the cookies. The city is like that, something I can pick up, but can't touch.)

From Ontario to waiting:

(My girlfriend, Shoshana, and I are taking a gap year after undergrad, and before what? Maybe a MA, or an MFA if we're lucky. Maybe law school. Maybe going back to our parents's houses and a drawn-out search for fulltime jobs. But, for now, we are delaying the onset of our adult lives by teaching English in Europe. We are both used to doing expected things, and this twelve-month detour feels at once predictable and illicit: it is a minor deviation that opens the possibility of a greater one, and, by taking it, we have made the intimate, almost furtive, discovery of how easy it is to give up, to let go, and step sideways out of life.

We wanted to go to the Czech Republic because Shoshana knew about Nick Cave in Prague in the '90s, but we were a decade-and-a-half too late. Poland was out of the question. Neither of us had heard of Slovakia until we saw it on a map. Hungary, under Victor Orban, frightened us. We found an ad for two positions at an international high school in Brasov, Romania on a message board. It was in Transylvania, and we liked the pictures of the surrounding hills, of "Brasov" spelled out in white letters on the ridge overlooking the city, like a smaller, sadder copy of the Hollywood sign, and the aerial shots of the market square.

We have been teaching there for four months. When we aren't teaching, we are trying to be writers. We spend our free afternoons scribbling in cafés and our evenings in pubs arguing about narrative, the importance of character, and what comes after post-modernism.

We get three weeks of vacation at Christmas, and we are using them to visit the Netherlands. Before I left for Europe, my mother told me that I had to go. Everyone on her side of the family is from Zeeland, a province at the southern end of the country wedged between the North Sea and Belgium. She wants me to see the province with its deep estuaries and narrow promontories of land linked by bridges, but, most of all, she wants me to visit Goes, the small city at the mouth of the Scheldt river in which she was born. She has arranged for Shoshana and me to stay with my great-aunt

Trijntje. The train to Goes leaves several times a day from a station that is a short walk from our hostel. The trip takes less than three hours, and Trijntje is expecting us, but we haven't bought our tickets yet.)

We spend our time going to museums:

(The Van Gogh museum, which is white walls. And tall. Open staircases. Glass balustrades. And mezzanines. Its column of light an unsettling respite from the dull weather. The Sex Museum, which is crowded and has a line that stretches into the street. We file through the rooms at a slow, almost stately pace, looking at sex toys behind glass, and walls of pictures: famous porn stars; the world's longest, obviously fake, penis; a man standing on a wooden stool to fuck a cow in a barnyard, completely naked except for a pair of boots, incongruous against the background of mud and straw. Wedged between strangers, and drifting along with them, none of it manages to be either arousing or offensive. It is at most puzzling.

We don't have enough money to go out at night. We barely have enough money for the museums. We smoke pot in our room and drink Heineken in the hostel bar, where we agree with the bartender—who is from Minnesota and learning Dutch so that she can get her citizenship—that it really does taste better here. At night, we fuck in that fervent, purposeless way that people do when they are drunk and stoned and don't know what they want from each other, not coming, but not stopping.

Applications to graduate school are due in January and February, but we have left them behind in Brasov. We are avoiding the future the way we are avoiding visiting Zeeland and Trijntje, avoiding deciding who we are, who we are going to be, and knowing that we are avoiding the decision makes us more determined not to make it.)

The day we go to the Rijksmuseum:

(It is raining, a steady, penetrating shower. I am soaked by the time we get there. They make us check our coats and backpacks at the entrance, and I walk through the galleries in my wet t-shirt, damp pants chafing my thighs. The rooms are cavernous and ice cold. They echo. My heat bleeds into the empty space. Vermeer's blues are frigid. I fold my arms over my chest and tuck my hands into my armpits, but my fingers still stiffen and start to ache. I can barely concentrate on *The Night Watch*. I wander. *The Great Wave of Kanagawa. Winter Landscape with Skaters.* I can't break out of myself to see the paintings.

In a secluded wing of the building, I find an exhibition of Rembrandt's etchings. Four steps down to low ceilings, carpet, and long, narrow rooms that snake back on themselves. It is dim and windowless, and each piece is lit by an individual light. The effect is of nighttime darkness and candlelight without the wavering of a flame. It is not warmer here, but I feel the cold less. And there are the etchings: smaller than the paintings, more manageable, not as demanding. Most are no bigger than a sketchbook page. A few are the size of a piece of watercolour paper. A sign explains that it sometimes took Rembrandt years to finish a plate to his satisfaction. He would refine a composition, develop a scene, modify the details of a portrait, occasionally completely rework the piece, and prints from the various stages of the process are displayed next to one another. Beside them, the muddy, gleaming metal plates still show the marks of the work. Adding detail to the print meant adding lines to the plate, etching ridges and impressions into the copper that caught and held the ink. The more Rembrandt worked a portion of a plate, the darker that area of the print became. I follow a figure, the edge of a jaw, a face as it develops across printings, as it becomes more definite, hardens, takes on depth and character, becomes the face of someone you might know, someone you might see, and the massing lines fill it with shadows. I am held by the images, fascinated enough by the refinements and reversals, the darkened rooms, and the artist revealed in these intimate transformations to forget the cold. I walk back and forth, from one end of the exhibition to the other, until Shoshana finds me.)

In Goes after Christmas, before New Year's:

(In an apartment in the middle of the city. She was briefly married, but her husband disappeared decades before I was born, and no one talks about him. He left her with a son, Reuben, who died in his 40s, "of drugs" my grandmother likes to say, and who everyone talks about, but never to Trijntje. I have been warned not to mention him.

Trijntje picks us up at the station. She is small, like all of the older women in my family, and only comes up to my breastbone when she hugs me: a cap of fine white hair and clear hazel eyes inspecting me.

"Welcome to Goes," she says.

"Hoose," I repeat, like "goose," not the verb "goes," pronouncing the "g" that is close to a throaty, drawn out English "h."

"Correct," she says, "Correct. The Dutch way."

I know that at least.

On the drive back to her apartment, she points out my great-great-grandparents' house and the church where my grandparents were married. It is late, and she serves us a light dinner: rolls, cold squares of ham and a plate of waxy gouda sliced and arranged by hand, the kind of minor extravagance that old people who are used to living alone on very little serve guests.

We fill the time with talk about relatives, family news. She wants to know about everyone. I find myself searching for details I have forgotten, trying to remember conversations I never paid attention to.

She puts us up in the second bedroom. It is a small room with a double bed, a student's desk tucked into a corner, and a dresser with a handful of framed pictures on it. More pictures hang on the walls. Not too many. Not like the shrine of an obsessive in a movie. Not enough to shock. Not enough even to be remarkable at first. The pictures are of a boy, and then a young, and then an ageing man. A large one by the door captures a younger Trijntje standing next to him in the white, glazing light of southern France. He is taller than her, as tall as me, and dark-haired. They are both deeply tanned. I wonder if I am imagining a washed-out pallor under his walnut skin.)

Reuben, Trijntje tells me, my son. This was his room when he was a boy. And adds with a thoughtful, pained fondness: he liked to stay here when he had his troubles.

At breakfast in a tiny dining room with a tile floor:

(Trijntje asks us what we are going to be. I tell her that we are still deciding. I talk about our grad school applications. Shoshana says law school is still a possibility. We are both reticent, equivocal, sheltering in our uncertainty. I tell her that we have thought about teachers' college.)

Reuben was a teacher, she says. He taught in a primary school in Middelburg, the capital of Zeeland, she says. Little children. Five-and-six-year-olds. He taught maths and gym and English. The children learned to count in English by singing. They painted pictures that he took home with him.

(I imagine big primitive splashes of color, crude shapes, lopsided, tender suns over leaning houses and barely recognizable tulips.)

He would bike from Goes to Middelburg in the morning and come back again in the afternoon when he was well. Always very fast. Always bent over.

Like he was riding into the wind even when there was none.

After passing the train station on a driving tour
of the villages around Goes:

When he went to university. In Rotterdam, says Trijntje. That was when the troubles started. When he was away. As a boy, he always liked to be busy. He had his sports, his clubs, his friends, of course. His studies. Always, there was something. He worked at a grocery and went to university to become a banker like his father.

(For sometime, the landscape on the way to Wissenkerke.)

They let them go and do whatever in Rotterdam, she says. He was a good boy, but he liked people too much.

(Low fields in succession.)

He did not understand. And I did not see until it was too late.

(The regular line of the dyke to the north. Silence. The small car. Discomfort closes down my sympathy.)

I remember, she says, when he caught the train with his things, his bags, and when he came back. How he looked. You could not think it.

After climbing the dyke to see the narrow sand beach
where the extended family swims in the summers:

(Looking out over the tufts of loosely-rooted grass, the sloping sand that glistens where it meets the sea, and the blue-grey water shading into the grey-blue sky, I imagine them gathering in the long clear light of the afternoon. Blankets. Big umbrellas stuck in the sand and coolers in the shade. An old hurt edging her voice as she points down the beach. Husbandless Trijntje and her fatherless son. I imagine her seeing Reuben singled out by the kindness of other parents.)

On the walk back to the car:

Reuben was always having accidents as a boy. So many scraped knees and bruises I could not count them, but he never complained.

When he was seven, he broke his arm. I don't know how. He tucked it into his side, like this, she says, for two days and never said a word. For two days. And I did not know it. He was always good at hiding things, she says.

(An involuntary, half-reflexive twist of the face, self-recrimination, guilt she keeps in secret, bitterness, and something I cannot understand, something held between her and Reuben.)

Interrupting a report about Syrian refugees on BBC World News:

Geitenneukers, she says.

(I don't know what the word means, but I can tell by the way Trijntje says it, how she lowers her tone, as if to keep it to herself, how her voice becomes soft and vicious, almost sensual with hatred, that it is not a word used by women, especially not by elderly women who wear clear, plastic rain caps buttoned under their chins, and who drink a finger of gin at night for their digestion.)

They bring drugs, she says. Bagger. (She makes a curt plunging motion with her thumb.)

Before, it was not so bad. They were in Rotterdam, in Amsterdam, but only in some places. Now, they go everywhere. Now, they are in Middelburg, Goes. They sell their drugs to everyone. And no one does anything.

I vote PVV, she says. Every time.

After the TV moves on, in one of the lucid intervals between fits of dozing during which her head slumps into the upholstery of her wingback chair:

I think he felt too much.

(Trijntje is measured, thoughtful, as if reproducing the moment she found her way to these words, returning to the first satisfaction of containing an impossible, obstinate truth.)

He cried too easily as a boy. At sad books. At dead pets. Never his. No. I never had the time for them, messing everywhere. Not with a boy on my own.

(A pause during which she wrestles with her memories.)

He cried for his cousin's dog, but he only played with it so many times on the weekends. He cried for the losses of his classmates.

And it was not like other children when he cried. It was too hard. Too much. He would not stop. And he would not be comforted. He did not want it.

(She is resentful, half-resigned and still bewildered by sadness.)

He pushed away my hands. As if I was to blame. And held himself.

(I imagine Reuben bending into his knees, taking hold of feeling and curling his tiny body around loss, around that sustaining core of hurt, the way I had curled myself around my heat in the Rijksmuseum.

I see him with walnut skin.

And Trijntje...)

Walking along the Havenkanaal, past the boats docked for winter, covered in tarps, melt water pooling in the fabric's depressions:

The summer after Reuben came home from university, he told me that he needed to go on vacation. He said he needed a break. He needed to get away. From what?

(We walk carefully, taking short steps, over the slick cobbles.)

It was not the time. He needed to stay with me. I needed to watch him. I watched him all his life. He went away to study and see what happened.

But when Reuben got an idea, I could never stop him, not even when he was a boy. So, I let him go. What else could I do?

(We stop and look out over the still canal water, viscous with cold, the colour of winter rain.)

He was gone for three weeks. He said he was going to the South of France, but how could I know? The first time he called was from Brussels to say that he was almost home.

He had been in Marseille for all three weeks, in a pension not far from the beach. I could see the sun on his skin. He did not talk about what he had done. He did not talk much at all. He was quieter, calmer than when he left. Satisfied. I think.

(Trijntje frowns and tugs at her rain cap. She is frustrated by the ugliness of the canal that should be frozen over and filled with skaters, by the grey water that should be a white ribbon, and by the memory of Reuben's inscrutable happiness.)

He slept too. Nine, ten, sometimes twelve hours a night. Before, it was six at most. Even as a boy. And he was always restless. He went to bed after me and got up before me. But now I had to wake him for breakfast.

He got a job working at a camp for children.

It was something to do.

(We turn back and return the way we came.)

One day, he told me he was going to be a teacher.

Drinking coffee in a Trijntje's apartment:

The summers were always the most difficult.

(The dining room table is covered in a white tablecloth. Over that, there is a second, lace cloth that Trijntje has stitched herself, and that is rough on my forearms when I rest them in front of me.)

In the fall and winter, he had his school, the children, but in the summer, with nothing to do...

(She makes a loose shrugging motion that means "of course," and whose looseness conveys something of the open, purposeless days that were so hard for Reuben to fill, something of his aimless, fretting dissatisfaction.)

It was best to go away. He visited Spain, Greece, England. One summer, we went back to Provence. Both of us.

We hiked in the hills and through the lavender fields in the Luberon. I still remember the smell of the air.

It is true what they say about the light.

(That night, I look more closely at the picture by the door. Reuben has his arm around his mother. It is the end of the day. They are sunburned through their tans. There is dust on their shoes and dust muddying the sweat on their legs. They are both smiling the same tired smile, the smile of two people who have walked a long distance, often climbing, over rugged terrain under a white-blue sky, who have pushed their tired bodies through the last hours of the afternoon, who are proud of themselves, pleased with exhaustion, sated with effort.

There is a date written in ballpoint pen in the bottom righthand corner of the picture. From what my mother has told me, I can guess that Reuben died of an overdose the following January.)

Rembrandt's Etchings

The next morning:

(Trijntje drives us to the train station.)

I still see, she says, how he looked when he left for Rotterdam.

(She touches my hand and lets it go.

I expect another story. There is nothing. We are leaving, and she is thinking to herself, but no longer aloud.)

Trijntje waits on the platform:

(I watch her tired face with its fringe of white curls under the rain cap from the window of the train. She becomes clearer, simpler as we pull away.)

On the train ride back to Amsterdam:

(I think of Rembrandt's etchings and of how he returned to them year after year. I remember walking up and down the rooms of the Rijksmuseum. The parade of drafts. The fine and searching lines. The deepening shade of the faces. I think of the etcher's hands gathering in darkness with detail.)

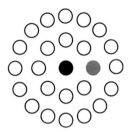

Tuesday: All Day

1. Patrick Philip wakes up and does not feel like a protagonist.

The alarm.

And that other urgency. Flinching bathroom light. He pisses loudly into the water and then reads the news online over breakfast. Raisin Bran and the last of the milk. Hillary leads. Panama Papers. Billions hidden. Protests in Iceland. Soggy now. The flakes dissolved into mealy sludge that is both satisfyingly sweet and nauseating. All quiet in Canada. The CBC reports on other countries' criminals. Not for the last time today, Patrick calculates: rent came out. And the Visa bill. Round down. Internet. Phone. How much for groceries? Coffee? The daily bleed of cash. He can't hold the numbers. And one course guaranteed for the summer. There might be more. "Depending on enrolments," the chair said, and looked apologetic.

Blurred slowness.

A sort of listless fumbling.

Not yet begun.

He bought Ellie a new laptop when hers died in the middle of a paper. A good one. Almost two months' rent now. This was three years ago. He had grants then. When he thinks about Ellie and the money, there is the dulling loss, and resentment. What else? The experience of watching himself begrudge a gift. That alone is degrading. The last swig at the counter. He spits the bitter grit of undiluted instant coffee crystals into the kitchen sink.

That taste at least is definitive.

Patrick showers after which he shaves and inspects his face: red. Pearled in the steam. Stress at the eyes. Pale under the flush of heat. Rounding a little, but still, when he turns in profile, the jawline that emerged with puberty.

He picks out jeans. His best pair. Dark. Tight across the thighs. Fresh from the wash, they cut into his waist. He prods a roll of stomach fat. They will loosen over the day, hike down, bind and stretch as he wears them. A black v-neck t-shirt. A blazer hides his gut, adds gravitas. Amanda Miller is meeting him at three. She wrote in her most recent email: "I wish to discuss my unfair grade." When he is teaching, he will push the sleeves of the blazer up his forearms.

He puts on an old blue parka and slings his bag over his shoulder. The strap cuts his chest. Still brittle, vulnerable with exhaustion, and hoping to catch the momentum of the day, he closes and locks the door.

2. Patrick rides the bus. A second coffee does not help.

The bite of cold (too cold for April) on showered dampness mellows to a steady ache in his hands and feet, numbs his face. Down Central. Libro Credit Union on the right. Artistic Esthetic Spa. Mugford's. The sun turns the sky to milk. Starbucks on the corner. University students lined up at the counter. He remembers Amanda Miller's email: "I am offended by your accusation." They buy tall, five-dollar coffees.

Boxwoods. Jas Shoes. LifeStyles.

In front of the Running Room, he waits and calculates: 20 exercises to mark this morning. Ten per hour. A hundred to go. Twenty after his first class. Summer dresses in a store window. Richmond Street is in shadow. Weak light touches the tops of the buildings across from him, the facade of In Fashion. Forty tonight. An easy day tomorrow and done for Thursday.

College and university students. The university students wear Canada Goose coats.

A young man with blonde hair and tired eyes smokes.

A young woman talks to a friend.

Patrick is no longer young.

The number 6 bus to the university. The young woman and the Canada Goose coats get on.

Patrick wants the number 8 to the college.

The wheeze of doors. Press and jostling and muddy heat. He grabs a strap. Textbook open on a lap. Listen. Nod lethargically. . Bob together when they cross the tracks. Elephants on the sign of Bangkok Pad Thai. Lean for the corner of Oxford and Richmond and drift into: is that Amanda Miller? Adrenaline. Catch himself at the next stop. Stare covertly. Start and stop along Oxford: the already leafing trees of Old North. Stately houses. Yellow brick. Listless shifting. He gets a look at maybe-Amanda in profile. No. And relaxes into a lurch at a red light at Adelaide. The Wolseley Barracks complete with rusting artillery. Superstore. Quebec Street. Patrick rehearses: "This is a clear-cut case of plagiarism. It is your responsibility..." Dozing around him. The purple and yellow sign of Planet Fitness. The heat is containing him now. A welcome painful tingle in Patrick's extremities. Highbury. And the turn to the college.

From the bus to the line for coffee in the food court. He checks his watch. Time to make two exercises gone before he orders a large double-double and sits down. He opens his laptop and arranges the exercise booklets and a stack of rubrics on the table. The line shortens. The buzz of many things gives way to single noises.

3. Patrick marks in the food court
and sometimes manages to concentrate.

8:44. He teaches at 10:30. He thumbs the stack and starts with Baylee Coe because she is a good student and it will be quick and easy, and it is: he circles "Clear expression," "Advanced thinking," "Well developed structure," "Free of errors" and scrawls, "Conclusion needs improvement. Well done!" 9.2. He stretches and sets himself to work. 8:47. Mia Borneman sits at the back of the class and resents him. Barely legible. No more coherent. 5.1. A private "Fuck you." The sound of someone walking quickly. Devin Kraeft. No face for the name. He struggles over a paragraph without punctuation. Loses time. 5.8. Mac Brch misspelled his own name. 9:14 Getting into a rhythm. Reading. Circling. Grading. Not thinking. He barely notices the bustle between classes. Better. Writes something encouraging. Drifts a little. Ellie on the couch. Grinning when he showed her his second chapter. There is, of course, the article waiting for revision and submission. At the back of his mind for three years. Commas are not periods! His supervisor said it was promising. No! Six months ago, Patrick saw him in the vegetable aisle at the supermarket. Explain! Middle aged with a beard. Like a bad Ginsberg joke. Paragraphing! Polite. His waning interest. Mild concern. "What are you doing now?" Grading. Patrick's shame-guilt-frustration breaking sometimes into rage. 10:18. 17 done. He can catch up in the next hour if they don't ask too many questions.

4. Patrick supervises and answers and marks
and answers and supervises.

Introduction to Business Communication's computer lab hour: they are doing a graded editing exercise. He takes attendance and reads the instructions out loud. "Good luck." Blue Jays cap in the back. Steve? "If you look at the instructions..." "Or listened." Cassandra McLeod is confused. "Read the instructions." "And understand them." Scott Young wasn't paying attention. "You are supposed to read and follow the instructions" "And try not to fail at life" Cruel. But true. Francis calls them the jellyfish of culture: "They are incapable of self-directed motion, but pack a vicious sting." "Alan, put away your phone" "~~For once.~~" Eric, he thinks. Blonde hair. The gym bro. Paige Li. "~~Andrea, eyes on your own screen.~~" But I will have to say it to everyone. Spend the hour surveilling the class. And why should I? Leon Maynard is late. "Find a computer and get started." "Yes, follow the instructions." "Alan!" "~~For fuck's sakes.~~" Settle finally into nervous concentration. He sits down at the desk at the front of the room. Adrian Wiseman wrote his name and the date and copied out two paragraphs of the question. Second row from the back. Might be there for the course evaluations. Likes to contradict me. Is it worth the complaint? Half-a-dozen emails and a meeting? In April? 5.0. Tito Desousa leaves early. Two more. Caught up. Everyone starts to get up at once. "~~What? No!~~" "Submit it the same way you submitted every other lab." "~~Like you did last week!~~" "Open the drop box." "~~Like you've been doing all term!~~" "Upload the file, check the academic integrity box, and click submit." "Andrew, you need to wrap it up." "As you have been doing all term, open the drop box, upload the file, check the academic integrity box, and click submit." "Fine, you can email it to me." "You'll get them on Thursday." "At the top of the syllabus." And into the loud, packed hallways.

5. Patrick marks in the office. The faculty talk among themselves.

The office is a big room with low ceilings and lines of cubicles. It is big enough that, between the partitions, the cubicles and the low ceiling, it is difficult to tell where or if it ends. Patrick sits at a cubicle he shares with eight other part-time instructors. The full-time instructors each have their own cubicle. He eats a granola bar and marks. Voices carry in the room. They fill the space between the top of the cubicles and the ceiling with a constant, fluctuating ecosystem of sound.

...

Francis Markham (full time), a large man in a sweater vest and button-down shirt who smells, sometimes unpleasantly, sometime comfortingly, of wet wool, finishes filing a workplace safety report on the mat that bunches under the break-room door.

...

Mike Fuller (part time) to Carolyn Davis (part time): "Have you heard yet?"

"Yes, they gave me three courses last week. You?"

"No. Not yet."

"I'm sure you'll get a few. They're slow this year."

Mike Fuller (part time) does not penetrate the armor of Carolyn Davis' (part time) complacency.

...

71

Patrick Philip (part time) thinks, "Three courses? She barely finished her MA." Hurt-jealousy-confusion, but there is marking. 18 to go.

...

William Holst (full time), a man in his late 50s wearing a navy suit and motorcycle boots complains to an audience of full- and part-timers by the photocopier: "I was telling them about the Cold War and they had no idea what it was. I told them that the US and Russia...They didn't understand a word of it. They just stared at me. So, I said, 'Imagine there's a red dog and a yellow dog, and the red dog hates the yellow dog...'"

...

"Two for now. You?"

"They're slow this year.

...

Francis Markham (full time) gathers momentum and digresses to Steven Maclean (part time) "Well...you know...when preparing them for the final exam...you have to keep in mind that I originally designed it as a metric of progression in three specific areas..."

...

"We're looking forward to it."

...

William Holst (full time) stands next to his cubicle and complains to Randy Morin (full time), Kathryn Snider (full time) George Cho (full time) and Ayman Sayed (full time) about the administration's treatment of part-time faculty: "We don't even have our own offices, but they have to share their cubicles. How many are there now?"

"Eight to a desk. Maybe nine."

"No one can work like that. And the administration doesn't care...We're nothing but operational costs...The more they cut, the better."

...

Patrick Philip (part time) takes a break and calculates how much money he can save this month by using bus tickets and walking instead of buying a pass. Nine to go.

...

Darren Monson (full time) perches a heavy haunch on the edge of his desk and holds forth on his decision to begin the Introduction to the Humanities course he is designing for students upgrading their GEDs with the Grand Inquisitor episode from *The Brothers Karamazov*, getting louder and more impassioned as he goes on: "We need to start off the course with a bang...dive into something that shows them the value of literature...one of the greatest hits of Western culture...a resonant statement about the nature of freedom and the necessity of faith..."

...

Patrick Philip (part time), Steven Maclean (part time) and Sarah Marcott (part time) decide not to think about how to teach Introduction to the Humanities when they get it next year.

...

Mike Fuller (part time) asks Patrick Philip (part time) about his summer courses.

"One."

"None."

"There are more coming, I think"

"I hope."

"Sorry. I have to..."

...

William Holst (full time) complains to Ron Mussen (full time) and Amanda Barfoot (full time) about his new Ford Expedition: "You wouldn't believe the gas bills," he pauses and adds, "but nothing beats it in the winter."

...

Patrick Philip (part time) remembers his meeting with Amanda Miller.

...

Mike Fuller (part time) wanders off.

...

Patrick Philip (part time), Ron Mussen (full time), Daren Monson (full time), Steven Maclean (part time), Kathryn Snider (full time), George Cho (full time), Sarah Marcott (part time), and Randy Morin (full time) mark quietly.

...

William Holst (full time) complains to Francis Markham (full time): "I don't care how bad it gets. I'm not retiring before I'm 80."

...

Patrick Philip (part time) is done. He has finished 21 (and 20 this morning makes 41) and he is about to teach.

6. Patrick talks to himself (and also to his class).

The beginning of the second last week of his pop culture class. "Today I want to start tying everything together." From the Frankfurt School to post-modernism and theories of identity and consumption. Last week they watched *Tropic Thunder*. "We have to ask what links these objects, these texts?" The thread he follows is irony. He loses most of them quickly. But then he never had them. He hikes up the sleeves of his blazer, and steps out from behind the lectern. It comes, slow at first, because it is the end of term, because half of them are checking their phones, because he forgot to buy another coffee, because he has been working steadily since 8:30, because he only had a granola bar for lunch, because there are forty exercises to go, and because he is meeting her in less than an hour, but it comes: that familiar, vibrant transport. Why he does this. For twenty minutes, he forgets himself in his words. After, Cody West wants to talk to Patrick about metal and politics. "What does he think of Napalm Death?" Patrick is flattered, but has to put him off. Amanda Miller is waiting for him.

7. In the time it takes to mark four exercises (five if he is on a roll), Patrick resolves nothing.

[SILENCE]

[.........] They walk past the receptionists. They walk through a locked door. They walk down a long hallway. [....................] [...............] [..............] She sits at the table. He sits at the table. They sit across from each other at the table. The table is pale grey. The table is the same color as the walls. [..] [....................... ....] She is hurt. She is insulted. He has hurt and insulted her. [........ ....] He reaches into his bag. He fumbles in his bag. He produces a stack of papers from his bag. He fans the stack of papers from his bag out on the table. He fans them out on the pale grey table with a flourish. He is firm. He is calming. He is almost apologetic. He thinks his confidence is parental. [... ....] [.........................] [.................... ....]

[SILENCE]

She bends. She bends over the papers. She studies the papers. [............. ....] Her finger presses into the papers. Her finger presses into the table under the papers. The table under the papers is the same color as the walls. [...] [.................... ....]

[SILENCE]

[..]

[SILENCE]

[..........................] [...................] [............] [...................] [...............] [............................ .....] [..] [..........................] [.......................... ....] She removes her finger from the papers. She removes her finger from the table under the papers. This does not change the color of the table. It stays the same as the color of the walls.

[SILENCE]

[....................................] [..............................] [................]
[..........] [................ ..] [..
] [.............] He pushes the papers across the table. He pushed the papers
across the table towards her. [.......................] She looks at the walls instead
of the table.

[SILENCE]

[....] [..............] [..........................] Her voice rises in pitch. Her voice
turns accusatory. [.............................] [..............] [................................
..........................] [.............................. ....] He touches the papers
that he has pushed across the table towards her. He taps the highlighted
paragraphs. He taps the table under the papers with the highlighted
paragraphs on them. [.................................] [............. ....
...................]

[SILENCE]

He looks up from the table. He looks at the walls. He second guesses
himself. He thinks about: the Chair. The possibility of more teaching. And
then comes the wincing cringe of shame-resentment-selfrecrimination, the
sharpness and frustration of irrational fear. He is smaller than the room.
He is smaller than the table. He is the smallness and meanness of taping
highlighted paragraphs.

[SILENCE]

She tears up. [....................................] [................] Her voice clogs with
emotion. Her voice moistens with emotion. Her voice whines with emotion.
[..................................] [........ ....] [..............] [...........
....
.......] He doesn't want to look at her. She doesn't want to look at him. They
don't want to look at the table. They don't want to look at the walls.

[SILENCE]

[............] [....] [....................................] [................................
] [......................] [.......... ....] [..............................]
[..............] [.......................] [.....................] [...... .] [................................
....] [................................
.....] He doesn't tap the papers. He doesn't look at the papers or at the table
under them.

[SILENCE]

[................] [...] He reaches into his
bag. He takes his notes out of his bag. He does not set the notes from his bag
on the table. He taps them as he reads them. [................................
..................] [.......................] [.......................... ....
....]

[SILENCE]

[..........] [................] [....................] [.............................] He puts his notes from his bag back in his bag. He turns the pages on the table. He turns a page. He taps a block of yellow. He turns a page. He taps a block of yellow. He taps a block of yellow. He is the smallness and meanness of yellow blocks. [.......
....]

[SILENCE]

[....................] [....] [.....] [..........] [...........] [..
..................] [......................................]

[SILENCE]

[.............................] [.................................] [.............] [.................
............................] [...............................] [...]
[...]

[SILENCE]

[....] [...] [............] [................................] [..........................] She is outraged. She is dramatic. She is performing sincerity. The sincerity she is performing is no less sincere because she is performing it. He is not performing.

[SILENCE]

[..] [.....................] [...
] [.............] [.................] [.....] [........] [.....]

[SILENCE]

He gets up from the table. She gets up from the table. They walk down a long hallway. They walk through a locked door. They walk past the receptionists.

[SILENCE]

The table behind them is the same colour as the walls.

8. Good news! Patrick marks at home, and goes out.

Patrick rides the bus home and sets up his grading on his kitchen table. He is slow, drained by the day, by Amanda Miller's recalcitrance, and weighed down by the inertia of his own pessimism. Thirty-nine to go.

He checks his email: "Dear Patrick Philip...I am pleased to offer you a section of Introduction to Business Writing 1000...May 1, 2016 to August 26, 2016..." That makes two courses. From $900 a month to $1,800. He can pick up some tutoring in May and June, a few summer school students in July and August. And there is what he has saved over the last eight months. If he is careful, frugal, he can finish the summer without any debt. Maybe even with a cushion for next year.

He marks quickly, painlessly, carried by relief and elation. Twenty-five done. He decides to treat himself to dinner.

9. Patrick celebrates, and forgets what he is celebrating.

Patrick goes to the Runt Club, a pub a block south of his apartment, where he expects to see someone he knows.

He sits at a table in the window and orders Sirloin Tip Fettuccine and a pint of Labatt Fifty. He marks five exercises before the pasta comes, 4 while he eats it, twice that after, slowing, but still effortlessly. Pint of Fifty. Francis Markham settles next to him. Patrick puts away his work. He complains about Amanda Miller. Francis commiserates. The jellyfish of culture. Pint of Fifty. Francis discusses his new pen. He is very particular about his pens. Pint of Fifty. Randy Morrin arrives. They debate utopianism in politics. Hope vs. realism. Patrick argues for hope. Francis is a realist. There has to be at least the possibility of change. Randy agrees in principle with both of them. Pint of Fifty. They discuss superhero movies. They talk about *The West Wing*. Pint of Fifty. And then about misheard song lyrics. Patrick is rocking back in his seat. Folded in warmth for a long moment. Emphatic. Lounging and hazy. Complaints about colleagues. Gossip. Grad school memories. Hiring? Pint of Fifty. Maybe next year. Who knows. Francis is careful. Randy is sympathetic. He bums a cigarette from Randy and they smoke on the patio. He remembers Ellie. He can feel the last pint destabilizing him as he drains it. It is time to go.

10. Patrick walks home.

Curb. Road. Between the cars. Wobbles. Another curb. The world rotates to his left. Worse than he thought. Catches a parking meter. Gathers himself. Swings. Sets out again. Undulating existence. Cuts through the Libro parking lot. Listing in open space. Now to the left. Now to the right. Walking quickly to keep up with his lean. Collides with the wall. Roughhard brick. Sudden surge. Hold. Can't. Vomits copiously behind a planter. Sour relief. Spits. Steadies a little. Pushes off. Staggers. Stops on the sidewalk to plot a line to his apartment. Tomorrow? How many to go? The numbers muddle. Teaching at 12:30. Ricochets off a telephone pole. Remember the alarm. Paved drive. Tangles in the bushes by the step. Tears free. And bangs through the front door. 1A. On the left. Be sure. Supports himself on the frame. Squints. Hard. Tight at his belt. He has to piss. He rummages in his bag. Papers. The book he didn't get a chance to read. Phone. Finds himself sitting on the floor. Stands. Unsteady. Front right pocket. Drops his keys. Bends. Takes an abrupt knee. Tomorrow? Drops them again. How many to go? Goddamn. Tomorrow. He opens the door.

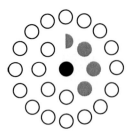

Metastases

Cancer cells spread through the body in a series of steps. These steps include:
1. *Growing into, or invading, nearby normal tissue*
2. *Moving through the walls of nearby lymph nodes or blood vessels*
3. *Traveling through the lymphatic system and bloodstream to other parts of the body*
4. *Stopping in small blood vessels at a distant location, invading the blood vessel walls, and moving into the surrounding tissue*
5. *Growing in this tissue until a tiny tumour forms*
6. *Causing new blood vessels to grow, which creates a blood supply that allows the tumour to continue growing*

When observed under a microscope and tested in other ways, metastatic cancer cells have features like that of the primary cancer and not like the cells in the place where the cancer is found.

Cervix, Primary Cancer:

At first ... a nagging ache ... a hardly noticeable collection of minor pains that have not yet realized the coherence of agony ... a discomfort that is distinguishable only in careful retrospect from the regular soreness of a winter spent building a base for her first attempt at an Ironman after the kids and a long recovery from a stress fracture in her left foot ... on one of the first runs of the spring ... climbing a hill in the obtuse light and the green only just coming back into the close-cropped grass of the park and the April bare trees not yet budding ... a spasm crones Liz to a stop and she hobbles home ... one foot ... her left foot that she has finally started to trust again ... and then her right ... after another ... injury is a falteringfalteringinterminablepresent ... a sharpness that does not unclench until the afternoon and leaves a residue of disorientation in her body ... holds her to a hidden brokenness... Dr. Karen Forsyth's auburn hair must fall in flat and heavy curtains when it is down, but it is never down ... Karen's voice is apologetic ... hedged in

... contained ... like her hair it is held back from the transformation that is taking place between them ... Stage 4 cervical cancer has its own time ... it has its own days ... its own months ... don't say, *left* ... say, *countable* ... say, *quantifiable* ... say, *it is like injury, like faltering and time is like distance in the spring morning* ... say, *she is limping through that drawn-out present* ... say, *days are like hills she is climbing through bare trees...* say, *it is this strangeness that settles into her hips* ... how long until she is home?

A 4x5 cm mass destroys her cervix and invades her bladder ... eighteen months of nothing ... count days like footsteps from that April run ... count days like mornings ... of what? ... *I'm so sorry* ... of waiting and repeating so that it can be read back to her, said back to her in several different variations with pauses to puzzle out their own script: pelvic pain, hip pain, bleeding or spotting between periods, pain or discomfort during intercourse, general malaise, mood disruptions or swings ... no bloating ... *Are you worried?* ... on a scale of 1 to 10 ... *Of course* ... she does not say that sometimes agony strobes through her and stilts her legs to comical stiffness ... she does say, *I can't run the way I want to, the way I am used to running, and that affects my mental health,* and she means, *I am less myself in the world* ... Karen withdraws her concern into the container of professional silence ... ties it back like her hair ... pelvic exam: never performed ... regularly scheduled Pap test: *some weird cells* ... Liz says it over the way she says her symptoms over, but to no one in particular ... *nothing to worry about* ... what is pain anyway? ... a waiting and repeating ... a waking in the body ... the rate of growth of a tumour is highly variable and depends on the tumour subtype, the location of the tumour, the blood supply to the cancerous tissue, etc... . six months for the gynecologist to find nothing on her pelvic ultrasound and nothing on the results the doctor bends over a counter to review ... researchers have yet to develop accurate models for predicting tumour growth and the kinetics of growth rates remain understudied ... the gynecologist tells her it might be musculoskeletal ... everything is careful ... the walls of every office she visits are a careful absence of colour ... how much running do you do? ... tumour growth rate is quantified by the unit doubling time (DT) ... how many answers given into the silence after her name is called without a question mark ... repeating: *nothing* ... her physiotherapist prescribes a stretching routine to open up her hips ... *Have you tried a gluten-free diet?* ... tension in her hip abductor muscles ... there is debate about whether DT is an accurate measure of tumour progression. It overestimates the difference in growth rate of slow-growing tumours and underestimates the difference in growth rate of fast-growing tumours. For this reason, researchers have proposed Specific Growth Rate (SGR) or percentage increase per unit time as a more reliable and valid metric of tumour growth ... no ... climbing still ... her chiropractor suspects a muscular imbalance to be treated with a series of spinal realignments ... her osteopath politely disagrees ... what is the doubling time of doubt? ... say, *Are you sorry Karen?* ... when does uncertainty turn ... repeating: malignant? ... nothing ... invades nothing ... no ... until it doesn't.

The second ultrasound taken alongside the biopsy is a confusion of grey ... Liz's uncertain eye is anchored here ... now there ... now ... now it is happening ... Liz nods and says, yes ... Liz lets herself be anchored to a point in that confusion by Karen's pen ... this revelation, like cancer, has its own time ... it opens the moment into a room for Liz to stand in the middle of and feel the space all around her ... *You have Stage 4A cervical cancer* is a location at the tip of a pen ... she stands in that room where the ink-flecked tip meets the image ... the fleck of ink is black ... the image is grey ... Karen is there with her ... Karen is not there with her ... the world goes on outside of the room ... time goes on outside of it ... Karen's body with its long brown hair and careful face is both there and not there ... time has been going on like that, separate from Liz, since that morning run through the bare trees, but now she knows that remove as the strangeness that settled into her and would not lift ... Karen's face is closed on the perfect circle of its own certainty ... there is a chair for Liz in the middle of the room that has opened in the moment ... Karen does not have Stage 4A cervical cancer ... Liz does not sit in the chair ... there is space all around her ... *I'm sorry* ... what is a word for presumption? ... no ... Karen's authority reaches through her arm and the pen in her hand into the confusion of the ultrasound ... what is a synonym for both defensiveness and refusal? ... the walls of the room are beyond Liz's reach ... the walls surround her ... what is a word for both there and not there? ... the room with the chair in the middle in which she does not sit is her childhood room ... the walls have no colour ... the walls are the colour of her earliest memories ... Karen says they need to talk about options ... Liz has been sent to this room at the tip of Karen's pen but she will not sit down in her childhood... radiation therapy paired with chemotherapy ... she will not sit down in the place that she has been sent to with her rage, in the room that is a trap at the tip of Karen's pen, in her childhood punishment and powerlessness ... there is the question of her pelvic lymph nodes ... Karen's face is a closed circle ... Liz can only say, *yes* ... Liz can only say, *of course* ... the pen will lift clear of the image ... the moment will close ... after ... there will be an after that room that opened inside of it ... a treatment plan ... a marathon of after ... familiar in its regimentation... but first there will be the long and faltering parking lot to cross through an afternoon that is also a morning.

The five-year survival rate of Stage 4A cervical cancer is 56% ... side effects include: nausea, fatigue ... include: repeating ... include: resistance ... it is important to remember that survival rates for women with cervical cancer are estimates, and they may not reflect individual prognoses ... repeating: the humiliation of diarrhea ... Karen is hopeful for both of them ... chemo fog ... how much of treatment is waiting to suffer? ... no ... how much is waiting through suffering? ... don't ask ... how much is hunching over spasms of shame? ... and remission is like a return ... to the sureties of her body... to a half marathon in early summer ... touching only the possibility of her earlier rhythm ... *are you sorry Karen?* ... but finding at least that familiar euphoria to shore her against her slowness, against the confusion of the drugs that flow from the grey surface of the ultrasound into the container of her life ... repeating: the pain returns weeks later ... like reality ... like waking from a dream of health ... the five-year survival rate of Stage 4B cervical cancer, cancer that has spread to distant organs, is 16.5% ... repeating: it is important to remember that survival rates for women with cervical cancer are estimates, and they may not reflect individual prognoses ... learn about statistics ... learn again what is countable and what is not ... pelvic lymph nodes ... *I asked her straight out, "How could this happen?"* ... her face closed in a circle ... liver ... right lung ... it happens ... always: that doubt ... a year and a half for her to get her diagnosis ... *I knew all the time* ... longer to grow like resentment, like rage that itself turns cancerous when it is curbed on itself, when it is turned inward and left to grow ... *I knew, Karen* ... before a second round of chemotherapy, a friend who is an oncologist offers to review her medical history, including the copies of the tests that Liz requests from both her GP and her gynecologist ... cramping always like anger, but, at least, this minor release into action ... repeating: waiting for the determination ... learn that radiotherapy can be palliative ... the friend calls on a summer evening when Liz is watching her youngest son Brendan's soccer game. He is playing in the U6 league and the kids, including him, are too young to play well, too young to understand the game and work together as a team. Their bodies are still too small for their heads. The ball stutters across the uneven field and the kids follow it in a strung-out crowd ... lagging ... *can you hear?* ... losing attention ... Karen ... over the coaches calling ... over the paralysis of wanting and not wanting ... *yes* ... *your first Pap smear came back ASC-H, not ASC-US ... just some weird cells ... ASC-H indicates atypical squamous cells that could be a high-grade or dangerous form of cancer ... someone missed ...* nothing ... *your gynecologist read the same paperwork and made a note that the test came back normal* ... repeating: missed, misread ... eighteen months to diagnosis ... when detected at an early stage, the five-year survival rate for cervical cancer is 92% ... nothing ... *this finding necessitates a referral for a biopsy* ... they should have caught this two years ago is outside of time . . . the game is shifting towards the far end of the pitch ... the goalie is drawing out of the net towards midfield ... small figures ... repeating: someone ... Liz ... *I know* ... wanting: nothing ... *I knew* ... shifting away.

Pelvic Lymph Nodes, Secondary Cancer:

After that afternoon when she was contained at the tip of Karen's pen, she tells her sons, Brendan and Luke ... who is three years older than Brendan and who therefore worries her more because of this, because he can understand ... *I knew* ... all four of them posed in the living room ... what time of day? ... what colour of light connects them? ... she explains in clear words that do not connect them ... does the light matter or the living room in which they are sitting? ... she says, *cancer* ... she says, *sick* ... she says, *medicine, not chemotherapy* ... she doesn't say, radiation therapy or five-year survival rate, through the deadening exhaustion of delivering her own diagnosis ... Luke and Brendan ... her hips are laced with dying and she is lifting the weight of their confusion ... they hug her on the couch, of course ... under the front window where she has sat down to be touched ... under what light? ... they cry, of course, in that way children have of crying until they are just crying, until they are wild with it, and long past mourning ... but holding to her still ... hands ... Mark hovers ... careful ... she is crying too ... your mother ... tentativeineffectual in his desire to help and not to hurt not to hurt not to hurt ... but the boys do hurt ... setting their crying into her ... hanging their grief from her dying hips ... memory lives in the bones of her body ... without meaning to ... hung like grief on the scaffold of her skeleton ... Luke and Brendan's not meaning to is as boyish and intentional as Mark's meaning not to ... time at least is alive in her ... her young sons crying out themselves ... the adjective to Liz ... James Stewart sat behind her through two years of public school ... grade two and three? ... a boyish hand drags sharply on the proper noun of herself ... the light no more certain now ... pulled out single hairs in sudden pricks of pain to soothe his boredom ... chased the girls at recess too ... a hot frustration with Luke and Brendan who hold to Liz like a muscle cramp ... Mark hesitates ... or was that someone else? ... the sharpness of being chased and sprinting hard across the fall ... why fall? ... the playground has itself stayed with her ... settled in her? ... that alone ... of course ... by tacit agreement we consign boys' transgressions to the secret histories of bone ... holding ... to the forgetting not forgetting of the body ... to the erasure of childhood from everywhere except the hidden berth resentment keeps inside of her ... James dated her best friend Sheryl ten years later ... Luke bumps Brendan or vice versa and the boys jostle back and forth across her hips ...

he liked to hold her head down when he came during blowjobs ... turn ... the moment ... of revelation inevitable ... jagged with pain ... and nauseous ... he is, Liz thinks, a doctor now ... a pediatrician ... they escalate ... is good, she imagines, with children ... turn ... the uncertain living room ... so fast ... so confident in force ... to the full-on pushing that leads to fighting ... like Mark with children ... consigned to say these clear and simple words ... calm down Calm Down CALM DOWN ... your mother ... the girls in particular that Mark still wants ... in what colour of light? ... his disappointment with their luck? ... this not connecting? ... this back and forth? ... of course ... her body? ... and will not have ... in the exhaustion of the room they find the forms they will carry forward ... the grammar of their relationship ... their going on ... the boys in their détente ... Mark in his hesitation ... in his not meaning and being careful ... that leaves Liz to manage Luke and Brendan in their grieving and not grieving and not ... in their boyishness ... in their bouts of crying that are as unpredictable, as impossible to refuse and as passing as weather ... learn that revelation is a moment the boys can close and forget ... waiting: in their not ... until they don't forget ... repeating: in their not ... until they hang once again from the hook of her dying ... hurt without warning ... learn that hate opens like a room in the noun of love ... learn that Luke and Brendan are like words out of clear skies ... are like atmospheric modifiers ... calm down ... Mark as well ... the April morning ... and that ... that holding ... of course ... learn that the faltering weight of cancer is the changing weather of grammar.

Liver, Secondary Cancer:

Mark stands in the kitchen ... after a run? ... in the wide clarity of the mid-afternoon that comes in through the windows ... after work? ... winter now and its white abundance of light that reveals but does not connect ... he is smiling across the shining granite countertop ... always now ... across the distance of her sickness ... his face drawn tight ... alive with satisfaction ... his long body fit ... as in (used with an object) to be adapted to or suitable for (a purpose, object, occasion, etc.), to be proper or becoming for, and also (used without an object) to be suitable or proper, to be of the right size or shape ... or not ... to himself ... to his enthusiasms ... Mark has been a runner and a swimmer since his teens and he has carried a boyish leanness into his mid-forties that seems at times like these to be an extension of the childish exuberance ... its own kind of abundant brightness ... he never entirely leaves behind at the public school where he teaches gym classes and runs intramurals ... childish in his disappointment when she said, *I can't. It hurts* ... a private withdrawal that is another kind of painful intimacy ... symptoms include: pain or discomfort during intercourse ... and Liz saying, *we can still* ... and they did ... without or not ... symptoms include: watching someone disappear into the loss that is her own disease ... and childish in the openness of his face ... the way he is himself at every moment ... the way he can be ... without regret ... in his disappointment ... Mark is happy when he is happy Mark is sad when he is sad Liz hurts when she is happy Liz hurts when she is sad Liz hurts when she hurts ... he tells her over the counter about taking the grade threes for a winter hike around the playground. He led them single file through close to a foot of new snow and they followed him down the white trench of his footsteps. In places where the wind banked the white against the fence, it reached to their armpits ... his voice is reaching out ... she imagines the line of small figures struggling after him ... symptoms include: solicitousness that is itself an absence ... listen ... follow the lean and confident line of his attention like the line of a pen through the welter of light ... but Liz hurts ... in the kitchen? ... in his fit? ... or not ... to that fact ... and her hurting is like a refusal... like a revelation ... like I can't ... Mark ... he tells her that he saw Joan Clayton by the gym door and said, *Look, there's Clayton bear* ... Scott Cruickshank and Mary Shaw crossing from the portables to main building were Cruickshank bear and Shaw bear ... the light in the kitchen is a substance she is struggling through to reach him reaching out ... this small thing ... he turned the hike into a bear hunt ... this minor joy in the winter morning ... his happiness now ... banked white against her ... the line of kids laughing and pointing through his smile ... symptoms include: knowing that she should be grateful to him for wanting to share himself with her ... for this impulse in him now ... but his delight settles between them like disappointment ... like regret ... like/as in unsuited or maladapted to ... he is Mark in this moment ... as in always ... and it hurts is a being there that is not being there ... in this light? ... an unfitting of the self ... in this kitchen? ... he has kept running through close to two years of her trying to run and not running ... five? ... no ... seven? ... marathons ... half-marathons? ... countless 10ks ... cool mornings drawing into the heat of the afternoon ... to which they often went on the weekends as a family ... how many times has she cheered him off? ... searched to see him ... really to be seen by him in his readiness ... through the crowd? ... to see him now ... how many times has she waited alone at the finish line? ... without the kids, or with them? ... how many times has she carried the long boredom of the hours between the beginning and the end of the race into this obligatory stasis? ... he tells her in the kitchen and Liz remembers through his telling: a different light ... alone with Luke and Brendan ... the risen sun burned hot on her stilled body. The risen sun whitened the pavement, extended the boredom of standing in her waiting, and forced the glow of rage slow ... a contained incandescence ... a rising likewise in her... a what? ... a secret/unseen/latent blazing out ... an over ... an abundance of light/heat ... that reached to and clarified the walls that held it in ... she was the limits of her skin ... her private self that lived alone now ... she was stretched over *DON'T DO THAT* ... she was her hand paused over a light bulb: the itching discomfort that comes before ... real pain ... real anger ... the crimson/the before that promises something ... *Brendan!* ... *Luke!* ... *Boys!* ... and this waiting in the sun for Mark as he is carrying his happiness towards her ... his face drawn tight with the suffering he chooses ... as in adapted or suitable to himself ... Liz can't choose the sun ... happiness/hardship/the hook of her hips ... Liz hurts when she hurts ... in the kitchen: his absence and solicitousness ... today in the kitchen: above all, his boyish and easy body ... that he lifts so effortlessly into its effort ... into this joy ... ... his lean body that she knows like her own with its long bare legs in the summer and its skin spackled with sun ... he could always outpace her ... he is outpacing her now ... alone at the finish line: learn that resentment is a solitude inside of intimacy ... always that interval ... that across ... listen ... his care ... and stilted tenderness ... be attentive to his telling ... hands that are conscious of their gentleness can give no solace ... the closer he comes the more alone Liz feels: *we can still* ... in the kitchen ... *can we?* ... no ... *I can't* ... no ... I hurt/alone ... as in with an object ... *Mark!* ... in the winter of my body ... and I won't.

Right Lung, Secondary Cancer:

Jen Carson sits opposite her in the living room. They have been friends for twelve years and Liz is on leave from the library where they work at separate branches ... chemo brain is a common term used by cancer survivors to describe thinking and memory problems that can occur during and after treatment ... Jen folds forward in the living room ... and says? ... called chemo fog ... less the words ... the words? ... less what? ... called cancer-related cognitive impairment ... Jen says while folded forward? ... called cognitive dysfunction ... than the voice with which she says the words ... *I can't imagine* ... and that saying that is itself a calm and urgent apology of sound ... Jen specializes in physical literacy and leads semiregular yoga retreats in her branch. *Bodies belong in libraries too,* she says. She believes in the importance of self-care, and, from the mat from which she leads these groups through their poses, she recommends ... Jen's hands are folded like her body ... they are folded like her words on their own kind of softness ... twelve years? ... how long ago? ... Jen's hands are tucked into their own apology ... being present in the moment ... Jen is leading now ... and that stretch of time is separate from Liz ... like the years are a room in a stranger's house ... like they are held in Jen's strange and careful hands ... *breathing from your diaphragm* ... a kind of drifting: a dismissive attentiveness ... Jen is delivering ... what? ... in the living/ordinary room? ... less the words ... than the sounds that are her condolences in advance ... you may learn new ways of doing everyday tasks to help you concentrate: *tea?* ... accept: I can't imagine ... accept: now ... accept: Jen's soft hands folded over her performance of care ... a therapist may help you learn new ways of speaking that help you commit conversations to memory and then retrieve those memories later ... Liz can't blame Jen for not imagining ... no ... she can't ... hold this pose: sound whose softness has folded the prospect of Liz's dying into it ... stressful situations can make memory problems more likely ... but she can ... she must ... and having memory problems may be stressful ... Liz stands over the glass coffee table with the teapot in her hands, bearing the hot weight of it like the twelve years of forgetting that Jen is holding in her hands that are folded/calm in her lap ... present in: the concern that slides away from her ... tucked around their apology ... to end the cycle you may learn relaxation techniques ... and standing there Liz experiences the sudden desire to bring the teapot ... of course it is a teapot ... of course it is her and Mark's handmade teapot with a pale green glaze from a potter who makes her own business cards out of handmade paper with a hand-carved stamp ... such as progressive muscle relaxation ... down hard on the glass of the coffee table ... such as mindfulness practices ... down hard on the softness of the moment and the sounds that are Jen's words ... on the condolences that Jen is offering like a gift and what that giving means ... the weight of the pottery down on it ... she wants to hear the decisive pop of the glass sheet ... the snap of the clay like a word in her hands ... a certain/final break ... clean ... before/followed by ... accept: your limitations ... accept: laughing about things you can't control can help you cope ... the bright and threatening ... careful ... kids' feet ... dogs' paws ... accept: you probably notice more than others do ... secret and blood/ sudden fear in the rug ... learn to manage ... before the catastrophe of light: but ... which is its own kind of acceptance ... always: but ... and ... she does not ... now ... not ever ... that restraint constant in life ... itself clean and tucked into her ... the pot settles with a soft click on the table ... grit of the unglazed bottom on the glass ... and she returns ... as if to a memory although not to a memory ... not now ... to her seat on the couch ... twelve years? ... to receiving once more the news of her death ... learn relaxation techniques ... Jen? ... to sitting down in this folded moment ... less what? ... called what? ... and these soft words that are the long and false civility of illness.

[Location Unknown], Secondary Cancer:

There is a separateness to sickness ... which is the solitude Liz feels in moments of connection ... but that is also the isolation of days spent on the couch when Mark is at work and Luke and Brendan are at school ... days of hours ... hours of minutes ... and she is hurting in the still house ... all runners are alone ... at the starts of races ... alone in the shoving ... the elbows ... the clipped heels ... the finding a way through the crowd of runners around them to their own pace ... this jostling ... like a difficult conversation ... like not being understood or listened to ... always: alone in their bodies ... Liz discovered as a girl: the line of her own race ... the still of the morning through which she moved through decades into the last moments of her easiness ... through the spring-bare trees ... always: alone in the suffering at the end ... at that reaching past herself that was/is herself ... Liz ... in her running ... discovered: what carried her ... into exhaustion and through it ... the substance of ... as in the concreteness of ... as in the material (essence) of ... her determination ... as in always: anger in its various mutations ... call it rage ... call it frustration ... Karen ... call it mornings of minor annoyances turned into miles until the stillness was her fury and she was beyond tireless ... *I am so sorry* ... with her hair tied back in that careful room ... *to have to tell you* ... the qualifier necessary ... careful like Karen's hair and the colour of the walls ... but that tone ... Jen folding her soft apology towards her ... how long ago? ... how long to go? ... that withholding ... settled like hurt like hate into her hips and will not lift ... a waiting and repeating ... *are you sorry Karen?* ... in this not yet ... in this still/separateness of sickness ... in this limping home ... balance is a trust in the body ... unbalancing is a failure of unconsciousness ... a falteringfalteringintoknowledge that is felt as a loss ... as a not forgetting ... no ... eighteen months from the onset of symptoms and that first rehearsal of her pain ... as a not ... knowing/I knew ... to her diagnosis ... as a no ... letting go ... or relenting ... as a repeating that expands from the perfect circle of Karen's face and the moment that opened between them ... to Luke and Brendan ... to Mark ... to *NO* ... *I don't* ... *NO* ... *I won't* ... *NO* ... there is a sharpness in the still morning of her body ... resentment/ transference ... and the condition produced by this ... a rapid transition ... as from one subject to another ... a negation ... that holds her to the line of herself ... Liz in the loneliness of her determination ... hating/hurting/ hating/hurting/hating/hurting ... until ... no ... she can't anymore.

R$_0$ Values of Select Airborne Viruses and Emotions:

R$_0$ or R-nought is **the basic reproduction number of a viral or bacterial infection and/or of an emotional state**. It represents the expected number of cases generated by one infected individual in a population where all individuals are susceptible to infection. R$_0$ applies exclusively to a situation in which no other individuals are infected, no individuals are immunized, and there are no deliberate interventions in transmission. It should not be confused with the effective reproduction number R. which represents the number of cases produced in a population where individuals may be immune and/or steps are being taken to control the spread of the infection. By definition, R$_0$ cannot be modified by vaccination campaigns, therapy or other interventions.

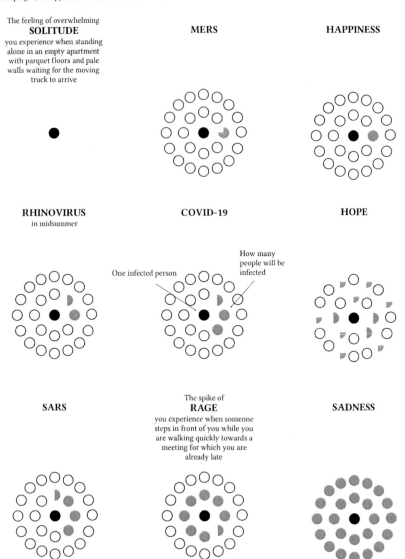

The feeling of overwhelming
SOLITUDE
you experience when standing alone in an empty apartment with parquet floors and pale walls waiting for the moving truck to arrive

MERS

HAPPINESS

RHINOVIRUS
in midsummer

COVID-19

One infected person

How many people will be infected

HOPE

SARS

The spike of
RAGE
you experience when someone steps in front of you while you are walking quickly towards a meeting for which you are already late

SADNESS

Life Maps and Assemblages

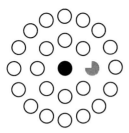

The Death and Possible Life of Daan de Wees

My grandfather, Daan de Wees, is dying. He has been dying for as long as I can remember. Lung cancer. Half of one lung removed and part of the other. Two rounds of chemotherapy. He stayed at the Cancer Center at the Grand River Hospital in Waterloo. Red brick. Long, empty lawns that we did not run across. Ash under his tan. My brother and I took turns blowing into a device that measured lung capacity. We watched a ping pong ball rise and dance in a clear plastic tube. A decline that stretched over a decade and was expected and predictable and slow and seemed to me at the age of fifteen like it would never end. But this is the end. And we are driving to Woodstock to watch him die.

It is February and it is snowing hard. Thick, damp flakes stream at an angle across the road. They felt the windshield between sweeps of the wipers. My father hunches over the wheel and concentrates. My mother tells us about my grandfather. She offers us solitary facts, fragments instead of stories, sentences that are truncated by grief and something more than grief, something that lies separate from but alongside it. Her words are hedged by omissions. The silence between then expands into the storm.

*

His life as it was told to me and it might have been:

He as born in the town of Goes in the province of Zeeland in the country of the Netherlands. Did he belong to a family of provincial merchants? To the sort of petite bourgeoisie who form the backbone of small market towns? To a family whose men each owned two suits of the same dull colour, one for weekdays and one for Sundays? Did these men wash themselves at basins before shaving? Did they stand stripped to the waist, their suspenders hanging in loops under naked bulbs? Was watching his father and his pale torsos polished by water why Daan kept this habit through his life? Did these men lean on the smooth elbows of their suit jackets when the shutters were closed against the North Sea wind

91

to talk about the prices in the markets of Middleburg, Bergen op Zoom, and Bredan? Did the particularly ambitious ones mention Rotterdam? Did the women who raised these men's children and oversee their households tell each other they were better off than farmers' wives, but still take an upright pride in boiling their own potatoes and milking their own cows? Did Daan learn to measure his worth before he learned to work with his hands? **He liked to say he had some gypsy blood in him. He pointed to his hair, which was thick, until the end of his life, and so brown into his sixties that it was almost black.** In his youth, did he also point at his skin and the way it held to the olive shades of summer and was burnished gold by the lamplight of long evenings? Did he offer this as an explanation of his life before the war and after it? Was this why he didn't like to work the same job for long? Why he was restless, not lazy, but easily bored? Did he say this to his father and his four brothers on those occasions when he returned to the small packing plant they ran on the outskirts of Goes after bouncing around the Netherlands, doing a bit of everything, making very little money, and coming back only because he knew they would give him work to do and a bed to sleep in so that they could disapprove of him? Was it a joke? An apology? Did he mean it and everything it implied? Was he hiding behind honesty or absurdity? **In 1935, he biked to Brussels to visit the World's Fair where he jumped from a platform wearing a harness tied to a rope. It was just like bungee jumping.** Did he go alone, leaving his brothers in the middle of the harvest with a mound of potatoes at the plant door? Did he bike down the fall lanes with the wind at his back, heading inland, racing the salt of the sea? Did he go with friends who laughed at the way he outsprinted them to their destination each day? Did they sleep in hedge rows with their coat collars turned up to their ears? Was this a story he told because he had seen a picture in a newspaper of the platform and a man poised at the edge with his feet in a harness? Because he liked the idea of the leap and what it said about him that he had made it? **My mother told me once that his gypsy blood explained the way they moved around in Canada, and the string of jobs he got and quit. She said this bitterly, but as if she believed it, or wanted to.**

*

When I was young, my grandparents lived in a rented house at the bottom of a hill in Woodstock. It had a front porch that they sat on sometimes and a basement that opened directly onto the backyard. There were cut glass dishes on the dining room table, lace in the curtains, lace in the spread drawn tight across my grandparents' bed, and an old-world hush in the rooms. They lived on his CPP. Small portions. Care. I remember clearly a bone-handled shoehorn in the umbrella stand and a cream-colored phone on the wall in the hallway whose cord stretched into the kitchen.

The basement belonged to him. The walls were lined with shelves that he had made out of plywood and two-by-fours. Fluorescent lights hung where he sprouted plants for the vegetable garden in the backyard. His work bench filled the room and crowded the shelves. For as long as I knew him, until he couldn't anymore, he made things: small things, like Jacob's Ladders for his grandchildren's stockings and the cribbage board my parents brought out when he visited. Big things, like the beds my brother and I slept on until we moved out. Things that took up their places in our lives and reminded us of Daan whenever we thought about them, like the stained-glass light that still hangs over my parents' kitchen table. He made a cradle for me when I was born, and then my brother used it, and then it was passed around my parents' circle of friends as they had their babies. Everyone who took it wrote the full name of their child, including their embarrassing middle name, and their date of birth in permanent marker on the bottom. The cradle was plywood, boxy and functional: you could almost see the plans he had cut out of a magazine. Most of the things he made were like that, not clumsy, but painstaking, the work of a man for whom life had become an effort. Who was himself contained. Focused. The basement was pressurized.

When I stayed with them in the summer, I watched TV in the living room until my grandmother sent me outside to play. I liked to kick the black walnuts that fell from the tree on the other side of the fence. I watched the neighbor kids through the fence. My grandmother had told me not to talk to them, and I didn't want to, but I wanted to understand why she had said this. Their yard was different than my grandparents'. Overhung by trees. Where grass could grow, the kids had worn it down to hard, dusty earth. Rocks. Clumps of roots. The kids themselves were dusty. Rings of dirt around their necks. Around their wrists. And there were more of them than I could keep track of. They went in and out of the house all day. And some of them belonged to the house. And some of them didn't. Plastic shovels and buckets. A Big Wheel trike. All bleached. As if they had been left out over the winter. Yelling in the house. Often a loud noise. A kid darted out. Hid behind a tree. Ducked under the porch. A woman stood in the open door. Come here. Come and get your spanking. The kid waited. I mean it. And then came. Crafty. Delaying. They disappeared into the house. One day there were donuts. Round balls coated in sugar. She distributed them from a lawn chair. Smacked if they reached. Share. Sugar mixed with the dirt on their hands. Pink palms. White grit at their mouths. Alone. The youngest one drove the Big Wheel across the yard. Easy on the dirt. Caught on the roots. He lifted and struggled. Kept going. I got bored and went back to kicking walnuts.

Questions gather around these memories the way they gather around what my mother told us on that wintery drive: why do the scenes I watched through that page wire fence always return to me in conjunction with my grandparents' house? With the low-ceilinged basement? And the work Daan did there? Why do these handful of fragments fold together like this? And why can't I reduce the way that dirt yard and the interior of that house overlap to the eight steps down from the kitchen porch to the lawn where I alternated between watching and kicking walnuts or the two steps up from the recessed basement door? To the simple fact of their physical proximity? Is what I watched through the fence connected by a subterranean logic to my mother's resentment? To her need to believe in Daan's gypsy blood? Was I looking through the diamond links into a poverty that I would later confirm had haunted my mother's childhood? Into a squalor that had only been held off? And the cruelty of want that hadn't? Was the dignity of the myth Daan had made for himself, its strangeness and exoticism, a necessary mercy? Was it lace stitched by hand and hung in the windows of a rented house at the bottom of a hill? Cut glass set out on a second-hand table? Tenuous and solemn in its sincerity? Or is this all a trick of my child mind? Of the concatenating logic of memory? Did I notice first the care Daan took at his work bench in the basement and then the plastic toys yellowing in the dirt yard and turn the one into the inverted reflection of the other? Am I seeing through the fence into that pressurized silence or into myself?

*

His life as it was told to me and it might have been:

In the late 1930s, he got married and joined the army. There is a picture of him standing next to his wife, Catharijne, in his uniform, his peaked cap tilted back. Is it a young man's leanness under the pressed lines of his clothes? Or the insipient sinew and bone of middle age? Is the secret of what is about to happen already contained in his body? Is his face already showing his age? Or is that the light? The peak of the cap deepening the hollows under his cheekbones? Are his and Catharijne's faces closed around their seriousness or flattened by discomfort? Are they happy inside of these official selves? **He was mobilized in 1939.** Was he in a reserve company that was called up? Was he already living in the barracks on a base? Among men like his brothers? Men he rubbed against sharply? Did he march to the border in a panicked rush through the night to fight in the spring of 1940 when the Germans invaded? Or faster still through the dawn to defend the Hague? Was he already there on the main defence line along the river Meuse?

94

Had he been there for months? Had he been waiting for an event that had seemed inevitable for so long that it caught everyone by surprise when it happened? Did he watch German paratroopers falling from the morning sky? Did he hear about them and the loss of all but seventy planes second hand? Days after the fact? Did he see a German tank crash through a hedge row and spin up mud through a hay field or find himself standing alone in the open afternoon staring at the two parallel rents in the earth? Did he fire his gun before folding this torn sod over it or throw it cold and clean into a canal? Did he send his uniform after the gun or plunge it into a barrel fire behind a barn? As he walked back to Goes in his bare arms and undershirt, did the magnitude of these losses lift him into a reeling lightness? **He worked at his family's packing plant. My mother tells us that he was part of the resistance, that he stood up to the occupation, and organized a strike. It was more serious, she says, and less romantic than it sounds.** Was the plant commandeered by the Germans who turned it into a munitions factory making bombs for the planes that flew out of the bases on the North Sea coast or was it left as it was except for the trucks who took away the produce and the men who told him to load them faster and swore at him in a language he understood without wanting to? Was it Dann who convinced his brothers and the five other men who worked alongside them to walk off the line? Did he tell them to follow him when he left his place? Or did he set his stubbornness in the service of another man's plan? Did the soldiers who came to break the strike single him out or did he step forward with the same brazenness that he told his father he had gypsy blood in him? Did he strike or was he struck? Did he take a knee or fold limp to the hard-packed earth in front of the plant doors where he had left piles of potatoes to bike to the world's fair? Did this happen in stunned silence? Did his legs and arms flop loose? His head roll? As the soldiers kicked his senseless body? Did he fend off their boots with his arms? Did he grunt until the sounds lost their shape and broke open into agony? Did his brothers recoil from the brutality of the beating? Did they think that he had brought this on himself? Did one of them slip away to find Catharijne or did they wait until the end of the day to tell her? Was this delay a mercy to them or to her? Did they lift his body into the back of the car that would take him away because they had watched what the soldiers had done to him and been glad that it wasn't them rolling in the dirt or because they were ordered to? Was the tenderness with which one of them lay his head on the seat and brushed Daan's hair out of his blank eyes a rebuke or an apology? Did they see that in moments like these we are all caricatures of ourselves? And Daan? Did he think it would work? Was he convinced? Did he convince the other men? Was it the confidence that he talked himself into over a month of evenings that made him do it? Was it the blind anger that he was used to bleeding away by leaving one place after another but that had been boiling in him since that bare-armed walk across the country and that now had a target? Stubbornness? Righteousness? An arbitrary sense of possession, the intolerable fact of the Germans imposing themselves on his family, on his brothers, on a building with their name on it in showy white letters that were touched up each year, but never by him? Was it an act of heroism or self-destruction? Daring or fatalism? Was there a difference? Did he realize that he would be sent to a labour camp for a year and half? That he would sleep shoulder to shoulder with two other men on a hard, wooden bunk and be grateful for their heat? That his bruises and the ribs that he knew were broken without needing a doctor to tell him would forget how to heal? Did those eighteen months cave him in with hunger or despair? Did they hollow his already lean body to the hopelessness of bone? Was his limping return to Goes a relief? His stoop a reproach? **In my mid-twenties, the same age that Daan was during the war, I visited the Netherlands. One of my great aunts drove me past the plant. It was a single-story brick building, smaller and lower than I expected. It had been abandoned decades earlier and left to decay: the roof and the windows were gone. She hadn't meant to show it to me. We were on the way to somewhere else and she sounded embarrassed when she pointed it out.**

*

We went straight to my grandparents' apartment. My uncle was already there, and met us at the door. My grandmother was behind him, tiny, reduced, making abrupt, confused movements. She cried into my mother who held her and looked at us over her head. My brother and I sat on the couch while my mother and my uncle talked about my grandfather: Did he have oxygen? A mask. Enough. The company would pick up the tanks after. They increased his morphine yesterday. The doctor isn't concerned about the dosage. He has an IV and can self-administer. Do we know? There's a chart. We want him to be comfortable. The nurse is checking in twice a day. The funeral home is being difficult. My mother talked sharply into the phone about extra charges, hidden costs. She said it was unethical. My father said we could cover it. She said we shouldn't have to. My mother and uncle went into the bedroom. We stayed in the living room. It wasn't time. It wouldn't be long. We would see him soon.

*

His life as it was told to me and it might have been:

My mother was born in 1947 and my uncle two years later. They emigrated when she was four. Did they pack their lives into a set of steamers trunk given to them by a relative or into a handful of mismatched, second-hand suitcases with battered corners and latches Daan wired shut to be safe? After the war and the years of deprivation that followed it, did what matter to them fit? Or did they agonize over what they left behind? Was emigration an exile or an escape? Did it take the definite shape of Daan's willfulness or did they live every day with their doubts? Did he spend the voyage standing in the bow of the boat smoking with his hand cupped over his cigarette to hide his seasickness or to separate himself from the passengers whose fantasies became more outlandish by the day? Did they land in Halifax or Montreal? How long did their legs take to relearn the steadiness of land? Did they wonder if it would ever lose its strangeness? Were the rocking train and then the rumble of the bus that carried them to Tavistock, Ontario at least familiar? Did they understand what it meant to be sponsored by a produce farmer named John Thorpe or had Daan cut short the explanation and made brusque marks for both him and Catharijne? Was the bunkhouse behind the barn they lived in for two years built with care or did they stuff newspapers between the boards to keep out the draughts and wake to blankets frosted by their breath in the winter no mater how much wood they fed the stove? Did they mind the hoeing and picking and weeding they did in the summer? Did the factory in Woodstock Daan took shifts in during winter remind him of the plant his brothers were still running in Goes? Did they talk about their work when they got together with the other Dutch families in the area on the weekends to drink coffee or did they turn to the certainties of home? Were some of these families from Goes? Were they relatives? Cousins? Second cousins? Did Catherijne and Daan already know their names and sometimes their faces? Was the dirty, boring labour on farms and in small factories a step down for them? Were they used to working for their fathers or uncles, to expecting shares in the business, and to giving as well as taking orders? Did they see that Daan was no better at taking orders than them? But that this work was a continuation of his life in the Netherlands? Were there times when they complained over their white cups and he sat back and busied himself with a cigarette? When he could not hide the fact that he saw their dissatisfaction as weakness and hardly tried to? Did this cost him friends? Or were there too few of them? Were they too closely connected, tied by the necessities of blood, Zeeland and the strangeness of this new place for any of them to hold it against him for long? Did they say to each other that that was Daan and how he was? Did they still have their old superiority to hold over him? Was he still the wayward son? The one who had worked with nothing to show for it and married late? Did they know that they would soon have new reasons to condescend to him?

97

That they would succeed? That they would get and keep factory jobs? Good union jobs with overtime pay and pensions? Or go on to build their own businesses? Or return to the Netherlands where they would buy houses and cars with the money they had made? Did they pour out that certainty with their coffee? When they said that was Daan and how he was, did they mean he wouldn't change, and they didn't expect him to? Did they recognize in him a version of their headstrong and exacting natures? Did they share his belief that there was a way to do things? And anything different was wrong? Did they pride themselves on their absolutes and the good sense to know when to keep them to themselves? Did they notice that even when Daan didn't say anything, his opinions, his denunciations, they were always denunciations, leaked out of him? And he often said something? Did they see as he leaned back and rolled his cigarette that his life had unfolded as a sequence of arguments? Did Daan carry the same aura of disapproval into these conversations that he brought with him into my parents' house? Did he inspect what the other men said the way he inspected the presents my brother and I gave him at Christmas? The crafts, the small, clumsy object that we created ourselves under the supervision of our parents, the paintings, coasters, pottery ashtrays? **We watched him turn what we had made over in his large hands, looking closely for flaws, mistakes.** Did these men also wonder if he would approve? Did they shrink imperceptibly into themselves before he lit that cigarette and announce his disagreement? Did he impose himself on those afternoons the way he did in our living room? Did he make his judgements matter? Was it after working for John Thorpe that they moved to Hamilton and Daan got a job as an industrial welder? Or did that come later? Did he like repairing the fuel tanks and hulls of ships? The space that contained and magnified him like a conversation with close friends? Was it this or the cigarettes that he rolled like words in his hands that set the cancer in him? Did he quit after a year and half because he wanted to or because his breath started to come hard and rasping? Because his coughs bent him into the memory of the camp? Did they move again and keep moving because he couldn't live with anything he couldn't leave behind? To Sarnia? To Windsor? For how long? Woodstock? St. Catharines? London? Petrolia? Sarnia again? Brantford? **And back to that house at the base of a hill in Woodstock. My mother has yearbooks from three different high schools and has lived with my father in the same farmhouse at the end of a long gravel lane outside of Owen Sound for almost five decades.** Is this continuity also an escape?

*

We checked into a hotel. My brother and I watched cable TV.

The next day, we went back to the apartment.

My grandmother hadn't slept. Her face had slumped and grayed. She went back and forth between the kitchen and the living room, asking if we wanted anything, until my mother told her sharply to stop it. She stood behind the reclining chair that faced the TV and held her hands in front of her, not like she was praying, like she had forgotten them.

There was another phone call to the funeral home.

My mother and my uncle talked about arrangements, what would happen after. They went into the foyer, but we could still hear them. My father looked sympathetic and incidental.

My mother and my uncle took turns checking on Daan.

I finished one book and started a second. My brother's video game died. He took the batteries out of the remote for it.

My father made sandwiches for lunch. He used ham, white cheddar and refrigerated tomatoes. He couldn't find the mustard. They were cold and didn't taste like anything.

The nurse came and went.

It was time.

My mother sat across from my brother and me. She wanted to prepare us. She told us he might not recognize us. She said this in her professional voice, the one she used with clients: the sentences came steady. Calm. Closed on themselves. They were only words. I felt empty and strange.

My brother went first.

I waited. My book was on the coffee table and I didn't pick it up.

He came out.

I went in.

The room was tiny, and I edged around the bed. My mother stood at the head of it, next to Daan, the oxygen tank and the IV drip. My uncle was beside her. Catharijne waited at the foot, in a narrow space between an armoire and a dresser, removed, a spectator, crying in a worn out, uncontrolled way. My father was in the door.

A white spread was pulled to Daan's armpits, and his arms lay on top of it on either side of his body. The sleeves of his pyjamas were rucked up to his elbows. His hands and forearms, the length of him under the padding of the bedclothes, were pared by sickness to lines of bone, knobs of joint and loose skin. He had always been clean shaven, but now he had gray stubble. Only the stroke of his nose and his eyebrows were the same. His head was propped on a pillow and he stared into the space in front of him without fixing on anything. His tenuous breathing, not loud, but difficult, and filled with interruptions, dominated the room. He lifted a hand and lowered it.

My mother directed me to a place at the head of the bed across from her.

"This is Andrew," she said. Every syllable was its own word. "Your grandson."

He rotated towards me. I took his hand. It was hot, at once tough and limp.

I didn't know what to say. My sure mother, my distant, reduced grandfather, my grandmother's weakened sorrow, and my father in the door: I didn't say anything.

Daan began to struggle. His mouth worked, his free hand plucked at the air, and he made soft, torn whistling sounds. My mother leaned down. He produced a short, blurred sentence. She repeated it: "Don't go for the buck."

"I won't grandpa," I said, "I won't."

I let go of his hand. His body relaxed. My father guided me out of the room.

That night, my uncle called the hotel, and my mother returned to the apartment. Daan died in the early morning.

We waited a day, and then drove back to Owen Sound.

My parents asked my brother and me if we needed another day off of school. They looked tired and concerned, realizing after the upheaval and uncertainty, the drives there and back in the snow, and their own grief, what it could mean for us. I said, yes.

When we were alone, my brother got mad at me. He said I was faking it. I didn't care about our grandfather. I just wanted the day off of school. I hadn't cried.

I pretended to be offended. I told him he was a liar. I said he made himself cry in the hotel. I knew him. I could tell. I didn't hold back. I was savage, and he left the room vibrating with rage, but he was right: Daan's death was a blank, an absence of feeling, and a test that I had failed.

*

His life as it was told to me and it might have been:

Was Daan a criminal in that minor, sordid way in which crime happens outside of TV shows, in real life, or did he do the sort of marginal work that meant he rubbed shoulders with criminals? Was this why immigration officials came to the house? **When they lived in Sarnia, Daan worked at a bowling alley. Some of the men there, including the owner, were using bowling balls to smuggle "things" across the border.** Did my mother say "things" because she didn't know or because she didn't want to say "drugs"? Using bowling balls? Hiding whatever it was inside of them? Was that possible? Had her child mind invented this the way mine had drawn together the dirt yard on the other side of the fence and my grandfather's basement shop? Was this a lie she had told herself then and repeated now? Had she learned in the telling to believe it? Was this why immigration officials visited their house? Had Daan watched the police arrest half of the staff and walk the owner out of his office above the lanes in handcuffs? Or had he arrived in the morning to find the doors chained shut? Did an officer see his name on the employee list and pass it on to immigration? Was he a suspect? Or someone who thought what he didn't know couldn't touch him? What kind of confusion was he living inside of when the caseworkers knocked on the family's door on a Friday afternoon? Did he invite them in and sit them down at the kitchen table where he had eaten his lunch a few hours ago? Or did they ask to come in with voices that told him it wasn't a request? Did the family join them around the table? Was my uncle too young to understand? Did he bang his feet on the rungs of his chair until Daan slammed his hand down and told him to go to his room? Or did the children watch from the safety of the hallway? Was Daan and Catharijne's broken English good enough? Had they answered these questions or ones like them so many times that the phrases came easily? By rote? Or was the language of bureaucracy beyond them? Did my mother have to stand at Daan's shoulder and translate the men's questions and her parents' answers? Did she ask in her clear and serious voice, in the clumsy Dutch she only spoke at home, where were you born? Town? Country? Religious affiliation? How long have you lived in this house? And before this house? And before that? Why did you move? How much do you make? Spend? What do you own? Owe? And your children? Schools? Did she have to draw out in precise and humiliating detail the short history of her parents' life in Canada? Were Daan's responses terse, contemptuous, barely contained? Or did he take the opportunity to explain himself? Did he answer for Catharijne? **In the pictures I have seen from that period, my mother wears her hair in braids on either side of her head. Her face is narrow, angular. Sharpness of eyes. Point of nose. Not even the tiniest excess of flesh.** Is she poised between her father and the possibility that he will explode? Did she ask him, Mr. de Wees, do you understand that these are very serious allegations? Do you know that your residency in this country is a privilege, not a right? Did she say in response, I don't know? Or did Daan's tone preclude translation? Did the two strangers sitting at the green Formica table that had followed her family from one place to the next for as long as she could remember look at her with irritation or pity? Did they look at her at all? Did she experience that peculiar dislocation that comes with saying words from a language you speak in a second language that you also speak? Did one familiarity transform another? Did she realize that she could not remember the country whose Gs she pushed out of her throat and whose Rs she tapped against her teeth? That Goes and Netherlands were a strangeness in her mouth? An emptiness in her mind? Was there black coffee made by Catharijne? Did they come to a détente? Did immigration monitor them for a year? Did they check in monthly? Did they interview Daan's new boss? My mother's and uncle's teachers? Or did they disappear out the kitchen door? **When my mother talks about the raid on the bowling alley and what followed it, her voice is light and distant, almost lilting, as if what happened is separate from her, as if it belongs not only to another time, but to another person, and she is repeating their words.**

*

Instead of a funeral, my mother and my uncle organized a commemoration of Daan's life. It was two weeks after he died, and we drove back to Woodstock for it.

The residents of the senior citizens apartment complex whom he had spoken to in the halls, my father's parents, my uncle and his second wife, some but not all of our cousins, and a few of the Dutch immigrants that Daan knew from the 50's, the ones who had stayed, who were still alive and who had kept in touch, came. They sat in rows of plastic chairs in the events room in the basement of the complex. The chairs were full, but the room was narrow, long and not very big.

My father explained the ceremony: "Daan wasn't religious, and he wouldn't have been comfortable with a church funeral. But we wanted to create a space where the people who knew him could come together to mourn and remember him, where we could gather to find comfort in our grief."

My brother read a poem.

I read a passage from Kahlil Gibran's *The Prophet* that my parents had picked out for me.

My father asked the audience to share memories. Some of them did. Most of the people who spoke were strangers to me. My paternal grandfather talked about playing cribbage with him at Christmas and ended crying freely.

My uncle said something.

My father told a story about meeting Daan for the first time. Musing, reaching for that intimacy when someone thinks aloud for an audience: "I remember how nervous I was. I was being introduced to the father of the woman I loved." Soothing, the words softened and rounded with feeling: "I wondered, what would he think of me? Would he accept me? I didn't speak any Dutch, and Daan was an intimidating man." Shifting to a storyteller's conversational lope, allowing for a second the possibility of a smile: "He sat me down and asked me who I voted for. And I thought, Wow. I was terrified.

But we talked for an hour, and he welcomed me into the family." Careful now, slowing into thoughtfulness: "What I learned to appreciate most about him was how he listened. Daan had very strong opinions, and he wasn't hesitant about expressing them, but he would always listen to what you had to say. He wouldn't always agree." Pausing, deepening his voice: "but he would listen."

My mother read a passage from a book. It described a traveler in the night, walking along a country lane. He saw the windows of a house shining in the distance. When he approached the house, he saw a family sitting at a table, plates of food, burning candles. There was an empty place. He stood in the darkness for a while, and then walked on.

My uncle played a tape of the Vienna Boys Choir singing "Amazing Grace". Catharijne sat in the front row.

No one expected her to speak.

*

His afterlife as I lived it and it might have been:

This was several years after he died, and we were driving again. The farmhouse was half an hour north of Owen Sound, and my family filled the twice daily trip with CBC radio and conversation.

My mother and I were alone in the car. I asked her what Daan did in the war. She was vague. I pressed her for details. I wanted to discover something dramatic, heroic. Instead, she told me that he used to hit them. I had suspected this. There were hints, and I saw his rage once: when my grandparents visited, they slept on air mattresses in the hallway. I was often up before the rest of the family, and, when I was, I would stay in my room, play music on a tape deck and read. This morning, the music woke him up. He stormed in and yelled at me in Dutch. He was shirtless, and his skin was an old man's skin, marked with blemishes, worn smooth in places, loose over withered muscles. Surgery scars. Purple shading to sick-gray. His body flexed around anger. He ripped the plug out of the wall and slammed my door. I was more surprised than afraid. I remember it because it was the one time that he forgot himself and I saw him exposed, frenzied, stringent and vulnerable.

When my uncle and my mother were bad, would he use his belt, fold it double, and strap them hard across their open palms? Bring it down on the backsides? When he was just angry, would he use his hands? A rolled-up magazine? The bone-handled shoehorn? Whatever was in reach? Did she have to lie to her teachers? Did she tell one of them that she ran into a door? Was she surprised when she was believed? Was this what was hidden inside of her terseness? Contained in the focus she kept on the road? He hit her was not what happened. It was what she was willing to say. I could guess at the rest, but I didn't have to: University. The first in her family to

103

go. My father. For whom every conflict ended with a discussion. Let's talk about it. Who loved John Lennon until he learned that he beat his first wife. Who gardened like Daan, nursing rows of peas and hummocks of zucchini through the hot summer, and who sang opera to himself while he crimped dough for pie crusts. Her long career as a support and then a social worker. The MSW she finished in two years. Her transition into management. The farmhouse which they have not yet left. Most of all, what she holds between herself and the world. The act of calm that transforms every meaningful conversation into a counseling session: I am listening. And I hear you. A withdrawal that composes the moment. Like irony without the laughter. How she is moral and remote.

My mother never spoke Dutch with my brother and me. She said it was because it had never developed beyond a child's Dutch, beyond diminutives and simple sentences. She spoke it reluctantly and badly with her parents when they visited. There were a few words, names of foods, "Drop," and a quality to the sounds my family used, our exclamations. We liked to make fun of my grandmother's accent and the polite way she refused seconds at dinner: "I have had yust more than plenty, thank you." There were Delftware plates in a row on the wall in a corner of the kitchen and above them a tiny print of Vermeer's *Milkmaid*. On a shelf, a clog that my grandfather had carved and worn in the Netherlands. One New Year's Eve, my mother fried Dutch donuts and sprinkled them with icing sugar. Another time, she invited her friends over for a rijstaffel. She cooked steaming mounds of basmati rice and they brought curries. But these were exceptions, the flotsam of a past she felt no obligation to: she created new rules and traditions, and filled her house with new memories.

The one thing my parents kept that belonged to my grandfather, but that he did not make himself and give to them, is a Dutch political poster. It is from the 1970s, and he must have brought it back with him when he and Catharijne returned for a year to Goes. It was produced for the Pacifist Socialist Party for the national election in 1971. In it, a naked woman stands in a field. She is facing the viewer, but her arms are thrown out wide, and her head is thrown back, and she is looking into the sky and laughing. Out-of-focus grass blurs the bottom third of the image into a gray-green haze. There is a black and white dairy cow standing behind her. The cow is looking at the camera. The sharp green letters across the bottom read: "PSP ontwapenend" or, in English, "Disarming PSP." It was meant to shame conservative Christians who supported the Vietnam war and opposed public nudity. It is visibly dated, an artifact from a different time and another way of thinking: the lines of the type, the tone of the colors, the woman's unruly pubic hair, the picture's primitive, exuberant version of natural freedom, its celebration of the body and the joyous rejection of the constraints of society belong to the past.

It was at the base of the narrow stairs that led from the kitchen to the basement in the house in Woodstock, and then on the inside of the closet door in the apartment where Daan died. My mother re-framed it and hung it in our rec room beside the pool table. My friends were always surprised when they saw it. They were used to posters of naked women, usually topless, sometimes bent over, arching their backs as they turned to look at the camera, their makeup overdone, their hair styles out of date, but they were used to these women in garages, shops, in the unfinished basements where their fathers drank beer and swore freely, not in a paneled rec room with a family game table and my mother standing there asking them what they thought of it. She liked to confront them with their prudishness, to challenge them. "That's what women look like, real women," she would say. "What's wrong with bodies? We all have them?" She was always smiling, aware of what she was doing, enjoying herself and her certainty. They would lower their eyes, hunch like boys do, twist their hands, shove them deeper into their pockets, and shuffle in place. She would watch them feel their discomfort. After she left, we would go back to our game of pool or the TV as if nothing had happened. We never talked about it. No one ever told me she was strange.

*

His afterlife as I lived it and it might have been:

My mother learned English faster than both of her parents. While they were still struggling, searching for words that never came, and forcing their tongues around the new syllables, she was losing the last inflections of her accent, and starting to talk with an easy fluency, as if she had been born here. She had just started grade school, but she became their translator.

Was Daan too proud to ask a child, let alone his child, for help? Did he chose an absolute silence? Or did he refrain from stopping her when my mother explained, "My father...?" Or did he develop a habit of speaking quickly in Dutch, and waiting, as if he couldn't be bothered with English, for her to translate what he had said? Were there times when he corrected her? Was Catharijne the kind of small and timid woman whose shyness made her seem even more diminutive than she was? Did she take my mother with her whenever she ran errands? Did they go together to the hairdresser, the grocery store? At the butcher, would she whisper the order in my mother's ear and push her towards the counter? My mother inherited Daan's height. She was five foot ten by the time she was sixteen, and that year she played on the high school volleyball team that won the city championship. Was she still going with Catharijne and speaking for her? Did she lean down to hear her mother's soft voice?

Were things different inside of the house? Did my mother wonder why she and Catharijne never talked like the mothers and daughters did in the books my mother read, about love and clothes and the people they knew, or the way my mother imagined her friends talked to their mothers, with a casual intimacy that deepened as they got older? Did Catharijne ever teach my mother about life? About being a woman? Did they ever find their way into moments of solidarity? They had their dogs. Two of them. A shepherd named Bubbles that died when my mother was twelve and then a bulldog cross they got at the pound. They named him together, a long name that they revised and added to every time they said it, and that made them both laugh out loud. They called him Winnie for short, and trained him together. They taught him to roll over and speak, to cover his eyes with his paws, and to sit on a chair at the dinner table like a third child with a napkin tucked under his collar. This was one of the few parts of her childhood that my mother will talk about willingly, without prompting, smiling, easy for a moment, and open.

For reasons that no one understands and neither of them will explain, Catharijne and my mother fight. They have done it for as long as I can remember. Bitterly. Sometimes for months. Where my brother and I see our grandmother, an old woman, the butt of our jokes, but only gentle ones, my mother sees an antagonist, perhaps an unwelcome reminder, and a constant frustration. When I asked her about this, she told me about having to talk for Catharijne, about having to do things for her, like she was a child. My mother was contemptuous, vicious with secret hurt. She said Catharijne wasn't as nice as I thought. I didn't know her.

After Daan died, Catharijne moved to Owen Sound to be near my parents. She had no friends in Woodstock who were close enough to keep her there, all of the other relatives in Ontario were distant, and my uncle lived in Texas and traveled a lot. She found a small subsidized apartment in a senior's building downtown. She is still living there now.

Every second weekend, my father picks her up on Friday evening on his way home from work, and she stays with my parents until Monday morning. The fighting has gotten worse. More intractable and abstruse. Catharijne and my mother never yell. They fight with withdrawals and refusals. They stop talking to each other for weeks at a time. Catharijne still comes out for the weekend. My mother won't speak to or look at her. They ride in the car, eat dinner, watch TV. They clean, garden, cook. Catharijne and my father play cards in the kitchen while my mother reads in the living room. They pass in the hallway, on the stairs. All without acknowledging each other. It is as if my mother wants to deny her in person. And Catharijne wants what? The farmhouse explodes with silence.

*

His afterlife as I lived it and it might have been:

When I drive back to Toronto from my parents' place, I like to stop for lunch at my grandmother's. Her apartment is filled with the few pieces of furniture she and Daan kept through the many moves: hutches, cabinets, the umbrella stand. The Formica table is long gone. There are lace sleeves on the arms of the couches. She feeds me sandwiches and Campbell's Gourmet soups from boxes. We drink Folgers instant coffee.

On one of these visits, when she and my mother are fighting, I ask her about it.

"Oh," she says, "your mother is angry at me again."

"Why?"

"Who knows." Catharijne looks confused, wounded. "She won't say."

Catharijne stops talking.

I can't tell if she is being evasive like my mother, if she doesn't understand, or doesn't want to, if she doesn't want me to understand. This is the one thing Catharijne and my mother can agree on, this willful silence, this obscurity that cannot be distinguished from ignorance: I don't know. They won't say.

On another visit, she tells me about Antwerp. She was born in Belgium and lived in the city in a flat with tall ceilings and false balconies until she was twelve. Her father was a partner in a large import/export firm with offices near the port. She told me about watching the ships and about playing games on the cobbled street in front of her house. She dreamed of being a lawyer, like her hero Marie Popelin, the leader of the Belgian League for Women's Rights. She was at the top of her class and sat in the desk closest to the teacher. And then one of her brothers threw a rock at a classmate. It hit him in the temple, she said, and touched hers with two fingers. Did she tell me this in her soft and tentative voice because she thought it was the turning point of her life? Was it? Was its significance absolute? A trick of her wandering mind? Or yet another dissimulation? Was it the chance occurrence that changed everything? Or nothing? And the boy it struck? The one whose folded limbs she could see clearly from eight decades and a continent away? Did he stand back up and stumble like a foal into steadiness? Or lie cantilevered and still? Did the rock crimp his left arm to his side and give him a shuffling limp? Did it cause him to labour over his words? Did his family threaten to take her brother to court? Was it going to go badly for him? And was that why her father moved them across the border to Goes? Or was the possibility of a court case a pretext? A cover? A way for her father to save face? Was it because irregularities had been found in the firm's books that they traded their third story flat for an old farmhouse with too few rooms? Did the children in the school that she walked to through the mud of the fields make fun of her accent? Did the teachers give her pitying looks and bad grades? Was it too different? Was she too old to change the texture of her voice? To learn curt new inflections for old words? When she returned to Antwerp at seventeen, did her childhood friends tell her that her Flemish sounded Dutch? Was the truth that she was neither Belgian nor Dutch? Was this why she dropped out of her last year of high school and started to work as an office girl? Why she took to returning on weekends to Goes? To that first dislocation? And a Saturday afternoon on Lange Kerkstraat through which Daan's lean body bent towards her like a question? Is it bending towards her now?

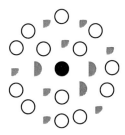

Weather Patterns

The first time that Aviva Green and Adam Mayer are in the same place together is in Dr. Märta Nilsson's graduate seminar in postmodern literature. The room is too small for the class, and Aviva and Adam are wedged in uncomfortably close to each other, but it is less a meet-cute than the product of a mistake. There are too many students in the program, and the classes are overenrolled. Aviva wanted the course, but only got in at the last minute because Dr. Nilsson agreed to take six extra students. Adam didn't want to take the course, but had to because the professor for the course he actually wanted refused to take the students that Dr. Nilsson agreed to admit. There is no good explanation for why they sit next to each other in chairs that are so close that their metal legs are interlocked and click together every time one of them shifts. Some of the students have met before, but none of them knows each other well. There are other seats in the room, but none of them is easier to get to or less awkwardly placed. Aviva resents being admitted late. Adam resents having to take the course at all. They could sit anywhere. But they don't.

*

The course focuses on novels written after the Second World War. Most of the books are American. Some of them are in translation. None of them are Canadian. The readings include Vladimir Nabokov's *Pale Fire*, Ishmael Reed's *Mumbo Jumbo*, Kathy Acker's *Don Quixote*, and Jorge Luis Borges' stories, which are not novels, but which are essential. Dr. Nilsson has an affection for Michel Tournier. She shares, albeit in an ironic, fastidious way, his fascination with German culture, and they spend a week discussing *The Ogre*. Aviva likes to pronounce the title with a heavy French accent. She makes a game of it, repeating "The Ogre" long after they have moved on to other books, enjoying the way the "g" grates in her throat. The novel is a blended retelling of both the Saint Christopher story and the Erlking legend as itself retold in Goethe's poem "Erlkönig." Dr. Nilsson tells them that Tournier studied philosophy at the Sorbonne and sat the agrégation in the same class as Gilles Deleuze. He failed. But he possessed a keen philosophical intelligence, and understood, she tells them at the end of what began as a digression and has now turned into a short, impromptu lecture, that "writing is itself always an act of interpretation." Dr. Nilsson is recovering from a foot injury. She complains about rehab and walks with a cane. It has a dull, flesh-coloured handle and a base with four rubber-shod feet like a tiny version of the chairs whose legs click together when Aviva and Adam move. Her Swedish accent is fitful, and strange to their ears. It has been softened by three decades of falls and winters in Southern Ontario and summers in Sweden, smoothed out, but only in places, and emerges, unexpectedly strong, on single words, so that when she tells them this about Tournier and his work the sound is itself uncanny, shifting and impossible to pin down.

*

Normally, every student leads a seminar on one of the books on the course, but, because there are so many students in the class, Dr. Nilsson assigns them to the books in pairs, and, because Aviva and Adam are sitting next to each other, across from and slightly to the left of Dr. Nilsson, they are assigned together to D.M. Thomas's *The White Hotel*. There is a storm blowing through the novel. A wild storm. A blizzard. The stars, in flakes of snow, come down to fuck the earth. The breaks in the middle of class are extra long because of the time it takes Dr. Nilsson to walk from the small room that only barely contains them and their chairs to the coffee kiosk at the far end of the building and back. She places her cane's four rubber-shod feet, takes a step, and then lifts her cane by the flesh-coloured handle and swings it forward. The motion is considered, almost formal. Aviva and Adam spend these long breaks smoking on the steps in front of the building. During one of them, they talk about the ice storm of the year before, the one that took down trees and power lines across central Canada and froze Montreal and most of eastern Ontario into a fairy tale, for a week. Aviva was in the last year of her undergrad at McGill. They heated the apartment with pine-scented candles, and the smell that reminded her simultaneously of the December that had just finished and six summers at camp went stale in the rooms while outside the storm turned everything into a brilliant, impossible mutation of itself. She left the apartment once, for cigarettes and food. She yawed wildly along the sidewalk. Her hands slid off ice-slicked cars, deformed parking meters, the handle of a door that had doubled in size. She didn't even make it to the end of her block before she turned back.

*

Aviva and Adam work on the seminar together in her apartment in a building whose carpeted staircase smells faintly of the liquid that drips out of torn garbage bags. They smoke and drink Diet Coke and talk through the night. Sometimes they talk about D.M. Thomas, but it is already November. They have done too much, and they have too much still to do. Final papers are looming. Aviva is supposed to be taking a correspondence course in Italian to fulfill her language requirement, but she hasn't opened the textbook since September, and the exercises are still wrapped in plastic. Neither of them believes in the program anymore, in the way Dr. Nilsson wants them to think about reading. Sometimes they talk about D.M. Thomas, but mostly they watch late-night TV and talk about life and the books that they love. The seminar happens, and, like everything else in the program, it is a minor success, but it feels like a disappointment. Talking into the morning in Aviva's apartment turns into a habit. Adam comes over at least once a week. He stays for the night and then a day and then another night. They don't go out. They don't do the work that they should be doing, the work that gets easier not to do the more of it there is. They call these interludes lost weekends. The conversation lags. It has to. They are spending too much time together. Adam takes books off Aviva's shelves and reads to her from them. He is trying to seduce her, though not in any concerted way, and, mostly, he likes the idea of reading to a woman; he likes the way Aviva lets him luxuriate in the sound of his own voice made strange, made resonant and sensual by too many cigarettes. He reads the passage from Michael Ondaatje's *The English Patient* about winds that Hana reads to Almásy out of the copy of Herodotus' *The Histories*. The second wind it mentions is the Africo. The Italian name for this wind is Il Libeccio because it blows out of Libya across Sicily into Rome. It is a sister wind to Lo Scirocco that likewise blows out of North Africa across the Mediterranean into Italy in the summers. Both originate in the Sahara, both carry and set down sifts of red desert sand, but it is Lo Scirocco, drawn north by a shift in the jet stream, that stalls a dome of simmering air over Europe to create the late summer heat waves that are getting worse each year.

*

It takes Aviva and Adam a long time to have sex. They are both more interested in striking the postures of seduction than in seducing or being seduced. And they often don't like each other. They agree about books, but they argue about small things. In the middle of an early January cold snap that freezes a second oval frame of frost inside the wooden rectangle of the picture window in Aviva's living room, they disagree about their favourite weather. Adam likes the summer, but only when it is dry. He likes impossible arches of white-blue sky. He likes high twenties. He likes low humidity. Aviva likes the fall, but only on the days when it is just right. She likes air to warm you with its coolness. She likes horizons turning to slate. She likes light softening to gold. When they finally do have sex, it is grudging, desultory, because neither of them can put it off any longer, and unexpectedly good. They click like chairs. And that is it. The feeling of it. Like they are connecting to something separate and outside of themselves. A chemical rather than an emotional event. It is CO_2. Two oxygen atoms covalently bonded to a carbon atom in a linear, centrosymmetric structure. O=C=O. The inevitable end product of respiration. The molecule itself is a balance of attractive and repulsive forces that form something permanent. A stable sharing of paired electrons. A colourless gas that is denser than dry air. It has a sharp, acidic odour at high concentrations. Since the beginning of the industrial era at the end of the 18th century, atmospheric CO_2 has risen from an average of 280 parts per million to over 410 parts per million in 2019. They agree. They disagree. And this agreeing and disagreeing accumulates to Adam and Aviva spending longer and longer stretches of time together in her apartment, to sex that is like a reprieve of good weather in the climate of their bodies, a shift in the wind that is blowing steadily through their lives, a break in the January storm.

*

They finish their MAs. Aviva takes an extra six months to complete her Italian course and graduates half a calendar year after Adam. This is a technicality, but they are at a stage in their relationship where technicalities matter. They take a year off before applying to PhD programs. They move in together and find jobs tutoring foreign students in English. The jobs don't pay well enough to be permanent, but they don't want them to be permanent. They know what they don't want. They are still learning how to want. One day in the fall, when she is still working on her Italian course, Aviva is caught in a rainstorm as she is walking home. It is a sudden, torrential downpour. It is so heavy that she expects it to stop as suddenly as it begins. But it doesn't stop. It goes on as she stands there. A drawn-out rush of drops. A blurred percussion striking every possible interval and the bare skin above her collarbones with a solid, almost stinging impact. Her body becomes a conduit for the rain. It runs off her like she is an open tap. And it is cold, but also heavy, and there is something unnameable and comforting about the density of the water driving into her.

And standing there in the rain and the sudden rivers, she remembers Brutus telling Cassius, "There is a tide in the affairs of men," in the fourth act of *Julius Caesar*. She read it in high school and then again not that long ago, in a summer course on Shakespeare's histories that she took at the end of her MA in which they debated whether it could or should be classified alongside the English history plays. The same month that she stands there remembering *Julius Caesar* in a downpour, a tropical depression forms in the Gulf of Mexico. It is strengthened by unseasonably warm waters in the Gulf and drifts slowly, almost lethargically, into eastern Mexico. September storms have saturated the ground in the mountainous, coastal states of Veracruz and Tabasco, and the soil is incapable of absorbing additional moisture. More than a meter of rain falls in a few days, causing flooding and landslides, and washing crocodiles into the streets of Villahermosa, the capital of Tabasco. At least 600 people are killed and approximately 500,000 are left homeless. The flooding is barely reported in Canada. It is mentioned briefly at a time when neither Aviva nor Adam is listening closely to the radio they like to leave on. It is noted in a paragraph at the bottom of a page in a section of the newspaper that Aviva skims. The headline, really the words "crocodile" and "Villahermosa," catch her attention, and she reads enough to get a general sense of the disaster. She reads the numbers that she will not remember. She pauses to imagine a slope shifting. Vague. Brown. Too broad to be fully grasped. Breaking free. Its weight gathering into a terrible momentum. Before she moves on. The rain that soaks Aviva and stings her bare skin stops as suddenly as it began. The clouds pass. They slip away like words in another room. She walks home down streets that are bright and shining with water. The next day she writes a poem about the rain. She puts it in a drawer and doesn't show it to Adam. The poem doesn't contain the rain or how it comforted her.

*

They both apply to PhD programs, and they both get in, although to different programs in different cities. The cities are only three hours apart by car, four by train, five and a half by a bus that stops in all of the small towns between the cities. They are both lonely at first. They miss the camaraderie of the last months of their MA. The new students are strangers who have read different books. Aviva and Adam visit each other every weekend and complain about their classes. The seminars are too competitive. The other students are pretentious. Well, as Foucault says... But does he? And there is sex. That, at least, is constant. Easy. They make friends. They laugh with those friends about how they didn't like them at first. Sometimes that laughter verges on flirting. Sometimes that laughter is flirting. The train ride feels longer every time. Adam cancels one weekend. Aviva another. Adam again. Again. And during a phone call in early December, he tells her that there is a conference on Saturday. He knows some of the people reading papers at it. There is a party afterwards. He has his own work. He can't come down this weekend.

And Aviva says, fine. Don't come. And he says, I won't. And a wide silence opens between then during which they both feel the receivers dead against their ears. The plastic turns warm and sore. They are separate. Alone. At the two ends of that tenuous dissolving connection. And then she says, Don't call. And he doesn't. Neither of them do. They think about calling, but only in empty moments with nothing in them. These naked segments of the day when they are stopped on the sidewalk or looking up from reading fill to the brim with the same warning silence that opened between them on the phone. And then it is too late. They have waited too long, and, because they haven't called, they can't call.

Ten years later Adam reads Jhumpa Lahiri's *Unaccustomed Earth*. The book ends with a trio of linked stories about Hema and Kaushik, a girl and a boy who share a house in Massachusetts for a winter and then go on to live separate, only rarely intersecting lives. In the closing pages of the final story, Kaushik dies in the Boxing Day Tsunami of 2004. He is on vacation in Thailand. Before the tsunami strikes, Kaushik, a Thai boy, and a Swedish tourist named Henrik row out into the ocean and along the coast. They stop to rest and Henrik swims ashore. When Kaushik lowers himself into the water to follow Henrik, his feet touch the bottom, and he lets go of the boat. His story and his life end here. His feet touch the bottom because of the drawback that occurs if the trough of a tsunami makes landfall before the crest of the enormous wave. In cases where this happens, the water along the shore runs back into the ocean, like low tide, but faster and further, retreating sometimes for hundreds of meters, revealing areas of the seabed that are normally submerged. This lasts for half of the tsunami's period, or about five to six minutes, and it is characterized by an ominous stillness as wave activity ceases and the ocean withdraws into silence. The earthquake that causes the tsunami is anticipated by another earthquake that comes earlier in the story, a tremor really, a sort of foreshock, at least within the logic of the narrative, during which the listless twenty-something Kaushik discovers his vocation as a photographer. Two earthquakes. A logic. Adam is disappointed by the story. He dislikes the easy symmetry, the way the tsunami is subsumed by its symbolic value and how the destruction he can barely imagine is transformed into a device. He complains to the woman he is sleeping with that "nature isn't narrative." He sells the book along with several others that he doesn't like enough to take with him when he moves, but he returns, sometimes, to the memory of the closing pages of that final story and to the warning stillness when Kaushik touched the bottom.

*

Aviva doesn't finish her PhD. She meets Daniel Irwin, who is three years ahead of her in the program, at the department Christmas party, and they start dating. There is a day several years later when she watches him read on the dock at her parents' cottage and then set down his book to work on the introduction to an edition of essays on neglected American modernist poets that he is editing. Everyone else is dozing in the heat or swimming or drifting aimlessly through the open hours of the summer day. She watches him from the deck of the cottage set down his book to work and pick it back up again. And she knows. She knows in a deep and certain way that she can't articulate and that is more compelling and durable because it stands outside of words. The book is Pevear and Volokhonsky's translation of *Anna Karenina*. It has been out for a few years, and they have both read the glowing reviews and wanted to read it, but they have only found the time this summer. They are reading it together and keeping pace with each other in their separate copies. They are on the third section. Levin has returned to his estate and begun to work with his muzhiks in his fields. He is cutting hay with them. He eats the muzhiks' food instead of going home for the midday meal and falls asleep in the shade of a bush. His men go on mowing. He wakes to see the field transformed by their work into neatly laid swaths of grass and rejoins the line of workers. Daniel is a little bit ahead of Aviva. He is closer to when Levin catches sight of Kitty in her carriage. But this doesn't matter. The late summer heat that drenches Levin in cooling sweat or how Aviva feels the same intensity in the sun that beats down on her on the deck don't matter. What matters is the way that Daniel puts down the book and picks it up again, reflexively, as if he is better, more himself, with it in his hands. Daniel gets a post doc. They get married. He gets a tenure track job at a small university on the east coast, and they move into a house with original hardwood floors and an endless series of minor problems that need fixing. Daniel works on his research. They have two children, both girls, whom she names after her grandmothers. In the middle of having children, Daniel gets tenure. When Aviva finally realizes that she won't finish the dissertation that she has thought about for years, but never started, she is between daughters, and the university where she met Daniel at a department Christmas party, the classes and those first few uncertain, hopeful years of her degree are far enough away that it doesn't matter. She doesn't resent Daniel who is still working steadily, doggedly, when he could, now that he has tenure, let up and relax a little. She doesn't regret what she sets down for good.

*

Adam finishes his PhD, but it takes him more than ten years, and he has to stand outside of the examination room and listen for almost an hour to the muffled sound of his defence committee debate whether to pass him or not. He teaches sessionally at several different colleges while he is working on his dissertation and keeps teaching like this after he finishes. He doesn't manage to pay much more than the interest on his student loans or to make it past the first round of interviews for a tenure-track position. Out of frustration, desperation, but also because of a kind of hopelessness that means he can do anything, he starts to look for jobs outside of the academy. The second one he applies for is as a copywriter for a consulting firm. The man who interviews him is old enough to be his father and has a shelf of novels on the wall behind his desk. They talk about books. Ted is a big fan of the Latin American boom. He took a course in contemporary Latin American literature when he was at university in the seventies, and he has been reading it ever since—Marquez, Vargas Llosa, Cortázar, and Fuentes, of course, but also Sabato, Roa Bastos, and Amado. Ted says the names like they are talismans, and Adam repeats them. Two weeks later, Ted calls him to tell him that he is hired. One of the books on the shelf is Vargas Llosa's *The War of the End of the World*, the original, oversized softcover edition of the first English translation with its garish cover—reds and purples, bronze type for the title, serious men with guns, and a woman's head thrown back, her mouth open in ecstasy. The Counselor's swarthy brooding face dominates the page. The climax of the novel takes place in Canudos, in the province of Bahia in Northeastern Brazil. It is an arid territory, and the closing pages of the book, when the Counselor's stronghold is finally overrun by the army, are filled with blood, but also with dust and thirst. Bahia is one of the regions of the tropics that are affected by extreme droughts during El-Niño Southern Oscillation events. A band of warm surface water forms in the eastern Pacific off the coasts of Chile and Peru, reaching as far north as Mexico. This mass of overheated water causes a change in atmospheric circulation that can weaken or reverse the trade winds and stop the rain from falling on Bahia. Climate models predict an increase in the strength and frequency of these events that may lead to decreases in crop yields of up to 89% and that will most likely render the state unfit for agriculture. There will be a shift in the oceans on the other side of the continent which is closed like a door. It will stop the rain. The spines of the books are turned out and *The War of the End of the World*'s is plain white. The reds and purples of the front cover are muted for the type that spells out the title and the author's name. Adam doesn't notice it among the other novels. He hasn't read it. He hasn't read most of the books on the shelf and none of them recently.

The truth that he is hiding when he talks so enthusiastically to Ted is that he hasn't read anything for several years. Not since finishing his PhD. When he was working on his dissertation, he didn't have the time or the energy to read for pleasure. And then, after his defence and the shame and relief of completing and the congratulations that came even though it didn't feel like a triumph and the ensuing confirmation of his suspicion that the possibilities of a PhD focused on late nineteenth century social protest novels had already been foreclosed, he stopped reading altogether. He tried to return to the books that he had loved before grad school, to the books that he had read to Aviva to seduce her, but there was always the sound of his committee arguing behind that door, of their tense voices reaching into the quiet hallway. And, when that had faded into a tolerable murmur that ached rather than hurt, there remained a particular scholarly way of reading, of parsing texts like they were puzzles to be solved instead of living inside of them, that was a habit of mind he couldn't break out of no matter how much he wanted to, and that robbed books of their joy. So, he stopped. Like the rain in a story he hadn't read, he just stopped.

*

Aviva raises their children and Daniel does his research. He is creating a massive a web-based archive called Other Modernisms that collects and annotates the published works and papers of the same group of neglected American poets on which he has been working since she met him. He wants it to be more than just a database. He wants it to be a virtual space where scholars from across the world can share their research and collaborate. He calls it a digital commons and pours himself into it. He puts on weight. He stops shaving. She likes the patchy fringe that grows to frame his rounded face. And she doesn't notice that he looks more tired than he should, that he sleeps less and talks more freely and fervently about the hypocrisy of his colleagues and the failures of the university until he doesn't sleep for a week straight and ends up sedated under observation in the psych ward of the hospital in which she gave birth to both their daughters. She keeps forgetting the visiting hours. She comes early or when he is too stupefied to recognize her. She is halfway through *A Visit from the Goon Squad*, the hardcover with the watery blue dust jacket with the Stratocaster neck in solid black with spidering white strings on it, and she tries to read it in the waiting room. She should like its broken narratives, the way it plays with time, perspective, point of view and the possibilities of the novel, but she can't track it. The shifts between stories, the leaps across decades, from the old to the new century, and from there into the future, the jumps from one narrator to another are gaps through which she slips out of the book into a blank and abstract panic. Slips. Except there is a force to it. An urgency. A momentum. Sitting in a plastic hospital chair she is carried out of the blue confines of the cover and the pages it contains into a spreading worry about Daniel, their daughters, everything.

At times like these, when she can't read or sit alone with herself and what is happening to her, she watches YouTube clips on her phone. She prefers political shows, news and commentary, shows that explain the world to her, that lay out problems with a calm outrage that insists there are solutions to them. She makes a point of watching *Democracy Now*'s Top US and World Headlines everyday. It is mid-August, and east of Baton Rouge, Louisiana, the floodwaters of the Amite River and its tributary the Comite River are rising. An inland sheared tropical depression heavy with moisture from the warm waters of the Gulf settles over the state and drops three times as much rain as fell during hurricane Katrina, reaching rainfall rates of two to three inches an hour at its peak. It causes a 1000-year flood that pours over banks, inundates twenty parishes, kills thirteen people, and destroys close to 60,000 homes. In recent years, scientists have begun to understand that the levees and spillways built to minimize flood damage have the opposite effect in the case of extreme flooding events. These systems of barriers, stopgaps, and safety valves turn normally meandering rivers into rushing torrents, maximizing the force of the water and increasing the magnitude of already massive floods by as much as twenty percent. *Democracy Now* covers the disaster as it unfolds. The destruction. The displaced families. The water that coils dense and frozen by its velocity in the frame. The tropical depression doesn't have a name. It is not a hurricane. It is not even a tropical storm. And it is not reported by major news outlets. Towards the end of the month, when the waters have ebbed, but the full scope of the damage, its enormity, remains to be grasped, Amy Goodman tells viewers that the Louisiana flood is the largest natural catastrophe in American history to happen in relative secret.

While Aviva sits in the plastic hospital chairs and watches clips on her phone, she rests the book she can't manage to read in her lap. It is slim for a hardcover, not heavy, but still solid. There is a softness to the matte dust jacket, to the linen pages, a luxurious, stabilizing materiality she can hold onto. The doctors say, psychotic break. Manic episode. They put Daniel on medication, and he returns to a semblance of himself, but with a closed wariness to his expressions. He can't go back to work. He resigns his position at the university without telling his colleagues. He packs up his office on the weekend when no one is around. They sell their house and move halfway across the country to live with her parents in a suburb north of Toronto. And it is sudden. And it is chaotic. And it is so unexpectedly easy. It is such a relief, this escaping from their lives, this giving up and letting go, this retreating along the incline of events, this receding from the crest of his mania and her barely contained panic that leaves so much wreckage behind it. The book is one of many things that get lost during the move. She notices it is gone when she unpacks the remnants of their library. She stands in a room filled with boxes and repeats the word "flotsam."

*

Adam gets promoted twice and then makes the jump to management. He gets married but doesn't have children. Daniel is doing better. He starts a company called The Agile Arts Agency that he describes as a digital humanities enterprise. He designs databases and websites for universities and research groups. He works out of a basement office in Aviva's parents' house. He gets a few clients by talking to friends from when he was a professor, surprises everyone, the friends who recommended him out of pity and even Aviva with the quality of what he produces, and lands a handful of larger contracts. His showcase project, the one he presents to prospective clients, is 1000 Letters, a hyperlinked collection of Gilles Deleuze's correspondence organized in a rhizomatic structure that he creates in partnership with Purdue University and The Université de Paris. He rents office space on the third floor of a walk-up on a side street in downtown Toronto. Aviva doesn't like the energy of the room, its stuffiness, the way the blinds are always half drawn and it is filled with a heavy, vibrating dimness through which the light falls in slats, but he is working. They are rebuilding their life. Adam transfers to the firm's headquarters which is in a glass tower two subway stops east of Daniel's new office. Adam and Aviva never run into each other on the street. They aren't connected on social media, and they don't know that they are living in the same city. Adam starts reading again. Aviva has never stopped. They both like to read the books that everyone is talking about. The prize winners. The novels of the moment. The books that let them feel connected to the broader world of culture and ideas that exists beyond their lives and that belongs in some way to the now-distant past when they started an MA together. They read Elena Ferrante's Neapolitan quartet when everyone else is reading it. Adam feels strange holding the books with their soft pastel covers on the subway. They look forward, with some trepidation, to the HBO miniseries. And, like their reading, their lives align, they click together: Aviva starts an affair with a partner at her father's law firm. A few months later, Adam sleeps with one of the interns who works on the same floor as him. Aviva meets Robert Sanders at a Best Western next to the airport when Daniel is at his office and the kids are at school. The sex is formulaic. It is as predictable as the hotel and bland to the point that she is vaguely offended by it, but she doesn't stop seeing him. Adam and Rachel Hill take long lunches, evenings, two days at a conference in Chicago. She is almost twenty years younger. They turn their age difference

119

into a joke, into something they can say into the silence that unfolds between them when they aren't fucking. None of it makes sense. The affairs. The hotels. The furtiveness. The moments of lightness, of freedom, that lift Aviva and Adam out of themselves. The sex that is both a necessity and an afterthought. The way that they read Elena Ferrante's novels together without knowing it over the same two months, and, while surfing YouTube late at night, click on the same clip of a climate scientist discussing melting ice caps and rising sea levels. His voice is careful, precise and urgent. It is the voice of someone who wants a large group of people to move quickly but without panicking, and it holds them for long enough to hear what he is saying: conservative estimates predict that the world's oceans will rise two to three feet over the course of the century. Some models suggest that an increase of as much as six to nine feet is possible. We may have already passed the tipping point. They sit with this discovery and the sensation of powerlessness that comes with it as the clip roles towards its end. The world is changing around them on a scale and at a rate they can barely imagine. A blue line on their screens breaks free of the x-axis. Tilts upwards. And it is at once terrifying and strangely reassuring. In the middle of eroding the lives they have made for themselves, this at least makes sense.

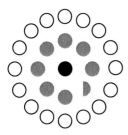

What We Think We Know About the Life and Career of Kathleen Scholler

Kathleen was born in northern Ontario. Her mother taught primary school and her father worked for the Ministry of Natural Resources. There must have been books in their split-level ranch, whose backyard ended at the bush, but not many, and we don't think her parents were readers. She was not a precocious or an avid reader. She has never talked about discovering *The Lord of the Rings*, about finishing *The Chronicles of Narnia*, or about re-reading *Little House on the Prairie* or *Swiss Family Robinson* until the spine cracked, the folded corners tore off and the pages fell out. The public library she went to must have been small, probably a single large room, likely a wing of a municipal building. In the corner, there was a carpet with a bright geometric pattern, beige metal shelves that went halfway up the cinderblock walls, a dangling mobile and two bean bag chairs, and that was the kids' section. Stickers on the spines of the books divided them into Toddlers (light blue), Preschoolers (dark blue), Early Readers (yellow), Young Readers (green) and Teens (red).

We have never heard her talk about that tiny library or about the hard, bright pride of moving on to the adult section.

*

She learned to ride in grade school and started show-jumping when she was twelve. Her parents rented her a horse, and made her muck out stalls, mow the lawn in the summer and shovel the driveway in the winter to pay for the horse, the lessons, and her equestrian wear. Afterwards, she remembered the work, the feel of her muscles—sore after riding or stiff in the cold—more than the jumping itself. She won ribbons and pinned them to a corkboard in her bedroom under the name of her horse spelled in big colourful letters her mother brought home from school. She has kept a picture of herself jumping. Some of us saw it on a side table in her living room when she was in graduate school, and a few of us saw it more recently on the shelves to the right of her desk in the second bedroom that she uses as an office. It has been there for as long as we have known her. Present but not obtrusive. In it, she is poised in a coat and breaches she bought with own money, leaning over the neck of her horse as it clears a jump, looking ahead, focused on the landing. The horse, her body, her eyes are all tilting forward. She is determined, untouchable.

In her teens, she went to an equestrian camp in upstate New York. She made friends with a pair of Colombian sisters and visited them during March break in Grades 10 and 11. These were the only international trips that she took in high school. The sisters met her at the airport in Bogota and they flew to the family ranch outside of Honda. The ranch had a private airstrip, and long, low buildings with red tile roofs and arched verandas overlooking the fields. The family had bodyguards who carried submachine guns and patrolled the grounds. They rode the trails through the hills. Dinners were served on the veranda. The parents called her Catalina and the servants called her senorita. One day, the guards let them shoot their guns. Kathleen tried an AK-47 because she had seen them in movies. It scared her so much that she had to shoot it again and again until the bolt clicked on nothing and she walked away breathless and shaking and wet-eyed under the high white sky.

We have seen the pictures of the trips that she keeps at the back of a small black album: the ranch house, the trails, the horses, her and the sisters and the guards posing with the guns. One of us pointed at the last one and asked Kathleen who the family was connected to. She looked uncertain and then surprised and then hurt.

*

Her high school years are mostly blank. She once mentioned Roland Michener Secondary School, and taking classes in French and English. She still speaks French and she has talked about doing translations. We imagine that it was a small school, built in the sixties or seventies of dun brick, modern then, but shabby now. She must have run on a weedy oval track, around a lumpy soccer field, under rusting uprights like the ones that some of us remember from our own small-town high schools. It was small enough that it had none of the cliques and divisions of city schools. Small enough that everyone knew each other well. Tight in the way compulsory communities are tight. Intimate. Narrow. She never talks about it. She could not have been remarkable.

We wonder if she was encouraged.

*

Some of us met her parents when they drove or flew down to visit her. They were smaller and greyer than in photos, as all of our parents have become smaller and greyer, transformed by age, but also by us, diminished when seen from new and fuller perspectives, from a greater distance, as people, now, as well as parents. They both wore hiking pants with cargo pockets (her father's unzipped at the knee to turn into shorts) and their faces were dry and tanned. We thought they looked like who they were, like they came from up north and belonged outside. They were reticent. They didn't ask us where we were from or what we worked on. Most of our parents were reticent when they visited us, unsure of themselves and of how they fit into our worlds, surprised by our confidence and by the reality of the lives they had only heard about and half imagined, but Kathleen's parents were different than ours, more reserved, and we noticed it. We saw them standing at the back of a room at a conference that she had organized. They were waiting to take her out to dinner. Her father said something to her mother. They looked around the room and only sometimes at the speakers; they listened for reasons to stop listening. This was the same defensive skepticism that we recognized in our relatives—What do you do? What good is it? Why does it matter? To me?—but theirs seemed more definitive, less vulnerable. When Kathleen took the lectern, they focused on her. They looked embarrassed. We could tell that they were seeing her mistakes. We saw them too. Each one stood out clear and irreversible: she stumbled. Her hands fluttered. Awkwardness. And elbows. And everything she said sounded like a question. And added up to a confirmation of something.

We watched her afterwards as she trailed after them, twelve again, sharp with need, aiming for grace, and arriving at clumsiness.

*

Her brother is an absence. He is in pictures, not many of those, and nowhere else.

We think this is notable.

*

Kathleen went to McGill. In first year, she took Robert Lerner's "Introduction to Canadian Literature: World War II–Present." He played music before each class started, alternative artists that she didn't know or had barely heard of, and every reading was paired with a song listed in the syllabus under the heading "Soundtrack." The course was organized thematically, and each week they tackled a big question. In the first class, "What is place? How is it reflected in literature?" Introducing his lecture on *Beautiful Losers*, "What makes a book Canadian?" Leaning seriously on the lectern, to begin a discussion of Klein's *The Hitleriad*, "Is satire adequate to horror?" He always returned, inevitably, by the end of the week, often by the end of a class, to the subject of his most recent book, *Making it Mean: The Creation of the English-Canadian Literary*

Canon: the social institutions that shape literature. He talked about publishers, anthologies and reading lists, about the people and the decisions that created classics. He liked to hold up the book they were reading that week and say, "In a very real way, you," taking in the class, "and I, make this mean."

We imagine Kathleen as the you to his I. We see her sitting in the front row, coming alive with a mixture of discovery and self-importance. She enrolled in a Double Major in Canadian Studies and English Literature, and she has been thinking and writing about the social construction of cultural value ever since.

*

Kathleen did well by writing papers that, at first tentatively and then with growing confidence, repeated what her professors said. She did well, but she never stood out. She was always second or third in the class after opinionated young men who talked in tutorial like they were at the bar and at the bar like they were in tutorial, and young women who looked more sophisticated than they were, who had the same clothes as Kathleen, but wore them better, and talked casually about books she hadn't read and places she hadn't been. We don't think she had many friends. She has never talked about friends. We can't remember names or stories. No one visited her. We know whose courses she took, but not if she had a roommate or went to Schwartz's Deli.

Denuja did her undergrad with Kathleen and followed her to graduate school two years later. When she arrived, she seemed surprised by Kathleen's friendliness and assurance, by her tacit closeness. Denuja was uncomfortable when Kathleen introduced her to us, cool, as if she had known Kathleen from a distance, and was used to feeling superior to her. We asked Denuja about Kathleen, but she was vague, evasive, and we stopped asking. We imagine that Kathleen spent those four years in Montreal on the fringes of other people's lives. We can place her on chairs she borrowed from other tables, leaning forward, hovering on the periphery of conversations, waiting for a chance to say something. And when she does? Everyone stops, and then starts again, or doesn't stop at all. We can see her listening intently, nodding sometimes, to someone who is not talking to her.

We know she watched and learned.

*

Kathleen met Ray Ianson in second year at a wine and cheese reception. Ray had a long face that shifted through several varieties of seriousness, and feathered, brown hair that fell in soft points over his forehead when he was reading. He was finishing a doctoral dissertation on novels written by poets, and he talked to her about his research as if she had read the same books he had and shared his interest in them. She noticed that he had delicate and expressive hands. We think Ray took her home that night, and she followed him, tipsy, euphoric with anxiety, and docile. We have seen Kathleen around people she is attracted to: she turns passive, almost blank, and pliable. We think she gives up herself, lets go, and it is difficult to watch. Ray liked to stay fit. Six mornings a week, he ran, and then did push-ups and sit-ups in the living room. He was showered and at his desk by 8 a.m. Kathleen tried to go with him once, but he didn't want to slow down, and she could barely walk the next day. When she was around Ray, she noticed things that were wrong with herself: the pucker of fat over her stomach, her bad skin, and the brown streaks in her blond hair. She got in the habit of bringing her laptop over to his apartment and working on the coffee table. Sometimes she could hear Ray typing in his office behind the closed door, other times there was silence, but she could always feel him—intent, producing. She had once seen a picture of Simone de Beauvoir and Jean-Paul Sartre at their desks. The caption explained that they wrote together for eight hours a day without talking or looking at each other. When she thought of that picture, and of herself and Ray, she felt serious and adult. This lasted until she discovered that Ray was sleeping with his French tutor. She told two of us this late at night. She was pale and soft around the mouth, blurred with emotion. They didn't break up. Ray pointed out that they had never said they were dating. She had met his parents, but she wasn't his girlfriend. He was right. She stopped working at his apartment. She saw him less, but she still saw him. They slept together on and off for years, whenever they were in the same city. Now, they are friends on Facebook.

We read an encouraging comment that Ray posted a few months ago under a picture of Kathleen finishing the Vancouver Marathon. Some of us posted similar comments. One of us liked his.

*

We saw Ray at conferences and noticed that Kathleen had adopted his mannerisms. She tilted her head to the right when she spoke, and said "of course" with a lilt and "we" with a conscious earnestness. She made the same sharp, intricate gestures with her hands. The resemblance was unmistakable.

We were disturbed by it, and we needed to point it out: one of us called him "Manthleen," and the rest of us thought this was juvenile, but also that Ray and Kathleen overlapped, like siblings.

*

We were close to Kathleen in graduate school, and we remember too much about her to write here. She started and joined things: a Canadian Literature reading group (started), a Medieval Literature reading group (joined), a Shakespeare reading group (joined), a conference on the topic of community (organized), and so on. She almost failed her comprehensive exams and broke down. She audited classes. She taught. She talked with authority. She tried on expertise. She embarrassed herself, but sometimes it fit. She spent her grant money on pant suits. She wore a tan one with a turquoise blouse one when she took the poet she wrote her MA thesis on out to lunch. She told us about a weekend in a hotel in Toronto with Ray, and how he offered to publish one of her papers when it was over and they were packing their bags. She edited a special issue of the journal her supervisor ran. She used the negative of a picture Ray took of her standing on a rooftop in Montreal holding a martini glass for the cover. She cropped out her head, but showed us the original. After that, she edited a slim volume of poems by an obscure Montreal modernist, and called it, proudly, "my book" in conversation. She read Bourdieu. We remember too much, but there is a constant that stands out, that connects everything, and that we return to because we can't understand or explain it. It is what we think of when we think of Kathleen and it is why we remember her: she had ambition. Some of us prefer to call it self-belief, others resilience. Pretension. We agree that part of it was naiveté, innocence, but not if it was deliberate. She wanted to be more than what she was, more than what we thought she could be, and that desire was as immune to her failures as it was to our disapproval. To shame. Was it determination? Perseverance?

We suspect it was a refusal, what Kathleen had separate from us, from her parents and Ray, from everyone.

*

Kathleen's supervisor for both her MA and her PhD was Fred Daniel, an experimental poet from the '60s who had become an academic in the '70s and who now presided over the territory where the avant-garde and the academy overlap. Every few months he would come to her apartment for coffee. She would clean the bathroom, dust and vacuum, arrange tea—although he never drank it—coffee and sugar on the kitchen counter, and pick up pastries from a Dutch bakery. We saw her several times, carrying the pastries in a cardboard box. She was vivid and concentrated and she didn't want to talk. He sat next to her on the stiff cushions of the same green settee that we sat on when we visited, and told her stories about the academics, writers and publishers that he knew. The personalities and animosities behind the articles. The partnerships that became feuds. Why someone won a prize and someone else didn't. Who hated whom. And why. Who had or hadn't slept together. And regretted it either way. Everything that he would soon put in his autobiography, and more that he wouldn't. When he left, the mugs stayed on the coffee table for a long time.

We can picture her there, alone in that tiny apartment, sitting across from a wall of shelves whose books are people, now, as well as books. The dishes can wait: she is thrilled and languid with importance.

*

Kathleen told us that she slept with a man in his sixties when she was in undergrad. She said he drove a convertible and was good in bed. Was this before or after Ray? Some of us doubted her. Why would she tell us if it wasn't true? This didn't make us think that she slept with Fred. Her adoration of him felt sexless. We wanted it to be sexless.

We understood that the commonplace magnitude of an affair would have diminished us.

*

She started running. Slowly. And alone. But regularly. On the paved paths along the river behind her apartment building. She went to Ottawa one spring and told us that she ran the half-marathon. Most of us didn't believe her.

We could've found the finishing times online, but we didn't bother.

*

In the second year of her PhD, Kathleen attached herself to Joan Turner, a medievalist who had just been hired by the department. Joan was young, and imperiously awkward, as if she had decided that social interaction was something she could excel at, when she chose to, and she often chose not to. She had spent a year as a visiting scholar at Oxford, had a degree from Princeton, and had packed her life with accomplishments the way she had loaded her CV with credentials: she had a black belt in Karate, an interest in late Victorian ceramics, a passion for Bergman, a copy of Escoffier's *Le Guide Culinaire* in the original French from which she had mastered three dozen recipes, and a long distance boyfriend who was as successful as her. Kathleen gave Joan advice about the city, and sometimes about life, and Joan let her. She ate lunch in Joan's office. They went camping together. Joan bought a house in the neighbourhood of tree-lined streets where professors bought houses, and Kathleen lived in it when Joan spent the summer in England. She showed us the small tins of caviar she was allowed to try, the shelves of feminist fantasy novels, and the collection of pottery vases she dusted once a week. They wrote an article together. Joan bought a dog, and Kathleen walked it when Joan was away at conferences, or visiting her boyfriend, or too busy. It was a Rhodesian Ridgeback, big and powerful and badly behaved, and Kathleen could barely hold it back. Joan would get drunk and call Kathleen late at night to fight with her. We don't know what she said to Kathleen. We didn't ask. Sara, her roommate, told us about the phone ringing until Kathleen answered it, and about the time she picked it up by accident and Joan started screaming at her. When Sara walked past Kathleen's door, she heard her whispering quickly and frantically, pleading. Afterwards, Kathleen would come out of her room and talk to her about nothing in particular, tomorrow's weather, the news, people they both knew, looking preoccupied, and holding onto things, the back of a chair in the living room, the lip of the kitchen counter, until she calmed down. Sara told Kathleen that the calls had to stop. Kathleen became helpless and confused, and Sara never brought it up again. Kathleen claimed she was bisexual. We thought saying this was something she did to seem more interesting, more sophisticated, like teaching herself how to make crème brûlée (the first time, she beat the eggs and the custard rose like a soufflé), learning rudimentary Spanish, and talking about the Nouveau Roman. It wasn't until much later that we began to wonder about her relationship with Joan. Friendship didn't explain the hysterical intensity of those phone calls or Kathleen's desperate loyalty. Had they been lovers? In secret? Touching a handful of times? When they had both been drinking and they could deny or excuse what passed between them? Some of us wonder if it was consensual.

We imagine a silent, guilty, fervent struggling.

*

Kathleen wrote her thesis on poet-critics—poets, like her supervisor, who wrote criticism and who often worked as academics—and it alternated between chronicling the careers of Fred and his friends, and extending the arguments he made in his articles. When she decided that she needed to finish it, she set herself up in the office she shared with three other graduate students. She read and wrote from 8 to 6 every day with a half hour break for lunch. It was summer, the other students were gone, and the building was empty except for the faculty who didn't work at home and who weren't on research trips. Silence. Sometimes footsteps in the high, old hallways. She shared a casual friendliness, greetings and short conversations with the other people in the building. She complained about the Beckett scholar who wouldn't acknowledge her when she passed him on the stairs. She developed the habit of mentioning articles in conversation.

We disliked the way that she said the names of the authors. It was familiar, offhanded, as if she knew them the way that she knew the people she nodded and talked to in the hallways, as if she knew them the way she knew us.

*

She got an interview. None of us saw the talk she gave, but we heard about it from friends, from acquaintances we met at conferences, in bits and confusing pieces that we assembled and tried to make sense of, never from Kathleen. We expected her to embarrass herself, but not only because of what her success would have said about us. She must have been the last candidate or the one from whom they expected the least. There may have been controversy. Did a friend of Fred's lobby for her, and others resist? We

128

are sure that the faculty was prepared to dislike her. We have been in rooms like that before, listening savagely, to disagree, to humiliate and destroy, or being torn down ourselves. Whenever we think about her in this moment, it is with a defensive cringe of shame. No sympathy. We hate Kathleen like we hate ourselves. Her carefully assembled confidence disintegrated. She tried to find an encouraging face in the audience. Nothing. Hardness. Doubt. Her talk hesitated to an end. The question period was worse. Someone asked her about Paul Gilroy's *The Black Atlantic.* She panicked. She hadn't read it. We think she answered as if she had.

We don't know what happened next, but we can see it, and Kathleen, desperately trying, and failing, not to become what the watching, vicious audience wanted her to be.

*

She got a post-doc at McGill with the help of her supervisor, and went back to Montreal. We didn't lose track of her, but we lost the details of her life. There was the distance, and Kathleen herself became vague, elusive. She changed her Facebook settings, hiding everything but her degrees and her current city. She didn't call anyone but Sara. Was she leaving behind a humiliation? Was she transforming herself? Or was it something else, something more mundane, but less predictable? We tried to imagine a new version of Kathleen, more professional, knowledgeable, poised, and couldn't manage it. Had she escaped us? Had she trapped us in our condescension? What we knew for sure we learned from Google searches: she became the reviews editor at a literary magazine, and recruited her friends and ex-students to write for it. She sat on a panel discussing "Poetry Today" at the city library. She taught a contemporary theater course that was written up in the student paper. She won a Fulbright Scholarship and was a visiting scholar at the University of Virginia. We noticed that that same year a professor moved from McGill to Virginia. We knew him and had seen him before, trailing small groups of female graduate students after him, and we included Kathleen with those women. She went to a conference in Paris. Those must have been precarious years. There was teaching, but not enough. What would happen after the grants and the scholarships ran out? Money was tight and there was a time limit on success. The possibility of failure, of a real and permanent defeat became more likely with each passing year.

We admit that we expected that the list of results from the Google search would stop growing, that what was there would fragment, that links would break, results would drop off and she would disappear. We expected her to resurface in a decade teaching at a CEGEP. Behind the results, the handful of successes, minor, most of them forgettable, there was a persistent, invisible striving, a conviction that we openly pitied, and secretly resented.

*

We don't know when the hard work started to pay off or when she met her girlfriend or how closely the two were related. Emily Morin was a professor who had written a pioneering study of Canadian feminist poetics and a handful of books of poetry in which she explored the radical alterities of the feminine voice. She was twenty-seven years older than Kathleen, a contemporary of Fred's, had shoulder-length grey hair with bangs cut straight across her forehead, and spoke in a commanding, meditative drawl. Where did they meet? We imagine a reading. We can put them together in a noisy room, standing, detached. We can't make them touch or speak. We have never seen them together in person. Did Kathleen listen to Emily with the same active adoration, nodding, prompting, making soft emphatic sounds of agreement, with which she had listened to Fred? Did she mirror Emily, adopt her mannerisms, her calm, deliberate gestures, and mimic her knowing maturity? They did a walking tour of the south of Spain? Paris? Friends' parties in Montreal? A dinner at a restaurant where you eat in the dark and are served by visually impaired waiters? Two weeks in Cuba? They went to conferences and sat on panels together. When Kathleen presents, we imagine Emily listening, Kathleen's quick, searching glances, and Emily's steady, encouraging reassurance. The room nods along with Emily. Kathleen still talked about canon formation, the social construction of literary value, and the way writers intervened in the reception of their work, but she increasingly focused on marginalized voices, on the groups who are rendered invisible by the dominant cultural institutions. She started to point to how aesthetic debates erase questions of politics and identity. Kathleen and Emily met before Kathleen made her Facebook page public again and began adding friends. Even then, it was several years before she mentioned Emily openly, and longer before she posted pictures of her. What we know we have guessed from her timeline: Emily is half of the *we* in a post about Andalucía. The person behind the camera for dozens of pictures. The gravity drawing Kathleen to conferences in Paris, Waterloo, at Black Mountain College.

We saw that, last year, they were in a cabin in Northern Quebec. Emily was roasting a duck basted in lavender honey and Kathleen was trying to convince her to watch *The Princess Bride*. They spent reading break with Kathleen's parents in Thunder Bay.

*

Things started to happen quickly, or time passed faster so they felt like they happened quickly. Some of them we missed, scrolled past or never saw, others we noticed and forgot. Some we remembered: Kathleen ran her first full marathon. And then her second. She turned a paper she gave on a panel with Emily into an article. She started editing for several online archives, and talked about the digital humanities. She added Facebook friends, people she knew, colleagues, people she wanted to know, until she had more than a thousand. She did a triathlon. She got a tenure track position at a university college that was affiliated with the university where Fred did his doctorate. She posted about early springs and mild winters. She tagged herself in pictures with mountains in the background. She decided to train for an Ironman. She started a blog called "Kat Tries" on which she wrote about training, races, and women in sport. She spent a term teaching in France. She posted links to articles about political issues: women in the academy, equal representation of female athletes in professional Ironman competitions, bike path expansion, LGBTQ rights. Idle No More started.

We followed the movement by checking her wall.

*

There is a pose that we think of when we think of Kathleen. It is how she sometimes presents herself and how we most often imagine her: her back is arched, but not too much. Her shoulders are up and back. She is turned slightly to the left or the right. The leg that is closest to the viewer is lifted, bent at the knee, the toe lightly touching the ground. Her hands are resting on her hips or they are raised and bent at angles that she has thought about. She is looking into the space behind the camera. The pose is practised. Exacting. But she strikes versions of it effortlessly, beside her bike at the top of a climb, on the patio of a hotel in Cuba, wearing one of the blazers she likes to teach in.

We have seen her refine it, repeat it with variations in countless pictures. We have watched her arrive at her effortlessness.

*

We only know her from social media and Google searches now: Emily still lives in her apartment in Montreal. She flies out for long weekends, and Kathleen visits her during reading breaks, over Christmas and for a month in the heat of summer. Kathleen has started building a website detailing the literary history of the region which she is going to use to teach her first graduate course. She is drafting a book proposal. She has joined the local triathlon club and leads the Friday evening recovery ride along the shore of a long, narrow lake under the reaching shadows of the mountains. She marshalled at the spring time trial. Her triathlon friends call her Kat and her colleagues call her by full name. They both like and respect her. She broke her leg in a crash last winter, and limped for three months in a brace, but she has worked hard at rehab, and she is already back on her bike.

We can tell from a distance that she has finally become herself.

131

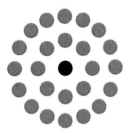

107 Missiles: An Autofiction in Fragments

1.

When I was in grade four, I asked my father to teach me how to fight. I was being picked on at school, and I thought that he would show me how to punch or elbow or apply an arm lock, that he would teach me the secret formula of toughness. He tried to pretend that I was joking, but I meant it. I was nine and this mattered. I insisted. He turned serious and told me it was better to walk away. "Violence creates problems," he said, "it doesn't solve them." I thought he was hiding something, deliberately holding back the tricks that he had learned and I hadn't, and I wouldn't leave him alone. He was on his hands and knees, weeding the garden in front of the house, pulling the plants, shaking the dirt off their roots and throwing them into a plastic bucket. The weeds wilted quickly in the heat. I pleaded and he relented. He took off his gloves and showed me how to sidestep someone and kick out their feet, how to lean left or right, use your hands to direct them, and dart out a leg. He invited me towards him. I rushed him and he tripped me onto the grass by the driveway. And again. And twice more, but I wasn't satisfied. I protested. It wouldn't work. It was too easy, too obvious, and I could tell that he was using his grown body to get the advantage over me.

2.

While I ran and tripped on the lawn in front of the house, my father smiled in the calm, detached way that he smiled at me when I did something that wasn't wrong, but that he didn't approve of or understand. He was serene. Unreachable. He looked like a character in the G.I. Joe comics that my brother and I collected: the latest issue of *Special Missions* had introduced three new Joes. One of them was a medic called Lifeline, a pacifist who got tangled in his parachute and had to be cut down, and who wouldn't engage in violence, not even when the Joes were ambushed and outgunned. The team was captured by river pirates, and they were forced to draw straws to pick a champion to fight for their lives. Lifeline drew the short straw. He faced down a hulking giant of a man, and the Joes thought they were going to die, they said it out loud in front of Lifeline, but then they discovered that the medic was a master of Aikido. The comic explained that it was "a Zen martial art with no offensive moves." "The purpose," the narration told my brother and me, "is to redirect violent energy away from oneself." The giant charged, and over and over again Lifeline sent him sprawling across the deck of the river boat. The men's bodies bent and arched. Black lines of force exploded out of them. The giant howled in frustration and Lifeline kiaied in letters that were dark and electric with the loudness of their cries. In the final panel of the fight, the giant sailed headfirst into the mast. Lifeline was turned with his back to the giant and bent at the waist at a 90-degree angle. His right arm was extended straight from his shoulder in line with his torso. The giant was flying over him with his limbs flung out and his mouth wrenched into a oval of rage. The mast was about to break off at the base.

3.

Even as a child, I could tell that what I saw in the climactic panels of that issue of *Special Missions* was impossible. Lifeline and the giant were posed like mannequins. Lifeline was too small. The giant was too big. Leverage didn't make sense of his wild flight or its shattering impact. I couldn't believe in it, in the effortlessness with which Lifeline sent the giant sailing over him or the force with which he landed, not the way I believed in the other Joes, in Duke, Snake Eyes and Roadblock, in swords that were razor-sharp, in guns that blasted everything in their path, in all of the dense and thrilling possibilities of violence, and in the salvation it offered.

4.

I was an obvious target at school. My family lived in a farmhouse in the country at the end of a dead-end gravel road, but we weren't farmers. We were separate from the community, and my parents ordered our lives according to a set of principles they had agreed on between themselves.

5.

The house we lived in was both old and new: in 1974, my parents bought fifty acres of mixed farmland and bush twenty-five minutes north of Owen Sound and left behind Toronto and the lives they had started to build there for good. The property was sandwiched between the escarpment that fell away on the south and east sides in a sheer face of limestone with a lip of turf curling over the top and a low forested ridge on the west. There wasn't any road access. They had to park their Volkswagen Bug on the soft shoulder where Concession 24 came to an abrupt halt. The car listed dangerously to one side and brushed its mirror against the cattails that grew in the ditch. They crossed the ditch on a plank and followed a faint and badly overgrown footpath that dipped down the ridge and cut through the swamp that separated the northwest corner of the plot of land from the end of the concession road before turning south and winding through pussy willow and dogwood to half a dozen small fields that had once grown corn and grain but were now filled with weeds and wildflowers and fit only for pasture. I imagine that the first time they saw it was in the late August afternoon. They were hot and tired from the drive and the walk through the swamp that had both taken longer than they had expected. The shadows were reaching out from the ridge and the light was turning yellow and catching the insects buzzing over and settling onto the tangle of weeds and grass and wildflowers that tugged at my parents' legs. I see the insects lift and set the air alive with the small and darting bodies as they wade through the fields. I imagine my parents stopping and standing there. In the middle of the first field. In that late afternoon light. In that wide and humming silence. And the knowledge of how far they are away from the car waiting by the road, how far from their lives in Toronto, from everything they have known until that moment. And deciding. This. This almost unreachable place. This half-wild solitude we can make our own. This is what we want.

6.

The property had a house and a barn and a paddock fenced in with falling down cedar rails that were the same dark silver as the barn boards. The house was the log house built by the original settlers, and it hadn't been lived in for more than half a century. The rooms were small and the windows were smaller and let in very little light. Everything about the house was dark and close and disappointing: decades of debris were drifted in the corners. The plaster sagged away from the lath. And there was the dust. Fine. Jet black. Almost a powder. Like soot but sharper in the mouth, danker and more pervasive. It hung a haze in the air. It coated their throats, settled into the seams of their clothing, and slipped off them like a sickly grey skin when they washed. And they didn't care.

7.

They took possession in the spring. They lived in a tent they pitched in the orchard, cooked on a Coleman stove balanced on a pair of sawhorses, and drank rusty water they pumped up by hand from the well behind the house. My mother worked at the Children's Aid Society in Owen Sound, and, for that spring, and summer, and into the fall, my father worked on the house: he tore out the plaster and lathe, the horse hair and newspapers the original owners had stuffed into the walls for insulation. He took it down to the bare logs and levered those free from the structure one by one. He numbered them with a blue crayon and rolled them onto a rough pile that grew as the house shrank. He made a deal with the county to extend Concession 24 through the swamp to the edge of the northernmost field. He cut and cleared the trees and the county crew laid down a raised roadbed and a narrow line of gravel on top of it that was soft and ticked against the side of the car but soon hardened into a pair of taupe ribbons. He brought in earthmoving equipment and had a new foundation pit dug on the far side of the orchard in a corner of a field overhung on the east and north sides by century maples. He had footings poured and built the cinderblock foundation walls and then borrowed a tractor with a bucket and backfilled the pit himself. He raised a ramshackle scaffold with a winch and a pulley and reassembled the numbered logs on the new foundation.

8.

By the late fall, when the frost was drawing fractals on the walls of the tent, fringing the blades of grass, and setting a stillness in the air that lasted into the afternoons, the structure that he had been raising slowly, one painstaking log at a time, had the rough outlines of a house: windows whose openings were the old openings or new ones he had cut out with a chainsaw, a corrugated steel roof, and chinking between the logs. An extension whose spruce board-and-batten siding was still new and gold in the slanting light contained the kitchen and above it the bathroom and master bedroom. The building sat in the middle of a sea of mud and stones from the excavation instead of a lawn. In the nights, the cold froze a crust over the mud. It crunched underfoot. In places, it would hold the imprints of my father's boots until they softened and blurred in the spring. Two of the doors didn't have steps and opened into midair. The short flight that climbed to the front door was an afterthought my father threw together with scraps of lumber left over from framing the roof. It leaned at one angle and shifted without warning to another when it took weight. Inside was worse, rougher, not so much in progress as hardly begun: plywood subfloors, a hole with a ladder in it instead of basement steps, studs and vapour barrier over pink insulation in the kitchen, wire mesh but no chinking in the gaps between the logs in the living room. No indoor plumbing. No running water. And no electricity.

9.

They struck the tent and moved into the half-finished house before the first snow fell. My father got a job as a counselor at Hincks Farm, a newly-opened rural treatment center for troubled teens southeast of Meaford. My mother left the Children's Aid and joined him there. It was long way away, more than an hour's drive in the summer over winding country roads, sometimes a white-knuckled two in the winter through snowdrifts and blizzards, and they worked on the house when they could find the time and muster the energy: they put up drywall and laid down brown speckled linoleum in the kitchen. My father added stairs to the basement and then cupboards to the kitchen with boards salvaged from the old house for doors. The summer came and he built a wraparound porch with four solid steps. The next spring, they spread a black layer of topsoil over the mud, seeded a lawn and put in a pair of raised gardens built with limestone and granite rocks that my mother collected from the fence rows and trundled back to the house in a clay-colored wheelbarrow.

10.

The grass came in slowly. And slowly the house began to look and feel more like a home. It became theirs, and, at the same time, it became less isolated, less cut off from the world: at first, they didn't have any way to clear the lane, so for several winters they parked at the end of Concession 24 and drove in on an old snowmobile they had bought from a neighbor. They towed groceries and then me in my car seat and snowsuit tucked in among the plastic bags on a toboggan behind the machine. But then my father found an old Massey Ferguson that was the same color as the wheelbarrow at an auction in Chatsworth and a snowblower to go with it. He carved a narrow white corridor through the drifts. Its sides were clean and straight and they rose with each snowfall until they were almost as tall as the car. In the fall of 1982, they raised and graveled the laneway so that it didn't flood in the spring. The following year, they paid the county to run hydro down the extension they had added to the Concession road. The poles cut at an angle through the fields and my parents replaced the kerosene fixtures they had salvaged from the original house with electric sconces.

11.

The phone came with the hydro and a party line started to ring loudly in the living room. It was a heavy black rotary phone with a pair of metal bells in its base. It sat on a dresser next to a reading lamp, and, from there, it rang out hard and bright and clear. It filled up the house with its ringing and could be heard through the windows when the sashes were lifted and the casements were cranked wide in the summer heat. Its ringing broke open the silence that had hung over the tangled fields through which my parents had waded on that first August afternoon with the grass tugging at their legs, the silence that had persisted through the construction, that had waited at the edges of the work for those moments when my father put down his hammer or his saw, when he settled a log into place and stepped back to look at what he was in the middle of building, that had waited patiently all that while to draw its blanket of stillness back over him, the farm and the half-finished house. The phone rang. And when it had stopped ringing, the silence was still there, but it was a different silence, a newer and, in its way, a deeper silence.

12.

The townships in Grey and Bruce County were some of the last places in Southern Ontario to get electricity. It wasn't until the 1950s that they began to run poles down the shoulders of the roads and it took until the end of the decade for the wires to reach the more isolated houses. The farmers called it "getting the lights" and it was the light that changed. That became steadier. Clearer. More reliable.

13.

At the end of "Privilege," a story that begins with the adult Rose lording the poverty of her upbringing over her more privileged friends and returns in a sentence or two to Rose's first schoolhouse, to the boys' and girls' outhouses behind it, the turds frozen to the floor around the hole, Shorty McGill fucking his sister Franny at recess, and the fights that engulf the entire student body at least two or three times a year, at the end of this story steeped in the cruelties of want and the realities of small town violence, Alice Munro describes the way the Second World War and the prosperity and development that it brought transformed the town. The story is set in West Hanratty, *Who Do You Think You Are*'s barely-veiled version of Wingham, a town in Huron County far enough south of us to feel like a long way away, but close enough that we knew it by name. I think of the end of this story and of its juxtapositions whenever I think of the transformation that came to the country north of Owen Sound more than a decade after it came to Huron County. I think of one passage in particular when I see the traces of this change in the lines of old poles leaning at angles along the backroads of the township and in the brown metal boxes in barns with coins wedged in where the fuses should go, a danger that has been threatening for so long it has disappeared, become impossible, quotidian and, like the silence, comforting. It reads, "When Rose thought of West Hanratty during the war years, and during the years before, the two times were so separate it was as if an entirely different lighting had been used, or as if it was all on film and the film had been printed in a different way, so that on the one hand things looked clean-edged and decent and limited and ordinary, and on the other, dark, grainy, jumbled, disturbing." What the war did to Hanratty, what the electricity did to the light, the phone ringing in the living room did to the silence: it made it cleaner and more definitive. It separated out all of the minor noises and messiness that had lived inside of it until then, the insects humming in the fields, the wind lifting the leaves of the trees on the ridge in a gentle silvering rush, the far-off grumble of a car on the concession road. It made it just silence, nothing more, simple and absolute, an absence of sound in which my parents could be alone with themselves.

14.

In the comics that I read, phones were important. They were worth fighting for. There was a briefcase that traveled everywhere the president went. Inside it, there were the launch codes and a satellite phone that the president could use to unleash a nuclear strike. The briefcase was called the football, and it was always handcuffed to the left wrist of a secret agent like a suicide pact, but it never stayed there. The anonymous agent in his dark suit and darker sunglasses always died. The football was always cut off him. The good guys always had to fight to keep it out of the hands of the bad guys. Sometimes, one of them heaved it like its namesake, sending it sailing in a desperate, lofting arc through a panel to land safely in a hero's outstretched hands. The second, equally important, phone was on the president's desk in the Oval Office. It was always red and the same heavy, solid shape as the rotary phone in our living room. Sometimes, it had a grid of numbered buttons. Sometimes, it had a single large button in the middle of the base. It always rang in emergencies, when the bad guys were winning and destruction was imminent. There were only two arrangements of figures in the room when it rang: in the first, the president and his advisors stood in conversation, often by the bay window looking out onto the lawn. The smooth backs of their suit coats. Their heads bowed in thoughtful conversation. The calm and careful work of government. Until. Until. The phone crashed through the force field of power and wrenched them into a reaction panel full of horror: their bodies startled into awkwardness, arms flung out, hands reaching without knowing what they were reaching for, mouths torn into the same oval as the mouth of the giant that Lifeline sent sailing wildly over him. In the second arrangement, there was only a single figure: the president sat alone at a desk that filled and dominated the panel. He was always upright and facing forward. Never bending to read or write. Never turning to look away. Always staring out at the reader. Sometimes, his hands were raised. Sometimes, his tented index fingers rested on his upper lip, on the depression under his nose. His brow was furrowed. His face was a mask of concentration. He was still. Everything was still. Almost frozen. Only the phone moved. Its receiver jangled on the base. It rattled. It danced. Sometimes, it was suspended in midleap above the cradle. In both cases, it went off like a bomb. I remember it haloed in the same lancing straight lines as an explosion. In long razoring strokes. When this phone rang out in the Oval Office, when its receiver jolted on the cradle, the sound of its ringing was transformed into visible force.

15.

Although the house became less isolated as they worked on it, it was only ever less so, and both it and my parents remained in their stubborn way set apart, emphatic in their shared separateness: to reach it, you had to drive up what the locals called the Kemble Rock, a promontory of the Niagara Escarpment that begins as a ridge of mossy boulders to the west and pitches up a limestone cliff as it swings eastward and rises to its full height. My parents' house sits on the plateau above the cliff, and the most direct route to it is up the road that climbs the Rock. It was gravel then, paved now, and the kind of steep that you only expect to find in real mountains, in the Rockies in Canada or the Alps in Europe. You first see it when you clear the village of Kemble: a low hump on the horizon, a wrinkle in the landscape that you think you could reach out and straighten the way you straighten a rug, but that thought is a trick of the distance and of your assumptions. As you approach the hill, it rears up, towers in a wall of trees to the left and a grey rampart curving away to the right. The road threads between the stone and the trees, bending right and then sharply left before disappearing into the forest on top of the ridge. The road seems too narrow. The shoulders pinch in and disappear. It is open to the right, looking out over a ragged patchwork of pastures, hayfields and barns, over Beckett's gun range with its long bank of earth backstopping the targets to the latticed mast of the radio tower, and you can feel the height accumulate as you climb. No matter how fast you are going when you hit the slope, the engine starts to labour, and, when you step on the gas, the car revs but doesn't buck forward, it holds more firmly to the speed that is slipping away, that keeps slipping slowly away, and doesn't accelerate. There is a moment when you wonder if you will make it. When the engine stutters. When it coughs out noises you are not used to hearing. But you do make it. You slide over the crest, and the car gathers itself and then shoots forward into the half-light of the trees.

16.

In winter, the Kemble Rock was never a sure bet. Too much snow or ice and we would stall partway up the hill, spinning the tires until we gave up, backed down and took the long way around, swinging wide of the ridge, driving through Wolseley and Lake Charles, to come at the house from the west. When we were kids, my father turned the Rock and the tension that always filled the car when we cleared Kemble and saw it rise in the distance into a game: he would tell my brother and me to start our engines, and we would pinch our faces up and start to make low revving sounds in the backs of our throats. These would begin in harmony with the engine and climbed in pitch and intensity well past what our little Volkswagen Rabbit could manage. Sometimes, he would let off the gas so that the car slowed and the engine sputtered. He would tell us in a mock serious voice to stop dragging our feet. When he did this, we would hunker down in our seats, lift up our legs so that not even the backs of our thighs touched the vinyl, and make the loudest noises we could manage, hums that buzzed in our sinuses and hurt if we held them for too long. He liked to toy with the gas, and, every time he let off, we redoubled our efforts. We knew it was a game, and we knew also that it was serious, that we might not make the summit, that we might get stuck or stall and have to back all the way down to the driveway at the base of the hill where we could turn around. When my father told us sharply to be quiet, we stopped humming and holding up our feet. We watched him from the safety of the backseat, from the safety of our childhood belief in our father's infallibility, as he hunched worried and silent over the steering wheel.

17.

The Kemble Rock that towered in the summer and turned almost impassable in the winter, the road after it that wound through an MNR woodlot whose trees grew right to the shoulder and that felt like it could turn into a pair of ruts or dead end at any moment, the intersection with an actual dead end sign where you turned right to the house, the sign itself that was shot through with bullet holes that rusted until the sign was illegible and the county replaced it and someone shot more holes into the new sign, the road that dipped down and ran through swamp and looked like it was going nowhere until you got to the end and saw the driveway, and the end of the driveway from which you could only barely see the house which was still a long way away and half hidden by the trees, all of these were barriers my parents placed between themselves and the world. No one ever stumbled on the house by accident, no one was ever passing by, no one just dropped in, and, when people came for the first time, they often said they were surprised they found it. The house's remoteness was unmistakable. It was defensive. It was a shield against something I still don't understand, against, in the way it imposed itself uniformly, everything.

18.

My parents had not created these barriers between themselves and the world, but they had chosen them by choosing the house, and behind them they built a life that followed a set of rules that were as precise and rigid as a religion, but that were theirs and no one else's. Like the house, the rules were both new and old. Some they invented for themselves. Others they borrowed, adopted, salvaged from the people they had met and the books they had read, but never without some kind of essential transformation that made them their own: they believed in the power of love, and my father would sing along to Lennon's "Imagine" when it came on the radio, but they weren't hippies. Hippies were lazy. They didn't work or own anything. My parents had their jobs and the house that was getting nicer, closer to what they had imagined when they bought it, closer to finished, every year.

19.

My parents believed just as firmly in peace and in the value of nonviolence as they did in the idea of love. In practice, this meant that they sat us down and talked to us or sent us to our rooms instead of spanking us when we misbehaved, and that we weren't allowed war toys of any kind. No guns. No green plastic army men to play with in the sandbox my father built for us behind the house. No action figures with weapons. No He-Man characters. No Voltron robots. No ThunderCats. Not even Transformers.

20

The G.I. Joe comics that my brother and I collected together and alternated between sharing and fighting over were an uneasy compromise between our parents' ideals and our nearly constant demands for what they denied us. Whatever was in them, they were comic books. We were reading. And our parents accepted them as long as we bought them with our own money. They accepted them, but they disapproved of them. Sometimes, my father picked up an issue and read enough of it to find something wrong. He told us that the bullets drawing lines after them like lasers, the acrobatics and narrow escapes were impossible. None of it was real. Guns didn't work like that. The world didn't work like that. His voice, when he did this, was dismissive, contemptuous—he expected more from us, from me, in particular, because I was the oldest. The feeling that we were throwing our allowance money away, that we were wasting our time on something worthless, something he thought was crude and objectionable, was part of the fun of buying and reading them. And we did it for the same reason that we played war in the orchard in front of the house in sight of the big kitchen window, dodging from one tree to the next, debating what counted as cover, and firing sticks and pointer fingers at each other instead of toy guns.

21.

People who knew my family said we were vegetarians, but we weren't. My parents had their own ideas about food the way they had their own ideas about everything. We ate chicken and fish. But no red meat. And absolutely no junk food. This meant no trips to McDonald's. No Kraft Dinner. No Zoodles. No candy. Nothing processed. And no sugary cereals. For snacks during recess, my friends brought pudding cups, or cheese and crackers that came in a plastic package with separate compartments for the crackers and the cheese, and a red stick to spread the cheese. I got vegetables and dip in ratty Tupperware or dark strips of fruit leather or sesame snaps from the new health food store on Main Street, food that I had to explain, that I had to defend.

22.

We had indoor plumbing, taps, a tub and shower, a washer and dryer, but no septic tank, and we used a composting toilet that my father emptied once a week. It was taller than normal toilets, and it always smelled a little. When my friends came over, I had to show them how to use the stool next to it to climb onto the seat. We didn't have a TV.

23.

The absence of a TV and the outhouse in the orchard, which we didn't use, were what all of my friends who visited me noticed. They were fascinated by the outhouse. What was for me a commonplace thing that I passed every time I took the kitchen scraps out to the compost heap by the garden, held an almost irresistible attraction for them. When they saw it sitting between a pair of apple trees with its back to the fence line and a halfmoon cut into its weathered door, they had to get a closer look. They stood in the open doorway and took in the dimness. The must. The spiderwebs furred with dust. The clean white roll of toilet paper that my father always kept fresh. The braver ones leaned over the hole in the raised seat and stared into the darkness. They wanted to pick out crumpled squares of stained brown paper, discover a turd still glossy on the top of the pile like the lumps of shit frozen around the hole in "Privilege," see someone else's shameful leavings, and recoil in delighted horror. But there was only a dense blackness that got heavier and denser the longer they stared into it. The hole. And the smell rising out of it: muddy earth that reminded you of worms and the undersides of rotting logs. A tang too. The high ammonia note of urine still singing through the swampy base. They stared, and walked away from it reluctantly, as if they didn't believe that it could be that shabby, that prosaic, as if the grey shingles and raw plywood would reveal something repulsive and thrilling if only they looked for long enough or in the right way.

24

My friends were fascinated by the outhouse, but it was the absence of a television that they remembered. Of all of my parents' negations, this refusal and the blank space it carved out of our lives was definitive. It was the one eccentricity that my friends couldn't forget or reconcile.

25.

We sat at a round table at the back of the classroom drawing on sheets of foolscap. The teacher was nowhere to be seen. Jim Brown, who lived on the shore road a few concessions away and sometimes biked over to play on the weekends, started to talk about me. He said I lived in a cave in the forest. I played along. I said I was raised by wolves. The fantasy got more elaborate: my family dressed in animal skins, we hunted for food, and we had only just discovered fire.

Will Dekker added as a crowning touch, "He doesn't have a television." He used the full word and pronounced each syllable.

"No. He does," said Steve Green. "He has a wood-burning television."

Will drew it in colored pencil: a box with knobs and rabbit ears and a slot on the side with orange flames coming out of it. A crude figure was feeding wood into the slot. You could tell it was me because of the glasses. Everyone laughed. I laughed with them because I had to, but it was loud, wild laughter: I was exposed, defenceless, surrounded by and trapped in my strangeness.

26.

Everyone forgot about the drawing, but the joke lasted for years. At my first high school reunion, a decade after we graduated, someone told it again. I responded with a story from before I was born: when my parents were still sleeping in a tent and my father was gutting the house, they used a plank across a crevice in the rocks behind the barn as a toilet. I saw the plank when I was a kid, mossy and too rotten to bear my weight, but there and unmistakable. By the time I told that table of old friends about it, I had learned how to make facts like this exotic, compelling, to take a kind of rueful, defensive pride in them. In Grade 4, I wasn't the smart kid, or the strong one, or the one who went crazy, turned red and freaked out if you bugged him too much, or one of the ones whose skin looked perpetually dirty and who we already knew were going to drop out of school and who we never talked to. I was unremarkable and different, and I didn't yet know how to transform the material of my life the way my parents had transformed theirs.

27.

The worst of the bullying always happened at lunch. We ate in the gym and then went out to play. When we started Grade 4, we were allowed to cross the road to the backfield, an acre with a baseball diamond, a soccer field and a row of mature pines at the back whose shade created a separate space, an outdoor room, where the girls sat in circles and everyone huddled when it rained. The teachers stayed near the road talking unless they thought kids were slipping through the hole in the corner of the fence to go to the convenience store down the street.

28.

It happened at lunch, but it spread out through the day, drawing everything, every moment and action into an order of which it was the center. Our favorite movie was Star Wars, and it was like the tractor beam that pulls them into the Death Star, invisible, irresistible. I watched my friends carefully, gauging their moods, the tone of their jokes, trying to predict if today would be bad, or if they would forget and go easy on me. Good days were a reprieve that reminded me of the bad ones.

29.

All morning I anticipated it. I feared it. I looked forward to it with a prickling, restless anxiety that was indistinguishable from excitement.

30.

It started in the gym with my friends picking on what I was eating, or my clothes, some of which my mother made and the rest my parents bought at the Sally Ann, or what I had said that morning. Sometimes, I tried insults of my own, but I was clumsy with words, and my friends worked together. Jim picked up where Will left off. Paul Boisvert defended both of them. Sometimes, out of frustration or because I was carried away by the reeling freedom of transgression and I couldn't help myself, I pushed it too far. I told Jim he didn't have a father when I knew it would hurt him. My friends became as serious as adults. They told me that was wrong, and they didn't talk to me for the rest of the day. Sometimes, I laughed along with them. Sometimes, I listened while they decided what they were going to do to me. Sometimes, I egged them on, not aggressively, not challenging them, quietly, almost slyly, saying, "I hope you don't tie my shoelaces together today."

31.

One time, Will stopped joking and explained, "We wouldn't do it if you didn't say that." He was remote, pitying, as if I should have understood this.

There was a way people behaved, and this wasn't it. He could have been my father on the grass by the driveway. He watched me. I didn't know what to say. And that was worse than the jokes.

32.

We finished eating. The teachers opened the gym doors and we walked past the monkey bars and crossed the road to the backfield. I walked ahead of my friends, feeling them fan out behind me, or in the middle of the group, or I trailed after them, lagging behind—it didn't matter. When we were far enough from the road and the teachers, they grabbed for me. I ran. I had to run. It was part of the ritual, but the attempt was half-hearted: I knew I couldn't get away, and my body was heavy, and I didn't try very hard. They were smiling and I was smiling. It still felt like a game.

33.

They caught me and pinned my arms. I struggled in fits and starts, in bursts. I told them to let me go. I could never sound like I meant it. My voice bubbled with laughter. I couldn't believe fully in my performance, in my resistance, or in what was about to happen. I flailed. I went limp. I said, I give up. I did for a moment. And then I threw my weight left or right. I tried to break free, but they hemmed me in and held me. Paul tripped me and put his knee on my chest.

34.

They liked to test how much pain I could take before I begged them to stop. They gave me Indian burns or took turns punching me in the shoulder. Paul would bend my fingers back. He went further than the others, past the point where it really hurt, until I seized with desperation, and pleaded for real. Frantic. I bargained. I threatened to tell. He ignored me. He stopped when he wanted to, never when I thought he would.

35.

They tied my laces together and let me up. They formed a loose circle with me in the center. I stumbled and fought to stay standing. They pushed me, sending me staggering, caught me or let me fall. They liked to help me stand and then trip me. If I refused when one of them offered me his hand, he would soften, reassure me, remind me that he was my friend: the fun was in making me trust them and then betraying me.

36.

On the worst days, they would spit on me. I don't remember who started it, maybe Jim, I want to say Paul. They stepped back. They always stood a few paces away: even in this, there were rules, a sense of fair play. They gathered phlegm from their throats, and sent gobs arching or strings stretching and spinning through the air. Thick and heavy, warm as the mouths they came out of, they landed with an audible plop, and stuck, and smeared when I attempted to flick them off. I pitched and flailed my arms, trying to shield myself and keep my balance. The muscles of my face flexed into an expression that I didn't understand, a grimace that was unique to these moments, and didn't belong to me.

37.

I don't remember how it used to end. If they got bored and wandered off. If it went on until the bell rang. I remember fighting to untie my laces so that I wouldn't be late for class. Most times, at the end of the lunch recess, I walked back towards the school with my friends, silent, absorbed with shame, storing up what had happened without understanding why I held it to me.

38.

Around my friends, I was solicitous, but tentatively, clumsily, and then too wholeheartedly, and my attempts to win their acceptance were often worse than doing nothing at all. I tried and failed in both small and big ways to fit in, to become unremarkable. I wanted to disappear into safety, but I never succeeded. Without a television or a radio that could pick up the Toronto stations, I always liked the wrong things. Or I liked the right things, but too late or too much or not enough. I was a beat. Off. A step. Behind. In my enthusiasms. For several months in Grade 2, I heard "light sabers" as "life savers" and didn't understand my mistake because I hadn't seen the movies and had only stared longingly at the toys in their plastic cases on the racks at the Sears in the new mall. I learned. I tried. And I kept learning and trying. But the solitude inside my laughter as Will drew my woodburning television and a caricature of me with my glasses feeding logs into the red and orange flames was a permanent condition.

39.

When I was alone, I slipped into daydreams that were elaborate fantasies of power and redemption, dreams in which I was stronger and better than my bullies. The bus ride home took the long way, following the shore to Big Bay and looping back to drop me off at the end of the route more than an hour after it had picked me up at school. I hunkered down into the green, textured vinyl, tucked my knees into the back of the seat in front of me, and imagined being bigger, tougher, more effortlessly capable of the brutal precision of violence. In my mind, I sent bodies cartwheeling. I dodged easily away from punches. I toyed with them. I let them slide past me by millimeters. I didn't run because I didn't need to. I stood my ground. When someone grabbed me, I broke their grip and threw them sprawling onto the grass or the root-knuckled earth under the pine trees. I beat Jim. I beat Will. I held Paul and I hurt him. I bent his hands back at the wrists. I folded them until his fingers touched his forearms and he writhed in pain. Curled into my seat, feeling the old diesel engine humming delicately through me, I did this with the same ease that Paul held and hurt me. I always stopped there. That was the limit of my sadism: returning the pain that had been inflicted on me. And I never pushed past this, past the feeling of Paul's tendons tightened to their limit, forced further, and the red cramp of his face as he fought to contain the feeling of what I did to him. I could never bring myself to imagine humiliating them. Even outlining us locked together, even touching the taut fibres of his body in these daydreams was difficult. Imagining it brought me too close to what my friends did to me during lunch hours, and it carried with it a nauseating shame that lingered long after the satisfaction of my fantasy had faded.

40.

I preferred imagining the throws to picturing myself holding Paul down and hurting him. I liked sending the bodies of my attackers hurtling away from me. Tracing the geometries of their trajectories. I liked seeing their limbs splayed in the air. Flung out. Purposeless. Flapping aimlessly. I liked the way they looked for a moment in midflight like the arms and legs of marionettes with their strings cut loose. How they were almost too awkward to be human. I often left my friends like this. Suspended. And I didn't imagine them crashing into the earth and folding over themselves. I was powerful. Untouched. Even by the consequences of my power.

41.

It was my daydreams that led me to my father kneeling by the garden in middle of the afternoon, pulling weeds with his gloved hands, shaking the dirt off their roots and throwing them into a plastic bucket beside him. I remember the sweat that stained his t-shirt, that drew damp patches in his armpits and wet lines across his front where his skin had folded over the fabric as he bent forward. I remember the way his smell mixed with the smell that lifted off the dark patches of disturbed earth, with the deep vegetal scent of the wilting weeds. And that frustration, that willfulness that sent me hurling myself at him again? And again? And again? That made me relentless in my insistence? I didn't believe in Lifeline or the giant sailing weightlessly over him to collide with the mast, but I believed in my father. I believed that he could turn my fantasies into reality. I was certain that he could save me. I was certain also that, every time he tripped me and sent me tumbling past him, he was refusing to do so, and I hated him for it.

42.

The bus dropped me off at the "DEAD END" sign. I walked down the road through the swamp, and then down the lane to the house. I read until dinner or I played with my brother or I worked on a fort I was building in a grove of cedars. I was laying sticks like xylophone keys across a pair of parallel branches and nailing them home to make a platform. I had found other suitable spots in the grove and made plans for more platforms after this one. The work was painstaking and tedious and could go on for as long as I wanted it to. On bad days, I snuck the ax out of the shed and chopped at an old stump on a fence line that was far enough away from the house for the sound of the blows to be muffled by the distance. The ax was dull but satisfyingly forceful. The wood was weathered and flaked away to cream white veined with the crumbling umber of rot. I was small. The ax handle was long, and the head was heavy. It took an effort to lift the tool, to heave it up into an arc until it caught its momentum, lofted, swung high, hung and half paused before it tipped slowly over its apex and came slicing down to chip another fibrous splinter from the stump. My arms hurt. My hands stung. My fingers turned numb. I swung. I thought about what had happened that day. I thought about what had happened the days before. Until I didn't anymore.

43.

I always put the ax back in the shed when I was too tired to lift it up and bring it down. I never tried to take it or the hatchet or the chisels arranged in neat a row above the workbench whose square ends still shone with the oil from the whetstone to school. I didn't. But I understood why kids brought things like these. Why they brought knives and guns. Why they hid them in lockers. In backpacks. Why they held them up, brandished them in wild desperation. I understood the fatalism of the gesture and that it was a gesture. That they meant NO. You have pushed me far enough. I am willing to do the worst thing. And I understood as well that the power of these weapons was not in the way that they wounded and killed, but in the way that they transformed time, in the finality with which they could break the past off from the future. I knew in the same the way that I knew when I needed to feel the weight of the ax in my hands, to feel the crude force of its impact, that they could change everything.

44.

In 1979, Ronald Reagan visited the NORAD command base in the Cheyenne Mountain Complex in Colorado. During the tour of the bunker, the generals showed him the tracking and detection systems they used to monitor the USSR. They explained that these systems could pick up an individual missile almost as soon as it was launched and track it unerringly as it flew over taiga and then the interminable icepacks of the Arctic Ocean, travelling halfway around the globe to its target. They could do this simultaneously for every single missile in the Russian arsenal. When Reagan asked them what else they could do, they said, nothing. Watch. Stare at the cascade of green dots blinking over the top of the world and fanning out as they travelled south towards their targets. Their state-of-the-art equipment, their banks of computers and the rows of grey-green screens which soldiers stared at around the clock meant that they could see the attack coming, but their only option was to absorb it. They could counterattack or not. They could launch before or after the Russian missiles landed. But there was nothing they could do to stop them. At the moment the missiles appeared on the monitors, they became inevitable.

45.

Ronald Reagan always hated the doctrine of Mutually Assured Destruction. He said it was a suicide pact. Russia and the United States were like two men sitting at a table. Each man, he liked to explain, held a loaded gun to the other's temple. They were each at the mercy of the other. They were each staking everything on the hope that the man across from them wouldn't pull the trigger. It was insane, he said. Intolerable. That the most powerful nation on the earth could be reduced like this to trusting its enemy. That his United States of America could be made abject. And what he saw in the Cheyenne Mountain Complex showed him that the doctrine that he already hated in principle was worse in practice than anything that he had imagined. Instead of the brain shutting off before it could even register the sound of the shot, what the generals showed him was a slow-motion apocalypse. ICBMs fired from northern Russia would take 25 to 30 minutes to reach their targets in the continental United States and they would be visible to American monitoring systems for close to the full duration of their flight. Within minutes of their launch, a phone would ring in the White House, and the president would be notified of the destruction bearing down on his country. He would be rushed to the underground bunker and forced to sit there in the stillness of a terrible knowledge, sit there at his desk in a replica of the Oval Office, sit at the center of a world that had spun out of control and wait as the minutes ticked by, sit and wait and watch the clock on the wall because there was nothing else that he could do. No other defence. No other plan. As the generals told him in their war-weary voices, there was nothing.

46.

Reagan's biographers speculate that this visit to the Cheyenne Mountain Complex and the realization that he had there, the understanding that the president would be utterly helpless in the face of a nuclear attack, combined with his hatred of the doctrine of Mutually Assured Destruction to shape his attitude towards Cold War military strategy and explained his unwavering commitment to the Strategic Defence Initiative that he announced in 1983 and that he pursued through both terms of his presidency.

47.

My father rarely talked about his childhood. It was as if the barrier that my parents had placed between themselves and the world also cut through his life and divided before the house from after it. The stories he told about growing up were generic and truncated: he had a friend he built forts with. I wanted to know what kind of forts. He told me, tree forts. He liked Will Rogers and cowboys. He rode his bike around the neighborhood. He wore a cowboy hat and a belt with a cap gun snugged in the holster for Halloween. The one story he told that stood out from the rest, that had enough detail to feel real, was about the time his older brother tied him up with rawhide as part of a game of cowboys and Indians and left him like that in the backyard. My father's brother had soaked the strips of rawhide in water to make them pliable. He tied my father's hands and feet. He was older and stronger than my father and the knots were too tight for my father to untie. I imagine my father lying on his side. His body is bowed backwards. His hands are bound behind him and his feet are tucked up so that he can reach the knots at his ankles with his hands. I can see him fumbling blindly. I can see him go limp and still when he gives up. Wet rawhide shrinks as it dries. It was a summer afternoon and my father lay on the grass in the full sun of an open sky. There was no one in the surrounding houses to hear him call out. His father was at work. His mother took tranquilizers and was dead to the world in his parents' darkened bedroom. The cords crimped tighter. His hands and feet started to tingle as a prelude to losing their feeling. He could tell it was only a matter of time. Someone found him. Someone cut the rawhide and set him free in a rush of pins and needles that was worse than the numbness it replaced. But he never told me who or how long he stayed there bent like a comma on the grass before they found him. The story was not about being rescued. The story was about the way that he lay there alone in the sunlight and the silence of a suburban afternoon. It was about the slow, inevitable bite of the rawhide. And his helplessness.

48.

My father continued to work at Hincks farm, and, by the time I was in school, he was lead manager of the treatment center outside of Meaford. My mother stayed there with him for a while, and then took a position running the Women's Centre in Owen Sound. They saw their jobs as one part of the larger project of making the world a better, safer, more just place, and, when they weren't working, they were both active in the peace movement. On weekends, they met with other young families, other social workers, artists, teachers, the owner of the local independent bookstore, to talk about peace and nuclear disarmament. The adults sat in the living room, and the children went upstairs or outside to play. Sometimes, there were activities that allowed us to contribute to the movement: one Saturday, we were given pages of doves with olive branches in their beaks to cut out and color. At the end of the afternoon, these were collected and glued to a red, three-panel display board that said "Stop Nuclear Proliferation" in white, official letters across the top.

49.

The red and white display was for a booth they set up at an expo that ran for a week in the building where women sold knitting, peanut brittle, fudge and jars of pickles during the fall fair. My parents and I manned it for three evenings. We handed out pamphlets with mushroom clouds on them and buttons that said, "No Bombs." We talked to the people who filtered past about Hiroshima and Nagasaki, about radiation poisoning, nuclear winter and "Star Wars." We told them stories about a secular apocalypse. They were mostly rural people, farmers, or the sons and daughters of farmers. The men hooked their thumbs into their belt loops when they walked and the women wore home permanents. They listened and rocked on their heels as they listened. They looked puzzled, amused and then politely superior. My father with his full beard and gentle voice, my mother with her long straight hair and professional manner, and me talking to them like a grown-up, were beyond their experience. What we were saying didn't belong to their world; it was real, but too distant to matter, too big and strange for them to change or worry about. No one disagreed, no one contradicted us, but no one was persuaded: they never took any of the pamphlets or buttons, and they always moved on, wandering down the line of booths, secure, untouchable, safe in their certainty.

50.

It was not until decades later that I learned that Reagan's plan for defending the United States from a nuclear attack was called the Strategic Defence Initiative. My father followed the lead of Ted Kennedy and always referred to it derisively as "Star Wars." He explained to me that it was a missile defence shield and that the president wanted to put lasers on satellites in space to shoot down incoming nukes. He told me this in the same superior, contemptuous voice with which he told me that the things that happened in my comic books were impossible. In a tone of voice that said that I, the president, everyone should know better. "Star Wars" wasn't just stupid and unrealistic. It was dangerous. Any progress that the United States made towards being able to reliably shoot down incoming ICBMs in midflight was guaranteed to push Russia to develop a response to the American countermeasures and ignite a new arms race. Why couldn't Reagan see, my father sometimes wondered aloud, that, for all of his talk of world peace, for every speech in which he called on scientists to render nuclear weapons impotent and obsolete, even the idea of a ballistic missile defence system was itself an act of aggression? The program would only lead to more and deadlier nukes, not less. It would only escalate tensions between the world's two superpowers and bring us one step closer to total destruction. It was crazy. The only sane course of action, my father said, and repeated in his calm insistent voice until the Cold War ended, was complete nuclear disarmament.

51.

The words that my father used, and I understood, but in a limited, childish way, got mixed up with what I knew about the Star Wars movies. I imagined a deflector shield surrounding the United States. It was a clear blue wall, like a translucent layer of sky, that reached up into the clouds. ICBMS that were hugging the landscape to hide from radar and avoid being shot down slammed into it and broke apart without exploding. They turned into showers of fragments falling harmless through the air. Some of the missiles tried to fly over it, but their engines laboured as they gained altitude, their rockets sputtered with the effort of lifting them, the flames flickered and went out. The long silver tubes tipped over backwards and cartwheeled end-over-end to their destruction. When I learned that there were missiles that flew into space, that took off almost vertically, exited the atmosphere, and then dove back, dropping like lawn darts with fins to guide their descent, my wall turned into a dome. The missiles struck it and rebounded. They hit it at an angle and ricocheted off. Satellites orbited above this pale blue dome. These were versions of the satellites in the comics I read, and I imagined their banks of lights blinking in the cold darkness of space. I saw their wide solar panels spread like wings. The tiny rockets that oriented them towards their targets. And the red lasers reaching out from them like lines of elongated hyphens to destroy the incoming missiles. Even in grade school I knew that none of this was possible. At the Science Centre in Toronto, I had seen a laser that emerged from a box that was as big as a car and ran through a tube that was as long as a room. The pink beam was paler than a flashlight. It had taken seconds, whole distinct heartbeats stretched out by excitement, to set the thin end of a cedar shingle on fire. I knew that none of what I imagined was possible. None of it was real. But I was still captivated by the idea of the unbreachable dome and the streaks of scarlet light reaching unerringly out through the darkness.

52.

The week after the expo, I sat beside Paul in art class. We were at the same round table at the back of the room that we had been at when Will Dekker drew my wood-burning television. While we worked on cutting out paper snowflakes for the Christmas display, I told him everything that I knew about nuclear weapons: just one could blow up Toronto. All of it. Including the CN Tower and Maple Leaf Gardens. The mushroom cloud would be taller than ten CN Towers. He was terrified and fascinated, the way we were all terrified and fascinated by vampires and Darth Vader. The USSR and the United States had thousands of them, hundreds of thousands of them. "Millions?" he asked, and I nodded. Enough to destroy the world a hundred times over. But the USSR was far away? They had missiles that could fly around the world, all the way to Canada. And we live near the Bruce Nuclear Power Plant. We had been there on a school trip earlier that year. We had seen replicas of rods, the concrete structures in which they kept spent fuel bundles, and brightly glazed dishes from the 1950s whose dye set off a Geiger counter. It was the biggest plant in the country. There had to be missiles pointed at it. And nuclear war could happen at any time. Now. Tomorrow. Anytime.

53.

We were both looking out the tall windows on the second floor of Victoria Public School, as if we expected to see white trails reaching across the sky. All of Paul's confidence, all of the reckless ease with which he broke rules, and his casual sadism were gone. He was uncertain, turned inward by fear. My knowledge made me powerful. I possessed something remarkable and captivating, like the time I snuck my father's high-powered bird-watching binoculars and traded the chance to look through them for the right to play on the best soccer team, the one with Will and Paul and Jim Brown, at recess. My friends had crowded around me, and I had decided how long and in what order they looked. I was fair. I didn't let anyone hog them. Paul asked me questions for the rest of the class, and I answered all of them. When I didn't know something, I made it up. I told him that the explosion would disintegrate the people who were too close to it and leave nothing but their silhouettes on the walls behind them. I told him that the radiation would poison the people who were miles away from the blast. I told him that the flesh of the survivors would peel off in strips. And the nuclear fallout would plunge the world into an endless winter. I luxuriated in the details of an elaborate and all-consuming apocalypse.

54.
That weekend, Paul's parents called mine. Paul wasn't sleeping; they mentioned nightmares. My parents discussed the phone call, and my father told me that I had to stop talking about nuclear war at school.

55.
Paul Boisvert was one of the boys who picked the teams, and always a captain—not bigger than the rest of us, but quicker and stronger and surer. Before floor hockey games in the gym, he bent the plastic blade of his stick into a hook. He would smack it hard on the floor. That was the signal to pass to him, and we all did.

56.
Paul had already been playing rep hockey for two years. He knew how to take a slapshot, how to lift your stick with his, put his shoulder into you and steal the orange ball. If you complained that he was rough in the corners or along the wall, he would say, "Toughen up buttercup," and grin; if you stood in his favorite spot by the goal, he would push you out of the way and call you a cherry picker. He scored a lot. Everyone liked him. He knew things about boyhood and about being liked that I would never know.

57.
Paul's ninth birthday was the best. All of the boys from the class were invited. It was in early November, and we played street hockey, getting hot and tired in the cold. We raced back and forth between the nets and barely remembered to keep score. There were hamburgers and chips and pop for dinner, and a Jabba the Hutt cake for dessert. It had thick green icing and quarters baked into it. All the red meat and sugar made me feel sick, but I didn't mind. We watched *Rambo: First Blood* twice, once that evening, and again in the middle of the night when Paul's parents were sleeping, huddled around the television

with the sound turned down. We talked about the movie until we fell asleep, and most of us went home and asked for Rambo knives for Christmas. It was one of those rare islands of happiness in childhood that float up and free of everything else, and that remain there, suspended in memory, untouched by anything that came before or after them.

58.

I never told anyone about what my friends did to me. I never managed to take what I stored up inside of me as I walked back towards the school at the end of the lunch hour and turn it into words. It stayed inside me. Secret. Inert but still dangerous. Like the spent fuel stored under the sun-bleached concrete dome that we saw through the bus windows on our tour of the Bruce Nuclear Power Plant.

59.

The nuclear waste produced by the CANDU reactors at the Bruce Nuclear Power Plant consists of plutonium isotopes (1%), uranium isotopes (96%) and a collection of minor actinides, such as neptunium, americium and curium. The exact distribution of the isotopes depends on the composition and concentration of the fuel and on the efficiency of the reaction process. CANDU reactors are unique in the range of fuels they can use. Although they are specifically designed to use naturally occurring, unenriched uranium, they can be modified to use enriched uranium, mixed fuels and even thorium. Because of this, they are ideally suited for using material from decommissioned nuclear weapons. When fed with this type of fuel, the nuclear waste they produce contains significant amounts of U-233 and U-238, uranium isotopes with half-lives of, respectively, 160, 000 and 4, 468, 000, 000 years.

60.

The exponential decay undergone by uranium isotopes can be described by the equation

$$N(t) = N_0 (1/2) t/t 1/2$$

where

N_0 is the initial quantity of the material ,

$N(t)$ is the quantity of the material that remains active and has not yet decayed,

$t1/2$ is the half-life of the decaying quantity,

t is the amount of time that has passed.

On a graph, this equation produces a curve that begins at the y-axis as an almost vertical line that drops sharply toward the x-axis and then stretches out into a gentle slope declining towards but never touching zero. The figure is unremarkable except for the units of time on the x-axis which, in the case of both U-233 and U-238, measure years in exponential units of ten, in geographical time that reaches forward, that dispenses altogether with the human moment of its making as it accelerates into the future.

61.
Ontario Power Generation, the company that runs the Bruce Nuclear Power Plant, is currently considering a plan to bury the nuclear waste produced by its eight reactors deep underground in a storage facility next to the plant. To entomb it in the same grey limestone that rises to the surface and pitches up north of Owen Sound to form the Kemble Rock and the plateau on which my parents' house sits.

62.
The bullying decreased over time, but more slowly than I hoped. There were good days and bad days. And then more good days than bad days. And then good months. Good years. Paul was the one who kept it up the longest, but even he became less violent over time, more casual about it, less committed to the extravagances of his childhood viciousness. By the end, he didn't even touch me. He fake-punched me to make me flinch and laughed at me when I did. He only punched me for real if I braced myself and refused to cringe away from him. And then he only hit me on the shoulder. With the first knuckle of his fist. Hard enough to bruise. But no harder than one of us punched the other in the arm if we were the first to spot an oncoming a car with a burnt-out headlight.

63.
My friendship with Paul was inconsistent. We would be close, and then he would drift away, sometimes for weeks, sometimes for years: I went to his house a few times. I saw the Big Rig wallpaper in his bedroom. He could name the trucks. We played video games. We played *Captain Power*, shooting at the screen with special guns when the show came on YTV. We talked about girls. I was tentative. I watched him to see if what I said was right. He was loud. He was eager. He said he was never going to get married. He wanted a different girl every week. He wanted a different girl every day. He wanted to sharpen his dick like a pencil so that he could write his name in their vaginas. He skateboarded. He covered the wallpaper with posters of skateboarders. We planned to build a halfpipe with the scrap wood my father kept in the barn. We never did. My parents noticed that I swore more when I hung out with him. He was the first one of us to buy Ice-T's

Power. He wore his hockey jacket and baggy khakis. The vice principal of our junior high school ran over his skateboard at the entrance to the parking lot. He said she did it on purpose. She sped up. She swerved to hit it. She denied it. And there was no riding skateboards on school property. He wouldn't let it go. He talked about it for days. He repeated himself. He needed us to believe it was wrong as fiercely as he did. He needed us to agree that something had to be done. He confronted her in her office. She suspended him for a week. We had a video dance in the gym. He asked a young substitute teacher to dance. She was taller than him. She had big tits. She laughed like it was a joke. She said yes. He didn't make the rep team. He was good. But not that good. He still played hockey. But not as intently. He started to change. He wore army surplus pants and plaid shirts. He grew his hair long. He bought a guitar. He bought a pair of fourteen-hole cherry Doc Martens. He smoked. He dropped gym. He took drama. The drama room at our high school had a carpeted floor and carpeted walls. You had to take off your shoes. He was always late for the next class because it took him so long to put on his boots. He started a band. It was called *Grind Orchard.* He was the lead singer. They played at the Christmas assembly. There were nine of them. They filled up the stage. They played noisy, distorted songs. You could tell the chorus because they all knew it. They played a grunge version of "Little Red Wagon." He shouted the lyrics at the top of his lungs. He wanted everyone to shout along. Some of us did. He threw himself around. He climbed onto the back of one of the bassists. They staggered across the stage. He rear-ended someone on the 6th Street hill. He had bald tires. It was raining. It was November. He said the brakes locked up. He hydroplaned. No one believed him. He drove to Toronto to see The Flaming Lips. The show was in a bar. He was seventeen. He begged. The bouncer let him in, but only after he wrote "Underage" and "Don't Serve" in permanent marker on Paul's face. He loved Screaming Trees. He tried to convince me they were good. He gave me a mixed tape of their best songs. I didn't want it. He made me take it. He played Algernon Moncrief in our Grade 13 production of *The Importance of Being Earnest.* He wore a three-piece suit and a bow tie. He stuttered for effect. He ate cucumber sandwiches on stage. He knocked over a section of the backdrop at the end of the first act. It smashed a copy of the Aphrodite of Melos that was part of the set. I was on the crew. I swept up the fragments during intermission. He apologized to the art teacher who had loaned it to the production. He organized coffeehouses in the basement of the library. He played Neil Young covers. He played his own songs. They were clumsy, sincere imitations of songs I recognized. I went to university. He went to Waterloo to work and play in a band. He was still eager. He was still loud. He wanted to be liked. And he was vulnerable because of that.

64.

I did a double major in English and Philosophy at Trent University in Peterborough. In the middle of the Fall term of my third year, I came back to Owen Sound for my grandfather's eightieth birthday. I left my parents and both sets of grandparents playing hearts at the kitchen table in the evening and drove to the east side Tim Hortons, the one at the top of the 10th Street hill. It was where we had gathered in high school, where we went when we skipped classes, and in the summer, filling the patio on long hot evenings. We went to find out who was having a party or to wait listlessly for something to happen. Paul was sitting in the smoking section writing and crossing out song lyrics in a notebook.We were both bored and wanted to do something.

65.

I left my car in the parking lot. Paul drove us to the liquor store to buy whiskey and then to Brendan Stewart's house outside of Keady. I hadn't seen Paul since high school, and I was awkward, closed off: I looked through the tape collection in his glove box. We smoked and blew the smoke out the barely open windows. He talked in a fast, excited way about Waterloo. He had a job in a coffee shop and bakery. He made the bagels. It wasn't that bad. They had different kinds. He listed them.

On the country roads, the car drove down the corridor of its headlights. I couldn't tell where we were going.

There was a window between the bakery and the coffee shop so he could talk to the customers and pick up girls while he worked. A lot of students came in. University girls. He liked university girls. He liked talking to them. They taught him things. His band was getting a lot of gigs. They were planning a tour: Toronto, Kingston, Ottawa, Northern Ontario, and as far into the prairies as they could manage. He wanted to know what I was taking.

I watched the shoulder of the road.

I told him.

He loved philosophy. A girl had left a copy of The Republic in his bedroom and he had read it over a weekend. And that opened me up. And I talked about Plato and the cave and the shadows dancing on the walls of the cave until we got to Brendan's.

66.

Brendan and Ben Huntley were sitting next to a bonfire on the front lawn. They said they were expecting more people, but they never came. We sat down with them and drank the whiskey and talked about friends we knew from high school, where they were, how they were doing, but mostly what we remembered about them.

We got a little drunk.

The day before, Paul had played a game of hockey at the Bayshore Coliseum, "For old time's sake," he said, and it had almost killed him. "Smoker's lungs," he said. He laughed about it, but not bitterly. I could see that he was getting heavy around the waist, and broader everywhere, in the hips and face, growing into his adult frame and the habit of drinking: he was not fat yet, but I thought he would be in ten years.

67.

"I used to beat him up in grade school," Paul said to the other two. "Remember," he said to me. It wasn't vicious. He was smiling, half-disbelieving and warm: it connected us, and I could see that, for Paul, it was a personal measure of how much had changed. "Remember how I used to make you flinch."

He fake-punched me and I winced.

I cuffed his head.

He caught my hand and we struggled.

He tried to bend my fingers back and I pulled away.

"I could take you now," I said. I was taller than him. I had lost weight since high school and watched my body change in bathroom mirrors. I rode my mountain bike along the trail beside the river from downtown Peterborough to campus, sometimes even in winter, did push-ups in my bedroom and liked to think I was strong. "I bet I could beat you in a wrestling match."

Paul didn't want to wrestle. His smile gave a little, became unsettled and apologetic. I could tell that I was asking him to become a version of himself that he had almost forgotten, someone I remembered more clearly than he did. It was ridiculous and juvenile, and I knew it. I insisted.

68.

We squared off on the lawn and circled, hunched, arms out, measuring each other. I was serious. I tried to be mean and focused. Paul was still smiling: he had not yet committed to his role and he waited for me. I lunged, driving with my legs, trying to catch him off guard. He grabbed my shoulders, angled me off him with his hips, and pushed me away. I felt his strength: his body was more solid, sturdier and harder, more substantial than mine, and he knew instinctively how to move. This was what I imagined I had, honest force, man strength. I couldn't beat him, and I kept trying.

Brendan and Ben watched us.

I lunged again, and he grabbed me again, but this time he held me. I worked to throw him off balance. My body felt light and remote. Paul leaned into me and wrestled me to the ground. He let me up. The grass was rough and slick with dew. I was hot, fatalistic. I tried several more times, searching for a weakness, not expecting to find one. Finally, he pinned me. I struggled. For a minute, he returned to his childhood sadism: he grinned and let me struggle, clamped down, eased off and clamped down. I fought him when I could, but I was helpless. He put his full weight on me.

"I'm done," I said.

He waited.

"Done."

He relaxed. He laughed and helped me up. I was disappointed, but not ashamed or embarrassed. I had lost, but I hadn't failed. This was predictable. It made sense, and it felt right and satisfying and unbearable.

We went back to the fire.

69.

Brendan and Ben went to bed. Paul and I stayed up drinking. He wanted to talk more about Plato. I did, quick, loosened by the whiskey, punctuating sentences with my cigarette, but it had been a year since I had read him, and I preferred Nietzsche and Rorty and the anecdotes professors told about Wittgenstein to the Greeks. I moved from *The Republic* to *The Birth of Tragedy*, monologued on the difference between Dionysian and Apollonian, and segued to Hegel. Paul was confused but fascinated. He kept saying, "Interesting," and he meant it. He nodded along with me.

We emptied the bottle.

"Schlegelmacherhauer," I said, "the Swiss-German idealist, is the most interesting." It was a joke my friends and I had made in a course on continental philosophy we had taken the year before. And I meant it as a joke. But Paul nodded, and I couldn't resist his sincerity: "Reality, Schlegelmacherhauer argues, is the collection of our shared thoughts about reality. The world is both communal and notional, a civitas of ideas. And history is the subjective collective coming to know itself of the community of mind. He was Hegel without the totalizing mania. As passionate as Schopenhauer. As radical as Nietzsche. The best of German philosophy. His *Discourse on the Phenomenology of the Common Mind...*" And so on. I almost believed myself, and Paul believed me. He listened and thought hard about what I said.

I talked until the fire burned down.

70.

We slept on the couches in the living room. At dawn, Paul drove me back to the east side Tim Hortons. In the parking lot, before I walked back to my car, he asked me the name of that book, the one he should read, and I couldn't remember.

71.

Paul's band never made it to the prairies. Jim Brown told me about Paul fighting a bouncer in Hamilton because the club owed them money. He had heard it was bad: something happened to Paul's face, he said, but he didn't know the details.

72.

Paul went to Europe. He wandered from France into Germany, and, from there, found his way to Western Poland and the city of Poznan. He ran an English language hockey school and lived in a third-floor apartment in a building with a pale-yellow facade for the better part of a decade. That was where he was when we had our ten-year high school reunion. He called the restaurant the reunion was at and the roomful of people shouted, "Hi Paul!" into the phone.

73.

The Strategic Defence Initiative that Reagan announced in 1983 left a long and complex legacy that runs like a thread through American politics. If you pick it up in the middle of the '80s, it will lead you out of the fog of the Cold War through the interregnum of the nineties into the fear and confusion of the war on terror in the new century. Teams of military scientists and engineers tested and rejected x-ray lasers, chemical lasers, neutral particle beams and hypervelocity rail guns. Some of these were mounted on satellites and tested in space, but none of them yielded more than mixed results, and, in the case of the x-ray laser test known as the CABRA event, the positive readings could be attributed to a faulty sensor. By the end of the '80s, the Strategic Defence Initiative Organization, the group tasked with bringing Reagan's vision to fruition, had shifted their focus away from lasers and energy weapons to a satellite-based interceptor system called Brilliant Pebbles that fired kinetic tear-drop shaped projectiles at incoming warheads. Brilliant Pebbles was found to be technically feasible by four separate military reports, but the project fell victim to the changing political climate at the end of the Cold War, and, in his State of the Union address, George H. W. Bush announced a shift in focus from the Strategic Defence Initiative to GPALS or the Global Protection Against Limited Strikes plan. Instead of aiming to stop thousands of incoming missiles fired specifically and exclusively from Russia, this new system's goal was to provide perfect protection from up to two hundred nuclear missiles fired from anywhere in the world. Brilliant Pebbles remained at the core of the GPALS system, but it was augmented by a new generation of ground-based missile interceptors and a cohort of low-orbit detection satellites called Brilliant Eyes. In 1993,

Bill Clinton shuttered the Strategic Defence Initiative Organization, created the BDMO or the Ballistic Missile Defence Organization, and shifted the focus of research and development entirely to ground-based interceptor missiles. Brilliant Pebbles and Reagan's dream of a space-based defence system were officially dead, but his deep-seated belief that the United States must find a way to shoot down incoming nuclear missiles lived on. In the mid to late '90s, driven by a Republican-dominated Congress whose members were rabidly committed to military development, the BDMO designed and successfully tested several generations of PAC-2 and PAC-3 Phased Array Tracking Radar to Intercept on Target or PATRIOT Missiles. In 2002, as part of a post 9/11 push to implement a fully functional missile defence shield, George W. Bush renamed the BDMO the Missile Defence Agency or MDA and widened its mandate. The MDA mission statement, written in 2002 and preserved on their website to this day, begins:

> *The Missile Defence Agency's (MDA) mission is to develop and deploy a layered Missile Defence System to defend the United States, its deployed forces, allies, and friends from missile attacks in all phases of flight.*

Development has continued on a series of ground-based interceptor missiles and the agency still funds research on a wide variety of defensive options, including mobile kinetic energy interceptors and airborne laser systems carried by high-altitude planes. The Boeing YAL-1 Airborne Laser, for example, is fired from a turret mounted on the nose of a refurbished 747. This rather commonplace plane is a far cry from an orbital satellite, but it and the experimental payload it carries to altitudes of up to 12 km nevertheless preserve something of Reagan's original vision of an arsenal of space-based lasers defending the United States from nuclear threats.

74.

From its inception, the idea of a missile defence shield faced staunch criticism from the scientific community. In the 1960s, when Edward Teller, the father of the hydrogen bomb, proposed using nuclear warheads to intercept and destroy enemy ICBMs, in effect canceling an attack with an equal, reciprocal force, physicists Richard L. Garwin and Hans A. Bethe argued, among other things, that rudimentary enemy countermeasures could easily foil even Teller's interceptor missiles and that any national defence system was fated to be technologically ineffective. Teller's idea was madness, they explained. But not for the obvious reasons. It wasn't overkill. It wasn't bringing a comically large gun to a fistfight. It was, for all its callous hubris, virtually guaranteed to fail. What Garwin and Bethe understood in the 1960s and what analysts of missile defence programs such as George N. Lewis, Theodore A. Postol and John Pike continue to explain to this day, is that the structure of the engagement places the defender at an insurmountable disadvantage. The problem is a simple one. You are trying to hit a relatively tiny object moving at close to the upper range of speeds reached by conventional rockets with another equally tiny, equally fast-moving object. It is like trying to shoot a bullet out of the air, missile defence system critics are fond of saying, with another bullet. This is difficult, but achievable. What pushes the task of reliably intercepting incoming missiles beyond the ever-receding horizon of the possible is the introduction of countermeasures. A country capable of producing an ICBM is also capable of outfitting it with any number of relatively simple countermeasures.

75.

In an article published three decades after and in the very same journal as Garwin and Bethe's initial critique of missile defence systems, Lewis, Postol and Pike list sixteen separate countermeasures falling under four distinct categories. The list is suggestive rather than exhaustive. Their point is that the range of possible countermeasures is limited only by the inventiveness of the enemy. More importantly, even the most rudimentary countermeasure requires a substantial increase in the technological sophistication of a defensive system that hopes to reliably defeat it. In mathematical terms, the technological superiority of the defensive system must grow exponentially in relation to the technological sophistication of the countermeasures deployed by the attacker. This relationship can be described by the first quadratic equation learned by students in high school:

$y=x2$

where

> *y is the threshold of technological advancement the defender must exceed to reliably intercept missiles , and*

> *x is the technological sophistication of the countermeasures deployed by the attacker.*

It is a simple equation with a remorseless logic. When graphed, it yields a parabola that resembles the curve expressing the exponential decay of radioactive material rotated counter clockwise by 90°. It is the slantwise reflection of the half-life of the uranium isotopes that are soon to be locked up in a storage facility built into the layers of limestone on which my parents' house sits. As it leaves the y axis, the line bends away from the x axis and transitions almost immediately from a steep curve to a nearly vertical cliff that breaks through the upper limit of the graph long before it reaches its right-hand side. The filament of safety escapes from every figure. It tilts out of reach. And Reagan's dream of rendering the world's stockpiles of nuclear weapons obsolete disappears with it into the emptiness above the page. That line bending upwards on the graph reveals in its ruthless simplicity the lie of missile defence, that it can never be anything more or less than a long con, a false and empty promise, leading, not to peace, but to war without end.

76.

My father ran the Hincks Farm rural treatment center until he resigned from the position in 1987 at the age of thirty-nine. He took several years off, during which he worked around the house, tending and expanding the gardens, planting and weeding long rows of vegetables in a plot on the far side of the orchard in which my brother and I no longer dodged between the trees playing at war. He experimented with canning, and taught himself to bake pies with lattice crusts and loaves of dense whole wheat bread sweetened with honey and moistened with cottage cheese. In 1989, he founded the Men's Program, a group counselling program for men who have abused their intimate partners. The program began as a single group that met on a weeknight in a conference room in the basement of the Owen Sound Children's Aid Society, but my father built it up from half-a-dozen reticent men sitting in a circle of office chairs in a mostly deserted building with the mid-winter darkness pressing against the small, high window at the end of the room to a collection of groups meeting across Grey and Bruce counties, in Wiarton, Port Elgin, Sauble Beach, Walkerton and Meaford, and a permanent office space in a storefront on the main street of Owen Sound a block down from City Hall. In 2002, he was awarded the YMCA Peace Medal for his work to end domestic violence in families and violence against women. Four years later, he retired, passed the management of the program on to one of the other counselors, and went back to the gardens that were now bigger than they had ever been and took more of his time with each passing year.

77.

My partner and I drove up from London, where we were both working on our PhDs, to attend my father's retirement party. It was in the middle of winter. The car was small and low to the ground. It had snowed through the night and into the morning. The plows had not yet cleared the highway. Long stretches of it were blown over, and cars in front of us had ground the drifts into a dense, half-frozen slush. Even when we kept our tires in the ruts, chunks of ice clunked against the undercarriage. The car shuddered. The engine laboured like we were climbing a hill. And we weren't sure that we were going to make it until we drove through Rockford, and a few minutes later the road dropped away into the valley carved by the Sydenham river, toward the city of Owen Sound.

78.

My father's retirement party consisted of two separate events: the first was an official ceremony and reception in the afternoon at the Men's Program office, and the second was a potluck at a friend's house that evening. Friends, family, colleagues and officials went to the first, and only friends and family went to the second.

79.

We parked behind the market and walked to the office. We hung our coats on the rack inside the front door. We talked to people I remembered from my childhood. We talked to people who recognized me from the pictures on my father's desk, but whose names he had only ever mentioned in passing and who I had never met before. After we were done talking, we discovered that there was nowhere to sit. We stood in a corner holding cups of lukewarm coffee from a stainless steel coffee urn and waited for the official ceremony to begin. We listened to the man who was taking over the program from my father welcome everyone and speak at length about what he had learned from working alongside him for close to ten years. He talked into a mic on a stand that hummed when his mouth got too close to it. He remembered the long winter drives to the Walkerton group and what he and my father had shared on them. They were colleagues, he said. They were friends. I watched my father watch the man who was replacing him as he talked. My father's eyes were clear and bright. We listened to Larry Miller, the Member of Parliament for Bruce-Grey-Owen Sound, give a short speech about my father's contribution to the community. Miller was a lifelong Conservative in the middle of his second term. No one in the room had voted for him. No one liked him. But everyone was impressed by him being there in that room with them and by what it said about my father. We saw Larry Miller hook his thumbs into his belt loops and rock on his heels. We listened to my father's colleagues talk about him one after the other through the humming of the mic. The small crowd laughed at their stories. My father spoke last. We listened to him thank everyone for coming. He told us how important this was to him. He sounded like he meant it. Like this moment and the people gathered together in this overheated room with worn grey carpets and too few chairs and fluorescent lights that made the darkness gathering in the late afternoon outside the floor-to-ceiling windows seem duller and heavier than it was. Like all of this, even Larry Miller, mattered tremendously to him.

80.

The speeches finished. The small crowd broke up into smaller groups. We left. It was too early to go to the potluck, so we drove around Owen Sound.

The snowbanks were low and dirty. The streetlights came on. I pointed out landmarks from my childhood. Neither of us pretended to care about them. It was something we did to fill the time. The whole city felt small and distant. Nothing we looked at mattered.

81.

We went to the potluck and sat on the end of a couch and ate off of plates balanced on our knees. We noticed that the people there were the same as the people at the official ceremony but friendlier and closer together. We listened to them talk about my father. About when they had first met him. About what they remembered from working with him. We listened to them talk about what his life as they knew it had amounted to. We leaned forward and listened carefully to a man who looked like he was the same age as me. He told the room about being fresh out of his Masters in Social Work Management. "I thought I knew it all." Everyone who had gone silent and leaned forward like us because he was a man with a loud voice who was explaining himself. "And then I sat in on one of your father's groups," he said directly to me. "I realized how much I still had to learn." To this day he was taking lessons from him. My father was one of the most generous teachers and mentors that he had met in his life, said this man with a loud voice who looked like he was the same age as me, whose name I hadn't caught over the noise of several conversations happening at once, and who I would never see again.

82.

The potluck went on. We talked a little. We listened more. We left after a few hours. It was late. We had to drive back to London. The plows had worked through the day. The roads were clear and empty. The car felt like it never stopped accelerating. The distance was a long silence stretching out behind us.

83.

My father had no qualifications for the work that he did for the duration of his life and that we gathered to celebrate at that office on Main Street and then in the crowded rooms of a friend's house. He did a BA in Environmental Studies at Waterloo in the second half of the sixties. Environmental Studies. Not psychology like my mother. Or social work. He got his first fulltime job at a halfway house for troubled teens in Toronto because it was the kind of position that no one wanted. You had to live in the house and oversee the kids twenty-four hours a day, seven days a week. He was hired at Hincks Farm because the organization was only a few years old and it was run by young people like him who cared more about who you were than what you had done. He never did anything to make up for his lack of training. He never went to any seminars or retreats. There were no long weekends away from which he came back tired but alive with new ideas. He never went back to school. And he never tried to teach himself all the things that he hadn't learned and didn't know. When my mother did a Masters of Social Work in the middle of the eighties, there was a shelf next to the desk in the upstairs hallway that she filled with books, binders of photocopied articles separated by beige dividers with colorful plastic tags, and bundles of class notes. My father never read anything other than novels. There were no textbooks or treatment manuals with pens stuck in them to mark his place on his bedside table or in the magazine rack next to his favorite chair in the living room. The handful of books on the metal shelf above his desk in the Men's Program office were outlined in dust. And in the early two thousands he was still using the little bit that he had learned about Erik Erikson in the Introduction to Psychology course he had sat through more than thirty years ago to teach the men he was counselling about childhood development and building healthy relationships with their families.

84.

When I tell people about his lack of qualifications, they look at me blankly. A tiny wrinkle of confusion creases their foreheads. Not so much a crevasse of uncertainty as the lightest of lines in the skin drawing tight between their eyebrows. They can't see what I have told them as a criticism. I try a different approach. I ask them to imagine that he was an electrician who did wiring in houses for three decades without any training or making any effort to teach himself the trade. And then they see it. Their eyes widen. The line deepens. Their forehead crimps and that single vertical slash multiplies into a constellation of brackets. They imagine a short fizzling into flames. The fire spreading slow until it roars to full life. Eats through the studs. Climbs the walls. Cascades across the ceilings. They see the house, the commonplace material object, turning into a silhouette of itself against the roiling red-orange of the conflagration, becoming more tenuous, until it collapses in a shower of sparks and a mushrooming cloud of smoke. This imagined destruction makes the way that people can be transformed into wreckage real. It makes it tangible. I remind them that my father didn't work with live current. He worked, first, with traumatized teenagers who were mostly homeless and living on the streets of Toronto before being taken into the Hincks Farm treatment program, and, then, with men who had been convicted of beating their girlfriends and wives. And the person I am talking to understands. But only because they don't know and have never met him.

85.

If I said the same thing to the friends and colleagues gathered together at his retirement party, they would never accept it. They couldn't deny the basic facts. The BA in Environmental Studies. The books in their outlines of dust. But they would refuse their implications. They are too close. Too close to him. To the narrative of his career. To the three decades of anecdotes they passed back and forth over the plates balanced on their knees. This is how stories work. They are shields to save us from what we don't want to see. And my father's story, as his friends and colleagues know and tell it, is perfect from beginning to end. A better bulwark than the Kemble Rock. As simple and impossible as the idea of missile defence. The lives of the people who he has treated, the lives of their partners and children, whole constellations of people have come hurtling towards him, already out of control, already tracking the trajectories of their destruction, and ricocheted off. All of them. Every last one of them has been sent cartwheeling away while he has stood there in the middle of the story of his life. Stood there alone, blameless and invulnerable.

86.

I wrote the preceding three sections in the middle of winter, in the same month when, almost a decade and a half earlier, I drove up to Owen Sound to attend my father's retirement party. I wrote them when there was a different snow on the roads, but it was the same depth and texture as the snow I remembered from that tense drive north along highway 6. I wrote them after being estranged from my father for more than a dozen years. I wrote them with what my father and others had told me and with my memories of my life when it still contained him. I wrote them all at once over several hours one morning in my office at the university where I teach. The door was closed. People walked by in the hallway. They stopped to chat in front of the mailboxes that are directly across the hall. Their keys jingled when they unlocked the small silver doors. I could hear their voices. Words. Sometimes whole sentences drifted into my mind like so many motes of dust, broke apart and disappeared. By the time I was done, I was late for a class and the light of a cloudless, midwinter noon was blazing through my window and washing out my laptop screen. I finished them, and, the following day, I moved on to the next section. I kept writing. But I couldn't move on from the details of my father's qualifications, from the work that he had done or the people whose lives had collided with and rebounded from his.

87.

Three months after I finished writing about my father's education and the work that he did, I contacted an acquaintance through Facebook who was an alumnus of The University of Waterloo, and who could access their graduation records. He confirmed that Clark Schneider, my father, graduated with a Bachelor of Environmental Studies in Geography in 1971. In the academic calendar from the year of his graduation, I read about the program he took, and the required courses that formed the core of its curriculum:

Year 1	Geography 101* Introduction to Human Geography
	Geography 102* Introduction to Physical Geography
	Five courses chosen after consultation with the department
Year 2	Geography 200* Biogeography and Ecology
	Geography: 201* Climatology and Geomorphology
	Geography 202* Economic and Urban Geography

and so on...

The man I grew up with could tell me the names of clouds. He could point at the sky and say "Cirrus," "Cumulus," "Cirrocumulus." He could pick out the grey angle of rain on the horizon. I could find no more of him than this in the calendar and its list of courses.

88.

This discovery was a victory, a vicious confirmation of my suspicions and his inadequacy. For the spring and into the summer, I had this degree to hold against him. I turned it over. I said "a Bachelor of Environmental Studies in Geography" aloud to myself in several different tones of voice. And I thought about what it told me about him, about the work that he had done and the story that he had written with his life, until saying it and thinking about it weren't enough.

89.

In the middle of August, I contacted the man who had taken over the Men's Program from my father and arranged to speak to him on the phone. I stood at the breakfast bar in my kitchen on a Sunday morning with my earbuds in my ears and my cellphone on the counter in front of me ticking out the seconds of the call. Sometimes I lifted the microphone to my mouth to make sure that I was heard clearly. Sometimes I let it dangle free, listened and took notes on a lined pad that sat next to the phone. He was the same man who had spoken into the humming mic at my father's retirement party about their long winter drives to Walkerton. He had been there at the beginning of the program and had worked alongside my father until his retirement. He was both my father's colleague and his friend. He was happy to talk. He walked me through the history of the program and what they did in the groups. He told me about how and why they did it. He described Ellen Pence's Power and Control Wheel. He went on a long digression about the nature of patriarchy.

I leaned on the wood of the breakfast bar and let his words flow over me. He finished and I told him what I had learned about my father's degree and his lack of formal qualifications. He agreed with me. He told me that my father had presented as a social worker. I was confused by how easily he said this and surprised by his confidence. He told me that my father had been good at pulling the community together. He explained that critical thinking around gender issues was more important than all of this counseling stuff. And what was most important of all was wanting to change the culture of men.

90.
I knew that I had to contact my father. I had to lay out what I had confirmed and allow him to respond. I told people that I needed to do this. It was necessary, I said, unavoidable. I had an obligation to do it, and I had my parents' shared email address, but I couldn't bring myself to send the email. I opened blank documents. I stared at the cursor blinking at the top of the page and closed them. I delayed through the fall and into the winter until I couldn't delay anymore: in the middle of the COVID-19 pandemic and the second provincial lockdown, when I and anyone who was not an essential worker was confined to their home, a year after writing those sections in one sitting in my office while fragments of what my colleagues were saying in the hall filtered in to me, I sent him a series of questions that I typed out at a different desk under a different window in the same February light. I formatted them in a bulleted list, and they were targeted, impersonal, terse: I asked him about his training and qualifications. I asked him about testifying in court and about the basis on which he had offered that testimony. My questions were meant to catch him off guard, to surprise him into revealing himself, to hurt him into honesty. They were an attack on his work, but they were more than that: each sentence was a projectile whose trajectory tracked through a fissure I thought I had opened in the myth of my father, a line I sent arching through his defences, bending towards the mystery of the man himself at the center of his solitude.

91.
His initial reply was brief. He told me that he and my mother were well and explained that they were perfectly situated for self-isolation. They were keeping busy with work around the house. They had a new Spinone puppy for company. He said that he was confused by my questions. He would need to think about how to answer them. I reiterated them and waited until several days later he sent me a PDF file about his work with the Men's Program that ran to four single spaced pages and was accompanied by a short history of the Program that he had written when he retired.

92.

In the fourth paragraph of the PDF, he responded to my questions about his training and qualifications. He confirmed that he had a BA in Environmental Studies, but explained that he did not go directly from it into working at the Men's Program. "Prior to engaging in the intensive Men's Program training," he wrote, "I had eighteen years of experience working in mental health that involved working with teens and their families. This also involved extensive on-the-job training as well as workshops in milieu therapy, group facilitation, psychiatric assessment, nonviolent crisis intervention, psychopathology, addiction..." With the exception of the "intensive Men's Program training," which his history of the Men's Group told me lasted at most two months and ended with a weekend long retreat, there were no details in these sentences. Eighteen years of experience, but nothing concrete. No names of programs. Courses. Certificates. Organizations. Instructors. Experts he learned from. Nothing tangible. Nothing that could be tracked down and verified. The words floated free, detached from whatever referents they might have had: "intensive" "extensive." Even the nouns were on the verge of turning into adjectives. The list of workshops itself tilted towards absurdity: a psychiatric assessment is a complex process that should only be carried out by an expert with substantial formal training. An assessment can be done by a doctor, a psychologist, a psychiatrist, a nurse, a social worker or a community mental health worker, but only a doctor, a psychologist or a psychiatrist can give a patient an official diagnosis. Psychopathology is a field of study with introductory, upper year and graduate courses, specializations and sub-specializations. Addiction is similarly complex. These sentences, the only sentences in the document in which he specifically addressed his training, were at once charged with resentment, and strangely casual, off handed, as if the words themselves were enough. And, for him, they were enough. He stopped his discussion of his qualifications there.

93.

Two pages later, he returned to the question of his training, and of why he felt equipped to do the work that he did with the Men's Program, but not to offer any additional details. He wrote: "Many of your questions [...] are aimed at personalizing [The Men's Program] to my experience. You say that I have no meaningful training or accreditation and you wonder how I felt I was equipped to do the work. I think the best way that I can respond to this is that I was asked by the community organizations on our advisory group and by my peers to take the lead in the program. I believe that I was placed in my position and worked in directing the Men's Program and My Dad's Group because of the trust given to me by my clients, my peers, my supervisor, my board of directors and the professionals I deal with regularly in all the complementary services and systems in our area. I began in trust, I continued in trust and I believe I never betrayed that trust."

94.

Trust is a "firm belief in the reliability, truth, or ability of someone or something[, a] confidence or faith in a person or thing, or in an attribute of a person or thing." The philosopher Carolyn McLeod explains that "trust is important, but it is also dangerous. It is important because it allows us to depend on others—for love, for advice, for help with our plumbing, or what have you. [...] But trust also involves the risk that people we trust will not pull through for us, since if there were some guarantee they would pull through, then we would have no need to trust them. Trust is therefore dangerous. What we risk while trusting is the loss of valuable things that we entrust to others, including our self-respect perhaps, which can be shattered by the betrayal of our trust." She lays out a set of generally agreed upon conditions under which someone may reasonably be trusted. "Trust is warranted," she says, "that is:

> plausible [...] only if the conditions required for trust exist [...],
>
> well-grounded, only if the trustee (the one trusted) is trustworthy [...],
>
> justified, sometimes when the trustee is not in fact trustworthy [...],
>
> justified, often because some value will emerge from the trust or because it is valuable in and of itself [...],
>
> plausible, only when it is possible for one to develop trust, given one's circumstances and the sort of mental attitude trust is [...]

She then points out that trust makes us "vulnerable to others—vulnerable to betrayal in particular" and to the results of that betrayal.

95.

In trusting, we take on the liability of relying on the person whom we trust and the risk of investing them with our trust. Trust shifts accountability and with it a measure of culpability from the person who is trusted to the one who trusts. It displaces responsibility. In the case of a betrayal, some of the blame rebounds towards the person who trusted. The inverse is also true. To be trusted is to be, at least in part, protected, immune. The trust. In trust. Trust. As in their belief in him. As in their confidence in him. As in their faith in him. As in yet another word he has closed around himself like a wall.

96.

On the final page of the PDF, he turned to our estrangement. He was as confused by it as he was by the email I had sent him several days ago. He said that he was willing to answer any questions I might have about it. He wrote: "May I dare to suggest that some insight for you is actually hiding in plain sight. I am here and I am willing to engage." He invited me towards him. The door, he told me, was open. The door will always be open. And because of that, he is untouchable. Beyond reproach.

97.

My father stands in the middle of the story of his life. He smiles a calm, detached smile.

98.

There is nothing inside of his smile.

99.

Paul came back to Canada and found work at Le Jardin des Découvertes, a French language daycare in Owen Sound. His father's side of the family were francophones from Timmins and Paul had always spoken a quick and slangy Canadian French.

100

He organized a campaign to create a French Quarter in the city by changing the street signs around the daycare from English to French. There was an article about it on the *Owen Sound Sun Times*' website. It included a picture of Paul and a copy of the letter he wrote to the city council. In the picture, he stood at a crosswalk and held up a lopsided cardboard stop sign made by the kids that said "ARRÊT" in white letters glued to a bright red background. He was paunchy and unshaven. He wore olive cargo shorts and a plaid shirt that was too big for him. He smiled enthusiastically into the camera. In the letter, he wrote clumsily about the need to foster diversity and promote bilingualism:

Dear Briana,

I am writing on behalf of Le Jardin des Découvertes, a French preschool on 23rd street East in Owen Sound. We are writing to inform you that we are very interested in creating an unofficial 'French Quarter' in Owen Sound where our preschool is located. In doing so, we were hoping that there might be a chance of changing the two 'STOP' signs around our school to bilingual 'STOP/ARRÊTE' signs; the first located where 23rd Street meets 8th Avenue East and the second where 23rd meets 9th Avenue. We feel the benefits are twofold.

The first is educationally. Studies have shown that children acquire a second language when the target language and culture is viewed positively within their own community. By changing the 'STOP' signs, we feel it would help our community move towards providing validation to French students all over the city, that French is part of our heritage, and that it is regarded highly within our community. In no way are we suggesting that changing a couple of signs from 'STOP' to 'STOP/ ARRÊTE' would be the ultimate solution to language acquisition, we are merely stating that symbolically, it would be more than another step in the journey of our cultural growth within the community.

The second benefit would be culturally. By establishing a 'French Quarter' in Owen Sound, even if it is unofficial, you offer something to the city that other places in both Grey and Bruce County do not have. Again, it is purely symbolic, yet it gives character to this wonderful city, and brings to light just how much French and French culture is part of this city. From a tourism perspective, imagine being able to say that Owen Sound offers a French Carnaval (as we are planning this summer) and to be able to say it is in the 'French Quarters' of town. Perhaps it will never overshadow the other wonderful events that take place in the city, but even Summer Folk started as a couple of bands just playing in the park.

Thank you again for your time and patience.

Sincerely

Paul Boisvert

101.

He presented the request to city council, and they voted 6 to 3 in favor.

102.

If you go to Owen Sound, you can find Le Jardin des Découvertes next to the École Saint-Dominique-Savio French language primary school in the same building it was in when Paul worked there. You can see his bilingual stop signs at the two corners closest to the school. They produce a moment of minor disorientation. Something familiar is made new and strange. And those signs at their intersections do mark out in their own small way a separate world in the middle of the anglophone city.

103.

Paul moved to the Northwest Territories. He bounced back and forth between there and northern Alberta, teaching French and English to Indigenous kids in isolated communities where it didn't matter that he didn't have a degree, while working on a BA in General Arts through distance studies at Lakehead University. He applied to teachers' college. The Faculty of Education took into account his teaching experience, particularly his work with students from marginalized communities, and admitted him to their B.Ed. with only a three-year BA. It took him the better part of five years to complete the two-year degree, but he finished it, and, the following spring, he was hired by Coast Mountains Board of Education School District 82 to fill the position of Vice Principal at Hazelton Secondary School in Hazelton, British Columbia.

104.

Hazelton is less isolated than Fort Good Hope in the Northwest Territories where Paul was teaching when he was hired. But it is still a small town set apart from the world at the junction of the Bulkley and Skeena rivers in the interior of northern BC just off a branch of the Trans-Canada highway between Prince Rupert and Prince George. The easiest way to reach it is to fly into the Prince Rupert airport, rent a car and drive east into the mountains along a road that rises and dips and rises, each time more steeply, testing the engine, until it dips one last time towards where the rivers meet and where Paul lives in a small house in the neighboring community of New Hazelton.

105.

Paul is considering a Masters of Education. He has already bought some of the books. But there is a hockey rink next to the high school and an oldtimers league that plays in the evenings. He likes the smell of the change rooms. He likes the way sound moves inside of the building when there are teams on the ice and no one in the stands. He likes to feel his muscles, to remember his strength without living inside of it, and, most nights, the books sit untouched on the shelf above his desk.

106.

I have read most of the speeches that Ronald Reagan gave about missile defence and nuclear weapons over the course of his two terms as president. His November 18, 1981 "Address on Strategic Arms Reduction Talks-START" or the "Zero Option Speech" in which he proposed the withdrawal of all Russian and American intermediate-range nuclear missiles from Europe. His November 22, 1981 "Address to the Nation on Arms Reduction and Nuclear Deterrence" in which he presented his MX Missile basing plan, renamed the missile the Peacekeeper, and declared that it was the "right missile for our time." His March 23, 1983 "Address to the Nation on National Security" or his "Star Wars Speech," in which he announced the Strategic Defence Initiative and officially inaugurated the missile defence program that, despite several transformations, consistent failures and concerted criticism from the scientific community, persists to this day. His speeches at the U.N., in Europe and Russia. His speeches in which he called the Soviet Union an "evil empire." His speeches in which he reported on the state of negotiations with Gorbachev. But I find myself returning over and over again to one of his lesser-known speeches, to his March 14, 1988 "Remarks to the Institute for Foreign Policy Analysis at a Conference on the Strategic Defence Initiative." There is no video of this speech. No footage of Reagan delivering it from behind his desk in the Oval Office or from a raised dais in front of a crowd. No Wikipedia page for it. Only a transcript on the Ronald Reagan Presidential Library and Museum website. He was coming to the end of his second term when he gave it. In less than a year, he would step down from the presidency and begin his withdrawal from the spotlight. His public appearances would become less and less frequent until, on February 4, 1994, he would close a speech to the Republican National Committee with the words, "Until we meet again, God bless you my friends," and retreat completely into the silence that carried him towards his death. His "Remarks to the Institute for Foreign Policy Analysis at a Conference on the Strategic Defence Initiative" is the last speech he gave to the organization he created and tasked with realizing his dream of perfect safety. It is the first of many last speeches. It ends:

> *Civilization's standards of acceptable conduct had changed. It's hard to say they changed for the better. We have the opportunity to reverse this trend, to base the peace of this world on security rather than threats, on defence rather than on retaliation. Those who say it can't be done, who stand in the way of progress and insist that technology stops here—I plead with them to consider what they're saying. For no matter how effective arms reduction negotiations ever are, we can never "uninvent" the nuclear weapon. We can never erase the knowledge of how to build a ballistic missile. If they were able to succeed in stopping SDI, then we would be left forever with that loaded pistol to our heads, with an insecure and morally tenuous peace based forever on the threat of retaliation.*

> *But the world is rapidly changing, and technology won't stop here. All we can do is make sure that technology becomes the ally and protector of peace, that we build better shields rather than sharper and more deadly swords. In so doing, maybe we can help to bring an end to the brutal legacy of modern warfare. We can stop the madness from continuing into the next century. We can create a better, more secure, more moral world, where peace goes hand-in-hand with freedom from fear—forever.*

107.
With freedom from fear—forever.

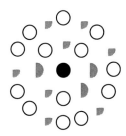

The House: North of Owen Sound

Location Description:

The house.   Sits.   Above the bay.   It was built in the 1970s.   The Kovaks.   Dan, Liz and the embryonic curl of Sebastian buy it from its first owners who buy it from the builders or build it themselves.   Neither Dan. Nor Liz.   Nor Sebastian know.   Or remember.   Where.   It sits. Above the bay north of Owen Sound.   On a shelf of land in the hamlet of Balmy Beach.   Between the paved lanes of Grey Road One and the shore. On the right when you are driving north.   After the Legacy Ridge Golf and Country Club with its low, fieldstone clubhouse.   And a wooded curve. Before the bridge over the Indian River.   The Trading Post general store And the plot of land where the feed mill.   Stands.   And burns.   Is partially rebuilt.   And doesn't stand.   Before the long and gently rising bend where the road turns inland. It is a flash of roof and light reflected off of shaded glass. Glimpsed through the trees: an irregular mirror laid over a matching clarity. You can miss it. If you expect it. If you turn your head. If you crane your neck. If you lean it just so. And you are quick and lucky. You can see down into the tall living room windows and catch its occupants unaware, Dan watching television or Liz lost in the private concentration of a book.   Low.   On a shelf of land north of Owen Sound.

It sits.   Above.

Before.

Secluded.

And exposed.

Exterior Features (Front):

The gravel lane turns off the paved road and runs parallel to it down a ridge dense with undergrowth, mature trees, and clumps of newly grown.   Cut to the ground.   And regrown.   Manitoba maple: angled trees.   Leaning

177

trees.   The lane is shorn up on the downslope by a wall of rectangular limestone blocks. The stones are in perpetual shade. They are blackish and coated with a damp, chalky residue. Sebastian pauses his play and lowers his nose nub to the stones, to the tickle of no touch: they smell of chalk dust and mould and a shadowed unhealthiness. The lane itself is almost as sheer as the ridge. In the winter, the Kovaks park one of their cars on the shoulder of the road next to the mailbox. In the spring, melt water engraves miniature tidal deltas in the gravel, draws delicate arboreal reliefs of silt. Branches fan through the crushed rock.   Most noticeable at the base of the slope.   Dan swears over a spinning tire.   Its blueglass trench. And frictionless whirr.   A full-throated, out-of-character FUCK. And from where he plants his feet to say that word the lane widens to a rough, gravelled rectangle with room enough for four or five vehicles. This is where they park the Subaru and his forest green Grand Cherokee, one and then two silver Volvos when the snow is off the ground. The ridge slopes from the pavement and then drops with the sharp vertical of a second rock wall to this rectangle. The trees that lean and the limestone dampen the noise of the passing cars.   The sound is muted.   The light is muted.   The air into which Dan's word disappears is inert: on the ridge and the lane, under the trees, and over the gravel rectangle.   North of Owen Sound.   A leaden neutrality registers nothing but the sound's.   The light's.   The air's.   Listlessness.   Leans.   Before.   Shorn up.   And exposed. The house faces the road and looks out through irregular mirrors onto the ridge and the shaded gravel.

Tall windows and secluded glass.   North.   Of tidal.   The house is translucent and reflective.

A quick and lucky flash.

The air is inert.

Listless.

And a muted nothing.

Under the ridge.

Façade:

Its southern end is one and a half stories. Its northern is two. The roof has an off-centre peak. And you can miss it. The long slope begins at the southern eave and rises leisurely over two thirds of the structure before making a short downward run. The shingles are black with grey speckles, granular and scattered with leaves above the bay. They are the original shingles and need to be replaced. The front is beige siding above flat rock that is a different grey than the shingles and that went out of fashion shortly after the house was built.   If you turn your head.   It is neither in bad taste nor tasteless, but gives the impression of a complex, premeditated error.   In private concentration.   Like men's animal print pyjamas, brown shag carpets, and what became of the hopefulness of free love: adolescent Sebastian prickles with opinions. He returns as an adult through the dappling trees after a long drive to the difficult and familiar relief of nostalgia.   To the delicate. Tidal.   Delta of memory.   Secluded.   And listless.   Leaden.   And exposed.   The garage is on the left.   Scattered.   With speckles.   And registers nothing.   The living room windows are on the right.   Replaced. And premeditated.   A line of weedy concrete patio stones runs from the garage to the front door stopping at a step flanked by two flat rock planters. The patio stones set the clipped rhythm of footsteps.   More bags.   No. Liz's palms crease with discomfort turning into pain.   This is it.   Neither tasteless.   Nor lucky.   Lock the car.   The flowers in the planters are untended and oppressed by the shade.   Before.   Brittle stalks of dead grass spike the petals in the high weeks of summer when they get what light they need to bloom.   To bloom.   And angle soft.   Neutral. And reflective.   The front door is originally a deep reddish orange. It is glossy, but it weathers over the decades that intervene between itself and what it becomes. It fades over these years to a Mediterranean clay.   To the memory.   And forgetting.   Of itself.   A colour whose gentle suggestion of warmth and drenching sun is at odds with the dim coolness under the trees.

Secluded.   In translucent listlessness.

A pair of opaque.   Elongated.   Lozenges of glass set in grubby. Set in granular and speckled grout.   Frame the entrance.

On the down slope.

Of exposed.

Foyer:

The door gives some resistance. It makes an airy shoomping sound.   Comes free.   And opens onto the foyer.   Grey.   Reflecting neutral.   And glossy.   It is only a landing. In its smallness welcomes and goodbyes are awkwardly cramped: people who want to be close find themselves too close and unable to draw back. Sixteen-year-old Sebastian hugs Liz to show her that he does not want to hug her. Indefinite scent imprinted in him. He does not hug Dan. He ages a decade to return. He does not hug Dan.   What became.   Muted.   And opaque.   Before a wooded turn.   Directly in

179

front of the door, three carpeted stairs lead up to the living room and, to the left, an equal three go down to the lower hallway.   Leisurely.   Cramped weeks.   Draw back.   The carpet is the same soft cream in the foyer as it is in the living room, the sitting room, the office and all of the hallways. It is short pile, scotchguarded, inoffensive and easier to clean than you might think.

In the secluded airy.   Leaden too.   Too close.   And leaning. Sebastian returns and remembers exposure.

Without remembering it.

Foyer (Cont.):

The carpet is covered with a clear plastic mat. Plastic runners go up and down the stairs. The plastic is tidy. The plastic is clouded with scuff marks and scratches from the dog's claws.   The plastic is plastic.   And soft cream.   In one corner sits a mud mat with Dan and Liz's street shoes on it. Her heels are in the upstairs closet. His runners are lined up neatly in the garage. The landing is screened from the living room by a flatrock wall that climbs halfway to the ceiling. It is the same rock as the façade. Warmer here under the incandescent bulbs. Harder here under the compact fluorescents. Shelves of rock project from this side of the wall and hold up: pictures of Sebastian now and then.   The dog.   And Dan and Liz standing side by side in Algonquin Park for inspection. The red rental canoe out of the shot. Forgotten too but for the faint water slap of its windward side.   Mid-lake.   The lean and tilt of weather.   Mismatched frames.   Pictures of varying.   Quality.   Sincere.   But amateurish.   Clumsily. Touching.   And not oppressed by shade.   There is a squat pottery vase among the photographs, a splash of cobalt blue and several desiccated branches of pussy willow: the velvety nubs catch what light they can.

Complex.   Neither clumsy.

Coming free.

Nor glossy.

Stairs:

The stairs to the living room are on the right, beside the rock wall, bordered on their left by a heavy maple railing that makes a ninety degree turn at the top step and is anchored to the north wall. Its end and corner posts are topped by globes, and the wood shines like cool honey.   Soft and cool.   What can.   The same railings are on the stairs to the second story.   And from the kitchen to the sitting room.   They are new in the moments Sebastian remarks on them. The original railings are white in their moments. The original railings are imitation wrought iron with plastic capped banisters and loosely rickety because.   They are not new.   And aluminum.   Now and then.   As a child.   As a young man.   As an adult in fits of nostalgic exuberance.   Allowing himself.   Dropping to this angled vertical.   Sebastian catches the end posts.   What can. With his inside.   Hand.   And leans out to take his turns at full tilt. He is new.   And he is not new.   Allowing now.   In his moments. And then.

He is the house.
Secluded.
Under the cool and windward honey.

Living Room:

A second set of stairs climbs the north wall of the living room to the upstairs and the bedrooms.   Bordered on the left.   Beneath these stairs, the plastic runner stretches from the top of the foyer steps to the entrance of the kitchen which is at the back of the house. Liz dislikes the plastic, but she puts it down because no one, not Dan or the dog, wipes their feet before walking through the living room. A pair of Lawren Harris' theosophical glaciers hang on the wall above the stairs.   Drenched.   And smelling of shade. Only Sebastian knows about Harris and his paintings. If he explains about Helena Petrova Blavatsky, about her bright red plaid dresses, the spiritual hierarchy, and the Toronto Lodge of the International Theosophical Society to his parents, Dan and Liz will doubt him without objecting, and then decide not to believe him. He does not explain.   On the left.   The plastic. Neither.   Registers nothing.   But registering nothing.   And they crane their necks to carve relief in the dimness under the trees.   The living room is the largest room in the house. The walls are eggshell white aged to butter and recede.   Lean out at full tilt.   Sharp they can.   The popcorn ceiling rises from ten feet at the south end to twenty above the north wall. It caps an airy excess of space so large that, when speaking to someone on the far side of it, they feel compelled to raise their voices even though they can hear them perfectly well. When they are closer, all the emptiness under it causes them to hush their words and restrain their gestures: they mind reflexively, like they are in a library or a church.   The muted and believes.   Mind. Your too close.   Self and lean.   Lean out.   Lean neutral.   And exposed in secluded neither.   Unless.   Several voices.   More than a family.   Fill the room with talking.   Off the paved road.   And parallel to maple.   North of Owen Sound.   New.   And not new.   You turn your head.   And lean.   Large banks of windows take up the south and west walls. They run in narrow rectangles from closed-in white wooden benches that double as chests to the eaves. Sebastian leaps wild from the benches. He raises his hand in defiance of the correction that does not come. He sprawls looselong. Trails a foot. Kicks clumsily against the limits of his ever-changing body. The benches hold extra bedding and the detritus of Liz's abandoned hobbies.   The benches do not believe him.   The windows do not believe him.   Thin, loosely woven linen curtains hang from pine rods to interpose a gauzy barrier between the interior and the outside world. The curtains interpose and do not believe him.   The walls do not believe him.   Remembering does not believe him.   And registers nothing. And recedes.   He does not explain.   The curtains deaden rather than diffuse the light that is already dappled by the trees. They grey the room. Closing them is like turning down the brightness on a computer screen. The curtains are pulled back and tucked behind brass hooks: the windows look out onto the slope of lane and the limestone wall that supports it on one side. Liz looks out but does not see. And the south lawn and the doghouse on the other.   Exposed.   And secluded.   They interpose.   And remember. Rectangular linen cushions and art books alternate on the benches.   That do not believe.   The books are stacked in glossy piles or leaned against the window frames to display their oversized covers: Dali, Rembrandt, the most obvious Impressionists, the least disturbing post-Impressionists, a complete record of Picasso's Blue Period, but nothing that contains his "Desmoiselles D'Avignon," Emily Carr, and at least one volume for each of the members of the Group of Seven.   Turned down and tucked.   It is not clear if the books are meant to be looked at or opened.   To be seen.   Or read. Whether they have been opened recently.

　　　Touching clumsy.   Leaning into neutral.   Neither listless.   They can.   And do not believe.   And catch.

　　　What light.

Living Room (Cont.):

Arranged with a haphazard precision around the cushions and books are pottery vases, teapots, and serving plates on hand carved wooden stands. These are not meant to be touched.   These are not meant to be secluded. Or exposed.   Neither dimness.   Nor airy.   The vases hold dried silver dollars, rattling milkweed pods, pussy willow branches, and several other plants neither Dan nor Liz can name without looking them up.   Clipped and dried.   Liz's gloved hands work the shears.   A rash cuffs her arms where her sleeves ride up.   I didn't.   The care.   And frustration of that.   Neither can.   Nor remember remembering.   Nor remembering relief.   An L-shaped couch upholstered in off-white canvas, a matching love seat and an armchair.   Complete.   And refused.   With a high back, softly iridescent fabric, and ebony arms and legs sit in the south-west corner of the room. The furniture is arranged in a square around a glass-topped coffee table with an oak frame in that listless and airy expanse of space. There are glass discs under the feet that print perfectly circular impressions in the carpet.   The glass is plastic.   And perfect.   A whimsically fluted.   Frozen in mid-liquid-collapse.   Hand-blown glass vase stands on the coffee table. It is almost three feet tall and contains more colours than anyone other than the artist has cared to count. Its mouth lolls. Its colours swirl and ooze and run muddily into each other.   Its colours are plastic. They are the private detritus of colours.   They refuse a simple beauty in the subdued light.   Premeditated.   And oppressed.   Carved out of dimness.   Neither.   Nor clumsy what can.   Above the bay.   After the wooded turn.   And what recedes.   Next to the vase sits a stack of tooled leather coasters.   Neither Dan.   Nor Liz.   Like.   Or will discard them. Beside the coasters is a guide to the birds of Southern Ontario and a pair of binoculars in their case that Dan leaves there: he looks out the window and likes to know what he is seeing.   Exposed.   And leaning into interpose.   Screened in shadow.   Perfectly circular and clouded with variety.   Damp stone smelling.   Of damp chalk dust.   And flat rock deltas.   A doorless.   Doorless.   Opening in the east wall gives onto the dining room.   And free love.   The fireplace is set on an angle into the north-west corner. It is an extension of the partition that separates the living room from the foyer. Its chimney is a course of rock that climbs the west wall to the ceiling.   A tucked.   And gauzy vertical.   The fireplace itself has frosted glass doors and has not been used for several years.   Dan holds Liz.   Does not hold Liz.   They hold in that not holding the memory of their embrace.   On the downslope.   Of what light.   They heat with natural gas and they have given up bothering to buy and stack firewood. There is an ornamental brass wood carrier with their last three sticks. Birch for decoration not burning. On the rock step in front of the fire, and a brass poker, brush and shovel standing in a polished rack beside it.   Smelling of smelling.   Only the poker shows any signs of use.   Dan stands.   And doesn't stand.   And adjusts an artificial Christmas tree.   Private green needles do not fall on this shelf of rock.   And land.   And rocks.   The tree to vertical.   Turns the screws.   Sebastien incandesces like a Noon

Room in the sloping.   Too quick.   Winter with the curtains thrown
open.   Sebastian frets.   Sebastian delights.   Sebastian dances elation.
Sobs.   Small.   Without explanation.   Unconsoled.   And small.
Under the listless trees.
      Secluded.   And refused.   Lights hang like luminous inverted
mushrooms from the ceiling.   What can.   Recedes.
      Leisurely.

Living Room (Cont.):

A wide screen TV projects from the wall midway between the entrances to
the kitchen and the dining room.   Subdued.   For inspection.   Inert.   And
inverted.   It is turned towards the south-west corner of the room, mirrors
the angle of the fireplace, and sits on a black particle board entertainment
console that contains a VCR, a DVD player and the manuals for all three
as well as the instructions for the digital cable whose box rests on top of
the set and keeps time in blocky green letters. It is here because they can't
manoeuvre the couch far enough back from the screen in the sitting room.
The basement is not Sebastian's room. They do not stop thinking of the
basement as Sebastian's. They do not put the TV in it.   Printed.   And
composed.   There are several videotapes next to the manuals: an amateur
recording of a casual friend's second marriage, documentaries of the 1999
and 2003 Hawaiian Ironmans that Dan has been given as gifts.   Four
unmarked.   Clumsy.   Black oblongs.   Replaced by DVDs.   By
nothing.   Beside these are bundles of cables and cords bound with green
twist ties. All four remotes are arranged in a neat row on top of the cable box
and refuse.   Forget.   And do not believe.   Secluded.   And exposed
in mid-listless collapse.   Large screen.   Flat.   Box.   Flat.   Box.
Box.   Books.   Replaced.   Lights.   Neither luminous.   And.
Neither forget.   Nor.   A brown.   Brown.   Leather.   Flat.   La-
Z-Boy love seat. In every way, from its marshmallow stuffing, to its touching
wear-and-tear, expressive of the intentional ugliness of masculine comfort,
that ostentatious refusal of beauty. Faces the television. The arm on the right
side, where Dan sits and rests the pan to pick his chicken carcasses.   An
unspoken détente.   I wish.   But I will.   And you can.   Shows signs
of distress and faint greasy discolorations. The lumpy couch, the inert and
seedy console and the darkly inorganic television.   Arranged.   Keeping
green time.   Its dead plane of screen, look impermanent, look mismatched
and mind-yourself, as if they are squatting in this corner and someone is
about to notice that they are an affront to the art books and pottery, to the

dried silver dollars and pussy willows, to all the creamy refinement and simple beauty, and take them away.   Overstuffed and ugly.   Too. Too close.   They what and can.   Would anyone object?   They do not belong.   To this cleanliness and order.   To its beauty and simplicity.   Printed with perfectly circular impressions.   Maneuvered and recorded.   That shows none of the deep-seated dirt.   Webbed scratches and.   Barely.   Perceptible patches.   Of.   Scrubbed. Spills.   None of the midway discoloured.   None.   Of the listless unhealthiness.   None of the shadowed neutrality.   Or.   The normal effects of habitation.   Sebastian.   Don't.   He does.   And doesn't. And does.   Even the dog learns to stay off the carpet.   Learns.   To keep the room and.   Its time.   That is meant for special occasions, for ceremonies of waspish observation and public concentration that Dan and Liz accept but do not like.   Dan.   And Liz do not.   Sebastian does and moves out.   They understand.   Are pleased.   And not.   That life is not a special occasion.

Pleased.   And reconciled.

To their sloping lives.

Neutral.

Secluded.   They concentrate, but do not believe.   And their believing is ostentatious.   And exposed.   To.   Books.   Box.   Box. Books.   Box.   Lights.   Box.   And beauty.

They understand and believe.

Neither forgetting.

Nor.

Subdued.

Dining Room:

The dining room is in the south-east corner of the house. Its hardwood floors are divided from the tile of the kitchen and the carpet of the living room by gently peaked, metal strips.   Gold.   That glows like honey and leans.   Sparkles likewise.   A large, rectangular table fills the room. The top is a solid span of scratched and lacquered pine. No matter how often it is wiped, it will not give up its insidious tackiness. In several places, there are regular markings where Sebastian's childhood pencil tip presses through his paper or wanders with a vandalous thrill off his schoolbooks and scores the wood.   What are you doing?   Don't.   Cups his hand to hide the digging tip.   Meltwater webbings ingrained with habitation.   The house.   And not the house.   The light markings and the deeper regular impressions, where he intentionally widens and excavates the surprisingly yielding material, are heaviest at the seat that faces the pair of sliding glass doors in the south wall.   East   Of intention.   Amateurish and north of exuberance.   The books are stacked in arboreal deltas.   The lights hang like luminous mushrooms from the eaves.   Darkly organic.   And dust.   Spikes through the leaves in what can.   The doors open onto the deck and the downslope of the gazebo, the lawn, and after that the tree, tree stump, wild grapevine and brush barrier that divides the property from the neighbours.   And books.   And box.   And secluded believing. Sebastian sits here.   Here.   So that he has something to stare at when he is thinking hard.   Avoiding thinking.   Not thinking at all.   He does not sit here because he is gone.   Don't.   He doesn't.   In secluded repose.   In neither tasteless exposed.   Lacquered.   And scratched. In the centre of the table, a white Lazy Susan with a saltshaker, a glass pepper mill and a handful of festive napkins left over from Christmas held vertically by a pair of miniature ceramic bookends, spins in rickety circles. Spins.   Past the rectangular turn.   And is not bought.   What can.   And became.   Refuses beauty.   There are four chairs, one for each side of the table: Dan and Liz.   Neither Dan.   Nor Liz.   Nor Sebastian.   Liz really.   Never invites more than one other couple to dinner. The two families crammed elbow to loud elbow. Enjoying the space and the silence of one person talking at a time because none of their friends' children live at home anymore.   Open.   But not pleased.   The peaked webbings of the house.   Spin.   And what is not the house. What.   Hangs.   Exposed.   The window in the east wall is high and small and gives some spotted.   Dappled.   Light for several hours in the morning, but withholds its view of the bay.   The listless, intentional water.   Unless you are a tall man and crane your neck.   Withholds what light it can.   If you are tall and quick and lucky. If you straighten out your spine, space out your vertebrae to look, you won't see more than fly specked glass in a grubby aluminum frame: Liz forgets to get up on a chair with her Windex and newspapers, and she is too short to notice that she has forgotten.   Forgotten the house.   That does not believe.   A chandelier hangs over the table.   The curtains interpose.   For an hour or two every morning, its teardrop prisms catch and refract the light from the window, but there is rarely anyone there to notice.   Sebastian is gone.   Remembering.   He is there at the table delving away.   And not gone.   The walls.   The books.   The light.   Are bare and the room feels emptily utilitarian. It is difficult to imagine it. To fill it with the damp aromas of cooked food and conversations. To crowd the table with dishes. To whirl the Lazy Susan jerkily. But it hosts its moments of genuine conviviality. Liz comes frazzled from the kitchen in the middle of one of her botched holiday dinners. She is calm through a successful Sunday brunch for a dozen good friends. She hosts more. Dan helps more. If the living room holds the ceremonies of middle-class sociability, the dining room contains its intimate reality.

Life refracted.

Climbs.

Neither private.   Nor can.   They forget.

This refined.

And too close.

Delta.

Kitchen:

North of the dining room is the kitchen. Its floor is large slate tiles separated by a finger width of pale grout that absorbs stains: roughly semicircular swathes in front of the sink, the stove and the fridge are rippled smog grey. The colouring of the tiles themselves is irregular.   Blue.   Bluegrey. Grey.   Rust.   Red.   Greyred.   Clay.   And they may be stained here and there, or that may be the original pattern of the stone. The effect of their variegation is to give the floor the natural, organic inevitability that Liz wanted, somewhat like the shelving water-slick rock, the darkened limestone of Indian Falls, and to remind the visitor that nature is uneven, only accidentally beautiful, and often unpleasing.   Nature withholds. It is insidious and water regular.   Oozes and runs.   To refuse.   A public.   And secluded beauty.   They put in radiant heat under the tiles.   North of conviviality.   In the premeditated winter, Dan eats his breakfast standing at the sink, which is a double stainless-steel depression under a window in the middle of the east wall.   Impatient.   Antsy, Liz says.   Repeats   Until it keeps the time of their marriage. His body a lean metronome matching her. He swings his weight from heel to heel. This window is lower and larger than the one in the dining room, and its two panes of glass are cleanly translucent.   Short.   Delicately lacy curtains hang from a brass rod above it. They are bunched behind two shining hooks. That are not brass.   Nor too.   Too close.   The aperture is deep and posed for inspection. There are small pots of herbs in various stages of growth arranged on the sill: basil, oregano, weedy chives, an experimental batch of lemon basil, a gauzy barrier, thyme in interpose, mint that is more delicate, its leaves less leathery and less pungent than the variety that grows by the river, and the swollen, spiky appendages of an aloe vera plant. Each pot has the tiny plastic placard that identifies the baby plants at the nursery taped to its side. The wedge that was stuck into the earth has been snipped off and the washed-out picture of a healthy, full grown plant is turned in to the kitchen. If, after a sip of his watered-down Gatorade, Dan shutters his eyes and leans into the brash warmth of the sunrise, if he leans wide to take in this accidental beauty, he is struck by a faint confusion of vegetable smells and rocks slowly back on his heels.   Remembering.   Not remembering. Angled maple.   Grape vines.   And brush.   This is the only room they renovate completely after buying the house.

Refusing.

Irregular light.   And speckled warmth.

Rock back.   Back.   To books.   Box.   Books.   Flat mat. And.

Intentional ugliness.

They both want the change, but not the disruption.   They tolerate. Resist.   Smile, of course, at the contractors.   They like the room.   But regret.   The long echo of those weeks through their lives.   That faint. Remembered.   Dust.   Noise.   Never faded.   Confusion of strangers in their home.

Their public secluded.

And private exposed.

Kitchen (Cont.):

Liz chooses the colours.   That do not ooze and run.   And the materials. Dan approves them. He researches the appliances and Liz decides if they fit her vision. She allows herself a restrained exuberance in the slate, which costs more than it adds to the room, in the sleek new fittings on the cabinets, in the satiny gloss of the cabinet's finish, and in the complex, muted cheer of the soft canary walls. She chooses the stainless-steel tap under the window for the elegant gooseneck of its spigot.   They stand in the stillness of the finished room.   They touch in it.   They hold each other and the separate resentments and frustrations of those six months.   Reflected.   Next to the tap, there is a second faucet on a long, flexible, metallic hose that they use for rinsing down the dishes and watering the plants on the windowsill. The flow of hot and cold water is controlled by a lever so elegant that it slips out of their hands at inopportune moments or returns, on its own, responding leisurely to gravity, not rising or leaning, to its shut off position. Restrained.   And registering nothing but arboreal deltas.   And flexible light.   To the left of the sink, the scales and measuring devices that

Dan uses when he is training are arranged in a line against the backsplash. The backsplash is slate.   Like the falls.   Like the floor.   Running satiny.   But composed of smaller tiles, four-inch squares, that alternate light and dark in a checkerboard pattern.   Allowed.   Light.   And less.   The countertop.   The butcher block.   Sits heavy on the vintage barn board facing of the bottom row of cabinets that she chose.   Muted glossy.   Neither scratched.   Nor exposed.   The counter begins at the fridge next to the dining room door and follows the south and east walls. It interposes a barrier between the kitchen and the sitting room and forms a ponderous, uneven horseshoe. Above it, the airy cupboards are finished in the same wood as the cabinets under the counter.   Finished.   And complete.   Canary water slips through maple.   Slopes secluded.   Into the shaded gravel and the house.   The appliances.   The stove.   The imposing fridge.   The dishwasher.   The closed in microwave.   Are a matching set cased in a buff stainless steel. Their muted metallic gleam registers movement in changes of tone but does not give off reflections. Gives off the nothing.   That Liz chose.   They are strikingly leaden. Listless and neutral.   Unnatural beside the wood of the countertop and the cupboards, hemmed in by the gentle, yellow walls.   Ponderous moments. And the falls.   Return.   Built.   And exposed.   Liz forgets and gets used to the freezer being on the bottom. She likes the ice dispenser and decides how best to arrange the moveable shelves.   The regular markings. And the disruption that does not believe.   Angled into neither.   They touch.   And hold.   And do not touch.   The dishwasher is next to the fridge. If they are opened at the same time, they bang together, and there are noticeable divots on both doors.   Noise.   Drops.   To limestone tile.   Dust.   Turns.   Shelving into simple.   The stove is at the end of the stretch of counter that refuses. And divides the kitchen and the sitting room. It has a smooth glass top with four ceramic burners that glow to ruddy, spiral life inside the glass. They heat up almost as quickly as gas and cool with the same tasteless speed. Liz is impressed by how easy the stove is to clean. Liz is annoyed when the dish cloth presses particles of food into the narrow seam between the stove top and its lip.   And wanders.   Into doubt.   Dan doesn't notice.   Or clean.   Dan isn't annoyed.   A clock in the centre of a clutch of gummy, inviting buttons keeps a different time than the digital cable box.   Dampened.   Green.   This Dan notices.   Dan notices often.   Remembers in moments.   Is annoyed by.   But puts off the embarrassment of misreading the manual.   The stove's oven is large enough to hold more food than Liz can cook. She wants for space when they host a potluck. When everyone touches. In the too. Too.   Kitchen.

Hemmed in by counters.
Whirling in moments that withhold.   And close.
Still they glow.
Tacky.
Restrained.   And imposed

Kitchen Contents:

There is a large drawer at the base of the stove in which Liz stores her cookie trays and muffin tins, the bread pans she hasn't and can't remember using, her cast iron and her non-stick frying pans.   Haphazard.   Shorn up.   For decoration.   The drawer sticks or the handle of one of the pans catches.   She struggles with it.   She pushes it in.   She pulls it out.   She doesn't touch.   And does.   Until it opens reluctantly. Refuses exuberance.   Less.   And less.   In listless composed.   Dan knows when Liz is cooking because the fan in the hood above the stove sends faintly perceptible vibrations through the house. He is annoyed and soothed by that running irritation.   I don't mind.   Of course.   But I do.   You.   The microwave is built into the cupboard to the left of the stove.   And presses and glows.   A circular glass plate in its bottom should spin on three small wheels, but one of the wheels has a slight flaw, stutters occasionally, and salts the powerful hum with an irregular knocking that is neither light nor oppressed.   Facing the road.   And speckled ruddy.   Liz sees into its interior with difficulty unless she stands on tiptoes. She climbs onto a chair to chip away at the bits of food fused to its plastic insides.   Teeters.   Climbs.   And forgets.   The bay that is built on a shelf of land.   And drops.   For what.   Whirling rippled cheer.   North of perceptible.   A cupboard door closes over the microwave. Liz shuts it because she has an ageing anti-nuclear proliferation activist's mistrust of radiation. She does not see how the black webbing in its window offers any protection.   Or trust.   The sloping light.   Built sheer.   Glossy.   Thrilled.   And tacky with scratches.   The cups and mugs are in the cupboard next to the microwave.   Abraded.   Glass tumblers imitate cut crystal.   Catch.   And do not refract.   They are dulled.   Clouded and arboreal.   With wear.   Plastic sports cups pushed to the back are plastic and.   Faded.   Two celebrate the Blue Jays' World Series wins in washed out detail. Dan sees Joe Carter jack-rabbiting around the bases after his home run.   Mismatched pottery glasses.   Irregular.   Rising slowly.   Some.   Small and muted. Earth toned.   Others glazed.   Water-slick.   They glow to life with

190

bright, primitive suns, whiskery cats and accidentally Christian fishes with blowsy spines.   Gauzy barriers.   Fluted porcelain cups in blues and greys dashed with vaguely Asian brushstrokes. Chubby, pottery goblets that do not glow and are so heavy that they always feel half full. Most of the cups have a chip here or there, a flint flake from the rim, or spidery cracks that are webbing by increments. Some of these fissures are studded with rubbery nodules of crazy glue. Liz buys the pottery cups in sets of four or six, but none of the sets are complete.   None arboreal.   Complex.   And faintly discoloured.   North of interior.   She catches cups.   Dashed with glass. Dulled.   Sebastian stands and grows in a different kitchen. He stands and stares at canary walls he does not remember. He thinks as a young man that life is a continuous slippage.   A mournful letting go.   Matched and unmatched.   And only accidentally circular.   The cupboards above the counter have a bottom and a top shelf.   The cups are on the bottom. And shelve.   Washed out.   Above them.   Above the maple.   Well out of daily reach, are a dozen mismatched wineglasses turned upside down, their bases sticking up like translucent, variegated mushrooms.   Dusty. And not.   Remembered.   These appear on special occasions: Liz has her friends over. Liz cooks a holiday dinner. Dan compliments her. But life is not a special occasion.   Arranged.   And studded.   They have been chosen.   And do not forget.   Next to the cups and wineglasses she buys are the mugs. Sincere and precise white cylinders with factory formed handles.   Conventional.   Desiccated branches.   Matte. And sheer.   Stamped with the logos of a variety of boards and service organisations above the bay: The CAS. The Bruce-Grey Board of Education. Summerfolk. The Gallery. Dan and Liz get them at Christmas parties, in volunteer appreciation packages or in exchange for donations. They do not like them, but they use them, and feel dimly guilty.   Oppressed by guilt under the trees.   If they think about throwing them out. Two dozen hand-made, lovingly distinctive pottery mugs.   Pastel teacups.   Small.   On the shelf.   Tiny and careful in the hand.   Liz calls them cute.   Or precious.   Or.   What can.   To heavy mugs.   In.   The colours of heft.   Commanding blues.   Earthy browns around.   Which Liz can barely wrap.   But wraps.   Her too.   Too.   Hands.   These are not white or perfect. These.   Are not accidentally beautiful.   These ooze and run.   Dan likes the big ones because they hold more than half-a-litre of water or Gatorade and Liz finds comfort in their bulk. She has bad circulation in her fingers.   White wax.   Skin that holds the pale ridge of the pinch: it is winter and she makes one mug of tea after another, sips each absentmindedly, cradles them until they cool, and pours the remainder of the bitter, puckering liquid down the drain. Liz picks out each mug except for the ones that Dan and Sebastian give her for birthdays and Christmases. They can't think of anything else. They have left their shopping to the last minute and drive or walk by The Artists' Co-op on Tenth Street.   The cups.   And mugs.   The shelving water-slick imperfect shapes.   And every other piece of pottery they own has the potter's signature scratched or stamped into its rough, unglazed bottom as surely as their personality is printed on the clay.   Rough impressions.   Pressed in the listless shade. This is what attracts Liz: no two potters and no two pieces are alike. Even the cheapest, most formulaic cups are guaranteed by human error, chance and the vicissitudes of the material to differ.   To doubt.   And print imperfect. This is why she displays them in the living room and fills up the cupboards: they stud the house with individuality. They have a meditative simplicity. She loses herself in running the sensitive pads of her fingers over ridges only touch can discern, seeking out and resting in depressions formed by the potters' digits, marvelling at the effortless precision of their idiosyncrasy. Marvelling.   In moments.   Of.   How long.   She fills with the satisfaction of having supported local artisans.   With.   The fading. Dropping.   Echo of that rightness.   Differs.   Touches.   The heft of her importance.

    Filled.   Filled up

With rough perfection.

And deadened rather than diffused.

    Secluded.   In a private concentration.   Compelled by light from shaded glass.   Individual.   Living.   In the vicissitudes of a beauty she chose.

    And exposed.

Kitchen Contents (Cont.):

Above the mugs: several pottery serving platters. A rustic colander holds cinnamon buns at brunches or rolls at dinners. A heavy bowl for Liz's curried chicken salad because she trusts its glaze to resist the staining spice. All of these are out of her reach. Dan lifts them down.   Imperfectly circular.   She pauses for an imperceptible beat as he turns away, reaching up for another dish or closing the cupboard doors, to savour their weight, their human material gravity.   Guaranteed by chance.   By marvelling. Mournful.   Meant to be touched.   She cradles.   Remembers.   And believes.   On the right, a motley assortment of plates: white plates. That are not plastic.   With chipped rims.   Slight flakes.   The ticks and nicks of use.   Sebastian forgets himself.   Shallow chunky circles in cheerful primary colours.   The absentminded remnants of several sets of Ikea dishes.   Square plates with inch-high sides, imitations of the restaurant plates Liz saw on the Food Channel and bought at Zehrs. In such moments.   To differ.   Matching long, narrow, rectangular plates that should serve dishes three ways, but that she uses for cheese and crackers or nothing at all.   And resist.   Blowsy flint.   Imperfect composed.   Exactly twelve porcelain dessert plates washed in eloquent dashes of sidereal blue and carbide grey.   Clumsily inorganic.   They rise.   Pushed.   And pulled.   Out of her reach.   Swirl and run. Ooze and brightly run.   Rippled with personality.   Cups and mugs. The perfect imperceptible dream.   Leaden.   And carbide.   Eloquent under the trees.   Beside these are bowls. Palm sized dessert bowls cradled in glass and clay. Shallow pasta bowls with authentic Carbonara, Bolognese and Primavera recipes printed next to baskets of produce in their bottoms: zucchini, tomatoes that might be poorly rendered eggplants and vice versa. Neither Dan nor Liz like these bowls, but they are eminently functional. Factory imperfect.   And profound.   They use them almost every day, reach for them reflexively, despite their dislike. Deep pottery soup bowls with flocks of migrating birds stamped.   Not pressed.   Into their sides. Half-a-dozen brightly pastel, plastic cereal bowls that give the impression of being microwaveable but are not: Liz catches Dan making his oatmeal in them and reminds him about the chemicals they release when irradiated. Annoyance mirrors itself between them.   She does.   He does.   Not. And disappears.

They rise reflexively.   And believe.

A warm.   Effortless.   And shadowed unhealthiness.

Leans out.

Into nothing at all.

They are.   And they are not the house.

Kitchen Contents (Cont.):

Liz's cooking hardware is next to the bowls: a handful of measuring devices. Sieves.   A pasta machine shining with an unworn stainless brightness. Rollers.   Elegant.   Basters.   Glow.   Meat and candy thermometers. Do not belong.   To glass.   To wood and plastic cutting boards.   Box. A pastry sheet.   Books and.   Two rolling pins.   Withhold.   A battery of metal, plastic and glass mixing bowls divide.   A juicer.   A tenderising mallet.   Insulated silicone gloves do not forget. Liz's only internet purchase and worth every second of irritation.   A manual ice-cream maker that she has neither the strength nor the patience to operate.   A hand-held mixer.   More colours run.   An immersion blender.   And here it overflows into the rest of the kitchen: her red KitchenAid mixer sits on the counter next to Dan's scale. Beside it rests a double-width wooden block of knives. The original serrated blades have been lost or broken or discarded and it is now filled with German or Swiss or French steel: two foot-long chef's knives.   A meat cleaver.   Liz stands at the counter and cuts up chicken parts.   Sections.   Ribs.   Likes.   In this private moment the heft followed by the tendinous resistance of the flesh.   Sixteen steak knives: two sets of eight that match except for the colour of their rivets. Paring knives.   Boning knives.   Bread knives.   Peeling knives. Chopping knives.   Knives with classic black handles.   Knives with green spongy grips to cushion the hand.   And the gritty length of a stropper that Liz slashes the knives over before she cooks although she doubts her amateurish strokes do much for their edges.   Doubts.   And does not believe in its resistance.   By the block is a blender: a heavy stainless steel base and a durable Pyrex glass jug with metric and imperial measures stamped along the raised horizontal ridges on its sides. There is a complete set, the deluxe set, of Lagostina pots and pans that Dan gives Liz at Christmas in the cupboards under the blender. They are used often but are not yet dulled or discoloured.   Desiccated.   Pushed to the back.   But not pulled.   Tucked.   Behind the pots and pans, sealed fastidiously in their boxes with scotch tape and protected by their original Styrofoam are a coffee grinder, a twelve cup coffee maker that they use exclusively for pot-lucks and parties, an espresso maker that is too difficult and involved to be worth the trouble, an electric crockpot, a pressure cooker, their old toaster, and, in the most remote, least accessible corner, a half-empty box of candy canes left over from Sebastian's childhood. Liz puts them away. The bowed sugar becomes incrementally more brittle by the month.   Less. Complex.   And listless.   Sealed.   In becoming moments.   Life is not.   Despite.   And neither.   Slips back nor returns.   To complete. The rest of the cupboards are taken up by large glass jars: white and whole wheat flour.   Rolled remote oats.   Mason jars of nuts, seeds, dried fruits, sugars.   Icing, granular brown, and white.   White and brown.   Least and most.   Remembered and forgotten.   Sea and table salt.   Two shelves full of tiny jars of spices that are for the most part too old to be used because Liz prefers the fresh herbs that Zehrs carries first but that can now be found in all of the local grocery stores, three small plastic bags of their favourite curry powder. White and red wine, and several varieties of balsamic vinegar. Canola, peanut, sesame and grape seed oil.   Catch and refract.   Believe.   And forget.   Olive oils for cooking, dressings and drizzling. Half a braid of local, organic garlic. Whole wheat pastas and two boxes of couscous. Carefully washed yogurt containers of both sizes beside a stack of lids. Next to these, a collection of unmatched Tupperware. Breakfast cereals that are all high in fibre and each contain at least one kind of nut and one kind of desiccated fruit. Liz's stash of dark chocolate Petit Ecoliers.   Books.   Canned goods.   Boxes.   Bags of dried beans and lentils.   Bags and boxes.   Soaps.   Detergents.   Cleaners. Disinfectants.   Deodorizers in.   Powder.   Liquid and aerosol form. Under the sink.   Silverware.   Tea towels.   Placemats Liz weaves at a workshop. Under these, a white table cloth and a green, Christmas-themed, vinyl table cover.   Paper and cloth.   Plastic and cloth.   Napkins with chunky napkin holders that are lathed from tree branches and lacquered to show the static eddies of the grain.   Bottles of red and white wine. Three narrow vials of Niagara ice wine that is too sweet for their taste, but which they nevertheless acknowledge is world class.   Pride.   For them.   Rye for Dan's father.   And vodka.   Gin.   Orange.   Mint and white chocolate liqueurs. Only the wine, which Liz uses for cooking, has been touched in months of moments.

White.   And red.   Books.   Brown and white.
Red brown.   Under.
Box.
And the white woven months.
Stutter occasionally.
Neither remember marvelling.   Mournful.   Nor narrow.
To tidal.   Forgetting.
Nor pull.

Sitting Room:

The north side of the kitchen opens onto the sitting room. A short person. Liz or Sebastian when he is small. Or a tall one.   Dan.   Sebastian when he passes Dan.   Dan alone.   Who ducks uncomfortably can look through the space between the counter and the cupboards over the back of the couch at the second TV and the office doorway.   What can.   Is elegant and eloquent.   Between the counter and the months.   Between misreading. The secluded light forgets.   Six steps to the left of the stove go down to the lower level.   Leapt by Sebastian.   Taken.   Always taken.   Two at a leaping time by Dan.   Go down.   And return.   A large, definitely polyester and possibly Persian inspired rug resists and covers nearly the entire floor. They vacuum it regularly, but it is permanently impregnated with dirt tracked in through the glass patio doors and dog hair.   Intimate. Leisurely imperfect.   Vegetable warmth presses and glows with a stainless beauty.   Trusts its glaze.   Dan rocks.   Rocks back.   To white and brown.   Confusion.   The patio doors are in the centre of the east wall. Dan and Liz leave them open in the summer. They place a specially cut dowel in the channel when they lock them.   Reflexively.   The cups are taken up. Lost or broken.   Toys scatter across the floor. They are stepped on. They are danced around on one foot.   They are plastic.   And not.   Gathered up. And put away for good.   The couch is snugged against the half-height south wall. Tucked away with its back to the kitchen. It is covered in places and not covered in others by a heavy southwestern blanket. Its white leather is cracked, abraded and worn down to raw, pilling patches. The dog's claws slit the arms and the cuts divulge strands of synthetic, fibrous stuffing. They reach.   And lean.   Alternate.   Loosely exposed.   Rickety and inert.   Nevertheless.   In front of the couch sits a solid but worn coffee table that dates from the same era as the house.   Slate.   And dust.   And an insidious tackiness.   That does not belong.   There is a stack of coasters at one end, a pair of remotes tucked into a canvas holder fastened to one of its sides, and stacks of magazines behind the glass doors of its base.   Complex.   And whirling.   Dimly in the guilt under the trees.   That does not believe.   Across from the couch, next to the door to the office, a new and then outdated widescreen TV, its futuristic design looking ahead of its time and the house and then quaintly misguided, complexly premeditated.   How different.   Yesterday's tomorrow is. Its sleekness turning boxy.   Its innovations becoming outmoded.   Its beauty difficult.   Neither.   Simple nor white brown.   Sits on a heavy, artificially aged chest. Its picture takes on an eye-straining opacity. And Dan notices it and complains. But watches it after runs or bikes with his feet up on the coffee table, the moist heat of his calves, the private concentrated warmth painting milky clouds of temporary masculine discolouration on the veneer.   Doubt.   Gives.   And hangs.   Leaden and secluded. Embarrassed by movement over the listless gravel.   There is a floor-to-ceiling built-in shelving unit next to the TV that holds a pair of metallic VCRs, one Beta and one VHS, several family pictures, and a collection of recent Canadian fiction in hardcover. A matching waist-high unit stretching the length of the west wall contains a respectable number of books that stutter occasionally: orange spined Penguins, several dozen early NCL editions that have nothing other than the extremity of their ugliness and the absurdity of their abstract cover art in common, and assorted softcovers from Dan and Liz's university courses in Russian and American literature. The books on these shelves, in the office and in the blowsy, intentional bedrooms are arranged alphabetically by author in categories: hardcover and softcover, non-fiction, fiction, poetry (there is little of this, a foot, no more than two, of shelf space, and it dates from a time when they were more adventurous or more susceptible to feelings of national pride and obligation, to restrained and clumsy exuberance, although Liz buys a copy of *Whylah Falls* when it features on Canada Reads and claims to enjoy it despite its undercurrents of misogyny), Canadian literature, international literature, Canadian history, and international history, art and general interest.   In categories and cupboards.   In collections.   White and accidentally red.   Complete. Pridefully, reflexively tucked.   Although.   The pictures on the walls are large.   Professional.   And of places they have canoed or would like to canoe: sunset in Killarney, a misty morning in Algonquin, the inverted limestone cones of Flower Pot Island and the dripping, totemic forequarters of a bull moose.   Normative in their appeal.   And predictably concrete. A gauzy barrier.   Tucked and turned down.   The room is scruffily inviting, unpretentiously lived in, scattered and dancing, comfortably ugly, and, because it is lived in but not thought out, suffused with a touching vulnerability.   Lean.   And reach.   Neither inverted.   Above the bay and the steady, irregular blue.   Clumsy and vulnerable.   They forget and believe.

Secluded.

They resist.   And are not exposed.

In the winter, the patio doors give the room a creeping chill. In the heat of the summer, the vinyl blades of a ceiling fan carve ineffectual circles in the humid air above the furniture.

A little precision.

Taken up with the air.

The Office:

The office door swings in and a plastic wedge holds it open.   Pushed to the back.   And restrained.   The office itself is deep and narrow. A small east-facing window draws attention to the lack of illumination without dispelling the room's obscurity.   Limestone deltas drop.   Dappled.   And diffused. With the exception of the window and its frame, the entire east wall is taken up by a plywood shelving unit that was built with the house and is painted the same colour as the walls.   The walls.   A course of rock.   And the small window.   The shelves.   Shelves filled with books, but for one shelf that holds the deceptively light boxes of computer programs, and accumulates both kinds of floppy discs, CD cases, instruction manuals and a nest of unused cables. And the bottom row of shelves that are stuffed to overflowing with old magazines.   Regular markings.   Touching leaden. He is a teenager. Sebastian hides a pair of pornos in the magazines. He buys them from a friend who stole them from the bottom of the stack under his father's bed.   Behind maple.   Mid-liquid.   And listless.   This before he moves into the basement. When he is still in the upstairs bedroom and he cannot trust Liz not to change his sheets, put away his clothes, straighten up his mess or find another plausible excuse for snooping.   Mind.   His muted too close self.   He is.   Misguided in the morning.   And neither. Secluded.   Nor.   A new computer with a large flat screen monitor and a cable modem sits on a glass-topped aluminum frame desk against the north wall.   Cut.   Reflecting.   And clouded.   The rods that support the glass are crimped here or there.   Brown and white.   Bent by Sebastian when he assembles the unit.   Loosely wrought in imitation.   Capped. Books.   And box.   Before he leaves, this is his second room.   Before. He plays games and writes essays on a series of faster and increasingly more impressive machines whose purchase he supervises, whose problems he fixes, and whose programs he updates. Both of his parents have always had what appears to him to be a genetic antipathy to computers.   Hushed. Or mismatched.   They are frustrated by the simplest of instructions, and, even after they grow accustomed to checking their email and surfing the internet, they approach the keyboard with a tentative wariness.   Too. Too.   Crystal.   As if they are certain that one of the keys is a self-destruct button, but don't know which one. Neither Dan nor Liz has any idea that, between the pair of hidden pornos and a pirated copy of *Leisure Suit Larry* labelled "*King's Quest III*: Saved Games".   Before.   And between the bus dropping him off and Liz getting home, on days he claims sickness, and during their evenings out, this room bears neutral witness to Sebastian's sexual awakening. They have no idea that the spots on the rug are not made by the dog or that when their son sits in the rolling, high-backed leather chair he feels a thrill of shame and the distant pressure, the faint oppression and shaded fading echo of adolescent compulsion, lust magnified by the room's narrow stuffiness.   Dim.   Listless compulsion. Hangs.   Inert.   And exposed.   The chair rolls on a translucent plastic mat.   Rolls and leans.   Incremental.   Like mushrooms.   The glass desktop is powdered with dust.   And smells of smelling.   There is the faintest ring to the left of the keyboard.   Faint.   And distant.   The walls are bare.   Walls.   Suffused.   And dashed.   With white neutral witness.   The room's only other feature is a maple veneer, two-drawer filing cabinet.   Parallel to misreading.   With bronze trim and a pair of bronze keys, one inserted in the lock and the other dangling from the ring that joins them.   Magnified.   And certain.   The cabinet contains bills, warranties, instruction manuals, newspaper clippings, Sebastian's new report cards. His old report cards. His shame and elation.   Shows improvement.   Excellent.   Excellent.   Registration and subscription forms, all of the papers that Dan has not stored in the fireproof portable safe in the back of their bedroom closet or in their safety deposit box at the Bank of Montreal.

> Books.   Books and.   Flat.
> Dust climbs.   Complete.
> And luminous.
> They are guaranteed by the light.   Perpetual.
> Under the trees.

Basement Stairs:

The basement door is open next to the kitchen stairs.   Propped open.   In its case by a deep blue Pyrex globe.   Plastic and.   Neither.   What can. Aluminum caps the lip of the first step and forgets.   Recedes.   But does not resist.   Its bronze finish wears.   Flares irregularly at the flick of the light.   Elegant with shame.   The landing.   The stairs.   And the basement floor are covered in dully iridescent orange indoor/outdoor carpet that feels like walking on new toothbrushes, that pricks a pleasant discomfort through socks and crunches softly, unpretentiously under shoes. Stainless.   It believes.   Dan shouts.   Go.   To.   Sleep.   Into a huddle of pre-teen boys.   Flares with a profound and iridescent rightness. And rolls back.   At the base of the stairs.   To the left.   The crawl space door neither divulges nor believes. It is secured with a latch and a combination lock threaded through the latch.   Refused.   But never closed because Liz can neither remember the combination nor where she puts the careful paper card on which she records it.   To.

> The right.
> To the basement.
> Soft.
> And half-forgotten.   Limestone shelves.
> To the gravel.
> Neither.
> In the flares.   And not light.
> They.
> Are clumsy.
> And compelled.

What We Think We Know

The Basement:

The basement itself is three rooms: Sebastian's bedroom and the furnace room on the east.   Above the bay.   The main room on west. The walls are drywall, and the ceilings are finished in acoustic tiles except for the furnace room which has a cement floor.   Bare.   Studs.   Pink insulation and vapour barrier.   The rooms shelve.   Forget.   And refuse.   The main room is Sebastian's playroom cluttered with toys. It hosts sleepovers   It is his TV room smelling of teenagers.   And it is empty except for a stack of boxes in the corner.   Dan's treadmill and cycling trainer.   A clock radio on a stool.   A small TV on a milk crate. And a dehumidifier.   Bare.   But never closed.   In the hot summer, the air is saturated with moisture, the dehumidifier whirrs ceaselessly away, and the gaseous mixture tastes, more than it smells, of chalk dust and the sweat that percolates over the winter into the carpet, and impregnates the walls.   The most remote and humid blue.   Hangs.   In the secluded air.   Hangs.   And glows.   Carves circles into interpose. Sebastian's bedroom door is closed. And stays that way. It has been years since he lived in the room. He lives in the room. And doesn't.   Although guilt stutters.   Regrets.   Occasionally.   Although.   They lean out into the faint and listless confusion under the trees.   His parents continue to respect the privacy he claims at fifteen when he responds. To a listless distant pressure.   To the gravity of feeling.   And moves himself into the basement.   Habit.   Hunched and hushed.   Stops them from prying. Not even Liz's intermittent fits of nostalgia will drive her to do anything more than vacuum the rug and change the sheets. The room alters as little as anything can when Sebastian leaves for university. A desk.   A window.   A bed flanked by side tables.   A dresser.   A bookshelf.   A bookshelf.   An end table contains.   A TV.   And VCR.   Fantasy novels by series.   Roleplaying rule books.   Forgotten Realms.   Existential philosophy.   Dostoevsky.   Anne Rice.   A hardcover history of the French Revolution.   The Second World War. The modernisation of Russia.   The unification of China.   The War of 1812.   The Red River Rebellion.   A history of Sarawak Township that Sebastian's parents gave him for Christmas remains.   Unread.   A Millennium Falcon.   An Imperial Walker.   A cup.   Of pens.   And pencils.   A desk lamp cranes its metal neck.   An incense burner. A pair.   Of pewter.   Bookends.   Bono in profile.   Nirvana in concert.   Pearl Jam's first album cover.   Screaming Trees.   R.E.M. Boxes of comics.   Sheets.   And blankets.   Worn out Doc Martens An electric guitar Sebastian plays.   Badly   And never pawns.   The room gives the impression of being half empty.   Amateurish.   Its swathes of open.   Airy.   Space.   Suggest removed furniture. Inevitable.   And angled into absence.   It has always looked like this. Vague.   Underused.   Vibrating in faint sympathy with the furnace and Sebastian's unformed self: he tells women that he lost his virginity on that single bed but reveals, much later, after more secrets, both true.   And false.   Vice and.   Versa.   New and not new.   That he never dated in high school, exchanging confidence for an inviting vulnerability when he is certain they will not think less of him, when they will feel privileged instead of betrayed. It is a trick he perfects, a strategy he refines in this room's subterranean solitude, in its private concentration after bush and house parties, campfires and long nights drinking coffee on the patio of the east side Tim Hortons, thinking hard towards sleep, solving himself like a problem, and puts into use when he shrugs off his shell of uncoolness at university: braggadocio and brash dishonesty followed by a revelation no less calculated for being sincere.   He is.   And is not.   Touching. False.   And true.   Solving privilege.   Until he is nothing.   Flat. Lacquered.   And exposed.   Sebastian and his parents fight and don't fight over keeping the basement door closed. They want it open so that the dog.   A different one.   The same one.   Can lie in the cool air and drain his heat into the concrete under the carpet.   Dim ridges.   And limestone.   Flash.   He wants it closed on principle and for the extra warning the door gives him when it hits the jamb. He moves out. Liz buys the Pyrex globe. And the door remains.   Open.   And closed.   Long after the arguments dissolve into a remembered.   Passing.   Irritation.

Inert.

Filled up with doubt.

This stainless depression withholds.   Returns.   And does not believe.

Hangs.

And recedes.

Blue.

And not new.

Crawl Space:

The crawl space runs east and then north in an L.   Static.   It eddies. Skirting.   Feeling.   And the reinforced cement pad of the garage. It is low enough to walk through uncomfortably.   Mismatched.   Hunched. Nose twitching.   Eyes smarting.   Hands fending off spider webs and shreds of pink Flamingo insulation.   Too.   Too close.   And tall enough to make crawling seem ridiculous. It contains the larger, messier leftovers of Liz's enthusiasms. The doubt and shame she chose: an easel, a box of paints and brushes that looks like a leather tackle box, canvases she stretches painstakingly and poorly over their frames, cattail reeds from a basket weaving workshop that are as dry and crumblingly useless as aging pulp paper, dogwood branches she ties together in a bundle, several boxes of wool and a set of potting tools daubed with globules of clay.   Project. But are not clear.   There are four bags of pink insulation.   Boxes. Boxes stacked at the very back years ago.   Object.   The bottom six inches of their cardboard sides buckling.   Unlabelled.   Sealed with packing tape. Their simple contents now a mystery.   Scrap lumber. Sheets of tongue and groove plywood leaning against the wall.   Warmth and confusion.   Two-by-sixes and two-by-fours.   Inert.   Mismatched lengths of moulding. Bits of pressure-treated wood Dan rescues from the scrap pile when the deck is being built.   Flaked cups.   Nodules.   And mugs.   The stakes with which he marks the edges of the gravel parking area in winter. A dilapidated rowing machine. The frame and box spring of Sebastian's old bed. His toys. His narrow guilt in boxes or stacked in neat piles.   Greasy discolorations.   Tarps.   Folding chairs. A pair of card tables.   A creeping chill in winter.   The deck furniture and the awning. Pool noodles. Sports equipment.   And dust.   Dust everywhere.   Dust coating everything in a shadowed unhealthiness.   And dust hanging in golden aureoles around the bulbs that light the space.

Bronze.   And narrow.   Press ridiculous.

And divulge.

Laundry Room:

A narrow hallway runs from the den to the west wall of the house where it turns south and climbs three steps to the foyer landing.   Remembers. The reflexive bay.   Two doors open north off the hallway.   The first from the sitting room gives onto the laundry room.   The carpet stops. Webbed and noduled.   White.   Gold speckled linoleum begins at the jamb.   Washer.   Dryer.   Scratched plastic washtub.   Dog food. Dog dish.   And dog water.   Cupboards that shelve and contain.   A broom.   A mop in a bucket.   Catches.   And leans.

Into neither angled.   Carbide.

Wandering.

Nor a red door in the shade.

The House: North of Owen Sound

Ground Floor Bathroom:

The bathroom is opposite the stairs to the foyer and next to the laundry room. It is narrow and deep.   Tucked.   And pulled.   It shares the laundry room's linoleum.   Toilet.   And sink.   Dusty.   Rose. Faded.   To dull liver.   To clay.   And slate.   Textured wallpaper echoes the premeditated tastelessness porcelain. Ugliness gives with time onto the comfort of a clouded floor.   And the toilet is opposite the door. A sink.   A cabinet   A brightly lit mirror.   Across.   From a waist-high window whose glass is covered with gauzy curtains that allow someone sitting on the toilet to observe the driveway and the south end of the parking area through them with surprising clarity.   The small room. Too close.   And open.   Too much its low and careful self.
     Like turning.
     Down.   The spotted light.   The passing irritation.
     Muted to a complex cheer.
     Complete.
     And parallel to remote.

The Garage:

Both the laundry room and the ground floor bathroom back onto the garage and insulate the house from sounds.   A step down from the back of the laundry room.   To.   The grubby coolness of the concrete slab.   Tilted to a pair of drains.   The concrete.   Hunches.   Deadened.   And tacky.   Avoiding.   Thinking at all.   Dan makes the step out of two-by-fours, plywood and a scrap of the basement carpet he discovered in the crawl space. It is his first project after they buy the house: a seeing through uncertainty. He curbs his clumsy hands. But still it rocks on the even floor. He shims it. He shores up disappointment. But the shims work free. He and Liz learn to forget.   Learn.   And grow used to the sudden intrusion of self-consciousness into habit as they tilt or.   Lurch.   Whirling. Tilt.   Lurch.   And believe.   Lean.   And forget.   Helena Petrova Blavatsky.   The intentional rock of the falls.   Plywood and two-by-four shelves.   The old vacuum and the new vacuum.   Mugs.   And stainless platters.   A skillsaw.   A jigsaw.   The old drill and the cordless drill. Insidious coasters.   An orbital sander.   A radial arm saw.   A table saw clamped to the top of a folding workbench.   Scales.   And measuring cups.   The remaining workbenches closed up.   Put up.   And pushed back.   A shop vac.   Bags of meditative cement mix.   Complete. Half-empty cans of paint.   Stain.   Varnish and urethane.   Narrow to shame.   Long drip-drools dried on the sides of the cans.   And.   The lids hammered closed with the butt end of a screwdriver.   A tack hammer. Paint trays that divide.   Rollers.   Stiff old and silky new brushes.   A bucket of mastic.   Tubes.   Of caulking.   And a gun.   A role of transparent plastic.   A chainsaw.   A pair of earmuffs.   A visored helmet.   A Weed Wacker with its safety shield stained chlorophyll green. A mower in the airy too.   Too much.   Its handle folded over next to bags of grass seed.   Fertiliser.   Rakes.   Snow shovels.   A snow blower. And a bag of salt Dan sprinkles into the blueglass grooves of the driveway in the winter.   Drenched in blowsy deltas.

Run.
To hunched and intimate reality.
Two green garbage bins and the recycling box stand.
Stand.   And can.
Secluded.
And free.
In passing conviviality.

Garage (Cont.):

Nine pairs of running shoes arranged on a length of green indoor/outdoor carpet next to the garbage bins and recycling boxes.   Above these. Above surprising clarity.   Habit   And self-consciousness.   Above all.   Raised up reflexively.   All three of Dan's road bikes hang from hooks.   Norco.   Teal Bianchi.   Cervélo.   Carbon fibre.   And. Spare athleticism.   Inhuman.   Precise.   Printed and complex. Equations of angles and flattened tubing.   Distilled by science.   Matching hybrids that he and Liz ride less than they expected.   Extra wheels. Inner tubestirespatchkitswaterbottlescomponentslubesandoils.   Two.   Pairs of riding shoes.   Shoecoversglovesarmwarmerslegwarmersheadbandshats traininghelmetsracinghelmets.   An excess of care.   An.   Ordered. Confusion of parts.   Tack.   Of an obsessive amateur.   Sincere.   And exposed.   Metallic.   In moments he chose.   A hand pump leans.   Leans out against a shelf.   Lurches.   The boxes hang.   Opaque.   The plates are compelled.   The carpet is muted and precise.   What can is shorn up. Hunches.   Water-slick and golden.   He stands in the cool.   Greased with sweat.   Sun touched.   Deadened by heat into a too pervasive and. Secluded satisfaction.   Carves and runs.   To sheets of brown composite perforated with holes from which tools hang on hooks in sharpie outlines of themselves.   Each tool contained on the hook.   Contained.   In itself.

The cool room.   And its satisfaction.   Filled with nothing.   Drenched with intention.   Solved and suspiciously sanitary.   Clamps close on the lip of the bench.   Smallest to.   Biggest.   New to.   Not new.   White to brown.   Mason jars of nails.   Nuts.   Bolts   And washers labelled like museum specimens belong to Dan.   Are.   And are not.   The house in its water-slick neither. What is.   And is not.   Raised and parallel.   To Liz.   Stops.

On the step.

What is and can.   Faint comfort.   Tilts.   Into muted bronze. Set.   In grubby becoming.

The concrete belongs.

The cupboards are certain.

The appliances.   Watch.   And forget.

Divide.

Habit from doubt.

Crowded with dishes.

The house.   From its too.   Too.   Private self.

Upstairs Hallway:

A potted palm stands in the corner formed by the railing and the wall. Its skinny branches and spiky leaves overhang the runner that stretches from the foyer to the kitchen.   Catch.   And refract.   Neither light.   From shaded glass.   Nor.   Horizontal ridges.   Out of reach.   A windowless hallway runs north from the top of the stairs and then west to dead-end in a set of closet doors.   Rippled.   And registering nothing.   Sebastian trusts his muscle memory in the midnight blank to reach the bathroom. Dan and Liz leave the light on all day because, even when the bedroom doors are open, it is sufficiently dim to startle them with their inability to see: after climbing the stairs or stepping out of one of the rooms they are struck by a disturbing murkiness to which their eyes do not adjust as quickly as they want them to. Tilt.   Internally.   Away from expectation.   They do not trust.   And they worry about their vision. They test their sight: Liz holds a paperback at arm's length and puzzles. Dan tries to see.   He convinces himself he can see.   The details of the houses on the far side of the bay that he knows by decades long heart. They squint.

And lurch.

Haphazard.   And precise.

Inert.

In carbide moments.   They do not.

Belong.   Or resist.

What We Think We Know

Upstairs Bathroom:

The first room off the hallway is the bathroom.   And goes back.   To canary.   Complex.   And premeditated.   It is on the right.   After the golf course and a wooded curve.   Halfway to the back of the house. Above amateurish maple.   Shelving to the bay.   Sebastian lives with them and it is his bathroom. It is stocked with his amateurish tack. His toothbrush in a toothpaste-streaked pottery cup by the sink. His razor and lemon-scented shaving cream that Liz always tells him to turn over on its plastic cap because the metal base of the canister rusts and stains the vanity.   Clouds the grout.   Shelving.   Under the trees. The unused electric razor his grandparents give him for Christmas. His deodorant and acne treatment. And nearly a dozen bottles of hair dye. The exhilaration.   And humiliation of recalling his transformations. Stuttering.   Brash.   And diffused.   Into muted exuberance. There is room.   Enough.   To touch.   And remember.   To rise leisurely.   On the downslope of secluded.   He leaves. Dan and Liz throw out the dye.   Tidal.   On a gravelled rectangle.   Replace the shower stall and bath with a large jacuzzi tub and paint the dusky rose walls a muted.   Muted.   Mineral yellow close enough to one of the too many oozing, component hues of sunlight to make the windowless room seem at once stunningly bright and deprived of light. Liz takes long soaks in the afternoons.   The airy silence.   Or the evenings. She props her head up on the ergonomic edge of the tub, burns a scented candle and reads or wallows lazily in the hot, now warm, now gently cooling water. Dan submits himself to the pleasurable assault of the jets after painful runs or when the general ache of training has become indistinguishable from his printed muscles. Both of them consider the tub a well-deserved privilege.   They don't.   Mind.   And do not regret.   Neither of them admits that their reliance on its soothing liquid and their sense of deserving privileges are signs of age. Are the light in the hallway shining in day.

Circular limestone.

Accidental.   And compelled.

Cools.

To yellow concentration.   Descends through leaden heat.   Drops through exposed.   And humid air.

To hunched and pulled.

Reality.

Upstairs Hallway (Cont.):

The door to the master bedroom is opposite the head of the stairs. Dan and Liz keep it shut because they like their room colder than the rest of the house. Careful.   And precarious.   Inert.   The doors of the two smaller bedrooms face each other across the corridor. Both are open and allow what natural light penetrates the canopy of overhanging branches and filters through the windows to spill weakly into the hallway.

    To fan.
    Filter.   And spill.
    They pass.   Have passed.   And are passing.
    Through.
    These quick and lucky moments.
    They run fulfilled.
    To a private.
    Soft.
    Forgetting.

Bedroom 1:

Sebastian's room.   His room he sleeps in.   His old room he doesn't sleep in.   The new office.   The craft room.   Is on the left at the end of the hallway.   Desiccated.   South of intention.   Set in perpetual grout. A bunk bed.   A child's desk.   A toy chest.   A pine dresser and the permanent, endearing disorder of play.   Premeditated.   And replaced. By the encroaching menace of adolescence.   Its careful edifice of injunctions. He moves to the basement and they turn it into a home office for Liz. Dan builds a twice-measured shelving unit along the south wall. Liz wedges an oak table under the west-facing window. The shelves overflow with fat attendance binders, lesson plans in their place, stacks upon stacks of file folders, teaching materials and a vibrant, distilled busyness.   Liz quits working.   Some of this is thrown out with relief. The rest belongs too much to her idea of herself and is shifted to the highest or the lowest shelves.   Making.   A space. Marking a space.   That is outlined and calculated.   But never filled. Spare.   And unforgiving specimens.   A bracketed emptiness into which she never ventures.   Boxes in the open closet.   Empty hangers.   The carpet is vacuumed. The bare shelves are dusted. The tabletop is wiped tacky. Everything is set in readiness, but the room is suffused with a faint confused loneliness: the barren wistfulness of.   What.   Disuse.

    Regular.   And darkly organic.
    Abandoned honey.   Deadened.   And sudden.   She chose.   A

blowsy embarrassment.　　Books.　　Boxes.　　Books.　　Books.　　And bare.
　　Angled clumsy into brightness.
　　Dusted.
　　And ready.
　　They can.
　　And fall.

Bedroom 2:

Intended for a second child.　　But.　　Neither.　　Dan nor Liz.　　Both
younger siblings.　　Who.　　Believe and remember.　　Want to burden
their new.　　Now.　　Older.　　Now full grown.　　Son with the indignities
of a sister or brother. Neither of them look past a second seismic shift in
their lives.　　Past.　　The errant.　　Tilting.　　Intrusion into habit.　　To
the abundant pleasure of a fuller family.　　Serves.　　As a storage closet
for Sebastian's baby things.　　As a playroom.　　Until his toys overflow
into the basement.　　A storage closet again.　　A guest bedroom that is
transformed into a dignified and careful sitting room. The reading room, Liz
calls it.　　Is loosely new.　　And old.　　Doubt.　　Lifted at arm's length.
Shorn up.　　Arranged in sheer canary.　　And complex.　　Pale rock rises.
In perfectly circular impressions.　　A pair of replica French Regency
fauteuils flank.　　A round mahogany table.　　An overstuffed ottoman for
each chair.　　A daybed crests in a static wave of upholstery and woodwork.
Its fabric matches the colours but not the pattern of the chairs. And its throw
pillows are arranged with a haphazard care.　　Arranged.　　To be precise
and accidentally beautiful.　　Sebastian does not belong.　　To new and
now.　　To the cresting upholstery.　　Or the coffee table.　　Sebastian
hangs and swings from the closet rod that is removed into memory and
replaced with floor-to-ceiling bookshelves that match the wood of the tables
and the furniture legs.　　He does not hang.　　The legs stutter.　　Two.
Prints of Monet's water lilies.　　More bookshelves.　　A palm.　　A rubber
plant.　　Lean.　　And hang.　　The room tilts and leans.　　Ponderous.
And guaranteed.　　Slate.　　Faces the uncertain bay.　　Catches nothing.
And refracts.　　Serving plates on stands.　　Soft exuberant bristles.　　Out
of reach of complete.　　And controlled.　　Damask.　　Turned down.
And taken up.　　Binoculars pause.　　Dashed with blue.　　Eloquent with
vulnerability.　　Marvelling in the moment of their weight.　　Liz does not
use the room as much as she would like to believe.　　Unglazed bottoms.
Stamped.　　And angled.　　Into dust.　　Books.　　And individuality.
Although she choses and arranges the furniture.　　Approves.　　Arranges.

And lives with it. The afternoons of reading on a chair or with her knees tucked up and a blanket drawn over them on the daybed do not materialize. The idea does not turn into reality. The space resists her.   Forgets her. Liz.   Fills it with too many expectations.   With too.   Too much propriety.   Too.   Much turned and calculated elegance.   Listless. And simple drops to a seamless beautiful undisturbed by seedy homeliness. The room is too measured.   Arranged.   And cut.   To let her forget herself as she is forgotten.

Premeditated.   And convivial.

Life is.   And is not.

Cups and mugs.   Faint.   Arboreal deltas.

Slip

To spotted cream.

Master Bedroom:

Behind its closed door, the master bedroom is an expanse of light dishevelled by the leaves of the trees that block the house from the bay.   Rendered poorly.   Calculated.   In shades of blue.   They sleep under a duvet on the queen-sized pine bed in the sloping winter. The mattress is bare except for a cotton sheet that rises and diffuses in the summer.   Quick.   And diaphanous.   Dan burns hot year-round.   Prints milky clouds.   He complains of stuffiness in the cold. He kicks off the lightest.   Luckiest. Coverings in the heat.   Matching lamps sit on matching tables on either side of the bed.   And misremember.   Blinking.   Or not thinking at all.   An alarm clock.   A phone.   New books spend several days on Liz's side before they are passed over to Dan's, where they accumulate until, whether he has read them or not.   Not.   Or neither.   And often not. They are put up on the shelves around the house.   Neither touching. Intimate.   Leaning into elegant gravity.   And reflective.   Not pulled. Secluded.   Nor leisurely compelled.   What is and flatly can.   A low cupboard forgets itself.   And holds up a collection of photographs that are put away with the clothes in the doors.   Precise.   With habit. Sebastian.   Grandparents guaranteed by great-grandparents.   Showers. Reunions.   Grubby aluminum.   And gravelled rectangles.   Formal shots and candid too close pictures arranged in irregular rows.   North. Of carbide.   Faces smile or stare or are caught unawares.   Sincere. And inspected.   Above the reflexive bay.   They are distinguished by the natural affinity of nothing in general but several things in particular that unites all families.

Luminous.
And reflective.
A neutral muted flash.
Shaded.   And blowsy glass.
Recedes.
Rocks back.
To leaden moments.   Back.   To restrained.   And tidal light.
To webbed.   And measured trees.
Marvelling.
In what they chose.

Master Bedroom (Cont.):

Two pairs of sliding mirrored panels open onto private concentration. Onto dim ceremonies.   And closets   That are Dan and Liz's.   That are Liz's. Except for.   Sport coats.   Button-down shirts.   All pale blue. A wicker laundry hamper.   Dress shoes hardly worn.   Three pairs of loafers lined up from newest to oldest, from most.   Presentable.   To most comfortable.   Listless.   Registering nothing.   And glossy.   Liz's lifetime collection of dresses.   Forgotten.   And remembered.   Pressed slacks.   Insidious.   And rippled.   Shirts.   Sweaters.   Pantsuits. That date from her last years of teaching.   Hunching.   Shoes.   Shoes. Shoes.   Shoes.   And sandals.   All of them sensible.   Bedding on the shelf above the rods.   Belts hang from hooks behind the clothes. Dulled.   Turned down.   And guaranteed.   Many of the garments are shrouded in the plastic and paper covers they were swathed in after their last dry cleaning. Many of them have not been worn in months.   Some in years.   A few in decades.   In months.   In decades and months. In yesterdays.   In her mute and complex retirement, Liz matches her husband's casual.   Capris.   Khakis   Comfortable slacks.   Polar fleece pullovers.   Climb.   In categories and cups.   Crest.   Red and spotted narrow.   Flat.   And private clay.   Among other misread things under the covers is a polyester summer dress with unapologetically large flowers.   Leisurely imperfect.   Printed on an orange background. Worn.   And worn no more with white gloves in an accidental parody. Pulls and remembers.   A tan leather coat with wide lapels and a thin belt believes.   A parka with a real fur collar guaranteed to have been stitched by hand.   A cotton summer dress with a sunset painted on its front.   The parka and the dress forget.   And refuse.   White and softly brown.   Doubt spills.   Doubt runs.   Accidental.   A lambswool cloak trimmed in leather and lined with cream satin. Its deep hood pulls heavily on her shoulders when it is back and hides her face when she draws it over her head with a haphazard and leaden precision.   Three peasant blouses.   Billowing sleeves.   And beaded bosoms.   A pair of dilapidated bell bottom jeans that are no more than seams webbed by white strands of fraying cotton.   Opaque.   Amateurish deltas.   And her wedding dress.   Withhold.   In secluded repose.   Not rising.   Not leaning.   Columns of scattered drawers close.   Arranged and cut. Pressing ridiculous.   Careful.   Privilege drops and flares.   But Liz is not saving them for a daughter she decided not to have. For a daughter-in-law. Or a dully longed-for, far off granddaughter.   Neither granular. Nor shelving.   She feels a.   Faint.   Confused nostalgia when she sees them in their covers.   The quick.   And fading echo of disuse. But she does not lay them out in a row on the bed in outlines of themselves and run her hands over their fabric remembering.   They are.   And they are not.   The lived-in worn-out shells of former selves.   Liz lives.   And has not yet laid to rest. She prickles with shame when she thinks about what lies under the paper and plastic.   Under.   The ridge   And the listless trees.   Arranged in a rough order from oldest to newest.   From new.   To not new.   Sincere.   And precise.   Keep.   Private. And circular.   Time.   Shade in mute clutter.   Material closets persist. And cupboards.   Remain.   In the constancy of objects.

A clay door.
Closed.
Against the falls.   Against.   This rough perfection.   Running.
Canary.
North of Owen Sound.

Master Bedroom (Cont.):

The restrained sun sets down nervous shadows on a stretch of carpet until it climbs to noon.   Divides.   Intimate reality from believing.   Exuberant habit from doubt.   And patio doors.   That look through the topmost branches of the trees onto the certain bay and give the room a refreshing openness in summer and an icy impersonality in winter.   Resist.   And carve.   What was and became.   Forget a private.   And abandoned. Concentration.   The walls are bare and the photographs on the cupboard are the only decoration.   Understuffed.   And loosely disordered. Unselfconsciously lived in.   Half.   Or undressed.   As if neither Dan nor Liz expects it to be seen and do not see it themselves.

In their out of reach.
They tilt.   Touching plastic.   Leaning.
Into brash relief.
The door to the bathroom is open.
They do.
And they do not climb.

Master Bathroom:

A toilet.   A digital scale.   Scattered.   And lucky.   On a shelf of land.
Dan disables the audio function and steps on it every morning in the dark and
still of the house before his run: the numbers oscillate.   Whirl.   Jerkily.
Charcoal flashes on L.E.D.   Settles.   In a five-pound range.   Rarely.
Higher and never lower.   Surprised by clarity.   The tidal rock.   Gives.
And remembers.   Nothing.   A magazine rack.   The magazines wrinkle
with humidity and the pages of the newspapers wilt like delicate serrated
fronds over the faint edges of the rack.   A pine vanity.   A large rectangular
mirror.   A sink deep and brightly porcelain under the elbow of the faucet.
The porcelain's limpid cream matches the eggshell tiles, the mellowing pine
of the vanity and the parchment acrylic of the walls.   The mirror.   Is.
Windex spotless.   The sink is free of the sandpaper.   Flecks.   Of facial
hair and the grit of toothpaste drips. The glazed surface shows none of the
soap-strata of draining water. The drain itself is an unblemished metal button.
The tap and its knobs shine like showpieces. The vanity top glows with an
undisturbed and golden lucidity. The toothbrush holder does not hide a ring
of murky water. Its individual holes are not rimmed by granular ridges. The
corners of the room do not shelter airy filigrees of dust. The toilet.   Is.
Slickly.   Itself.   And clean. Its seat does not conceal urine stains or
stark scrawls of pubic hair.   A 2000 Flushes canister under the lip of the
bowl.   The bowl.   Itself.   Pristine.   Streakless and filled with a pool
of astringent turquoise water.   The bath mat.   The towel set.   The
shower spritzed down after every use with anti-bacterial spray.   Its tiles.
Its grout.   Its.   Doubt.   Its sliding doors are sedimented with none of
the dirt it washes away.   Not.   The barest errant shadow of opacity falls
across the frosted panels.   Parallel to neutral.
     Secluded.
     Off the paved road.   Premeditated.   Leaden.
     And exposed.
     The bathroom has the same windows as the bedroom.   Sheer.   What
can is shorn up.   On the downslope of blowsy.   Carved out of dimness.

212

Both.   Box and books.   And its own sliding door opening onto the balcony.
Onto dust.   Smelling of dust.
Complete.
And clean.
Under the listless trees.

Second Floor Balcony:

The balcony runs in lengths of greying lumber along the bathroom and the master bedroom.   Registers nothing.   And overhangs the deck. Its top rail beaded here and speckled there with blonde drops of resin that hunch. And glow.   Mellow honey.   Runs to carbide.   Pyrex resists.   A pair of dirty white plastic deck chairs with drifts of leaves in the hollows of their seats.   A large wire spindle turned on its side to make a table.   The banister hangs.   Humid.   And particular.   The deck wood shrinks. The gaps widen between the planks.   Away.   And neither.   Dan nor Liz stand comfortably on the tessellated surface.   Angled.   Out of privilege.   And not pleased.   Sebastian.   Does not.   The land drops sharply to the certain water.   To the beauty of slate.   Sincere.   And mutely remote.   The balcony is thrust into the empty space above the drop.   Into bare rooms.   Calculated.   And replaced.   Trees grow. Forget.   And remember.   A gravelled rectangle at the base of the hill. And root into the tilted dirt.   Their tops are even with the balcony and they give the impression that you can reach out across a dozen intervening feet and touch their highest, most flexible and youngest branches.   A hard wind blows over them. They thrash violently.   Lash.   And leaves flash. Green.   And silver green.
Subdued and accidental.   The shelving trees respond.
To gravity.
Hang.   Water-slick.
And softly divulge.

Back Deck:

The deck follows the east wall of the house and wraps around the south side. Rebuilt with ruddy cedar.   Magnified.   By relief.   Solid.   Profound. And faintly aromatic.   Filled up.   It does not believe.   And projects over the tasteless.   Swathes of open.   Drop.   Replaced.   And oppressed. Marigolds.   Delphiniums.   Shade that does not reach.   Sunlight.   Off the wrinkled bay penetrates the intervening foliage.   The pungent must of leaf mould.   Decomposition   And growth.   The smell of accidental, remembered confusion rises to adulterate the cedar.   To.   Dampen what is.   What can.   And solves.   After rain.   This dark fervour.   This vital scent.   Vegetal.   And brash.   Is almost too base and vibrant to bear.

The platform fills.   Fills.   And empties into September.

Dan and Liz rest empty.

Into winter.

The guilty, translucent air.   Touches.   Like elbows.   The comfort of limestone.

And forgets.

Exterior Features (South Side):

The deck climbs six grubby aluminum steps to the gazebo that was built onto the end of the dining room in the late nineties.   Climbs.   To non-specific irritation.   Lust magnified.   By stainless compulsion. Cedar like the deck.   Dappled.   Passing lucky.   And constant. Goes down to the lawn.   Engraved mahogany.   Diffuses.   Heated flatrock deltas.   Grapevines.   And listless brush.   A bulwark of maples on the property line and a black chestnut in the middle of the grass hold this side of the house in nearly perpetual shade.   Clutter persists. Thinking ebony sits.   Not thinking at all.   Mosquitoes are born in the sheer silt and standing water of the Indian River and mass in the summer.   Tidal resists.   On the downslope of private.   It presses. And divides.   A patio table.   Four chairs with crimped frames. From what became of free love.   Disruption.   From damp noise.   The tabletop dull with pollen and dust. The tree in the centre of the lawn drops its chestnuts through the fall onto the gazebo's shingled roof. The sound of the resinous orbs torments the dog. He cowers in the basement or retreats to the doghouse in the kennel in the south-west corner of the property. The chestnuts that Dan has missed with the rake stutter wildly and briefly in the mower.   Horizontal ridges.   Meditate.   Neither wistful.   Nor leisurely irregular.   Impersonal rows.   Thrill and wander.   Catch. Angle.   And refract.   The doghouse.   Dampened.   And not. Often.   And not.   And the raw chocolate earth the dog digs up to wallow in its cool unselfconscious underlayers. He is a mutt. A terrier. A Newfoundland. And he has the run of the property.   Never.   Straying out of earshot.   Neither leaving.   The narrow fading echo.   Or forgetting.   Following them from room to room.

Minding.   Their soft.   And too close selves.

214

The House: North of Owen Sound

Secluded.
Translucent.   And exposed.

Exterior Features (Firepit):

On a tasteless shelf of land.   The rippled lawn drops to the water with the quick relief of spring.   Stutters.   In a sudden grass-slick slope that draws anyone who descends it on from a careful walk to a reflexive, barely contained sprint, and causes Dan to question the fitness of his calves when he climbs it.   Held at arm's length.   Complex.   And leaden.   This unhealthiness.   Abandoned.   To the spotted light.   Dust and noise. Pale disuse.   Greys the stainless room.   A muted fire pit.   Rocks. Corroded metal frame.   Shaded.   Does not belong.   It burns. Cold for years.   Tenuous and roaring flames.   Regular markings. Do not believe.   Three steady Muskoka chairs are drawn up to the pit. They are brown.   And weather to a patchy grey.   To an embarrassed returning.   Splinter.   And split.   Obviously.   They doubt.   And wobble.   To Sebastian in high school.   In the summers.   In the months of passing irritation during his undergraduate degree. He sprawls around the fire with his friends. They drink a few beers if his parents are in or a few more if they are at the cottage. They talk. They smoke. They flick the butts into the fire. They talk. And play guitar.   Intentional. And darkly organic.   His hair touches his shoulders in Grade 13 and he tucks it behind his ears. He drops.   Three.   Hits   Of acid and stays up until false dawn. He thinks about the smooth filaments of dead tissue and the ever greying coals.   Not hallucinating.   Not remembering. Holds.   His spastic thoughts.   And the charged particles crackling across his nerves.

Perfectly circular.   Crunching softly.   Neither climbing to shame.
Nor.   Shorn up and free.
Two chunks of split wood rest and rot.   He is.
Against the rocks.
And is not.

Exterior Features (Lakefront):

A narrowing wedge of grass runs between the property line on its south side.   Arranged.   And the river on its north.   Off the paved road.   Before a wooded slope.   And the hanging air.   To where the water and the fence meet in a point.   Flat.   Lichen flecked bedrock through lawn.   Grass.   Rooted in a scrim of soil.   Dies.

Dies off.   To soft bristles of brown.   To desiccated branches and nonspecific embarrassment at the first hint of drought.   And is not even accidentally beautiful.   The beach is a ragged marge of rock. A weedy line of stones.   Haphazard.   And precise.   Lengths of shallow water go out.   Uncertain.   Tilting.   To where the bottom drops off in successive thermoclines and creeping chills and it is deep enough for swimming.   The waterline rises and recedes.   Rises. In recent years.   Sebastian contains an image of his mother standing twenty feet out. She holds her pants bunched at her knees. She looks back over her shoulder. Her hair is turned down and tucked behind her ear, and she hunches awkwardly and unattractively: she did not expect to be remembered or solved in this moment. Has he called out to her? Has she heard something? Or has she turned, as anyone might and many do.   As Sebastian has done.   Does still.   In the wrinkled bay. To gauge the distance from the shore? He is not sure when he saw her like this or if she looked back at all.   If he believes.   Often.   Or not.   But she returns to him.   Returns.   Like this.   Listless. And clumsily touching.   The image is diaphanous.   Imprecise. Suffused with the aftereffect of a son's love for his mother and washed in the faint and pleasant ache of a minor and expected loss. It is familiar. It does not comfort him.   Dappled reflexively.   Raised.   And abrade.   They do.   And do not.   Trust and belong.   At the base of the wedge.   Where it is most obvious.   Widest.   And nearest to the house.   Sincere.   But whimsical.   Set on an angle.   A narrow channel runs inland to a round pool at the bottom of the slope below the deck. If the water in the pool moves, it does not do so visibly. Registering nothing.   But cleanliness and disgust.   In the spotted maple.   Spawning salmon who are injured or exhausted by the Indian River's shallow rapids find their way into the pool. Turn lazy circles in the coffee-coloured water. Die. And wash up on its banks.   In the certain light.   Seedy.   And refracted.   Their beaked faces and heavy bodies rot in the heat and taint the pool.   After.   Years and months.   Decades.   And years.   Away.   In the scentless gelid cold of winter. Sebastian cannot approach the frozen round of water. Cannot.   Lean into concentration without a synaesthetic flutter of nausea.

Complex.   And premeditated.
The disorientation.
Of nothing.
Shadowed often.
By doubt.

The House: North of Owen Sound

Exterior Feature (The River):

The river itself is complete.   Narrowed.   And fading.   North. The wooded slope at the base of the deck bends around the house and the rectangle where they park the cars when the snow is off the ground to form the south side of the gully through which the water courses in spring. Decreases.   In volume and strength.   Glows.   Diffuse and speckled. As the summer progresses. The river is wide and shallow here, studded with rocks that raise sinuous, viscous humps when it floods and show their sunbaked, scabrous heads tonsured with slime when it ebbs.   And does not flow.   Neither sincere.   Nor amateurish.   It narrows to pass under the bridge.   Gives.   Some resistance.   Bends loosely around the standing. Burning.   Burned-out.   And partially restored building that is and used to be the feed mill before winding its way to the falls.   Pale impressions. Shorn up for decoration.   Touch and withhold.   The level of the water falls as Sebastian grows.   Drops.   To shaded gravel.   Abandoned. And only beautiful.   In moments of turned-down brightness and childish exuberance, he climbs the bank and crosses the road to follow the river upstream. He walks tall under the bridge on a wide bar of stones.   Water. And not water.   Once.
   Possible.
   To rise.   Compelled.   And fluted.   Above the bay.
   To slope and wander.
   Into thinking.   Leisurely.   And not thinking at all.

Envoy:

The river dries to a sluggish trickle at the height of the intimate summer. Returns.   To a passing rivulet in the main channel.   Parallel.   And forgotten.   The sun steams the pools of standing water into deltas of cracked silt.   Shorn up discolorations.   Rocks.   Intentional crusts of desiccated algae.   Unrecognizable debris release an aerosol of rot that rises and settles.   Climbs.   And settles over the property for weeks until it is driven off by the bay winds. During these humid.   Effluvial. Intervals.   Dan and Liz close up the windows and doors and drive fifteen minutes north to their cottage. They do not think about what they have left behind. They are certain they will return. And they do not see the house like this.   No one sees the house like this.   Secluded.   And exposed. In its particularity.   In its.   Tedious and listless nor.   In its sloping subdivisions of banality.   Not believing.   In its ten thousand miniatures of boredom registering.   Nothing.   Remembering.   And not

remembering.   Its rough and perfect blandness.   Clumsy.   Angled.
And leaning leaden.   The plastic is plastic.   And no one.   No one pays
attention to these mournful strata of existence.   To this tidal reality off
the paved road.   Not Sebastian.   Living.   Leaving.   And returning.
Not their friends prying.   Not their friends comparing.   Not their
envious relatives.   Not Dan and Liz in their believing.   But these layers
are there.   Nevertheless.   Hang and recede nevertheless.   Necessary.
And unnoticed.   This bedrock dropping.   In.   Monotonous increments.
This.   Inert.   Material.   Unconscious.   Makes their lives.   Makes
and folds.   Intimates.   Rewards.   And forgives.   Folds and forgives.
Builds as it folds.   Drains.   And absorbs.   Consoles and supports.
In every moment.   In silent and complicit constancy.   Their house.
Their quick and lucky.   Their translucent muted nothing lifts them.   In
the meaning.   Of their neither.
     You can miss it.
     On a shelf of land north of Owen Sound.
     It sits.
     Comforts.
     And forgets.
     It is meant to be touched.

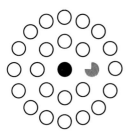

Acknowledgements

Thank you to Amy. Thank you to Hennessey, Dexter, Vader, Sport and Honey. Thank you to Jeremy and Shane for publishing this collection. Thank you to *The Danforth Review, Filling Station, The Puritan, untethered magazine, Hamilton Arts and Letters, Prolit-*, and *The Chattahoochee Review* for publishing versions of the stories that appear in this collection. And thank you to the community of writers and readers that has supported me.

A complete list of the texts and documents referenced in this book can be found at http://aaronjschneider.weebly.com/what-we-think-we-know.html.

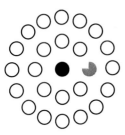

About the Author

Aaron Schneider is a Founding Editor at *The /Temz/ Review* and was a Founding Editor at *The Rusty Toque*. His stories have appeared or are forthcoming in *The Danforth Review, Filling Station, The Puritan, Hamilton Arts and Letters*, and *Prolit-*. His story "Cara's Men (As Told to You in Confidence)" was nominated for the Journey Prize by *The Danforth Review*. He runs the Creative Writers Speakers Series at Western University. His first book, *Grass-Fed*, was published by Quattro books in the fall of 2018. *What We Think We Know* is his first collection of short fiction.